# La Citadelle des Neiges

Ouvrages de Matthieu Ricard

*Plaidoyer pour le bonheur*, NiL, 2003
*L'Infini dans la paume de la main*,
avec Trinh Xuan Thuan, NiL, 2000
*Le Moine et le Philosophe*,
avec Jean-François Revel, NiL, 1997
*Moines danseurs du Tibet*,
Albin Michel, 1999
*Himalaya bouddhiste*,
La Martinière, 2002
*L'Esprit du Tibet*,
Le Seuil, 1996

Écrits et traductions du tibétain :

Dilgo Khyentsé Rinpotché,
*Le Trésor du cœur des êtres éveillés*,
Le Seuil, coll. « Points Sagesse », 1996
Dilgo Khyentsé Rinpotché,
*Autobiographie d'un yogi tibétain*,
Albin Michel, 1998
*Les Cent Conseils*,
Padmakara, 2003

Matthieu Ricard

# LA CITADELLE DES NEIGES

Conte spirituel

NiL éditions

ISBN 2-84111-327-2

*À K. P.*

# L'enfance au village

Détchèn naquit à Khorma, un hameau de l'Est du Bhoutan, au pied de l'Himalaya. Un moine des environs l'avait baptisé Détchèn Dorjé, « Félicité de Diamant ». Tout enfant déjà, il avait le pressentiment qu'il était possible de comprendre le monde. Il sentait en lui la présence d'une force qui ne demandait qu'à s'exprimer. Il ne savait pas très bien quelle direction lui donner, mais l'espoir brillait en son cœur comme une petite flamme.

Parfois, il avait l'impression de ne faire qu'un avec ce qui l'entourait – l'herbe humide, les branches agitées par le vent, les falaises multicolores, les insectes qui courent sur la terre brune, les martinets qui fendent le ciel avec des cris perçants. Il se fondait alors dans le monde et l'embrassait tout en le respirant.

En d'autres occasions, tout lui apparaissait comme une vision lointaine, une image incertaine. Il ne comprenait guère pourquoi, et restait pensif aux abords du village, contemplant le paysage, interrogeant les choses.

Il n'avait connu d'autre vie que celle de Khorma, un hameau d'une vingtaine de maisons et d'une centaine d'âmes. Pourtant, bien des choses qui, pour les villageois, allaient de soi, le troublaient. Lors des travaux des champs, par exemple, il éprouvait un malaise incontrôlable à voir souffrir les animaux : les bœufs que l'on attelait toute la journée pour les labours, les vers de terre lacérés par le soc en bois des charrues, les mules au dos meurtri par de pesants fardeaux...

Il n'aimait pas non plus que les hommes, enivrés par le *tchang*, la bière de millet, perdent la tête. Les bagarres, plus que tout, lui étaient un spectacle insoutenable. Pire encore, il entendait dire qu'ailleurs des peuples entiers s'entretuaient. Il ne comprenait pas comment on pouvait en arriver là.

Les sourires, les paroles douces, les gestes de bonté l'emplissaient d'une joie comparable à celle que l'on éprouve en inspirant une bouffée d'air pur. Ses yeux brillaient et il sentait alors croître en lui une force de vie nouvelle. C'est ainsi, pensait-il, que les choses doivent être.

Lorsqu'il s'en allait ramasser du bois mort dans la forêt avec les autres enfants du village, il préférait donner sa collecte plutôt que de voir ses camarades réprimandés par leurs parents s'ils revenaient les mains vides : cela le peinait plus que de se faire gronder lui-même. Tout petit encore, un jour d'hiver où il avait beaucoup neigé, il revint à la maison presque nu, sans le manteau que sa mère lui avait taillé. « Il y a dehors un petit homme transi de froid », annonça-t-il. Interloquée, sa mère alla voir : Détchèn avait soigneusement emmitouflé de son manteau un petit buisson à silhouette humaine.

Les parents de Détchèn étaient de bonnes et braves gens. Sa mère, Palmo, nom qui signifie « Glorieuse », tissait presque toute la journée des tissus multicolores aux motifs complexes et chatoyants. Il lui fallait une année entière pour terminer trois grandes bandes de tissu *kishotara* ; assemblées, elles formeraient un splendide vêtement porté, les jours de fêtes, par les femmes de bonne famille. Son travail fini, elle irait vendre le fruit de ses efforts au *dzong*, ce bourg construit autour d'un fort situé à une heure de marche de Khorma. Le *dzong*, siège du gouvernement local, abritait aussi un monastère. De sa vente, Palmo tirerait une bonne somme, avec laquelle elle achèterait de l'huile, du sucre et du riz rouge, lequel ne poussait pas à l'altitude élevée de Khorma. Elle rapporterait aussi des bottes en caoutchouc, des lampes de poche et quelques autres objets manufacturés en Inde.

Le père de Détchèn, Péma Dorjé, « Lotus de Diamant », s'occupait des bêtes – un bœuf et cinq vaches – et des travaux des champs, secondé par ses cinq enfants, deux garçons et trois filles. Les terres n'étaient pas très riches, mais elles donnaient de l'orge, du sarrasin, du millet et du maïs, qui constituaient l'essentiel de leur nourriture. Vers la fin de l'été, recouverts des piments mis à sécher au soleil, les toits du village, faits de longues lattes de bois noircies par le temps, viraient au rouge vif.

Palmo faisait aussi fermenter le *tchang* et distillait l'alcool dont l'odeur envahissait, le soir venu, chaque maison du village. Les hommes étaient habiles à travailler le bois avec le long couteau qu'ils arboraient fièrement à leur ceinture. La construction des maisons était l'occasion de fêtes et de cérémonies religieuses. Des moines venaient tout d'abord bénir les lieux. Détchèn ne saisissait que confusément le sens de leurs cérémonies – d'autant qu'ils ne faisaient guère d'efforts pour expliquer aux paysans le sens de la religion, n'étant souvent eux-mêmes pas très instruits ! –, mais leur musique et leurs chants l'émouvaient, leur présence l'attirait. Ensuite, on choisissait sur le calendrier un jour favorable au commencement des travaux. Lorsqu'on célébrait l'édification de la charpente, le *tchang* coulait à flots. Détchèn se rappelait le jour où son oncle Wangchouk s'était mis à danser sur le faîte du toit à la manière d'un équilibriste, chantant à la ronde : « Je suis Vishvakarma, le dieu des Artisans ! » Détchèn et ses amis l'avaient contemplé avec une frayeur amusée, s'attendant à ce qu'il dégringole du toit, mais pas du tout : le dieu des ivrognes devait veiller sur lui ! Enfin, un lama invité pour l'occasion consacrait la maison et plus particulièrement la pièce dédiée au temple familial.

Avec la nuit venait le silence. L'éclat falot des lampes à huile durait peu : le village entier ne tardait pas à s'endormir. La quiétude des ténèbres semblait pénétrer chaque chose. Elle n'était rompue de loin en loin que par le concert des chiens aboyant soudain sans raison, ou parce qu'un de leurs semblables du hameau voisin était venu rôder en territoire interdit.

Toute la famille dormait dans une grande pièce ; les aînés sur de larges banquettes basses disposées le long des murs et recouvertes de laines bariolées, les plus jeunes sur des nattes posées à même le sol. Dès les premières lueurs de l'aube, les choses ne traînaient pas. On allumait le feu de bois dans l'âtre, la fumée envahissait la pièce principale et la bouilloire chantait, prête à verser du thé chaud sur les flocons de riz concassé ou sur la farine d'orge grillée enrichie d'une noix de beurre. Palmo se prosternait trois fois devant la statue du Bouddha, offrait sur l'autel familial sept bols d'eau claire, puis allumait un bâton d'encens ainsi qu'une lampe à beurre. Elle ne savait ni lire ni écrire mais connaissait par cœur de nombreuses prières et les apprenait à ses enfants. Elle leur racontait également des histoires fascinantes, comme celle du grand ermite Milarépa dont le corps était devenu verdâtre à force de se nourrir d'orties, et qui pouvait voler dans les airs et traverser des rochers. D'une voix douce et mélodieuse elle chantait aussi des versets des enseignements du Bouddha :

*Qui a la compassion est Bouddha,*
*Qui est sans compassion est démon de la mort.*

*Sans commettre le moindre acte nuisible,*
*Pratique parfaitement la vertu,*
*Et maîtrise complètement ton esprit :*
*Tel est l'enseignement du Bouddha.*

Lorsque Détchèn se faisait gronder pour avoir fait une bêtise ou lorsqu'il avait du chagrin, il accourait spontanément auprès de grand-mère Yangchèn, une femme au grand cœur et à la langue bien pendue qui ne craignait pas de faire valoir ses opinions sur les gens et les choses ; les villageois jugeaient plus prudent d'écouter ses sermons que de la contredire. Elle consolait Détchèn mais lui faisait aussi la leçon, s'appuyant sur des dictons dont elle possédait un répertoire inépuisable : « Seul l'insensé met sa main dans le feu en espérant ne pas se brûler. Sans avoir goûté les larmes, tu n'apprécieras pas le rire. »

Le tir à l'arc était la grande distraction des hommes du village. On installait aux extrémités d'un champ deux planches étroites distantes d'une centaine de mètres l'une de l'autre sur lesquelles était dessinée une petite cible colorée de la taille d'une soucoupe. Après avoir tiré, les archers s'attroupaient autour de la cible. Totalement insouciants du danger, ils attendaient l'arrivée de chaque nouvelle flèche qu'ils évitaient d'un rapide mouvement du corps si celle-ci venait à passer trop près d'eux. Lorsqu'une flèche touchait la cible et, plus encore si elle se fichait en son centre, les membres de l'équipe victorieuse se livraient à une danse rituelle et entonnaient des chants de victoire.

Au fond, la vie au village n'était pas si rude

que ça, mais Détchèn avait le sentiment, encore confus, que ce n'était pas ainsi qu'il souhaitait passer toute son existence.

Un jour, dont le souvenir se grava pour toujours dans son cœur, arriva un homme que les villageois semblaient particulièrement heureux d'accueillir. C'était Jamyang Nyima, « Doux Soleil de la connaissance », un demi-frère de sa mère. Cela faisait des années qu'il vivait dans les montagnes, là où il gèle souvent la nuit, même en plein été. À la veillée, au coin du feu, il parla de la Citadelle des Neiges, un lieu hors du monde, si loin des hommes, si près des dieux. Quelques fidèles du village y étaient allés en pèlerinage. Jamyang, lui, y vivait depuis douze ans. Il racontait la beauté sauvage et la paix immuable de l'endroit. Il insistait sur la présence là-haut d'un être hors du commun, un maître spirituel appelé Tokdèn Rinpotché, dont il était le disciple. Jamyang parlait de lui, la voix pleine d'amour et de respect, comme de celui qui guidait sa vie spirituelle avec sagesse et compassion. Jamyang n'était ni un moine ni un homme marié, mais un ermite, un méditant qui avait passé de nombreuses années en retraite. Il émanait de lui une assurance tranquille et une grande gentillesse. Tandis que Détchèn l'écoutait, son esprit s'envola vers les montagnes enneigées, imaginant ce que pouvait être la vie là-haut, se demandant à quoi pouvaient bien ressembler un maître spirituel et une existence d'ermite. La possibilité de vivre d'une autre manière commençait à se faire jour en lui.

Le lendemain matin, à l'heure du thé, il trouva son père et Jamyang en pleine conversation au coin du feu, leurs mains tendues au-dessus des braises chaudes. Lorsque Détchèn s'approcha, son père lui dit : « Jamyang va bientôt repartir dans les montagnes. Veux-tu l'accompagner ? » Le jeune garçon sentit son cœur bondir de joie. Il se voyait déjà traversant la grande forêt, arrivant auprès des ermites de la Citadelle. Comme la plupart des enfants du village, il respectait ses parents et se soumettait sans mot dire à leurs injonctions, même quand cela ne lui plaisait qu'à moitié. Cette fois-ci, c'est avec un grand sourire qu'il acquiesça. L'aventure promise le remplissait d'excitation.

Les parents de Détchèn avaient remarqué

que, dès son plus jeune âge, leur fils était d'un naturel calme et bienveillant et qu'il aimait s'asseoir longuement en compagnie des moines et des ermites de passage au village. Ils voulaient donc lui donner une chance de se familiariser avec la vie spirituelle.

« Tu nous manqueras, ajouta son père, et c'est vrai que nous avons besoin d'aide pour les travaux des champs, mais, si tu t'adonnes à la vie spirituelle, nous ne pouvons rien souhaiter de mieux pour toi. Et puis tu te souviendras de nous dans tes méditations et tes prières. Nous serons fiers de toi. »

Détchèn avait quatorze ans.

Sa mère prépara son balluchon. Pas grand-chose, à vrai dire. Une pelisse de laine brune et un bonnet pour l'hiver, une couverture à longs poils, un bol en bois pour le boire et le manger, un sac de cuir souple contenant de la farine d'orge grillée – la *tsampa* – et du beurre. Elle y ajouta des provisions pour la route qu'elle rangea dans un panier rond vanné par son mari avec des fibres de bambou teintes de couleurs vives.

Jamyang quant à lui emportait des vivres qui leur suffiraient à tous deux pour plusieurs mois : un sac de *tsampa*, deux sacs de riz rouge, une outre de beurre, un panier d'osier carré rempli de maïs concassé et d'une vingtaine de briques de thé compressé. Il y avait aussi un grand pot de graisse végétale destinée à l'offrande de lampes dans le temple. Jamyang et Détchèn prendraient deux mules pour les trois jours de leur périple afin de porter tout cela.

Le moment du départ venu, Palmo donna à Jamyang quelques billets froissés. Non qu'il y eût quoi que ce soit à vendre là où il allait, mais cela lui permettrait d'effectuer de menus achats lorsqu'il croiserait des nomades de passage qui descendraient au *dzong* dans la vallée. Elle se réjouissait de l'avenir auquel son fils se préparait, mais on voyait des larmes perler au coin de ses yeux. Détchèn était le dernier de ses enfants, celui auquel elle avait prodigué ses plus tendres soins. Excité par l'aventure, Détchèn ne comprenait pas encore qu'il ne verrait sans doute plus sa famille pendant un an ou deux. N'empêche qu'il eut lui aussi un pincement au cœur lorsqu'il se mit en marche avec Jamyang et leurs mules.

Les villageois interrompirent leurs activités pour leur souhaiter bonne route et longue vie. Les frères, les sœurs et quelques camarades de Détchèn les accompagnèrent jusqu'à un petit col. Au sommet, il se retourna. Sa mère, sa grand-mère Yangchèn et quelques parents se tenaient encore immobiles devant la maison à les regarder s'éloigner. Pour leur dire au revoir, Détchèn agita au vent une longue écharpe cérémonielle de soie blanche que sa mère, en signe de bon augure, lui avait passée autour du cou au moment de le quitter. Au village, quelques écharpes décrivaient, en réponse, des arabesques porteuses de souhaits affectueux. Puis, le col franchi, Jamyang et Détchèn perdirent le village de vue.

# Le voyage dans la forêt

Tout était devenu tranquille. Devant eux s'ouvrait un chemin ardu, une longue ascension de trois jours vers les hauteurs enneigées. Ils marchèrent deux heures en longeant la rivière, puis pénétrèrent dans une jungle luxuriante, peuplée d'arbres immenses formant une voûte d'émeraude d'où ruisselaient çà et là des flots de lumière. Les sous-bois touffus étaient parsemés de troncs d'arbres morts, de mousses et d'orchidées, traversés de ruisseaux qui se ramifiaient et s'étalaient en formant d'interminables marécages boueux.

Un bâton dans chaque main, ils sautaient de pierre en pierre – en espérant qu'elles ne roulent pas sous leurs pieds –, passaient le plus vite possible sur un tronc d'arbre étroit et à moitié pourri avant que celui-ci ne s'enfonce sous leur poids, puis repéraient aussitôt le tronc suivant ou une pierre à peine visible qu'ils atteignaient d'un bond. C'était tout un art, et mieux valait ne pas être distrait ! Généralement, cela ne se passait pas trop mal car, sans qu'il y paraisse, au fil des années, pierres et rondins avaient été disposés aux bons endroits par d'innombrables voyageurs et bergers. De plus, comme la plupart des gens du pays, Détchèn avait un sens remarquable de l'équilibre et ignorait le vertige. Les deux marcheurs et leurs mules allaient donc bon train.

« Ces chemins marécageux sont comme le *samsara*, le monde de la souffrance, expliqua Jamyang à Détchèn pendant l'une de leurs rares haltes. Pour le traverser, tu dois t'appuyer sur deux bâtons, la sagesse et la méthode. L'un ne peut aller sans l'autre. Avec un seul bâton, tu auras tôt fait de perdre l'équilibre et de te retrouver le nez dans la boue. » Détchèn n'avait encore aucune idée de ce que signifiaient sagesse et méthode, mais il se tint coi.

Non loin de là, le bourbier débouchait sur un chemin qui serpentait vers un monticule tapissé d'une belle mousse verte illuminée par les rayons du soleil perçant la voûte des grands arbres comme autant d'épées de lumière. Le lieu invitait au repos. Jamyang et l'enfant s'assirent pour souffler un peu. Ils ne furent pas longs à allumer un feu et à préparer du thé dans la bouilloire cabossée que Jamyang avait détachée de la selle de l'une des mules.

Tandis qu'ils se restauraient, Jamyang poursuivit : « La sagesse, c'est de comprendre que tout ce que tu vois, tout ce que tu ressens, est aussi éphémère qu'un rêve, une illusion, une goutte de rosée, un éclair dans la nuit, une bulle à la surface du torrent. La méthode, c'est d'être empli de compassion pour tous les êtres ; en gros, c'est d'avoir bon cœur. Sans sagesse, tu perçois tout de travers, et sans compassion, ta sagesse ne vaut pas grand-chose. »

Peu à peu, les mots prenaient davantage de sens pour Détchèn ; mais cela restait quand même un peu compliqué pour un garçon de son âge sans la moindre éducation.

« Quand tu chemines par ces sentiers difficiles, continua Jamyang, tu comprends mieux la loi de cause à effet. Si tu es distrait, si tu fais la moindre erreur, ta chute sera très désagréable. C'est pareil dans la vie : si tu agis sans réfléchir ou, pire, avec méchanceté, tu récoltes naturellement des problèmes, sans compter le tort que tu fais aux autres. »

Ça, c'était déjà plus clair. Détchèn se souvenait du jour où il s'était bagarré avec ses camarades du village, et de la tristesse qu'il avait ensuite éprouvée. Une autre fois, il avait menti pour échapper à une punition et s'était senti très mal à l'aise, comme si le monde ne tournait plus rond.

Détchèn se réjouissait d'avoir tant à apprendre. La découverte d'idées nouvelles se mêlait à celle de la grande forêt, dans laquelle il ne s'était jamais aventuré jusqu'alors. Cette dernière était peuplée d'oiseaux aux chants étranges : le toucan dont les appels sonores et mélodieux résonnaient dans toutes les directions, la pie himalayenne dont l'immense queue ondoyait, telle une écharpe de soie bleue glissant sur la verdure, quand elle s'envolait soudain, quelques mètres devant eux. De gros papillons passaient comme des fleurs de velours emportées par la brise.

Il y avait aussi des ours, mais heureusement ils n'en rencontrèrent pas. Plusieurs hommes du village portaient sur leur visage les profondes cicatrices de leur face à face impromptu avec la bête. Du moins ceux qui avaient survécu.

Détchèn se mit à songer aux *migueu*, ces « hommes sauvages » que des étrangers venus un jour dans son village appelaient les « abominables hommes des neiges ». Ces visiteurs insolites voulaient à tout prix voir un *migueu*, ce qui avait beaucoup fait rire Détchèn et ses amis. Tout le monde connaissait quelqu'un qui connaissait quelqu'un dont le grand-père ou le cousin avait rencontré un *migueu*, mais personne au village n'en avait vu de ses propres yeux.

À vrai dire, Détchèn redoutait davantage les sangsues. Elles grouillaient par milliers. Telles de fines langues noires, elles se dressaient, ondulantes, sur les feuilles des bas-côtés et les herbes du chemin, comme si elles avaient pressenti votre passage, ou bien elles se laissaient tomber sur votre tête depuis les branches des arbres. Tous les matins, Jamyang et Détchèn se frictionnaient pieds et mollets avec du sel afin que les prédatrices ne s'incrustent pas dans leur chair. Mais il y en avait toujours quelques-unes pour se glisser sous les vêtements. Leur morsure était indolore sur le moment, et Détchèn ne s'apercevait de leur présence que lorsque le sang coulait le long de ses jambes ou perçait au travers de sa chemise. Les mules, elles, n'avaient guère de moyen de se défendre et se retrouvaient vite ensanglantées, surtout aux endroits où leur peau est fine, sur les pattes, autour des yeux et dans les naseaux.

« Les pensées vagabondes sont comme ces sangsues, lui dit Jamyang, on ne les voit pas venir et quand on les remarque il est déjà trop tard : elles ont envahi notre esprit. Elles sont comme le feu qui couve sous les braises. Les braises, ce sont nos habitudes, nos penchants invétérés, il suffit que les événements de la vie les attisent pour que les flammes de la colère ou de l'envie resurgissent. »

Détchèn portait des chaussures de toile que sa mère lui avait achetées au *dzong*. Du temps de ses grands-parents, personne au Bhoutan ne mettait de chaussures, pas même Ourgyen

Wangchouk, le roi du pays. Détchèn se rappelait avoir vu au *dzong* une vieille photographie toute jaunie sur laquelle le roi et sa cour se tenaient debout, pieds nus, aux côtés de dignitaires étrangers arborant le costume de leur pays. Son père lui avait raconté que ces émissaires, venus en grande pompe de l'Inde qu'ils occupaient alors, s'étaient comportés avec pas mal d'arrogance. Mais les Bhoutanais n'en furent nullement impressionnés ; ils se moquèrent même des visiteurs à face blanche, qui repartirent très fâchés.

Détchèn, quant à lui, appréciait ses chaussures. Jamyang lui raconta que lorsque son père était allé en pèlerinage au Tibet, il y avait trente ans déjà, ses compagnons et lui s'étaient enveloppé les pieds de bandelettes de tissus pour affronter une semaine de marche dans la neige et franchir les hauts cols. Une fois arrivé au Tibet, il s'était procuré des bottes tibétaines en feutre multicolore, pourvues de semelles de cuir rigide. De retour au pays, il ne les avait plus jamais portées, mais la famille de Jamyang les avait conservées en souvenir.

Cela faisait douze heures que Jamyang et Détchèn peinaient sur un chemin étroit et fangeux, sinuant sous la frondaison de l'épaisse forêt. L'alternance de montées et de descentes semblait ne jamais prendre fin. Les descentes, dont certaines menaient jusqu'au bord du torrent, étaient presque pires que les ascensions, car il fallait ensuite regagner toute l'altitude perdue.

La nuit tombait et il commençait à pleuvoir. Jusqu'alors, il n'y avait eu aucun endroit où s'arrêter pour camper, mais Jamyang savait qu'ils approchaient d'un hameau accroché à flanc de colline.

Dans le crépuscule, une trouée s'ouvrit soudain dans la végétation et de petits champs cultivés en terrasses apparurent. Une gorge profonde, en contrebas, fendait la vallée boisée d'une entaille vertigineuse. Sur le versant opposé, une grande cascade plongeait dans le torrent, telle une écharpe de soie blanche se déployant lentement sur la muraille sombre.

Le hameau comptait en tout et pour tout deux maisonnettes. Sous l'auvent d'une grange s'empilait une grande quantité de bois. Am Phourba, la paysanne qui régnait sur le foyer, accueillit Jamyang comme s'il était un parent proche. À l'instar de la mère de Détchèn, elle tissait de superbes *kishotara*, dont la vente permettait de subvenir aux modestes besoins de la famille.

Une dizaine d'années auparavant, alors qu'il traversait le torrent à gué, son mari avait glissé, se cognant violemment la tête sur un rocher. Depuis, il éprouvait constamment une grande fatigue et avait peine à travailler. Il faut dire aussi qu'il était devenu un peu simplet. Mais il faisait la cuisine et cultivait les petits lopins de terre entourant la maison. La fille aînée, Drolma, s'occupait des trois autres enfants et veillait à tout, tandis qu'Am Phourba tissait.

Après avoir aidé Jamyang à décharger les mules, Détchèn, fourbu et trempé, s'assit devant l'âtre de la cuisine, regardant le père préparer une soupe de pâtes fraîches qu'il venait de découper sur une grande planche polie par l'usage. La pâle lueur d'une lampe à huile révélait à peine les murs noircis par la fumée.

Jamyang donna des nouvelles de la vallée, puis extirpa de ses sacs quelques achats qu'Am Phourba lui avait demandé de rapporter : des écheveaux de soie de toutes les couleurs, une douzaine de boîtes d'allumettes, trois rouleaux de corde, une pelle en fer et un sac de sel. Après avoir avalé avec délice plusieurs bols de soupe chaude, Détchèn, épuisé, ne fut pas long à s'endormir sur une natte de paille à même le plancher, la tête sur son ballot. Jamyang le protégea d'une couverture.

Am Phourba recouvrit son métier à tisser d'une grande étoffe, son mari jeta de la cendre sur les braises et bientôt la maisonnée s'endormit. Seuls le tic-tac d'un gros réveil indien, qui indiquait une heure approximative, et le lointain grondement de la rivière peuplaient le profond silence de la nuit.

Aux premières lueurs de l'aube, tout le monde était debout, excepté les deux derniers-nés, encore endormis dans le lit de leurs parents. Il fallait raviver le feu, disposer les offrandes sur l'autel, aller chercher le bois et l'eau, préparer une collation et sortir les bêtes.

Am Phourba, quant à elle, se retrouva

bientôt assise devant son métier à tisser. Sa navette allait et venait comme par magie. De temps à autre, la tisserande nouait sans hésitation de nouveaux fils de soie aux couleurs éclatantes, ayant clairement à l'esprit la complexité du motif qui naissait sous ses doigts. Tout en œuvrant, elle conversait avec Jamyang. Détchèn observait en silence.

À un moment donné, Jamyang se tourna vers lui : « Ce métier à tisser est un enseignement à lui tout seul. La chaîne, vois-tu, montre qu'en ce monde toutes les choses sont reliées les unes aux autres. Si tu tends ou relâches l'un des fils, ton action se répercute sur tous les autres fils. La navette, elle, représente ton esprit et la motivation de tes actes. C'est elle qui crée la beauté ou la laideur de la trame de ton existence. Selon que ton esprit est bien ou mal intentionné, selon qu'il fait passer dans la chaîne de tes actes les fils de soie de l'altruisme ou le crin de l'égoïsme, il fera de ta vie une magnifique étoffe aux couleurs resplendissantes ou une toile rêche tout juste bonne à faire une camisole.

— Oui, mais je ne suis pas seul au monde,

réagit Détchèn. Les autres interviennent dans mon tissage, ils m'aident ou ils m'entravent. »

Ce à quoi Jamyang répondit : « C'est à toi, le maître d'œuvre, d'intégrer dans ton travail leurs actions, leurs espoirs et leurs craintes, afin de fabriquer un tissu suffisamment grand pour tous les vêtir. »

Les deux pèlerins reprirent leur route après le thé du matin.

Ce jour-là, la forêt était ensoleillée et ils allèrent d'un bon pas. Vers midi, ils parvinrent à un autre hameau où on leur offrit de bon cœur un humble repas. La situation dans ce village était pourtant loin d'être facile. Les femmes et les enfants travaillaient dur, à la maison comme aux champs, tandis que les hommes ne se fatiguaient guère : et pour cause, à partir de trois heures de l'après-midi, ils étaient tous ivres car ils distillaient un fort alcool de riz dont on sentait partout les relents. C'était un triste spectacle. « Telles sont les illusions de ce monde, murmura Jamyang. Les êtres aspirent au bonheur mais lui tournent le dos. Appâtés par de brèves sensations de plaisirs faciles, ils s'en retrouvent bien vite prisonniers, voués à la morne répétition du besoin. Regarde ces hommes esclaves de l'alcool. Il en va de même de nos habitudes mentales. Nous obéissons passivement aux impulsions qui traversent nos esprits comme des refrains qui n'en finissent pas. Et pourtant, la transformation de l'esprit est une aventure si passionnante ! » Jamyang réfléchissait à voix haute ; Détchèn écoutait pensivement.

Puis ils retrouvèrent la forêt et, au bout d'une heure de marche, dépassèrent quelques yaks qui paissaient dans un sous-bois marécageux. Détchèn en fut surpris : d'habitude les yaks vivent dans les hauts pâturages, domaine des nomades. À qui pouvaient-ils appartenir ? Bientôt, ils aperçurent un petit groupe de cabanes, habitées par deux familles tibétaines. Les parents avaient fui l'invasion chinoise plus de trente ans auparavant avec une douzaine de yaks, et, depuis, vivaient chichement dans ces huttes précaires. Ils offrirent à Jamyang et Détchèn du petit lait, qu'ils avaient en excès durant la saison d'été, alors qu'ils barattaient le beurre à longueur de journée.

Le soir venu, nos amis trouvèrent une clairière au bord de la rivière, et se disposèrent à y passer la nuit. Ils rassemblèrent du bois mort pour allumer un feu et étalèrent sur le sol plusieurs couches de ramilles de pin dont les longues aiguilles formaient un tapis moelleux. Après s'être restaurés de thé chaud et de maïs concassé, ils s'allongèrent sous la voûte des arbres que les flammes teintaient de rouge. Un grand-duc ponctuait de temps à autre le silence de son « bouh ! » grave et guindé. Avant de sombrer dans le sommeil, Détchèn resta quelques instants les yeux grands ouverts, plongeant dans la nuit sans rien y saisir. Des images du village et de ses proches flottaient dans son esprit. Il voyait ces derniers réunis dans la salle commune, en train de se demander ce qu'il advenait du petit Détchèn.

Le matin du troisième jour, Jamyang et Détchèn émergèrent enfin de la grande forêt. Ils longeaient à présent un torrent tumultueux qui dévalait la vallée. Ses bouillons d'écume se heurtaient à d'énormes blocs noirs qu'ils lissaient depuis des siècles, tourbillonnaient autour de fosses invisibles et éclataient en poussière d'argent où souriaient toutes les couleurs de l'arc-en-ciel. Ils firent halte dans une prairie accueillante pour faire bouillir du thé et consommer leurs dernières galettes de sarrasin. Durant les heures qui suivirent, la marche fut plaisante. Ils rencontrèrent les premières plaques de neige. Le sentier devint abrupt et se mit à zigzaguer parmi d'énormes rochers. L'ascension prit une bonne partie de l'après-midi et ils durent s'arrêter fréquemment pour reprendre leur souffle.

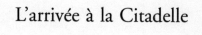

# L'arrivée à la Citadelle

La végétation changeait rapidement. Gentianes jaunes et bleues, edelweiss et genévriers avaient remplacé les essences tropicales. Nos voyageurs atteignirent un plateau verdoyant traversé par un torrent qu'ils durent franchir à plusieurs reprises en jouant les équilibristes sur des troncs d'arbres jetés en travers de son cours. Enfin, ils gravirent un col en pente douce couronné de drapeaux de prières qui flottaient au vent.

Là, Détchèn découvrit un immense cirque de parois rocheuses surmontées de crêtes aux neiges éternelles, qui formait un cercle presque parfait enserrant une plaine de bruyères et de forêts de sapins. Au milieu serpentait une rivière aux reflets bleus. Sur la droite, à une demi-heure de marche, posé sur un éperon rocheux, un petit temple, miette d'or sur les montagnes noires, étincelait au soleil.

Du paysage tout entier se dégageait une impression de paix et de majesté immuable. Détchèn pensa qu'ici devait être le « bout du monde ». Les deux pèlerins se prosternèrent trois fois dans la direction du temple, puis restèrent quelques instants silencieux, s'imprégnant de la puissante beauté du lieu. Jamyang regarda Détchèn et annonça à voix basse, plein de respect et d'émerveillement : « La Citadelle des Neiges. »

Montrant respectueusement le temple de la main, il ajouta : « C'est là que demeure Tokdèn Rinpotché. » Puis il expliqua à Détchèn : « *Rinpotché* signifie "très précieux". C'est la façon dont on s'adresse à un maître spirituel. On n'utilise son nom personnel que s'il est nécessaire de l'identifier par rapport à d'autres maîtres. Tokdèn Rinpotché a passé vingt ans au Tibet, auprès des plus grands sages de son temps. Puis il est venu méditer à la Citadelle des Neiges. Il vit ici en retraite depuis plus de trente ans, recevant la seule visite de disciples ou de quelques pèlerins. »

La Citadelle des Neiges était en effet un lieu

sacré situé à l'écart de toutes les routes et de tous les villages, l'un des grands lieux saints où avait médité Padmasambhava, le « Maître né du Lotus », connu également sous le nom de Gourou Rinpotché, qui, aux VIII$^{e}$-IX$^{e}$ siècles, fit fleurir le bouddhisme au Tibet. Plus tard, sa compagne spirituelle, Yéshé Tsoguial, « Reine de la mer de Sagesse », se livra à l'ascèse dans une grotte perdue au milieu des neiges. Le petit temple où vivait Tokdèn Rinpotché avait été construit à quelques mètres de la grotte de Padmasambhava.

Détchèn marchait d'un pas léger, empreint d'une allégresse toute nouvelle. Chaque pierre, chaque arbre lui semblaient chargés d'une présence vive. Les cimes enneigées étaient bordées de collines qui s'inclinaient vers le centre de la plaine. Elles ressemblaient à des éléphants couchés offrant leur dos à qui voudrait le gravir, ou à des lions fièrement campés défiant le voyageur intrépide. La plaine elle-même dessinait un lotus à huit pétales, et le ciel se découpait au-dessus des crêtes blanches à la manière d'un *gakhyil*, un « cercle de joie ». De petits lacs couleur turquoise constellaient les prés comme autant de coupes d'ambroisie. Des écharpes de brume enveloppaient les versants et s'accrochaient aux parasols des grands pins. Pics crénelés et arêtes déchiquetées s'élançaient vers le ciel, telles des vagues déferlantes figées dans la pierre.

Chaque roc, chaque grotte, chaque rivière portaient une histoire. Ici un ermite avait médité, là un saint avait laissé l'empreinte de son pied dans le rocher, là encore résidait une divinité du lieu. La terre était sacrée, le ciel était sacré.

Jamyang et Détchèn levaient sous leurs pas des faisans bariolés qui s'envolaient à grand bruit d'ailes. En dehors de leur maître spirituel, seule une vingtaine d'ermites habitait le cirque.

En un rien de temps, le ciel se couvrit et il se mit à neiger. Alors que leurs vêtements commençaient à blanchir et que le jour baissait, l'homme et l'enfant atteignirent un hameau d'ermitages en bois, construit en demi-cercle au bord d'un petit lac entouré de grands rochers plats. Ils pénétrèrent dans une cabane un peu plus grande que les autres, qui servait de lieu de réunion.

Quelques ermites étaient assemblés autour du feu où chauffait la soupe du soir. Ils accueillirent les voyageurs avec une gaieté tranquille. Personne ne parlait haut et fort comme au village, les conversations se tenaient à voix basse, se mêlant au murmure de la bouilloire.

Le dîner fut frugal. Un bol de *thoupa*, du bouillon de nouilles dans lequel on avait mis à tremper des légumes séchés. Après avoir échangé quelques nouvelles, les ermites se retirèrent pour se livrer à leurs pratiques du soir.

Détchèn apprit que d'autres ermites étaient en retraite solitaire depuis plusieurs années. Ils se consacraient entièrement à la vie contemplative, et seul leur maître spirituel venait de temps à autre leur rendre visite. On déposait des provisions et du bois devant la porte de leur ermitage.

Fourbu mais comblé, Détchèn dormit d'un sommeil réparateur dans un coin de la salle commune. Il fut réveillé, bien avant l'aube, par le son cristallin des clochettes des ermites qui, chacun dans son ermitage, commençaient leur journée de méditation par des prières. Au lever du soleil, Détchèn découvrit la beauté lumineuse du cirque de montagnes habillées d'un fin manteau de neige.

Il allait bientôt vivre l'un des moments les plus décisifs de son existence : la rencontre avec un maître spirituel. Malgré son jeune âge, il pressentait l'importance, la richesse et la solennité du moment. Son attente était à la fois grave et joyeuse, un élan intérieur empreint de respect et de curiosité.

# La rencontre avec le maître

Jamyang vint le chercher et ils gravirent ensemble le chemin abrupt qui menait au petit temple. Sur le seuil, Détchèn sentit son cœur battre plus fort. Puis, une fois soulevé le rideau protégeant l'entrée, il fut introduit dans une grande pièce. À gauche, un petit autel abritait des statues d'argile aux couleurs surannées et des textes sacrés devant lesquels étaient disposées des offrandes. Le plancher de bois sombre et patiné reflétait les ombres et les lumières. Quelques *thangka*, des peintures sur étoffe encadrées de brocarts délavés, ornaient les murs. Un léger parfum de pin et de genévrier mêlé d'encens flottait dans la pièce. Mais Détchèn ne percevait rien de tout cela. Émerveillé et timide, il portait toute son attention à un homme âgé au visage serein dont les cheveux blancs étaient auréolés par la lumière de la petite fenêtre contre laquelle il était adossé.

Jamyang et Détchèn se prosternèrent par trois fois et s'assirent aux pieds du maître, qui se tenait sur un lit bas couvert d'un tapis de laine. En peu de mots, Jamyang raconta l'histoire de Détchèn. Le maître sourit, le regarda avec bonté, et dit *shatsa*, cette exclamation qu'une mère attendrie réserve à son enfant.

Il émanait de ce sage une force de paix bienveillante, et sa simple présence conférait au lieu un calme comme le garçon n'en avait jamais connu. On aurait dit que chaque chose, chaque instant portaient la sérénité du maître. On n'entendait rien d'autre que le léger bruissement des grains du *mala* qui défilaient lentement entre ses doigts, petites perles de bois lustrées par la récitation de millions de mantras. La prière lui était aussi naturelle que la respiration.

Tandis que Jamyang et le maître s'entretenaient, Détchèn s'imprégnait de chaque image et de chaque parole, comme on boit à courtes gorgées l'eau pure d'une source. Il fut convenu que le jeune garçon reviendrait le lendemain matin pour recevoir ses premières instructions spirituelles.

Le maître donna sa bénédiction à Jamyang. Lorsqu'il apposa longuement ses deux mains sur la tête de Détchèn, ce dernier sentit une douce chaleur pénétrer son corps et l'emplir d'un bien-être indicible, comme si l'amour du maître s'écoulait de ses paumes à la façon d'un nectar lumineux, dissolvant toute peur et faisant s'épanouir le meilleur de lui-même.

Jamyang et Détchèn prirent congé, reculant à petits pas, comme à regret, évitant par respect de tourner le dos au maître, les mains jointes en un geste de gratitude.

En repassant le seuil du temple, Détchèn fut ébloui par l'intense luminosité qui inondait soudainement le paysage intérieur qu'il venait de découvrir. En silence, l'homme et l'enfant descendirent le chemin, attentifs à la présence du maître dans leur cœur.

Ils allèrent trouver lama Dorjé, qui faisait office d'économe pour la petite communauté. Ce dernier conduisit Détchèn vers une cabane en bois de sapin noirci par le temps qu'avait laissée vacante un méditant reparti dans sa province natale. Une lucarne créait un clair-obscur accueillant dans lequel on découvrait une couche basse recouverte d'une épaisseur de feutre gris, une table rectangulaire et un coffre en bois brut qui constituaient le seul ameublement. Sur deux étagères reposaient quelques images de divinités peintes sur papier, des photos de maîtres jaunies par les ans, une statue de Padmasambhava et sept bols d'offrandes en cuivre rouge. En dépit de la simplicité de l'endroit, Détchèn ressentit une grande joie. Il n'avait jamais eu de chambre à lui. Ce petit ermitage était maintenant son royaume, un havre de paix où il pourrait s'initier en toute quiétude à la pratique spirituelle. Ses parents, ses frères et sœurs et ses amis lui manquaient et il pensait souvent à eux avec affection et nostalgie, mais, étrangement, cela ne l'empêchait pas de se sentir parfaitement à l'aise dans ce lieu lointain et cette vie nouvelle.

Le lendemain était jour de pleine lune. Une demi-douzaine d'ermites – ceux qui n'étaient pas en retraite fermée – s'était rassemblée sur le terre-plein devant les ermitages pour y faire une offrande d'encens. Des branches de genévrier, trempées dans l'eau du petit lac, avaient été empilées sur un feu de bois où grésillait de la farine d'orge, du beurre, du miel et de la mélasse. Il s'en élevait d'épaisses volutes odoriférantes dans lesquelles les ermites visualisaient des offrandes infinies : fleurs multicolores, joyaux étincelants, nourritures aux cent saveurs, parfums et musiques emplissant les cieux, dons sans limite aux Bouddhas du présent, du passé et du futur, soulageant les souffrances de tous les êtres, leur apportant paix et félicité.

Détchèn passa le reste de la journée assis dans la prairie, découvrant peu à peu le somptueux paysage qui allait s'offrir à lui pendant des années. Une petite rivière aux eaux cristallines serpentait au milieu de la plaine ovale, cette même rivière qui, sitôt franchie la « porte » du cirque, dévalait les gorges vertigineuses que Détchèn avait gravies jusqu'à la Citadelle des Neiges. Comme autant de joyaux épars se dressaient, ici et là, des éminences rocheuses serties dans des bosquets de conifères. La majesté du lieu tenait surtout au cercle parfait de montagnes altières, impressionnantes parois rocheuses couronnées de neiges éternelles, plus lumineuses que le ciel.

Outre le col par lequel Détchèn était arrivé, une autre issue perçait ce cirque grandiose : un sentier abrupt menait vers les hauts plateaux au nord de la Citadelle, à la frontière du Tibet. Un jour, Détchèn emprunterait à son tour ce chemin pour se consacrer à la plus profonde des aventures spirituelles, la retraite contemplative, mais il ne le savait pas encore.

Le lendemain matin, il se prépara à recevoir ses premiers enseignements. À l'aube de sa deuxième rencontre avec Tokdèn Rinpotché, il ne ressentait plus l'attente devant l'inconnu qu'il avait vécue la veille, mais une dévotion naissante, faite d'admiration et de confiance. Il se sentait comme un apprenti menuisier à qui l'on va confier ses premiers outils et un bloc de bois brut, comme un jeune fermier plein d'ardeur à qui l'on donne un lopin de terre.

Le décor n'avait pas changé. Tokdèn Rinpotché attendait Détchèn assis dans la lumière dorée du matin, comme un sage qui n'a rien à perdre ni à gagner, mais tout à donner. Détchèn se prosterna et s'assit aux pieds du maître, sur le bois luisant. Celui-ci terminait ses prières du matin. Après quelques instants de silence, il dit : « Le marin doit traverser l'océan tant qu'il a un bateau ; le voyageur doit chevaucher vers les contrées lointaines tant qu'il dispose d'un bon cheval. Tant que tu possèdes cette précieuse existence humaine, pense à parcourir le chemin spirituel, te rapprochant sans cesse de la libération du monde de la souffrance et progressant vers l'Éveil ultime.

« Réfléchis bien au sens de la vie humaine, si précieuse, si fragile. Il est difficile de réunir les conditions propices à l'épanouissement de la réalisation spirituelle. Il est facile de dilapider sa vie, jour après jour, dans des activités sans fin. Rares sont les êtres qui rencontrent les enseignements du Bouddha, le Dharma, et plus rares encore ceux qui s'y intéressent. Trouver la Voie revient à découvrir un joyau inestimable : ne le gaspille pas ! Utilise-le pour exaucer toutes tes aspirations et celles des autres. Persévère dans la pratique spirituelle ! »

Tout en parlant, le maître regardait Détchèn avec une force calme d'où émanait, presque physiquement, une grande bonté. Il ajouta :

« Prends ton temps. Médite sur ces pensées et reviens me voir demain matin. » Détchèn demeura assis quelques instants encore, avant de prendre congé, s'imprégnant des paroles qu'il venait d'entendre et de la simple présence du sage.

Il descendit dans la vallée et s'assit au bord du ruisseau. Les eaux vives cascadaient entre de petits îlots herbus encapuchonnés de neige et enveloppaient les cailloux bruns de nappes transparentes. Il voyait la vie se déployer, parfois insignifiante en apparence, parfois lourde d'un avenir incertain : les bergeronnettes hochant la queue au bord du ruisseau, les insectes affairés, si vite emportés par les flots ou écrasés sous les pas distraits des humains. La vie avait-elle un sens ? Il n'y avait jamais trop réfléchi. Au village, la vie consistait à s'occuper des animaux, à ramasser du bois, à vagabonder avec ses jeunes compagnons. Quel était le sens de cela ? Détchèn restait perplexe. Une tristesse inexplicable s'empara soudainement de lui. Qu'allait-il advenir de lui ? Saurait-il être heureux ? En dépit de toutes ces interrogations qui le préoccupaient et le laissaient songeur, il sentait que les paroles du maître, telles des graines, ne manqueraient pas de germer dans son esprit, puis de mûrir en une compréhension plus claire et plus vaste.

Le jour suivant, le maître enseigna de la même façon, sans avoir recours à un texte, puisant directement aux sources de son expérience. Il répéta lentement, à trois reprises : « La vie des êtres s'écoule comme une cascade de montagne. »

Il demeura un moment silencieux, et poursuivit : « Ne laisse pas ton existence s'écouler en vain ! La vie est courte, incertaine et semée d'embûches. Elle passe comme le torrent qui court vers la mer, comme le soleil et la lune qui glissent vers les montagnes du couchant. Qui sait combien de temps il vivra ? Il n'y a pas de temps à perdre.

« La mort frappe les jeunes comme les vieux. Toi et moi, nous pouvons très bien mourir ce soir. La mort est certaine, seule son heure est imprévisible. On ne sait, de la mort ou du lendemain, qui viendra le premier. Sois toujours conscient de l'impermanence des choses.

Lorsque tu méditeras, cela t'encouragera à pratiquer avec assiduité. »

Tel fut l'enseignement de ce troisième jour. Les instructions de Tokdèn Rinpotché étaient toujours à la portée de tous. Qu'il s'exprime avec fermeté ou avec douceur, la simplicité et la profondeur de ses paroles parlaient au cœur de chacun, du plus érudit au plus ignorant.

Détchèn revint s'asseoir au même endroit que la veille, un petit coin qu'il aimait bien, près de la rivière, et contempla d'un œil neuf le paysage ensoleillé et l'eau qui coulait, rapidement, pour ne jamais revenir. Il comprit en la regardant que chaque instant vaut son pesant d'or. La vie lui parut aussitôt infiniment plus riche !

Les jours suivants, Tokdèn Rinpotché expliqua à Détchèn les lois du karma, comment chaque pensée, chaque parole et chaque acte ont des conséquences en termes de bonheur et de souffrance. Il lui expliqua le non-attachement et le renoncement : « Ce n'est pas à ce qui est bon qu'il faut renoncer, mais aux causes de la souffrance qui sont enfouies dans notre propre esprit : la malveillance, la bêtise, l'avidité, la vanité et la jalousie. »

Détchèn comprenait parfaitement qu'on ne pouvait être heureux au prix de la souffrance des autres. Tokdèn Rinpotché lui donna alors ses enseignements sur la compassion, qui constituaient clairement pour lui le fondement de toute pratique spirituelle : « Fais preuve de bonté et de générosité ; rien d'autre n'a d'importance. Ce qui n'est pas inspiré par le bien d'autrui ne vaut pas la peine d'être accompli. Cultive l'amour et la compassion. C'est une pratique exempte de tout danger et de toute déviation possible.

« Si quelqu'un tombe à l'eau et se trouve emporté par le courant de la rivière, ne vas-tu pas lui tendre la main ou souhaiter qu'il puisse s'accrocher à une branche ? Le *samsara* ressemble à une rivière tumultueuse qui emporte les êtres de souffrance en souffrance. Ses flots sont alimentés par l'ignorance et les autres poisons mentaux. Les mains tendues sont celles de la bonté aimante et de la sagesse qui permettent aux victimes des infinies vicissitudes de l'existence de rejoindre la rive de la libération. »

Plus il passait de temps en présence de

Tokdèn Rinpotché, plus le jeune garçon voyait grandir son admiration et son amour pour son maître. Ce dernier était l'exemple vivant de ses enseignements. Sa bonté et sa douceur coulaient des profondeurs de son être. Les mots de Jamyang résonnaient en Détchèn : « On n'a jamais envie de quitter le maître. On voudrait se fondre en lui, comme un flocon de neige qui tombe dans un lac. »

Dans sa cabane, Détchèn méditait de son mieux. Il ne doutait jamais du chemin, mais parfois de lui-même et de sa capacité à le suivre. Il lui arrivait d'être envahi par un profond sentiment de découragement. La destination était claire, mais saurait-il l'atteindre ? Il avait envie de pleurer, il voulait quitter son ermitage, il était tenté d'abandonner ses résolutions et de repartir au village. Pris dans la tourmente, il se sentait mal dans sa peau. Mais ces doutes ne duraient guère ; nuages chassés par le vent, ils laissaient bientôt place à la sérénité, semblable au ciel clair où brillait le soleil de sa pratique spirituelle. Après coup, ces moments d'abattement ne lui apparaissaient plus que comme de mauvais souvenirs, des distorsions de la réalité dans le miroir des fabrications mentales. Son désarroi passager devant l'ampleur de la tâche et la lenteur de ses progrès suscitait en lui une détermination farouche, semblable à celle du grimpeur qui redouble d'ardeur en contemplant la distance qui lui reste à gravir. Il appréciait alors d'autant plus la qualité de chaque instant qui passe.

Au début, il avait eu bien du mal à dompter son esprit vagabond. Il faisait le tour du monde dans sa tête et entretenait des dialogues imaginaires avec ses amis du village ou avec d'autres dont le souvenir l'irritait un peu. Il essayait en vain de réduire ses pensées au silence. Il lui semblait même qu'elles se multipliaient ! À peine croyait-il en être venu à bout qu'elles resurgissaient avec force, créant chacune sa propre fantasmagorie, se bousculant en lui comme les eaux d'un torrent impétueux. Mais à force de persévérance, son esprit se mit à ressembler peu à peu à un fleuve large et paisible.

Détchèn avait désormais appris à connaître les autres ermites, qui lui prodiguaient une attention paternelle. En raison de son jeune âge, il était devenu leur mascotte et ils aimaient bien le taquiner, tout en l'encourageant dans sa pratique. L'un d'eux, lama Dorjé, l'avait, au début, quelque peu intimidé. Il avait une grande barbe hirsute, fait assez rare chez les Bhoutanais, qui sont généralement imberbes, et roulait de gros yeux courroucés chaque fois qu'il regardait Détchèn. Mais ce n'était qu'un jeu, et aussitôt lama Dorjé éclatait de rire. Un jour, pour l'amuser, il montra à Détchèn comment attraper des *abra*, ces jolis rats des champs de couleur brune. Il souffla vigoureusement dans l'une des ouvertures du tunnel souterrain où l'*abra* se terrait et enjoignit Détchèn de bloquer l'autre sortie avec la manche de son manteau. Presque aussitôt, l'*abra*, fuyant le souffle chaud à odeur humaine, s'engouffra précipitamment dans la manche grande ouverte. Une fois attrapé, il se laissa d'abord cajoler sans résistance, mais finit par planter ses dents acérées dans la main de Détchèn, qui lui rendit derechef sa liberté. Lama Dorjé lui raconta que les *abra* creusaient de nombreuses caches où ils entassaient leurs graines, mais qu'ils les perdaient souvent. En effet, au moment de les enterrer dans la prairie, ils regardaient le ciel pour repérer sous quel nuage se trouvait leur cachette, afin d'être sûrs de la retrouver plus tard !

L'*abra* était la proie favorite du *dremong*, sorte de grand ours noir. On dit qu'après avoir attrapé un *abra*, le *dremong* le serrait sous son bras. Par chance pour l'animal terrifié, lorsque l'ours s'emparait d'un deuxième *abra*, il le mettait à nouveau sous son bras et, ce faisant, laissait échapper le premier !

Il y avait aussi un vieux moine tibétain qui avait dû fuir le Tibet trente ans plus tôt, lorsque les Chinois avaient envahi son pays, et Phuntsok, âgé de vingt-cinq ans, qui venait de fuir le Toit du Monde avec pour tout bagage un ballot de livres précieux. À deux reprises, ce dernier était tombé aux mains de l'armée chinoise alors qu'il tentait de passer la frontière et avait croupi plusieurs mois dans une prison après avoir été torturé. Un jour, il avait enfin réussi à déjouer les gardes-frontières et à franchir les cols enneigés. Depuis, il pratiquait paisiblement à la Citadelle des Neiges.

# La femme de la forêt

Un matin, alors que Détchèn se promenait dans la forêt qui couvrait le versant sud de la vallée, il entendit une voix de femme chantant une mélodie d'une grande pureté, portée par le silence des bois. Ravi, Détchèn s'arrêta pour mieux entendre et discerner le sens des paroles :

*Les pensées de bonheur et de souffrance, de désir et d'aversion*
*Ne sont autres que la vacuité lumineuse de l'esprit.*
*Sans altérer ce qui surgit,*
*Regarde sa nature :*
*C'est la grande félicité.*

Guidé par la voix, Détchèn arriva bientôt en vue d'un petit ermitage à l'orée d'une clairière.

Sur la terrasse, une femme aux traits sereins était assise en méditation. Craignant de troubler sa contemplation, Détchèn se tint respectueusement à distance.

La femme lui fit signe d'approcher et l'accueillit avec un large sourire. Son regard lumineux reflétait un mélange de bonté et de certitude quant à la futilité des choses de ce monde. Elle demanda à Détchèn d'où il venait et ce qu'il avait fait jusqu'alors. Puis, après un moment de silence, elle lui dit : « Tu es jeune, mais avec le temps tu comprendras que les plaisirs et les séductions du monde, bien qu'attirants au premier abord, tournent souvent à l'aigre. À l'inverse, les premiers pas sur le chemin spirituel sont un peu ardus, mais le voyage devient de plus en plus plaisant à mesure qu'on progresse. »

Détchèn prit congé discrètement, et, tandis qu'il s'éloignait, le chant reprit.

*Le corps : impermanent, telles les brumes de printemps.*
*L'esprit : insubstantiel, tel l'espace vide.*

*Les pensées : évanescentes, telle la brise dans l'espace.*
*Sans trêve, songe à ces trois points.*

Cette femme et la sérénité qui émanait d'elle avaient profondément impressionné Détchèn. Elle avait suivi un chemin bien différent de celui des autres villageoises, asservies à des tâches sans fin et souvent maltraitées par des maris alcooliques. Détchèn en conçut une admiration accrue pour le chemin spirituel et, de retour aux ermitages, s'enquit de l'histoire de la retraitante.

Lama Dorjé lui raconta qu'elle venait du village de Doumré, à deux jours de marche de la Citadelle. Sonam Wangmo, « Force du Mérite », était l'aînée d'une famille de six enfants. Toute jeune, elle avait dû s'occuper de ses cadets et vaquer aux travaux du foyer. À l'âge de seize ans, ses parents avaient songé à la marier. Cela aurait fait un homme de plus à la maison (parfois, les jeunes filles partaient dans leur nouvelle famille, mais souvent aussi le jeune marié rejoignait sa belle-famille).

Sonam Wangmo était très jolie et les prétendants ne manquaient pas. Les soirs d'été, certains n'hésitaient pas à s'introduire par les fenêtres du grenier pour la surprendre dans son sommeil, une coutume chère aux jouvenceaux des campagnes bhoutanaises. Certains d'entre eux lui plaisaient bien, mais la vue des grands-mères édentées assises sur le seuil des maisons, celle de sa propre mère, prématurément vieillie par une vie de labeur, et la fréquentation des hommes dominateurs qui dictaient la vie de la communauté ne lui avaient guère donné envie de suivre les traces de ses aïeules.

Un jour, un lama était passé au village, accompagné de quelques disciples, tous en chemin vers la Citadelle des Neiges. Sonam Wangmo n'avait pas osé l'aborder, mais faisant cercle autour de lui avec les autres enfants, elle l'avait observé avec une curiosité respectueuse, tandis que ses parents et plusieurs villageois lui offraient thé et nourriture. Puis tous avaient reçu la bénédiction du lama et lui avaient souhaité longue vie et bon voyage. Le souvenir de ce visiteur, qui n'était autre que Tokdèn Rinpotché, était resté vivant dans l'esprit de la jeune fille.

Son oncle et sa tante lui avaient raconté leur séjour à la Citadelle où ils avaient reçu des enseignements du maître. Ils lui avaient parlé de la vie là-haut, une vie qui lui semblait autrement plus prometteuse que celle qui l'attendait au village. Non seulement elle échapperait à la servitude de la vie ordinaire, mais la possibilité d'un épanouissement profond s'offrirait à elle. Se dédier à la contemplation est un choix respecté que nombre de femmes font au Bhoutan, mais on ne s'attendait guère à ce qu'une fille belle comme Sonam Wangmo prenne une telle décision. Un beau jour, pourtant, alors qu'un groupe de pèlerins s'apprêtait à monter vers la Citadelle des Neiges, elle en profita pour demander à ses parents la permission de les accompagner. Son souhait recueillit l'approbation de tous. En fait, cette randonnée prévue pour quelques jours se révéla être sans retour.

Parvenue à la Citadelle, Sonam Wangmo s'était aussitôt sentie chez elle, parfaitement à l'aise. Elle éprouvait le sentiment libérateur d'être sortie d'une situation sans issue. Lorsqu'elle avait rencontré Tokdèn Rinpotché, son cœur s'était ouvert davantage. Les quelques paroles qu'il avait prononcées ce jour-là flottèrent longtemps dans sa tête, à la manière d'une musique que l'on aime. Elle s'était vite décidée : elle ne retournerait pas au village. La veille de leur départ, elle avait annoncé à ses compagnons de voyage qu'elle souhaitait demeurer quelque temps auprès du maître. « Dites à mes parents de ne pas s'inquiéter. Tout ira bien. » Dès qu'ils furent partis, elle avait éprouvé une merveilleuse légèreté.

Tokdèn Rinpotché devint à la fois un père et une mère pour elle. Sonam Wangmo aimait profondément ses parents, mais, aussi bienveillants fussent-ils, ils ne pouvaient offrir à leur enfant la sagesse qu'elle avait trouvée chez son maître.

La jeune fille était restée quelques mois à proximité du sage, recevant ses enseignements, puis, sur son conseil, elle s'était installée dans le petit ermitage de la forêt. Voilà maintenant cinq ans qu'elle y habitait. Ses parents et certains de ses frères et sœurs étaient parfois venus lui rendre visite, chargés de provisions et d'une cape doublée de longs filaments de laine qui lui permettrait de braver les rigueurs de l'hiver. Ils étaient restés quelques jours, tout à la joie de voir la jeune fille si épanouie, puis ils étaient repartis rassurés, secrètement remplis d'admiration pour sa force et son choix.

Lama Dorjé avait parlé d'une seule traite. Le vieil ermite et le jeune homme restèrent pensifs, méditant sur le sort de tous ces êtres que les flots de la vie emportent jour après jour, comme des bouchons ballottés sur un fleuve ; ils mesuraient le bonheur de ceux qui avaient eu la bonne fortune et la détermination nécessaires pour accomplir leurs aspirations les plus profondes. Détchèn fut tiré de sa rêverie lorsque le rideau de la porte s'écarta. Jamyang lui annonça que Tokdèn Rinpotché l'appelait.

La nuit était tombée. Une lampe à huile éclairait faiblement le visage du maître. Devant sa table, un petit brasero rougeoyait dans un pot en fonte. Citant un sage du passé, Tokdèn Rinpotché dit à Détchèn :

« On peut faire du beurre avec du lait parce que le lait contient déjà de la crème, mais personne n'a jamais obtenu du beurre en barattant de l'eau. L'orpailleur cherche l'or dans les pierres, non dans les bois. Pareillement, s'efforcer d'atteindre la bouddhéité n'a de sens que parce que la nature de Bouddha est inhérente à tous les êtres. Sans cette nature, tout effort serait vain. »

Il poursuivit : « Mais il ne suffit pas de prendre conscience du potentiel que nous possédons tous, encore faut-il le faire fructifier. Seule la chaleur d'une résolution enthousiaste peut faire fondre la gangue qui entoure notre être et permettre à l'or de la bouddhéité de briller de tous ses feux. Cette diligence doit être constamment nourrie par la confiance en la sagesse du maître, et par la certitude que sa compassion n'abandonne jamais le disciple. »

Puis, après un silence, il sourit à Détchèn en disant :

« Voici plus d'un an que tu vis auprès de moi. Malgré ton jeune âge, tu as fait preuve de détermination et de constance dans ton désir de pratiquer le Dharma. Tu as foi en ton maître et dans les enseignements du Bouddha. Je pense que le temps est venu pour toi d'aller faire une retraite dans la montagne. Que penserais-tu de te rendre à Néuring, dans la grotte de la "Reine de la mer de Sagesse", près des deux lacs sacrés, le lac Blanc et le lac Noir ? Tu resterais là-haut le temps qu'il faudra pour que ta pratique progresse. Je subviendrai à tes besoins. Souviens-toi des paroles du Bouddha : "Je t'ai montré le chemin de la délivrance. C'est à toi de le parcourir." »

Détchèn acquiesça avec joie. Il appréciait à sa juste valeur l'importance du moment et ressentait un mélange d'exaltation et de gravité devant l'aventure qui l'attendait. Il était comme le marin qui, pour la première fois, va partir seul en mer, maître de son navire mais ne comptant plus que sur lui-même dans le calme comme dans la tempête. Il éprouvait une immense gratitude envers celui qui l'avait conduit jusqu'à ce rivage, celui dont les enseignements et les bénédictions continueraient à le guider tout au long de la traversée.

Lorsque Détchèn prit congé ce soir-là, Tokdèn Rinpotché lui apposa longuement les mains sur la tête, priant pour que le garçon soit libre de tout obstacle extérieur et intérieur et qu'il goûte le fruit de sa pratique spirituelle. Plein de confiance dans son maître, il s'endormit en imaginant les lacs et l'immense espace.

Il s'éveilla le lendemain animé d'une énergie nouvelle et d'une sensation de légèreté qui lui donnait envie de chanter, de bondir, de s'envoler. Il fut convenu que Jamyang, lama Dorjé et deux autres ermites l'accompagneraient jusqu'à la grotte de Néuring pour l'aider à s'installer et porter les provisions. Il fallait prévoir que, durant les mois d'hiver, la neige couperait Détchèn du reste du monde. Son départ fut fixé à la semaine suivante, au dixième jour du cinquième mois lunaire, après la célébration annuelle de la naissance de Padmasambhava.

À l'occasion de cette cérémonie, présidée par Tokdèn Rinpotché, tous les ermites de la vallée, sauf ceux qui avaient fait vœu de ne jamais quitter leur cellule, se réunirent pour célébrer une journée durant un magnifique rituel d'offrandes, ponctué de méditations chantées et de récitations de mantras. Parmi eux se trouvaient des retraitants, hommes et femmes, que Détchèn ne connaissait pas encore, et qui étaient descendus d'ermitages accrochés aux contreforts de la Citadelle. Sonam Wangmo, la grande méditante de la forêt, vint aussi et prodigua à Détchèn conseils et encouragements. Ce fut une belle et joyeuse fête spirituelle. De généreuses offrandes de nourriture, de fleurs, d'encens et d'eau parfumée au safran avaient été disposées devant l'autel. Les chants, où se mêlaient les voix graves des hommes et celles, hautes et mélodieuses, des femmes, se succédèrent toute la journée. Le sentiment de communion spirituelle qui émanait du maître et des disciples renforçait la confiance et la force intérieure de Détchèn : il se sentit plus de courage que jamais pour entamer sa retraite de montagne. Il appréciait pleinement sa chance d'avoir rencontré un maître spirituel et des compagnons d'une telle qualité.

Détchèn rassembla ses quelques effets dans un gros balluchon. Juste avant le départ, il alla offrir une écharpe cérémonielle de soie blanche à Tokdèn Rinpotché et reçut une dernière fois sa bénédiction. Ce dernier lui donna une belle cape en laine qu'il avait portée pendant quelques mois. Quand Détchèn s'en envelopperait dans sa grotte, il ressentirait ainsi de façon palpable la présence de son maître. Les ermites lui firent quant à eux de petits cadeaux de nourriture, qu'ils accompagnèrent de leurs prières et de leurs vœux de succès pour sa retraite. Puis Détchèn et ses quatre amis se mirent en route.

Le soleil matinal illuminait le sentier escarpé qu'ils gravirent en quelques heures. Puis ils traversèrent les hauts plateaux et atteignirent enfin les deux lacs. Un peu au-dessus du lac Blanc, perdu dans les éboulis de roches, s'ouvrait la grotte où Yéshé Tsoguial, « Reine de la mer de Sagesse », la compagne spirituelle de Padmasambhava, s'était longuement livrée à l'ascèse et à la méditation. En la voyant, Détchèn se rappela ce poème d'un maître du passé que Jamyang avait recopié pour lui :

*Si tu aspires à la solitude des montagnes,*
*Des grottes accueillantes s'ouvrent à flanc de falaise*
*Sous des sommets drapés de brume.*
*Demeurer en ces retraites est source d'une indicible joie, temporelle et ultime.*

Les pèlerins déposèrent leurs fardeaux à l'entrée de la grotte et allumèrent un feu de bois mort pour préparer le thé. Puis, après s'être restaurés, ils entreprirent d'aménager la grotte qui n'avait pas été habitée depuis longtemps. À l'aide de pierres plates, ils remontèrent le mur écroulé qui en fermait l'entrée, ménageant une lucarne et une porte basse devant laquelle ils suspendirent une lourde étoffe. Ils rassemblèrent ensuite une bonne quantité de bois mort qu'ils empilèrent dans une cavité voisine. Finalement, et non sans quelque appréhension, ils laissèrent Détchèn sur d'ultimes souhaits de progrès spirituel. Mais ils savaient que Détchèn avait la trempe d'un bon retraitant et ne s'inquiétaient pas outre mesure.

# La retraite dans la grotte

Après leur départ, Détchèn ne se sentit plus de joie. Il contemplait avec émerveillement sa petite grotte et le paysage environnant dont l'immensité lui dilatait le cœur. Désormais il était seul avec sa pratique spirituelle, seul avec les jours et les mois qui s'offraient à lui comme au paysan un champ fertile. La présence de son maître nourrirait chaque instant, sans que nulle autre préoccupation ne vienne envahir son esprit.

Il aménagea un petit espace dans un coin de la grotte, déblayant les pierres et les branches mortes. Puis il étendit de l'herbe sèche sur laquelle il posa son tapis de feutre et la cape de Tokdèn Rinpotché. Dans une niche du rocher, il plaça une statuette de Padmasambhava que lama Dorjé lui avait donnée et disposa autour quelques offrandes.

Puis il s'assit, le buste bien droit, et formula la promesse suivante : « En accord avec les conseils de mon maître, je poursuivrai ma pratique jusqu'à ce que naissent en moi des expériences méditatives et une réalisation spirituelle profonde et durable. Je n'aurai d'autre compagnon que la solitude, et les enseignements de mon maître seront mes seules pensées. »

Il se trouvait dans l'état d'esprit d'un artisan qui s'apprête à réaliser son chef-d'œuvre. C'était le début de l'après-midi, vers la fin de l'été. Le soleil baignait l'entrée de la grotte et réchauffait les dalles de rochers. Détchèn sortit s'asseoir devant sa nouvelle demeure, savourant la plénitude du moment. Il formula ce vœu du fond de son cœur : « Dans cette vie comme dans les vies suivantes, puissé-je continuer à progresser sur le chemin de l'Éveil et dédier jusqu'à la plus infime parcelle de moi-même au bien des êtres. » Il poursuivit par cette prière :

*Si je reste en bonne santé,*
*J'utiliserai mes forces pour m'adonner à la pratique spirituelle.*

*Si je tombe malade,*
*J'utiliserai mes maux pour augmenter ma compassion envers ceux qui souffrent.*
*Si je vis longtemps,*
*J'utiliserai chaque instant pour accomplir le bien d'autrui et le mien.*
*Si ma vie touche à sa fin,*
*Je vivrai au mieux le moment de la mort pour obtenir une renaissance favorable à la quête de l'Éveil.*

Il commença sa retraite le soir même.

Jour après jour, il s'immergea de plus en plus dans la pratique, méditant tout d'abord quelques heures par jour, puis augmentant progressivement jusqu'à effectuer quatre longues séances de pratique : l'une avant l'aube, la deuxième le matin, la troisième l'après-midi, et la dernière après la tombée de la nuit.

Au réveil, il s'asseyait le dos droit, car une posture corporelle équilibrée facilite la concentration et évite de succomber à la torpeur comme à l'excitation mentale, les deux défauts majeurs qui nuisent à la clarté et à la stabilité de la méditation. Il commençait par invoquer les bénédictions de Tokdèn Rinpotché et des maîtres de la lignée spirituelle. Il suscitait ainsi en lui une profonde dévotion qui, souvent, lui faisait venir les larmes aux yeux. Puis il ravivait sa diligence en pensant à l'impermanence de toute chose, à la fragilité de la vie humaine et à la nécessité de lui donner un sens. Les êtres vivants se comptent par milliards, mais combien prennent seulement conscience de la valeur de leur existence ? Et, parmi ceux qui s'engagent dans la pratique, combien persistent et atteignent l'Éveil ? Ces derniers sont aussi peu nombreux que les étoiles de l'aube.

Détchèn ressentait aussi de façon aiguë l'extrême vulnérabilité de la vie, ce qui la rendait d'autant plus précieuse. Il réalisa que le monde ordinaire n'apportait que des satisfactions éphémères et limitées, et que le cercle vicieux du *samsara* ne se romprait pas de lui-même. Il fallait s'en arracher et, dans ce but, développer la même détermination qu'un prisonnier qui ne songe qu'à s'évader.

Il lui semblait évident que, pour atteindre ce

but, il n'était pas question de faire n'importe quoi : toute action a des conséquences, et celles-ci dépendent de l'intention et de l'attitude qui l'inspirent. Pour développer une vigilance continue, il devait être pleinement conscient que la souffrance résulte des actes nuisibles, et qu'elle ne peut que croître tant que l'on agit de façon négative. Il devait clairement distinguer les actes positifs des actes négatifs, accomplir les premiers et se garder des seconds, aussi anodins fussent-ils. Il était maintenant convaincu que tout acte, toute parole et toute pensée, même les plus infimes, devaient être dédiés au bien des êtres.

Il prenait refuge dans le Bouddha, dans son enseignement et dans la communauté de tous ceux qui suivent le chemin de l'Éveil. Du plus profond de son être, il développait la compassion et l'amour altruiste. Puis il visualisait au-dessus de sa tête Vajrasattva, le Bouddha de la purification, brillant comme une montagne enneigée frappée par mille soleils. Un nectar s'écoulait de son corps, purifiait Détchèn de toutes ses taches et dissipait les voiles de son ignorance. Ensuite, Détchèn offrait mentalement aux Bouddhas du passé, du présent et du futur toutes les merveilles de l'univers : joyaux, forêts et montagnes, fleurs et essences médicinales, amoncelés dans l'espace. Il unissait son esprit à celui de son maître et demeurait autant qu'il le pouvait dans la parfaite équanimité de cette fusion spirituelle. Il ne manquait pas de conclure cette séance de pratique en dédiant les bienfaits de sa méditation à tous les êtres.

À l'aube, il se restaurait de *tsampa* ou de riz concassé trempé dans du thé chaud.

Durant la matinée, il se consacrait aux multiples visualisations de divinités symbolisant divers aspects de l'Éveil et à la récitation de mantras. Il apprenait ainsi à développer une vision pure du monde et des êtres. Chaque forme devenait déité, chaque bruit le son d'un mantra et chaque pensée un reflet de la sagesse. Après avoir déjeuné d'un repas simple, il lisait les vies des maîtres du passé ou des enseignements qui l'inspiraient.

L'après-midi, il s'absorbait dans la nature de l'esprit, c'est-à-dire la présence éveillée, limpide et lumineuse, qui se manifeste dès lors que l'écran des pensées se dissipe dans le ciel de la simplicité. Le soir venu, il récitait de nombreuses prières pour le bien de tous les êtres, puis s'endormait en unissant à nouveau son esprit à celui du maître.

Détchèn était confiant : s'il pratiquait avec énergie, jour après jour, mois après mois, les qualités spirituelles se développeraient en lui comme le miel s'accumule dans la ruche à mesure et en proportion de ce que l'abeille butine de fleur en fleur. Il pratiqua ainsi pendant tout l'été. Savoir que la grande *yogini* Yéshé Tsoguial avait médité en ce lieu lui était une profonde source d'inspiration. Il est dit qu'un mois de méditation dans un site béni par un maître du passé permet de faire autant de progrès qu'une année passée dans un lieu quelconque. Ici, pas un instant n'était ordinaire. En dehors des périodes de méditation, durant le repos, les repas ou toute autre activité simple à laquelle il s'adonnait, l'inspiration du lieu demeurait comme une présence invisible. Ce sentiment était renforcé par les traces tangibles du passage de la sainte : l'âtre en pierre dans lequel elle allumait son feu, le coin sommairement aménagé où elle s'asseyait, et même le muret qui fermait la grotte.

Détchèn aimait beaucoup les alentours. Il sortait quelquefois et allait s'asseoir au soleil sur un large rocher plat au-dessus du lac Blanc, pour emmagasiner un peu de chaleur. Au nord de la grotte, des éboulis dévalaient en pente raide dans le lac. À l'est se déployait un étagement de chaînes de montagnes dont les plus lointains sommets se fondaient dans le bleu profond du ciel. Devant, au sud, la pierraille laissait place à une pente herbeuse parsemée de rhododendrons en fleur. De loin en loin, le chant d'un pinson des neiges, les cris d'un couple de choucas ou l'appel d'une marmotte rehaussaient la perfection du silence.

Un jour, Détchèn contempla longuement un papillon posé sur une fleur qui oscillait doucement sous la brise. Il butinait, puis, sans raison apparente, l'instant d'après s'envolait, voletait de-ci de-là et revenait déployer ses belles ailes bleues sur le pistil orange. Ce manège, répété à plusieurs reprises, évoqua en Détchèn les instructions que Tokdèn Rinpotché lui avait données sur la façon de stabiliser son esprit : « Commence par observer le va-et-vient de ton souffle. Après une douzaine d'inspirations et d'expirations, ton esprit se calmera un peu. Concentre-toi sur un objet extérieur, une image du Bouddha par exemple, ou garde ton esprit centré sur lui-même. Lorsque tu t'aperçois que tu es distrait par des pensées nouvelles, reviens vers l'objet de ta concentration comme le papillon vers la fleur. Si ton esprit se fatigue et que ta concentration se relâche, laisse-le simplement reposer dans son état naturel, préservant cette liberté intérieure, sans encourager les pensées ni tenter de les supprimer. Contemple la nature même de l'esprit. A-t-il une forme, une couleur, une localisation ? N'y trouvant rien, demeure à l'aise, détendu, dans cet "introuvable". Laisse les pensées se défaire à mesure qu'elles se forment, comme un dessin tracé du doigt à la surface de l'eau.

« Parfois, fais naître en toi un puissant sentiment de bienveillance et de compassion inconditionnelle à l'égard de tous les êtres, et laisse ce sentiment envahir ton esprit tout entier. À la fin, dédie les bienfaits de cette pratique à tous les êtres.

« Ainsi, peu à peu, au fil des jours et des mois, ton esprit deviendra plus clair et plus stable. Il ne sera plus emporté comme auparavant par les vagues des pensées négatives qui sapent ta paix intérieure. Il deviendra libre des flots de pensées qui nous entraînent, impuissants, vers l'avidité, la haine et la souffrance. »

C'est ainsi que Détchèn apprit à travailler sur son esprit comme on assouplit son corps ou comme on prépare une terre avant de la cultiver. Quelques mois s'écoulèrent dans la paix de la pratique spirituelle.

Puis vinrent les premières neiges. Détchèn se prépara à être bientôt coupé du monde. S'il arrivait qu'en été de rares pèlerins montent jusqu'ici pour rendre hommage au lieu saint de Yéshé Tsoguial, aucun être humain ne pouvait y accéder l'hiver.

Il allait faire très froid, mais la grotte était bien protégée par la masse du rocher et si exiguë que l'air se réchauffait dès que Détchèn faisait bouillir l'eau du thé.

Un matin, plongé dans sa méditation, les yeux mi-clos, Détchèn eut le sentiment qu'il se passait quelque chose – il avait dû inconsciemment entendre un bruit. Il souleva le rideau de la porte et sortit. À une cinquantaine de mètres de lui, près de la source qui ne gelait jamais, même au cœur de l'hiver, une panthère des neiges s'abreuvait, accompagnée de ses deux petits, nés au printemps. Elle n'avait pas vu Détchèn qui, parfaitement immobile, l'observait avec une prudente fascination. Ce félin farouche et rare évite l'homme et d'ordinaire se déplace surtout la nuit. Bien que Détchèn n'eût jamais entendu parler d'accidents, il n'était guère rassuré.

La mère et ses petits repartirent au bout d'une dizaine de minutes. Lorsqu'ils furent sur le versant opposé, de l'autre côté du lac, Détchèn ne put résister à l'envie de manifester sa présence. Il cria « Ohééé !... » Les trois têtes se tournèrent instantanément, et les animaux s'immobilisèrent, le regard fixé sur la grotte. Au bout d'un temps qui parut fort long à Détchèn, la mère reprit sa marche et, suivie de ses petits, s'en fut comme si de rien n'était.

Cette rencontre rappela à Détchèn une histoire que lui avait racontée lama Dorjé. Un grand maître nommé Jamyang Khyentsé Wangpo était venu du Tibet afin de méditer dans cette même grotte de Yéshé Tsoguial. Il était accompagné d'un disciple, et tous deux avaient passé l'hiver dans la caverne, encerclés par la neige. Un jour, le lama avait soudain dit au disciple : « Cache-toi derrière moi et ne bouge sous aucun prétexte. » Puis il s'était drapé dans sa large cape brune et, assis bien droit, était entré aussitôt en concentration profonde, les yeux grands ouverts. Le disciple se tenait derrière son maître, presque entièrement dissimulé par la cape de ce dernier. Un bruit s'était fait entendre à l'entrée de la grotte et, chose inconcevable en cet endroit l'hiver, un tigre était apparu. Il s'était arrêté devant le lama et l'avait regardé, en grondant d'un air courroucé et en balançant nerveusement sa queue. Imperturbable, le sage méditait, avec une expression noble et insondable. Au bout d'un moment, qui pour le disciple avait semblé un siècle, le tigre avait poussé un puissant feulement, la gueule grande ouverte, puis, tournant le dos, s'en était allé. « Tu peux sortir, avait déclaré le maître, il ne se passera plus rien. » Plus tard, il avait expliqué à son disciple qu'il ne s'agissait pas d'un tigre ordinaire, mais d'une manifestation de la déité gardienne du lieu sacré, venue honorer le grand lama à sa façon tout en le mettant à l'épreuve.

Détchèn se demandait comment il réagirait s'il se trouvait confronté à pareille situation... Qui sait, un tigre lui rendrait peut-être visite un jour ? Au Bhoutan, on avait vu ces félins errer jusqu'à plus de quatre mille mètres d'altitude, soit à peine plus bas que Néuring.

La méditation de Détchèn progressait. L'isolement, accru par la neige, renforçait sa concentration et son engagement. Affranchi des préoccupations du monde ordinaire, il n'avait d'autre pensée que sa pratique. Il lui arrivait de rester de longs moments absorbé dans la nature même de l'esprit. Parfois, il rafraîchissait son inspiration en lisant quelques conseils et chants d'Éveil laissés par de grands contemplatifs, tel celui-ci :

*Le rayonnement de la conscience éveillée,*
*libre d'élaborations,*
*Est directement perçu au-delà l'intellect.*
*Puissé-je me garder de nouer le ciel avec le lasso*
*de l'investigation*
*Et exceller à demeurer spontanément dans*
*l'état naturel !*

D'autres fois, son esprit était envahi d'une dévotion douce et puissante envers son maître, sentiment qui l'emplissait de chaleur et de félicité. Comme l'écrivait l'un de ces maîtres :

*Lorsque le soleil de l'ardente dévotion brille*
*Sur les sommets enneigés des quatre corps du*
*maître,*
*Il fait jaillir le torrent des bénédictions :*
*Engendre donc une foi ardente.*

À maintes reprises, Détchèn dissolvait son esprit limité dans le vaste Éveil du maître et reposait sereinement dans cette union. À certains moments la présence de son maître était si vivante que des larmes de joie et de reconnaissance jaillissaient de ses yeux.

Le printemps finit par revenir. Les neiges commencèrent à fondre, les perdrix blanches sortirent de leurs gîtes, et les marmottes se réveillèrent de leur sommeil hivernal. Ici et là, des fleurs perçaient le sol dégelé ; de nouveau la nature respirait.

Vint pour Détchèn le temps de se livrer à une pratique que lui avait transmise Tokdèn Rinpotché et qui consistait à extraire, par la méditation, l'essence des éléments naturels. Il s'exerça à toute une palette de visualisations, au cours desquelles il s'imaginait absorbant la force élémentale des forêts, des montagnes, des océans et du ciel. Pendant un mois, Détchèn vécut tout d'abord de l'essence de fleurs et de plantes médicinales, puis de minéraux et, finalement, de l'essence du ciel qu'il respirait comme une nourriture. Curieusement, il ne maigrissait presque pas. Au contraire, il se sentait plein de vigueur et avait l'esprit clair et lucide. Il se rappela ce poème d'un yogi d'antan :

*De même que le lion des neiges ne craint pas*
*le froid des montagnes,*
*Que le vautour ne tombe pas du ciel*
*Et le poisson jamais ne se noie,*
*Le pratiquant ne peut mourir de faim.*

Vers le mois de juin, un après-midi, il vit venir au loin un homme qui se dirigeait vers la grotte. La silhouette lui semblait familière. Lorsqu'elle se rapprocha, il reconnut Phuntsok, le jeune moine qui avait fui le Tibet quelques années auparavant. Pourquoi venait-il ainsi le voir, alors qu'il le savait en retraite ?

Phuntsok apportait une lettre de Jamyang. Cette dernière disait en quelques mots que Tokdèn Rinpotché n'était pas en bonne santé et qu'il conseillait à Détchèn de revenir auprès du maître.

Détchèn fut pris d'inquiétude et éprouva un profond désir de revoir son maître. Ce soir-là, Phuntsok campa dans une grotte voisine et il fut convenu qu'ils redescendraient ensemble le lendemain matin. Bien avant l'aube, Détchèn conclut sa retraite par une cérémonie d'offrandes et formula du fond de son cœur des prières pour la longue vie de Tokdèn Rinpotché et de tous les détenteurs des enseignements du Bouddha. Puis, avec l'aide de Phuntsok, il emballa ses quelques effets, et tous deux se mirent en route. Juste avant que ne disparaissent de leur vue la grotte et le lac, il se retourna pour les regarder une dernière fois en formant le souhait de pouvoir consacrer le reste de sa vie à la pratique spirituelle.

# Le corps d'arc-en-ciel

La descente s'effectua rapidement et les deux hommes furent bientôt en vue du temple. Détchèn rejoignit ses amis qui étaient réunis dans la salle commune. Ils avaient l'air grave et parlaient à voix basse. Un mois plus tôt, Tokdèn Rinpotché était tombé malade, et son état s'était aggravé. Après les avoir écoutés, Détchèn monta vers le temple et arriva en présence de son maître. Alors qu'il se prosternait devant lui, il remarqua tout de suite le visage émacié de Tokdèn Rinpotché. Celui-ci accueillit pourtant Détchèn avec un grand sourire et le bénit chaleureusement. Détchèn s'enquit de sa santé. Rinpotché répondit qu'il était à présent très âgé et que son corps illusoire allait bientôt subir la loi de l'impermanence. C'est pourquoi il avait pensé qu'il serait bon que Détchèn redescende afin de recevoir ses derniers conseils. Il demanda à son disciple de lui relater sa retraite et sembla satisfait de ce qu'il entendit.

Depuis son retour, Détchèn rendait visite à Tokdèn Rinpotché plusieurs fois par jour. Il restait assis en sa présence et participait aux quelques conversations qui se tenaient ; presque toutes avaient pour sujet la pratique spirituelle. C'est dans ces moments que Rinpotché prodiguait à Détchèn des conseils et des indications sur les exercices contemplatifs qu'il lui faudrait accomplir dans le futur.

Un après-midi, alors que le maître et le disciple se trouvaient assis seuls au soleil sur la petite prairie située devant le temple, au bord de la falaise, un arc-en-ciel se forma sur le sombre rideau de pluie qui drapait le fond de la vallée. « Regarde bien cet arc-en-ciel, remarqua Tokdèn Rinpotché. Il est présent, avec ses couleurs riches et somptueuses, et pourtant, il est insaisissable. Il brille dans l'espace, mais il n'est pas différent de l'espace. Il semble exister de lui-même, mais si, derrière toi, le soleil cesse de briller, il s'évanouit sans laisser la moindre trace. En vérité, il résulte de la réunion éphémère de nombreuses causes et conditions. Comme lui, le monde est un réseau infini de relations qui apparaissent de multiples façons.

« Il en est de même de ton esprit. Tes pensées semblent concrètes et contraignantes, mais, si tu les examines bien, elles n'ont pas plus de consistance que cet arc-en-ciel. Il est aussi vain de s'attacher à nos sensations que de courir après l'arc-en-ciel pour s'en faire un manteau. Considère que tout ce que tu vois, entends, sens, goûtes ou touches est semblable à un arc-en-ciel, au reflet de la lune sur l'eau ou à une image dans un miroir. Reconnaître la nature ultime de l'esprit, l'Éveil, la conscience pure, libre de fabrications mentales, c'est réaliser l'état de Bouddha ; ne pas la reconnaître, c'est être dans l'ignorance. Disciple bien-aimé, que la durée de ta vie égale celle de ta pratique ! »

Détchèn avait absorbé les paroles de son maître comme des gouttes de nectar.

Cependant Tokdèn Rinpotché s'affaiblissait de jour en jour. Bientôt, il eut du mal à se lever. Tous les ermites de la Citadelle s'étaient rassemblés pour accomplir, matin et soir, des cérémonies dédiées à la longue vie de leur maître. Un jour, Tokdèn Rinpotché les appela dans le temple et leur donna un enseignement.

« Comme les jours et les nuits qui s'enfuient, la vie s'écoule inexorablement. N'est-il pas miraculeux, après avoir dormi, de s'éveiller vivant ? Cette vie est plus fragile qu'une bulle sur l'eau. Penser qu'on va d'abord terminer tout le travail entrepris, puis se consacrer au Dharma, est puéril. Il faut comprendre qu'on n'a pas de temps à perdre, comme si l'on était touché au cœur par une flèche. Faute de quoi, on risque fort de sombrer dans le marécage des illusions du monde, les préoccupations ordinaires liées à la joie et la peine, au gain et à la perte, aux louanges et au blâme, à la renommée et à l'anonymat.

« Soyez vigilants dans votre pratique et dans chacune de vos actions, maintenez constamment votre conscience en éveil, que ce soit en marchant, en étant assis, en mangeant ou en dormant. Vous devez arriver à l'état que décrit le grand Milarépa :

*Effrayé par la mort, j'allais dans les montagnes.*
*À force de méditer sur son heure incertaine,*
*J'ai conquis l'immortel bastion de l'Immuable.*
*À présent, ma peur de la mort est bien dépassée !*

« Par-dessus tout, cultivez l'amour altruiste et la compassion. L'esprit plein d'amour, mettez-vous au service des êtres, en pensée et en acte. En particulier, ne vous nourrissez pas de la vie des autres. Pour qui est imprégné de compassion, consommer de la viande est aussi effroyable qu'une mère qui dévorerait la chair de son propre enfant. Comment pourrait-il être juste de tuer des créatures désarmées et inoffensives ?

« Quelque activité que vous entrepreniez, dédiez-la au bien des êtres, et une fois votre tâche terminée, offrez à ces derniers les mérites que vous aurez acquis. C'est ainsi que vos actes produiront des bienfaits à long terme. Déposée sur une pierre chaude, une goutte d'eau s'évapore en quelques instants ; versée dans un lac, elle dure des siècles.

« On a vite fait de confondre un simple aperçu de la nature ultime de l'esprit avec une réalisation parfaite. Ne soyez pas impatients, ne vous laissez pas leurrer par quelques expériences méditatives, méditez simplement jusqu'à votre dernier souffle. Unissez constamment votre esprit à celui du maître et demeurez naturellement dans la parfaite simplicité de cette union. C'est l'essence de toute pratique spirituelle, et c'est ce qui vous permettra de reconnaître la nature ultime de l'esprit. »

Tous les disciples réunis sentaient bien qu'ils recevaient là le dernier enseignement de leur maître. Chaque instant était comme une pépite d'or qui fondait lentement dans leurs cœurs. L'enseignement terminé, ils restèrent silencieux quelques instants, puis Tokdèn Rinpotché leur fit signe de prendre congé. Lentement, ils défilèrent un à un devant lui et, les yeux ruisselants de larmes, reçurent sa bénédiction.

Tous ensemble, les ermites le supplièrent de

rester dans ce monde pour le bien des êtres. Tokdèn Rinpotché répondit qu'il serait sans doute encore là jusqu'au dixième jour du mois lunaire, dédié à Padmasambhava, mais qu'il ne promettait rien au-delà.

Les disciples sortirent respectueusement à reculons, les larmes aux yeux, les mains jointes sur leur cœur, priant que la vie de leur maître soit prolongée et, si elle ne l'était pas, qu'ils puissent le rencontrer à nouveau, vie après vie, jusqu'à ce qu'ils atteignent l'Éveil.

Au dixième jour du mois, on prépara une grande cérémonie d'offrandes. Tokdèn Rinpotché demanda à ce qu'elle eût lieu dans la salle commune, près des ermitages. Il souhaitait rester seul en méditation. À la fin de la cérémonie, les disciples envoyèrent lama Dorjé présenter une ultime requête au maître afin qu'il reste en vie. Tokdèn Rinpotché la reçut en souriant et hocha la tête sans rien dire.

Le soir venu, Tokdèn Rinpotché annonça à Tendzin, son fidèle serviteur qui l'assistait depuis vingt ans, qu'il souhaitait demeurer seul et ne plus être dérangé. Tendzin allait fermer la porte de l'extérieur, et personne ne devrait l'ouvrir durant les sept jours à venir. N'osant poser de questions ni contrevenir aux ordres de son maître, Tendzin aida Tokdèn Rinpotché à s'asseoir et à s'envelopper dans sa grande cape de laine. Puis il se retira à petits pas, le cœur lourd. Avant de passer le seuil, il regarda une dernière fois son maître, qui, en dépit de sa faiblesse, s'était assis bien droit en posture de lotus, les yeux grands ouverts, fixés dans l'espace devant lui.

Tendzin ferma la porte, fixa fermement la cheville du loquet en bois puis, après être resté quelques minutes seul dans la nuit étoilée, conscient de l'importance du moment, il descendit aux ermitages pour faire part aux disciples des instructions du maître.

Durant ces sept jours, les ermites, hommes et femmes, partagèrent leur temps entre méditations et cérémonies d'offrandes. Le matin et le soir, ils récitaient des prières tout en circumanbulant autour du temple où Tokdèn Rinpotché était entré en méditation.

Détchèn, quant à lui, restait le plus souvent

assis sur une petite corniche herbeuse à côté du temple, se livrant à la méditation de « l'union à la nature du maître spirituel ». Au bout de cinq jours, il fut pris d'un irrésistible désir de savoir ce qu'il advenait de son maître. Il n'aurait pas songé un instant à ouvrir la porte, mais, alors qu'il n'y avait personne alentour, il s'approcha d'une petite fenêtre d'où l'on pouvait regarder à l'intérieur, entre les deux pans du rideau. Ce qu'il vit le laissa bouche bée et l'emplit d'une stupeur émerveillée. Le corps de Tokdèn Rinpotché, toujours assis en posture de méditation, était entouré d'un halo lumineux. Il semblait plus frêle que d'habitude et se découpait comme une silhouette dans la lumière. De petites lueurs multicolores dansaient comme des flammèches sur ses vêtements. Après quelques secondes qui lui parurent une éternité, Détchèn eut peur d'être surpris et regagna prestement la corniche pour reprendre sa méditation, l'esprit bouleversé par ce qu'il venait de découvrir.

Il se garda bien d'en parler à quiconque. Il craignait d'avoir fait quelque chose d'inapproprié, mais il voulait aussi garder cette vision dans son cœur comme un précieux trésor.

Lorsque les sept jours furent écoulés, les plus anciens disciples de Tokdèn Rinpotché et son fidèle Tendzin montèrent en procession vers le temple. Chacun tenait des bâtons d'encens et des écharpes cérémonielles de soie blanche. Non sans hésitation, ils poussèrent le loquet et pénétrèrent dans la pièce. Détchèn restait à distance, le cœur battant.

Tendzin et les disciples s'arrêtèrent avec un émerveillement craintif devant la couche de Tokdèn Rinpotché. Il n'y avait plus que la grande cape brune, vide, posée sur le lit comme si elle enveloppait quelqu'un. Lama Dorjé s'approcha et écarta doucement les pans de la cape. À l'intérieur, il ne trouva que les cheveux et les ongles du maître : celui-ci avait dissous son enveloppe corporelle en « corps d'arc-en-ciel », un fait que seuls les plus grands saints du passé avaient pu accomplir.

Détchèn se glissa furtivement dans la pièce. Un parfum subtil y régnait, ainsi qu'une indescriptible atmosphère de paix et de communion spirituelle. L'émerveillement ne laissait place à aucune autre pensée.

Par la suite, Jamyang lui expliqua que seuls les yogis qui ont parfaitement réalisé la « Grande Perfection », c'est-à-dire la compréhension ultime de la nature de l'esprit et du monde des phénomènes, peuvent atteindre le corps d'arc-en-ciel. Les pratiquants qui ont fait l'expérience de l'union de la forme et du vide deviennent capables de dissoudre les éléments grossiers du corps – terre, eau, feu, vent et espace – et les cinq agrégats – forme, sensation, jugement, volition et conscience – en lumières de cinq couleurs correspondant aux cinq aspects de la sagesse – la sagesse de la réalité ultime, la sagesse semblable à un miroir, la sagesse toute égalisante, la sagesse qui distingue toute chose et la sagesse tout accomplissante.

La nouvelle se répandit rapidement dans la communauté des ermites. Quelques jours plus tard, elle atteignit les villages des vallées et les nomades des hauts plateaux, de sorte que de nombreux fidèles affluèrent vers la Citadelle des Neiges et campèrent par centaines aux alentours du temple. Durant sept semaines, de grandes cérémonies d'offrandes furent accomplies en hommage au maître défunt.

Détchèn y participait parfois, mais il préférait méditer dans la solitude. Il éprouva un profond désir de retourner en retraite afin d'approfondir davantage sa pratique. Il choisit un petit ermitage à proximité du lieu où son maître bien-aimé était parti en corps d'arc-en-ciel.

Il y demeura une année, dans la paix de la contemplation.

Quelques heures de sommeil lui suffisant, il se réveillait vers trois heures du matin. Il invoquait son maître avec une telle dévotion que son regard se brouillait de larmes. Il lui semblait alors si présent qu'il sentait de manière presque palpable la main qui s'était si souvent posée sur sa tête et revoyait son regard lumineux comme un sourire qui l'emplissait de félicité et de confiance. Maintes fois dans la journée, il renouvelait le vœu de progresser vers l'état de Bouddha afin de devenir capable d'aider réellement les êtres, puis reprenait une à une toutes les méditations qu'il avait pratiquées dans la grotte de Néuring, afin de les approfondir, de les rendre plus claires et plus stables.

Puis, ayant conclu sa retraite, il sortit de son ermitage au petit matin et contempla le paysage devant lui. Soudain, il réalisa que si le maître n'était plus dans son corps, assis dans le petit temple, il était désormais partout. La plaine enneigée lui rappelait le maître ; les grands arbres dont les cimes oscillaient au vent lui rappelaient le maître : tout était le maître sous mille formes différentes. Les sons, le souffle du vent, le murmure du ruisseau, les appels des oiseaux... tout résonnait comme la voix du maître. Même le profond silence de la nuit était saturé de sa présence. L'esprit du maître brillait derrière chaque pensée, comme la lumière qui permet de voir les formes et les couleurs.

Détchèn se sentit empli d'une force sereine. Désormais, le maître serait toujours avec lui, où qu'il soit, quoi qu'il arrive. Il pouvait partir sans crainte d'abandonner ce qui comptait le plus dans sa vie, sans peur de perdre quoi que ce soit : dorénavant, ce qui lui était le plus cher était dans son cœur.

Il en conçut une joie immense. Le monde

entier reflétait la présence du maître, et l'univers se lisait comme un livre d'enseignements dont chaque page le comblait. Il ne se sentait plus étranger dans le monde, il appartenait à toute chose. Il se rappela l'image du filet de perles qui recouvre le palais d'Indra, le Dieu et la mythologie de l'Inde : l'univers tout entier se reflète dans chaque perle, sans que la perle s'agrandisse ni que l'univers rétrécisse.

Maintenant, il pouvait redescendre. Quelle différence cela ferait-il d'être ici ou ailleurs, puisque la bonté et la sagesse du maître étaient partout présentes ? Il pourrait partager son nouveau savoir avec ceux qui lui étaient chers, avec les habitants de son village et, qui sait, avec d'autres encore.

Mais comment manifester tout cela ? Par la force de l'exemple sans doute. Il se devait de laisser briller à son tour la lumière du maître qui miroitait en lui comme une montagne d'or se reflète sur les ailes des oiseaux qui la contournent.

Détchèn décida donc de revenir à Khorma.

# Le retour au village

La descente fut rapide. En deux jours, Détchèn arriva en vue du village. Il s'arrêta quelques instants pour contempler de loin les lieux familiers de son enfance et la maison de ses parents. Des enfants jouaient sur le chemin et quelques paysans liaient des bottes de foin. Apercevant sa silhouette, ils se demandaient qui pouvait bien être ce pèlerin qui descendait des montagnes du Nord par un chemin si peu fréquenté. Son allure leur était vaguement familière. Mais Détchèn était maintenant un jeune homme ; il avait beaucoup changé. Enfin, quelqu'un le reconnut et s'écria : « Détchèn ! » et aussitôt plusieurs villageois vinrent à sa rencontre. Les voix répercutèrent la nouvelle : à peine Détchèn arriva-t-il à proximité de sa maison que sa mère accourait déjà vers lui pour le prendre dans ses bras. Il se retrouva très vite entouré de ses frères et de ses sœurs qui poussaient des exclamations de joie.

Chez lui, Détchèn alla s'asseoir au coin de l'âtre où se tenait grand-mère Yangchèn. Elle l'accueillit avec un bon thé qu'il dégusta près d'elle. Sa sœur aînée préparait le souper. Bientôt, son père revint des champs et la famille au complet fêta ses retrouvailles.

Les jours qui suivirent, Détchèn reçut de nombreuses visites et alla aussi de maison en maison voir ses amis et ses proches. Tous manifestaient leur bonheur de le revoir et leur admiration pour ce qu'il avait accompli durant les trois années passées à la Citadelle des Neiges. Détchèn continuait à pratiquer de son mieux. Il se réveillait bien avant l'aube et méditait alors que la maisonnée dormait encore. Durant la journée, il passait quelques heures en méditation devant l'autel familial. Le reste du temps, il aidait les siens aux travaux des champs.

Un jour, après les semailles, les villageois lui demandèrent de leur donner un enseignement sur la pratique du Dharma. Détchèn n'était pas un érudit, mais il leur parla avec cœur de la vie spirituelle, s'inspirant des instructions qu'il avait reçues de Tokdèn Rinpotché. Il leur donna aussi de simples conseils de vie, fondés sur les paroles du Bouddha.

« Écoutez ! La vertu suprême, c'est d'avoir maîtrisé son esprit. La qualité suprême c'est l'amour altruiste. Inéluctablement, les bonnes et les mauvaises actions viendront à maturité. À chaque instant, gardez cette question présente à l'esprit : "Que dois-je faire de façon à n'avoir aucun regret au moment de mourir ?" Si des amis vous font du tort, ne laissez pas le ressentiment vous gagner l'esprit. Ne maltraitez pas vos parents âgés ; servez-les avec respect. Ne battez pas le bétail et les chiens de garde ; soyez bon envers eux. Tout le bonheur des êtres provient de leurs pensées bienveillantes, et tout leur malheur de leurs préoccupations égoïstes. Par amour envers tous les êtres, développez du fond de votre cœur le désir d'atteindre l'Éveil pour leur bien ultime. »

Détchèn passait aussi de longs moments en compagnie de grand-mère Yangchèn qui était devenue très frêle. Elle lui demandait souvent de lui parler de la Citadelle des Neiges et aimait particulièrement les anecdotes sur la vie des maîtres. La santé de grand-mère Yangchèn se dégradait et Détchèn passait beaucoup de temps auprès d'elle. Il lui tenait la main tandis qu'ils bavardaient ensemble. Lorsqu'elle s'affaiblit davantage, Détchèn prit l'habitude de s'asseoir simplement à ses côtés et d'accomplir ses pratiques spirituelles en silence ou à voix basse. Puis arrivèrent les derniers instants. Détchèn lui donna quelques conseils pour l'aider à partir sereinement et l'accompagna avec tendresse jusqu'à son dernier souffle. Dès que Yangchèn eut cessé de respirer, Détchèn invoqua les Bouddhas de toutes les directions de l'espace, et visualisa la conscience de sa grand-mère comme une petite sphère de lumière qui s'élevait de son cœur jusqu'au sommet du crâne. Là, sa conscience s'échappa par la fontanelle et, telle une étoile filante, alla se dissoudre dans le cœur d'Amitabha, le Bouddha de la Lumière infinie. Détchèn visualisa ensuite que Yangchèn renaissait dans la Terre pure de Grande Félicité où elle recevait les enseignements du Bouddha et continuait à progresser vers l'Éveil.

Des moines du *dzong* furent invités pour la cérémonie de crémation qui eut lieu à quelque distance du village, à l'endroit réservé à cet usage. Comme de coutume, la famille offrit un repas champêtre à tous les parents et amis venus des environs, une centaine au total. Ensuite, pendant quarante-neuf jours, le temps durant lequel la conscience erre dans le *bardo*, l'état intermédiaire entre la mort et la renaissance, trois moines récitèrent des prières dans le temple familial et, chaque vendredi, jour de la mort de Yangchèn, effectuèrent des cérémonies d'offrandes élaborées.

Trois mois passèrent.

La vie au village était loin d'être désagréable et Détchèn savourait la présence des siens. Pourtant, il n'avait nulle intention de redevenir paysan ou de fonder une famille. Il décida de se rendre en pèlerinage dans les grands lieux saints du Bhoutan et annonça à ses parents son désir de prendre la route et de renouer avec sa vie d'ermite.

# Le barde vagabond

Muni d'un petit sac de provisions, Détchèn se mit en route vers la province du Boumthang, située à une quinzaine de jours de marche du village. Il fallait passer plusieurs grands cols et traverser d'immenses forêts de pins noirs et centenaires. De longs filaments de lichen vert pâle flottaient sur les branchages. C'était, disait-on, la chevelure de milliers de fées célestes, les *dakini*, celles « qui voyagent dans le ciel de la vérité ultime ». Parfois, il surprenait un petit panda rouge accroché à une grosse branche ou un daim musqué qui détalait, effarouché.

Un matin il découvrit, du sommet d'un col, la grande vallée de Boumthang. Comme il y posait son regard, le soleil dessina un arc-en-ciel dans la bruine qui enveloppait les bosquets sombres. Ici et là, le rougeoiement des champs de sarrasin alternait avec la houle d'or pâle des blés ondoyant sous la brise légère. Un grand monastère couronnait une éminence rocheuse. Au loin, un autre, plus majestueux encore, laissait deviner son imposante masse blanche en bordure de la forêt, à l'extrémité de la plaine. C'était Kujé Lhakang, le « Sanctuaire de l'Empreinte du Corps ».

Pour l'atteindre, Détchèn dut marcher pendant deux heures au bord d'une large rivière aux eaux pures. Puis, empreint d'une ferveur respectueuse, il gravit, presque à la verticale, les abrupts escaliers de pierre qui menaient à la relique la plus sacrée du pays. Au fond du temple principal se trouvaient en effet une grotte et, profondément enfoncée dans sa paroi, la forme d'un corps. On dit que Padmasambhava, lorsqu'il visita le Bhoutan au VIIIe siècle, médita en ce lieu et, s'adossant à la roche, y laissa l'empreinte de son dos.

Détchèn se prosterna de nombreuses fois, offrit une centaine de lampes à beurre avec les oboles qu'il avait recueillies lors de son périple, et resta à méditer une bonne partie de la journée en cette grotte bénie. Les jours suivants, il rendit hommage aux nombreux temples et chapelles qui parsèment la vallée. Puis il poursuivit son voyage.

Plusieurs mois durant, il alla de lieu saint en lieu saint, d'ermitage en ermitage, s'arrêtant parfois des jours ou des semaines dans un village. On lui offrait l'hospitalité, il aidait aux travaux des champs ou récitait les écritures sacrées dans le petit temple familial des villageois. D'un tempérament joyeux et bienveillant, Détchèn était l'ami de tous. Attentif aux personnes âgées, il les aidait à s'asseoir au soleil près des grosses meules de foin lorsqu'il faisait beau, et remettait de l'ordre dans leur masure. Familier des enfants, il leur racontait toutes sortes d'histoires. Par exemple celle du roi Tchika Raja, venu du Tibet dix siècles auparavant sur une machine volante ressemblant à un immense oiseau en bois. En atterrissant, l'aéronef avait fait un grand bruit, « tang ! », que tout le monde avait entendu des lieues à la ronde. Depuis, on avait baptisé l'endroit « Plaine de Tang ». Après avoir converti la population à la bonne loi, le roi avait réparé son engin et était retourné au pays des Neiges. D'aucuns disent qu'il s'agissait de Padmasambhava en personne.

Détchèn avait gardé les cheveux longs de ses retraites et les nouait en une longue queue de cheval qui flottait dans son dos. Il portait la robe de toile rouge foncé des ermites et, autour du cou, un petit reliquaire en argent rouge ainsi que son *mala*, rosaire fait de graines de *bodhi* polies et noircies par l'usage. Il avait fière allure et les jeunes paysannes se plaisaient à le taquiner. Bien qu'il ne fût pas insensible à leurs charmes, il n'avait guère l'intention de se fixer quelque part et de devenir le jouet des passions humaines.

Détchèn était doté d'une belle voix aux intonations pures et mélodieuses. Le soir, au cours des veillées, il chantait des poèmes spirituels appris lors de son séjour à la Citadelle. Les familles s'assemblaient pour l'écouter, inspirées tant par la beauté du chant que par la profondeur des paroles. Parfois, en fin d'après-midi, on apportait du thé et des grains de riz grillés, mélangés à du beurre et du sucre, et le village entier s'asseyait en rond dans la cour d'une maison ou sur une prairie fleurie pour écouter Détchèn.

Détchèn devint ainsi un barde vagabond, répandant par ses chants l'amour et la sagesse du Bouddha. Parfois, il disparaissait quelques semaines dans un ermitage rencontré en chemin et se livrait à la contemplation le temps que duraient ses provisions.

Au bout de quelques mois d'errance, il parvint à la capitale, Thimphou, qui comptait vingt mille âmes. Détchèn n'avait jamais vu une aussi grande ville. Les belles maisons de pierres blanches, aux boiseries hautes en couleur, bordaient les berges d'une rivière aux eaux transparentes. L'édifice majestueux du *dzong*, immense forteresse moitié monastère, moitié résidence du gouvernement royal, dominait le paysage.

Sur la place du marché, les étalages regorgeaient de mangues et d'ananas venus d'Inde, et d'une foule d'objets dont la variété le surprenait. Détchèn se mit à chanter et fut bientôt entouré par une petite foule amicale. Bien que ne comprenant pas toujours le sens de ses chants spirituels, tous étaient impressionnés par la sérénité de ce poète aux cheveux longs, si jeune et d'apparence si sage. Certains lui firent offrande de quelques billets froissés, pour l'aider à poursuivre son pèlerinage. Puis il se mit à la recherche d'un cousin dont il avait une adresse approximative et le trouva peu avant la nuit. Il fut accueilli avec l'hospitalité chaleureuse coutumière aux Bhoutanais. Chaque jour, il retournait chanter sur la place du marché. Puis, alors que l'on commençait à parler de l'ermite chanteur, on ne le trouva plus. Il avait repris sa vie de vagabond.

Partout au Bhoutan, il suffit de s'éloigner des villages, de monter vers les hauteurs pour trouver une communauté d'ermites, un ermitage délaissé ou une grotte accueillante. Selon son inspiration, Détchèn y restait quelques jours ou quelques mois et se consacrait à la méditation. En partant, il ne laissait derrière lui que les cendres de son foyer et les traces de ses pas. Dans les campagnes il se mettait au service des autres, dans les ermitages il se recueillait avec joie dans la contemplation. Il était libre dans ses pensées et libre dans ses actes. Il n'avait qu'une seule pensée, une seule prière :

*Aussi longtemps qu'existera l'espace,*
*Aussi longtemps qu'il y aura des êtres,*
*Puissé-je moi aussi demeurer*
*Pour dissiper la douleur du monde.*

Les héros de ce conte, bien que fictifs, sont inspirés de personnes réelles. Leur histoire est une mosaïque d'événements vécus dans un passé récent ou lointain par moi-même et par d'autres. La Citadelle des Neiges existe, mais j'en tairai le nom. Le « bout du monde » doit rester ce qu'il est...

B 7



PENGUI

ALL THA

Pramoedya Ananta Toer is the author of more than thirty books, including *The Fugitive, The Buru Quartet, The Mute's Soliloquy,* and *The Girl from the Coast*, and is published in more than thirty countries. He has been called "Indonesia's Albert Camus" (*San Francisco Chronicle*). The *Los Angeles Times* compared him to James Baldwin and Dashiell Hammett, and he is listed in the updated edition of the classic *Lifetime Reading Plan* among the likes of Bertolt Brecht, Graham Greene, and John Steinbeck as one of one hundred authors everyone should read. He has been profiled in *The New Yorker, The New York Times*, and other major publications around the world. He is the recipient of numerous international literary awards (such as France's Chevalier Award and the highest award in Asian letters, the Magsaysay Award) and freedom-of-speech awards (such as the PEN Freedom-to-Write Award and the Hellman-Hammett Award. He lives outside Jakarta.

Willem Samuels also translated Pramoedya's *The Fugitive, The Mute's Soliloquy,* and *The Girl from the Coast*, among other works.

PRAMOEDYA ANANTA TOER

# ALL THAT IS GONE

*Translated from the Indonesian by*
WILLEM SAMUELS

PENGUIN BOOKS

PENGUIN BOOKS
Published by the Penguin Group
Penguin Group (USA) Inc., 375 Hudson Street, New York, New York 10014, U.S.A.
Penguin Group (Canada), 10 Alcorn Avenue, Toronto,
Ontario, Canada M4V 3B2 (a division of Pearson Penguin Canada Inc.)
Penguin Books Ltd, 80 Strand, London WC2R 0RL, England
Penguin Ireland, 25 St Stephen's Green, Dublin 2, Ireland (a division of Penguin Books Ltd)
Penguin Group (Australia), 250 Camberwell Road, Camberwell,
Victoria 3124, Australia (a division of Pearson Australia Group Pty Ltd)
Penguin Books India Pvt Ltd, 11 Community Centre,
Panchsheel Park, New Delhi - 110 017, India
Penguin Group (NZ), cnr Airborne and Rosedale Roads, Albany,
Auckland 1310, New Zealand (a division of Pearson New Zealand Ltd)
Penguin Books (South Africa) (Pty) Ltd, 24 Sturdee Avenue, Rosebank,
Johannesburg 2196, South Africa

Penguin Books Ltd, Registered Offices:
80 Strand, London WC2R 0RL, England

First published in the United States of American by Hyperion 2004
Published in Penguin Books 2005

10 9 8 7 6 5 4 3 2 1



THE LIBRARY OF CONGRESS HAS CATALOGED THE HARDCOVER EDITION AS FOLLOWS:
Toer, Pramoedya Ananta
[Cerita dari Blora. English]
All that is gone / Pramoedya Ananta Toer ; translated from
the Indonesian by Willem Samuels.—1st ed.
p. cm.
ISBN 1-4013-6663-5 (hc.)
ISBN 0 14 30.3446 4 (pbk.)
I. Title.
PL5089.T8C4713 2004
899'22132—dc22 2003056675

Printed in the United States of America

# CONTENTS

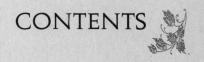

# PREFACE

Pramoedya Ananta Toer was born in 1925 in the town of Blora, East Java, in what was then the Dutch East Indies. His parents were educators and fervent nationalists and their home was a veritable hive of activity. In addition to taking care of the needs of their own nine children, they also provided room and board for sometimes up to a dozen other children. Then there were the servants required to manage such a large extended family, along with all the assorted relatives, business acquaintances, and vendors who were constantly stopping by at the house. Further, in pre-independence Indonesia, the Toer home and the school where Pramoedya's father was principal were the loci for much of the town's nationalist activity. Needless to say, Pramoedya grew up in a world where discussion, conversation, and storytelling were an integral part of daily life.

One can intuit from Pramoedya's semiautobiographical work, including the stories found herein, that it was his father's determination and resolve that gave the author the strength to survive the periods of detention and imprisonment as a political prisoner that he would later suffer—first under the Dutch; then, for a briefer time, under Soekarno; and last, for more than fourteen years, under the Soeharto regime. At the same time, one may also conclude from these same works that it was his mother who exercised a stronger influence on the writer's world views. It was also her bedtime tales that filled him with the desire to record stories of his own making. And it was she who became the inspiration for the many strong women characters one finds in so many of Pramoedya's works.

A number of Pramoedya's longer works are now available in English translation, including the four-volume *Buru Quartet, The Fugitive, The Girl from the Coast,* and *The Mute's Soliloquy.* Until now, however, the English-language reading public has been deprived of a single-volume, single-translator rendering of a collection of the author's early short stories, for which he first gained his fame in his home country. Of the author's early short prose works, most all Indonesian critics would agree that *Stories from Blora* (Cerita dari Blora) and *Dawn* (Subuh) best represent the author's early literary output. In this collection, we include seven of the eleven stories that originally appeared in *Stories from Blora* and one of the three stories ("Revenge") that originally appeared in *Dawn*. The choice for this selection was based on a list of the author's personal favorites.

In the United States, Europe, Australia, and elsewhere Pramoedya is best known for his longer prose works, especially the ones earlier mentioned, but in Indonesia the author is more highly respected for his skill as a short-story writer.

Unlike in the West, where the novel is prized as the ultimate in literary form, in Indonesia, just as high a value, if not higher, is placed on the short story, the novella, and poetry. While this might very well reflect the fact that it is virtually impossible for an Indonesian author to survive from his earnings as a writer, it does not completely explain the reason why so many authors choose to express themselves through the medium of shorter literary works. A possible answer might be the orality of Indonesian culture. In Indonesia a gifted speaker or an enchanting storyteller is likely to enjoy a level of popularity unimaginable in more literary-based countries. In Indonesia, short stories and poetry in particular are made not just to be read but to be read out loud, and to be shared with friends and strangers—just as parents share the historical memory of their family with their children.

This aspect of orality is highly evident in Pramoedya's work. In reading his stories, one can easily imagine the author relating them to his children, just as his own mother had once done for him to drive away his childhood fears.

—Willem Samuels

# ALL THAT IS GONE

# ALL THAT IS GONE

THE LUSI RIVER skirts the southern edge of the city of Blora. In the dry season, its bed of stone, gravel, mud, and sand heaves upward to expose itself to the sky, leaving scattered shallow pools. But when the rainy season comes and the forested hills are covered by clouds and the sun refuses to shine for forty to fifty hours, the river's greenish water changes to a mud-clotted yellow and rises to a level of twenty meters or even higher. The peaceful current becomes a crazed torrent. The river, swirling through its course, clutches at and then rips out clumps of bamboo from the banks like a child pulling weeds. It fells the levees and sucks into itself the bordering fields. So suddenly, the Lusi transforms itself.

From my home one can see groves of bamboo, blackish green in color, the tops of which weave and twist gently when the wind blows. When I was a boy, the dance of the tips and the whistle of the staves as the wind rushed through them never failed to frighten me. I can recall running in terror to my mother, burying my head in her lap, and starting to cry. Even now I can still hear her chiding me, "Whatever are you whining for?"

Her hands, no longer the soft hands of a girl, stroke my thin cheeks. Between my sobs, I gasp, "The bamboo is crying, Mama!"

Taking my head in her hands, she pulls me to her lap and tries to reassure me, "No, my baby, it's not crying. It's singing to you."

And then she starts to sing, something soothing and sweet, a folk song perhaps that rocks me, sways me, and then finally drowns my fears. Often it is her gentle voice that lulls me to sleep. Sometimes, as she sings, I run my fingers through her wind-tousled hair. I play with the lobes of her ears and the diamond-studded earrings that adorn them until finally, I hear her calm, sweet voice: "Come now, you're sleepy. I'll put you to bed." Hearing that, I open my eyes as wide as possible, hoping to persuade her to continue the song, but more often than not I find myself unable to keep my eyelids raised. But all that is gone now, vanished, along with the riverbanks and the clumps of bamboo that the high waters of the Lusi drag away.

Once, during an afternoon nap, I dreamt I found a one-cent piece, and when I awoke I clenched my fist for fear of losing the money I had found in my dream. I jumped out of bed and ran to find my mother. "Mama, Mama!" I called to her in joy, "I found a one-cent coin!"

She smiled at me, taking pleasure in my delight. "Wherever did you find it?" she asked. "Where is it now?"

I stuck out my fist and yelled, "Here it is! Right here in my hand!" But upon opening my fist I found my hand completely empty.

"Where did you say it was?" my mother asked me softly.

I stood there, dumbfounded by shock and disappointment. I wept as a great feeling of emptiness entered my chest.

My mother laughed and coaxed me gently: "You were only dreaming. You're awake now. Don't cry . . ." But I continued to sob.

My mother lifted the edge of her blouse to dry my tears. "Hush, be quiet now . . ." From the fold in her waistcloth, she took out a half-cent coin and handed it to me. I played with the coin in silence, as I tried to repress my lingering disappointment.

"It's late," my mother told me. "It's time for your bath. Nyi Kin will help you."

I removed myself from Mother's lap, but when I didn't immediately make my way toward the bath, her features darkened and her voice—no gentleness there now—grew stern: "Go on, off with you!"

Her tone, harboring no room for protest, made me reconsider an appeal. Slowly I walked away to look for the servant.

I can still see Nyi Kin quite clearly. Like so many women in this world, she had been forced to marry a man she didn't even know. And all that the marriage gave to her was syphilis, an illness that left her with an intense dislike of men. The disease destroyed her relationship with her husband and caused them to divorce. It robbed her of one of her eyes, wasted her beauty, and caused deterioration in one of her hip joints. When she walked she dragged her leg.

During the day Nyi Kin had little time to bemoan her fate; chores took up most of her attention. But when night came and her painful weariness made it difficult for her to sleep, it was then she mourned her loss.

Nyi Kin's arranged marriage, illness, and divorce had taken place before she came to work at our house. Perhaps it was because she had no children of her own—the syphilis had eaten her womb—that she showered so much attention on me. Even now, whenever I think of her, no matter where I am, I can feel her love and affection.

Sometimes Nyi Kin would stroke my cheeks as if I were her own child. When carrying me, she'd hide her face behind the long scarf she always wore around her neck, but then suddenly pull it away and pucker her lips. "Boo!" she'd say.

No matter how many times she did this, I'd always break out in giggles. Such pleasure that little game gave me. And she too would laugh with delight, but then just as suddenly stop the game and refuse to show her face. When I finally succeeded in pulling the scarf away, I'd find her staring vacantly. The precarious nature of her existence seemed to emanate from her reddened eyes. Hastily she'd pull my face against her own and hold it there for a long time; I imagine now that she was dreaming of the children she longed for but would never bear.

Nyi Kin always set aside part of her wages to buy snacks,

most of them going to me. It wasn't until later that I learned my mother paid her just 80 Dutch cents a month.

Like my mother, Nyi Kin was always telling me stories, but they were different from the ones that Mother told, which were about Asian war heroes. Nyi Kin's stories were about talking animals who had created for themselves kingdoms in the jungle. I can't recall how old I was when she told me these tales, but I do remember that she would remark how good the people of yore must have been to be able to understand the speech of animals. People these days, she said, are too sinful. They're cruel and unkind to one another, which is why, she also told me, they can't understand what animals say.

She talked about her own experiences as a girl and about an incident that had taken place when she was only a few years older than I was at the time. That particular story I would ask her to repeat again and again. She never refused, and each time I listened with surprise and awe. This is how the tale went:

*"I was just a girl at the time and the* bupati *who governed the Blora regency was Ndoro Kanjeng Said. One year, for some reason, our area experienced a double rainy season. The Lusi River rose over its banks, and our safe and peaceful city was soon buried beneath the muddy floodwaters. Because the city square lies on high ground, that bit of land became an island in the midst of a large sea. All the people in the area were herded by the rising waters to the square. They brought their children, their buffalo, and their cattle with them. Those who didn't leave their homes quickly enough risked being swept away to the river's mouth.*

*"Down and down the rains came, and soon even the regent's home was jammed with people. So then what he did was he went*

> *out of his house with a whip in his hand, and walked to the water's edge, which was already lapping at the city square. He lashed the water with his whip and said a prayer. And slowly, very slowly but just as surely, the waters began to recede and finally retreated to the banks of the Lusi."*

I remember that story very clearly. Nyi Kin had about twenty-five tales that she would tell me again and again, but to me they always seemed new and I never failed to listen with rapt attention. She told me about babies crying in the rain and how courageous the regent had been, how willingly the people served him, and how they had bowed to him when he came out of the house to save them from the flood.

Her story put me in awe of the regent. By the time I was born, he was long dead and buried. Even so, the mere mention of his name, Ndoro Kanjeng Said, evokes a kinder world that still lingers in the memory of the people of Blora.

Other stories that Nyi Kin told were about the gods and cacodemons that roam the world by day and night in search of people who are not on guard. Or, when looking at the clouds, she would recant fantastic tales from the *Ramayana*—how Dasamuka had hidden behind the clouds in wait for Sita and about his struggle with the great *garuda* bird Jatayu, who tried to stop him.

She told me about the heroes of the *Mahabharata,* too. She told them in a simple yet beautiful way. I was able to understand some of what she told me and stood in awe of the greatness of people of olden days. Looking back now, I see that I was like many people, both now and then, who would rather think about the past than deal with the present.

Important moments in life are not easily erased from memory, even that of a child. Such moments remain until the end of one's life. I remember one time when it was dark in the house and I was crying. My home was far from the closest power line and when night fell, the house grew gloomy inside. I remember Mother taking me outside that night. The dew made my body damp and shiverish, but it also helped to assuage the emptiness I was feeling inside. Maybe I had just been hot, I don't know, but Mother kissed my chin and whispered softly to me, "Oh, my little darling, why do you cry so much? Don't you know your mother is tired from working all day? Go to sleep, my baby. Tomorrow the sun will bring a new day and with it a new sky and new air. Then you can play to your heart's content."

The timbre of my mother's voice helped to soothe my feelings. I embraced her and gave her breasts my tears. She held my head against her chest, and I listened to the beating of her heart. As she began to sing, my fidgeting eased. The night's cool air and the dew seemed to make her song all the more poignant. After that, I don't remember what happened; when I next opened my eyes the sun was high in the sky and outside was the new day my mother had promised. I had a new day, a new sky, new air, and a new song, too. But all that is gone now, vanished from sensory perception to live forever in memory.

I remember the time when Nyi Kin suddenly disappeared. "She's sick," the other kids told me, but even so, I couldn't understand why she had left without saying goodbye. I looked for her everywhere but couldn't find her. I started to cry. I must have cried for at least two hours. Mother tried to calm me by offering me a banana, but that did nothing to check my tears. I felt an incredible emptiness inside me. Mother kept telling me: "Nyi Kin's gone home, honey. She's not feeling well, and when a person's sick you can't be near her or you'll get sick, too."

Mother's words did little to fill the vacuum inside me either. I kept on crying until exhaustion finally forced my body to sleep. When I awoke, the emptiness was still there and I started to cry again. Tears fell from my eyes like the drops of liquid that used to seep from Nyi Kin's hollow socket, the one she would wipe with the tip of her scarf.

Gradually, the emptiness abated and finally disappeared. Other things came to occupy my mind. Even so, at times, when I suddenly remembered Nyi Kin, I would ask again, "When is Nyi Kin coming back?" But Mother's answer was always, "She's still ill."

At that age I didn't know that Nyi Kin's house was not far from ours, only six or seven houses away. It wasn't until years later that Mother revealed the real reason Nyi Kin had gone: Nyi Kin liked to take spices from the kitchen, she said, and my mother would not allow thievery of any kind.

Nyi Kin was replaced by a younger woman. I was three years old at the time and had a baby sister who was one year old. Because I slept with the servant, I always woke up at five in the morning. She had to rise early to cook the fried rice for my parents' foster children—who weren't really foster children, but children whose parents had placed them with us—before they left for school. The two of us would squat together beside the hearth while frying the rice. When any crisp rice stuck to the bottom of the wok, I'd ask her for it and eat it right there.

I can't remember the servant's name, but I do remember that she, like Nyi Kin, was very fond of me. She had been raised on a farm and had once been married to a farmer, but after their crops failed they had separated.

An incident involving that servant took place when I was three or four years old and is still remarkably vivid in my mind. One morning I asked her for the crackled rice, which I then proceeded to nibble on while sitting on my haunches in front of the hearth. Our kitchen was not in the house but in an attached structure, the roof of which was made of corrugated zinc with upturned edges that had been fixed to a set of stakes. Seen from the inside, the roof had a triangular-shaped hole at each end, and it was through one of those holes I saw the most amazing thing. At 5 A.M., the sky looked completely dark from inside the kitchen, especially when one was facing the fire. But that morning, while I was sitting there, I looked up at one of the holes and saw a big head peering inside. I could make out a beard, eyebrows, and a big white moustache, but the face of the creature looking at me was black, even blacker than the sky outside. I didn't do anything. I just sat there in the predawn light, looking at that big face as I nibbled on my crackled rice. I didn't say anything either and, in the days that followed, the face began to appear regularly.

Finally, one day, when seeing the face, I pointed at the window and said to the servant, "Look! There it is! I told you! There's a big black head peeking at us again!"

The servant raised her head to look at the hole beneath the roof and started to laugh at me. "Of course there is," she said dryly, "but *I* can't see anything."

"But I saw it," I told her. "I saw a head, a really big head."

"Well I didn't," she said with just as much certainty. "What did it look like?"

"It was black. I saw a black face."

"You're fibbing. There's nothing out there."

I was unable to make her believe me; and our little conversation died right there.

Once I told Mother about what I had seen, but she didn't take me seriously either. As a matter of fact, she frowned and looked at me as if she were angry. "Has someone been telling you stories about devils? Who's been telling you about devils?"

At that age I already knew about devils, and I asked her: "Do you think it was really a devil I saw?"

"Who's been telling you those stories?" she asked suspiciously.

"Nobody. I saw him myself, Mama."

"You mustn't lie. Who taught you to lie? Nyi Kin, or is it that new servant? Tell me."

"Nobody, Mama, I saw him myself."

When Mother went off to question the servant, she responded with what I told her: "Every morning he tells me he sees the devil out there, but whenever I look up at the hole, I never see anything."

"Well, you must not tell him stories," Mother warned her.

"Oh no, ma'am, I'd never do that."

"There's no need to scare him."

"Oh no, ma'am. I wouldn't do that."

After that I stopped telling people about the face I saw through the hole beneath the roof every morning. But then one morning something happened even more out of the ordinary: That day, I was in the kitchen and I saw the head peek inside and then, a moment later, a monkey almost as large as myself jumped down from the hole. It leaped at the servant, who took off running around the central hearth. In the firelight I could see fear distorting the servant's features, but for whatever reason she neither screamed nor called for help. As the monkey tore around the kitchen, it grazed against me but didn't stop to bother me. It seemed intent on catching the servant. The two of them ran around and around in circles, one playing the hunter, the other the prey. But then, all of a sudden, the monkey vanished—I don't know where it went—and the servant collapsed on her haunches completely out of breath. I stared at her in silence. When she finally stood, I saw that there was a plate-size puddle of water on the ground where she had been squatting.

"You wet yourself," I commented.

The servant looked down at the puddle shimmering with the reflections of the firelight. She tossed some ashes on the pool of urine and walked away.

This experience was so overwhelming for me, I felt that I had to tell someone about it. It made me excited just to think about retelling it. When the other kids awoke, I ran in to tell them, but seeing that my mother was also awake, the desire to do so suddenly vanished. I didn't have the nerve. I knew my mother would say I was lying.

Later, after my father and the other kids had gone to school, the house was quiet. It was then that the servant approached my mother. "Ma'am, I would like to quit today," she said.

"But why? Aren't you happy here?"

"It's fine here, ma'am, but . . ." She didn't continue.

Mother didn't try to make her change her mind, and that very same day the servant left, never to return. I wanted to tell Mother what had happened, but I didn't. So, for the rest of the household, the servant's departure left little impression at all.

A few years later, when I finally did tell my mother about the incident, she cleared up—or at least thought that she cleared up—the mystery: "That would have been the Suryos' monkey," she told me. "They used to let it run loose in the morning." Memories differ, it seems. Our neighbor, Mr. Suryo, did indeed once own a monkey, but as I recall, that was not until a few years later.

Wherever that monkey had come from, it no longer mattered. The monkey—the one with the big head, white eyebrows, beard, and moustache—that had chased the servant was gone. It vanished like the banks of the river and the groves of bamboo dragged away by the floodwaters of the Lusi.

My father was the principal of a private school, and in the morning, when I'd see him getting ready to leave, I'd ask him to take me along. He'd almost always say no and I would start to cry. I don't know why, but there was an emptiness inside me that always made me want to cry.

"When you're big, you can go to school too," my parents would tell me, in an attempt to get me to stop. That usually helped to cheer me up.

"Can I really, Mama? Can I, Papa?"

"Why of course. And you can go to college in Surabaya, or to Batavia, or maybe even to Europe!"

After I had calmed down, my father would kiss me on both cheeks and get ready to leave. Only then could he safely walk away. Even so, I'd sometimes run after him, forcing Mother to follow me out to the road to try to make me stop. When this happened, I would start to cry again. But if Mother again said no, and absolutely forbade me to go, I dared not protest.

I remember well the feeling of what it was like when my father was not at home. I had a paint can to which my mother had fastened wheels and a string, and I'd pull it behind me wherever I went. There must have been something inside the can, because it clattered and clanked as I pulled it behind me, but the sound it made seemed to soothe my fears and encourage delight. But that, too, is gone now, just like the riverbanks and the clumps of bamboo that are dragged away by the floodwaters of the Lusi.

Usually when Father returned from school he would be laughing and in a good mood. Coming into the house, he'd always call out my name first and then that of my one-year-old sister. Then and only then, after kissing me and seeing that I was well, would he change his clothes and sit down to eat with Mother at the dining table. I'd join them but I ate on my feet, standing beside Mother. She would take a spoon of food from off her plate and put it in my open mouth. Then I'd run around the room and not return to my place until the mouthful of rice or whatever it was had been chewed and swallowed.

"Tastes good, does it?" my father would usually ask. And I'd answer with a laugh, "Gr-e-ea-a-t!"

My father never ate very much, not more than half a plate. Very rarely did he eat all the rice that my mother served him. But before my father had finished and left the dinner table, my full stomach would have already made me start to yawn. That's when my father would say to me: "You're falling asleep on your feet. Off with you; it's time for bed!"

Only when he said that would I realize that I was drowsy, but that didn't make me want to go to sleep. Mother always had to trundle me off to bed and stay with me, patting me on the thigh, until I fell asleep. I could see her hazy shape through my half-closed eyes. A smile revealed her small but evenly shaped teeth; a glow of love and affection radiated from her almond-shaped eyes.

But that too is gone now, carried away long ago, leaving with me only memories and feelings of wonder.

My mother, whose father was a Muslim cleric, was quite devout. I have no memory of my grandfather or what he looked like, but I remember Mother praying each and every day, except for the times she was pregnant. With her body almost completely enclosed in a pure white robe, only her face and fingers were visible when she prayed. Sometimes she held a rosary in her hand. When she was praying, I wouldn't dare approach her. I always waited outside the room where she prayed until she finished.

"Why do people pray, Mama?" I once asked her.

"To obtain God's blessings," she told me. "You pray for those who have sinned, that they return to the good and proper way. You pray for safety and peace. When you're bigger you'll understand why. You're still little. It's better for you to play than pray."

As to why this was, I never enquired further.

On nights when my father wasn't home, I'd often be awoken by the sound of my mother reciting her prayers. With Mother's clear and lilting voice, her prayers were like songs for me that kept the dark and silent night at a safe distance. Whether she was singing or praying, her voice was a pleasure to hear. And in the morning, when I woke up, if my father wasn't home yet, she would still be in her room praying.

One time, in the middle of the night, when I was awakened by her prayers, I went to her room. "It's late, Mama," I said to her. "Why are you still praying?"

Taking my chin in her thumb and forefinger, she pulled my head to her lap. Not saying anything, she kissed me instead. I could feel the warmth of her breath as she pressed her nose against my cheek.

She then began to pray again, but now her voice was hoarse and shaky.

"How come you're still praying?" I asked again.

"To make sure your father is safe. To keep him away from temptation." She looked at me quizzically. "Shouldn't you be in bed?"

I answered her question with one of my own: "How come Papa isn't home?"

Once again, she answered my question with a kiss that she pressed firmly on my cheeks.

"Where is Papa?" I asked again.

"Working," she finally said.

"But why is he working so late?" I asked.

"Because he has lots of work to do."

"When is he coming home?"

"When you wake up, your father will be home. Come now; it's time to go back to sleep."

She took me back to my bed and sang me a lullaby. When I woke up she was still praying, but her voice had now regained its clarity. To my ears, her voice didn't seem to be human at all; it was the sound of purity itself. I wanted to ask her whether my father had come home, but I didn't have the energy to get up, and I fell asleep again. I dreamt of my parents and my little sister.

In the morning when I awoke again I ran to find Mother. "Where's Papa?" I asked her.

"Your father has gone to school."

"Did he come home?"

"Yes, he did and before he left he looked in on you. He kissed you and then went off to school."

"Why doesn't he stay home and play with me?"

"Because he has to make a living so that he can buy clothing for you and food for the family."

I stopped pestering her, but late that day, when my father came home, I ran up to him and asked him, "Why didn't you come home last night? When I woke up last night, you weren't here."

My father laughed, but his laughter seemed hollow to my ears. On his face was a look of false cheer. My mother sat motionless in her chair, her head bowed.

"Mama stayed up all night praying!"

My father's laughter died immediately.

"Why don't you stay at home and play with me?"

Father laughed again. This time his laugh didn't sound false, but he still wouldn't answer me. We went to the dining table, and while we were eating I asked him, "Papa, can I go out with you at night?"

My question caused him to chuckle. "You're still too young," he said. "When you're big you won't have to go out with anyone at all. You can go anywhere you want, all by yourself."

I suddenly marveled at the miracle of age. His promise made me jump with joy.

"And can I go to Grandma's alone?"

"Of course you can. But not just yet. You're still too small."

"That's enough," my mother said in reprimand. "Stop asking your father so many questions. He's tired and wants to take a nap. And you should take one too."

That conversation, that incident, that too is gone, carried away and not likely ever to return.

In my mind's eye I can see clearly a day when I was afraid to approach my mother. It was a Sunday morning, and my parents' foster children had all gone off to a picnic site where the young people in our small town liked to gather. The house was quiet. Father was gone; only my mother, my sister, and the servant were at home. Feeling lonely, I went to find my mother and found her lying beside my sister on the bed. My sister was asleep, but my mother was staring up at the mosquito net that hung over the bed.

"Mama!" I called to her.

She didn't answer me; she didn't even move. With a great deal of effort I managed to climb up and onto the bed, and then I saw that my mother's eyes were red. Now and again she would wipe them with the flannel of my sister's blanket. I didn't know what to say. I sat there, silent for quite a while. I was frightened. Finally, with my voice trembling, I asked, "Why are you crying, Mama?"

It was only then that she looked at me. She pulled me to her side and hugged me.

"Why?" I asked again.

"It's nothing, my baby."

For some reason, right at that moment, I remembered a time, a beautiful time, when we'd gone to Rembang by train. There, looking out to the sea's horizon, we watched the ever restless and ever pounding sea whose every wave roared as it rushed to the shore. The horizon's base was a deep blue, almost black in color; closer to the shore it was a lighter blue; and at our feet, where the water tickled and rippled as it licked our skin, it was yellowish with churning sand.

"When can we take the train again?" I asked her. "When can we go to Rembang and look at the sea?"

My mother said nothing. It was as if she too were suddenly feeling the rush of the wind singing through the pines that line the Rembang shore.

My grandparents, my mother's parents, lived in Rembang, and upon hearing the name of her hometown Mother started to cry. Not knowing why, I asked her yet again: "Why are you crying?"

She sat up and kissed me repeatedly. Her tears felt cool on my cheeks. She spoke slowly as if attempting to control her voice: "We're going to leave Blora, my darling, and stay in Rembang forever."

"Why forever, Mama?"

"Don't you like the sea?"

"I do, Mama. Sure, I'd like to live by the sea," I consented happily. "When do we move?"

My happiness seemed to make my mother cry even harder.

"Soon," she said.

"When, Mama?"

"I don't know, I just don't know, but you'll be happy there, won't you?" My mother wiped her tears with my sister's blanket.

"Sure I will. Papa's coming too, isn't he?"

My question startled her. I saw that she was staring straight ahead, not even blinking or looking at me. I don't know why, but the look on her face suddenly made me afraid, and I started to bawl. My mother kissed me again and said softly: "Hush, don't cry . . ." Then my sister, startled by my shriek, also began to cry. Mother immediately put her to her breast. For a time, as she nursed my sister, she said nothing more, but her eyelids trembled and her gaze flitted from one place to another.

Finally, she told me, "Your father will be going to Rembang too."

"That's good," I told her, "because if Papa doesn't go, I don't want to go either. I'd rather stay here. Where is he, anyway?"

"Papa's at work."

I then repeated the question I had once asked her: "Why doesn't Papa ever stay home and play with me?"

"Because he has a great deal of work to do."

"But he's always working, Mama."

"Yes, he is," she said flatly.

When hearing her say that, I felt something grab me inside but could not quite figure out what that something was.

By this time I had stopped crying, and I asked, "Why were you crying, Mama?"

Not answering my question, she instead asked me listlessly, "Have you eaten?"

"Yes, but when Papa comes home I'll eat again. I like eating with you and Papa. It's so late and he's still not home . . . He'll come home tonight, won't he? Won't he?"

"Probably. He'll probably be home tonight."

"Did he come home last night, Mama?" I asked her.

"Yes, he came home last night, but you were already asleep. You didn't hear him, that's all. He even went to your bed and kissed you four times."

I laughed with pleasure.

"You were praying last night, weren't you, Mama?" As I asked that question, I heard, somewhere in my memory, Mother's prayers from the night before.

"No," she said, contradicting me. "I spent last night darning. You were asleep and Papa was reading. The other kids were asleep, too. And now it's time for you to sleep."

"If Papa comes home, wake me, Mama. You'll wake me, won't you?"

My mother coughed. I asked no more questions. I watched her finish nursing my sister, after which she stretched out silently and stared upward toward the top of the mosquito net. I still didn't say anything. I saw that her eyes were red, but I didn't say anything more. Then I too fell asleep.

When I awoke, Mother was still beside me, silently staring

at the mosquito net. Her eyes had lost their redness. Before getting out of bed, I asked her, "Is Papa home?"

My mother's body twitched slightly. She turned over to look at me.

"No, he's not, honey. But you slept for a long time, didn't you? That means you must be in good health. Now get out of bed and ask the servant to give you a bath, okay?"

I wanted to see my father and would not put off seeing him any longer. I refused and began to whine. "No! I want Papa. Where's Papa, Mama?"

"He'll be home soon, honey. Take your bath. When you're clean, he'll come home."

When I still didn't budge, my mother spoke more firmly: "I said call the servant to give you your bath."

This time I didn't care about the harshness of her voice.

"I want Papa!" I demanded. "Where's Papa?"

"He's working," she said stiffly. "Now take a bath!"

When I ignored her, her resoluteness suddenly disappeared. Kissing me affectionately, she got up and lifted me from the bed. She placed my feet on the floor, and after kissing me on my chin, spoke to me lovingly. "Papa will be home soon. But you have to take your bath. When you've had your bath, Papa will play with you. It's getting late. When Papa comes, I'll call you. Now go and take your bath."

The affection in her voice softened my rebelliousness, and slowly I stumbled off to find the servant.

After my bath, when I found that my father still wasn't home, I felt that familiar emptiness and began to cry again. This time I brushed off my mother's promises and bribes of food. I refused her coaxing and pleading.

The night grew later and later and still my father didn't come. With that feeling of emptiness welling inside me, I cried and would not stop. I screamed and felt as if I could go on screaming forever. My mother took me outside, but even the cool night air had no effect on the emptiness I felt. I knew that my crying upset my mother, but I wasn't going to be assuaged by her display of patience and care. She spoke softly and lovingly, but I continued to call out for my father. Even when her voice grew angrier in tone, I still continued to wail. The night deepened.

Between my outpourings of tears and screams I heard my mother invoke the name of the Most Powerful and beg for His forgiveness. But I continued to cry and to call for my father. It was pitch-black outside. When I cried, Mother never tried to threaten or frighten me; she attempted to ease my heartache with kind words and swaddle me in her affection. But this time it was of no use.

Finally, in desperation, my mother called for Dipo, one of my foster brothers, and told him to find my father and bring him home.

"Where should I look for him?" Dipo asked.

"I don't know. Just keep on looking until you find him. Tell him to come home, that his son is having a fit."

My mother, with the weight of my body in her arms, went back into the house. My tears began to subside, but after a time, when my father still hadn't returned, I began to scream and wail again. Then, I remember—it's like seeing through a fog now—my mother carrying me into the front room. She also carried a lantern, which she held up to the clock on the wall.

"It's three o'clock in the morning," she said, perturbed.

With the lamp still in her hand, she went to the back room.

"Papa! Papa!" I screamed again.

"He'll be home shortly, my baby. Now go to sleep!"

But my father still didn't come and I cried again, sometimes sobbing, at other times screaming.

Finally my father did return, with Dipo trailing behind.

"Papa, Papa!" I screamed. I don't know how many times I called for him.

My mother went to my father and without saying a word handed me to him. She then walked silently off toward her bedroom.

"Papa . . ." I sobbed again.

My father held me to his chest. His clothes, cool from the night air, felt damp to the touch. Slowly but surely, my tears subsided and then, finally, were gone, leaving small shudders that racked my chest. Walking with me in his arms, my father said to me: "My boy, my boy. Don't cry. Papa's here, isn't he? Now go to sleep. Sleep. It's late. Listen. Isn't that a rooster?"

I listened carefully and, sure enough, I could hear the crowing of a rooster.

"It's almost dawn," he said slowly.

The morning felt so silent. The heaving of my chest subsided and finally stopped. My father carried me to Mother's bed. I heard her crying faintly, her head buried beneath the pillow. Even as my father stroked her hair, she continued to cry. My father said nothing; my mother was speechless too. The only sound was my mother's sobs, which caused my own heart to tremble. Moving silently and with great care, my father left the room, carrying me outside and into the cool early morning light.

"Why must you cry so much?" he asked me.

"I waited for you and you didn't come home," I said half in

tears. "Mama said that when it got dark you would come home, but you didn't come."

"But I'm home now, aren't I?" he said softly. "So now it's time for you to sleep. Come on . . ."

My father sang slowly. His deep voice was both soft and soothing. After that I don't remember what happened, but when I awoke I found my father asleep beside me. A short while later, sleep robbed me of consciousness again.

When I next awoke, the sun was high. Because it was a holiday, my father hadn't gone to work. I found him and my mother sitting, facing each other, in the front room. After the servant had given me my bath, I ran back into the front room. "You're not going away again, are you, Papa?" I screamed at my father.

My mother looked at my father, who laughed and chucked me under the chin. "No," he said, "I don't have to work today. You're not going to cry again, are you?"

"Mama was crying again yesterday," I told him.

My father looked at my mother, but she didn't say anything. He said nothing either. I began to shout and scream happily as if nothing had happened between them and nothing were happening around me.

"Mama said we're going to Rembang," I announced.

My father looked at my mother again but still said nothing.

"I'm going, and the baby, too. We're going to see the sea. You'll come with us, won't you, Papa?"

Once more my father turned toward my mother but then turned back to me. "Of course I will. When do we leave?"

I looked at my mother and asked her coyly, "When are we going to Rembang, Mama?"

She didn't say anything. She seemed incapable of answering.

Her almond eyes reddened and glazed. A moment later they were pools of water, but just as a teardrop began to fall, she quickly wiped it away with the hem of her blouse. Not understanding what was happening, I began to scream and cry again. Something felt wrong inside, and when my mother rose from her seat and left the room, I began to scream louder. I ran after her and pulled on her sarong.

"Why are you crying, Mama?"

My mother picked me up, rocked me slowly in her arms, and then carried me away. But still she said nothing. She carried me to my bed and there laid her face on my chest. My father stayed where he was.

Yes, that incident too stands out clearly in my mind. But that part of my life—like the riverbanks and clumps of bamboo swept away by the Lusi River—is now gone.

Every year at Lebaran, at the end of the fasting month, Father would buy a load of firecrackers. He'd also give me and my sister and my mother and the foster kids a set of new clothes and some spending money. We'd set off the firecrackers on the ground in front of the house and all the neighbor kids would come running over to watch them explode.

Such an immeasurable sense of delight those holidays gave me, but that same sense of delight was not always evident in the look on my mother's face. The holidays seemed to be a sad time for her, especially after my father began to spend less and less time at home.

Gradually, I grew used to my father's absences and no longer threw a fit every time he left. Mother no longer was forced to send one of the boarders out to call him home. For a very long time I didn't know where my father went when he was not at school. My mother never asked him where he went. She never said anything at all when he left and never greeted him when he returned. It seemed like whenever my father left the house Mother was off somewhere working, in the kitchen, the back room, or the garden.

I, too, rarely asked my father where he went. When I did ask him, his answer was always, "Work." And if I followed that question with another, such as, "Can I come along?" he wouldn't even turn to look at me as he answered me: "No, you may not. When you're older, you can go out by yourself. Now go and play with the others." Then he walked quickly away.

On the Lebaran holidays my mother would watch us kids setting off firecrackers from her chair in the front room. She never said anything, but her lips moved constantly as a rosary passed through her fingers. Once when I did approach her she told me: "You should not play with firecrackers on Lebaran. Our religion forbids it. Firecrackers are used for Chinese celebrations and have no place in Muslim ceremonies."

Regardless of my mother's opinion, my father continued to buy us firecrackers for Lebaran, that is until one of the kids got hurt. After that, he never bought them again.

Then, one day, something really important happened. My grandfather, my mother's father, died and my father rented an automobile to take the family to Rembang. I don't really remember what happened there, but after our return to Blora, my mother was different. She seemed to droop, to lose all her strength. She mourned the loss of her father, I knew, but I also sensed there was something more. In the week after her father died my mother cried continuously.

"Everybody has to die sometime," I heard my father say in an attempt to calm her. "That's what life is about."

But Mother wasn't ready to receive that kind of solace, and her bouts of crying grew worse. I see now my mother must have felt that she had lost her last refuge, the only real place she had to run to outside of her religion.

A week went by, and if at that time I could have better expressed myself, I'm sure I would have said that Mother had finally surrendered herself to some greater force. When Father left the house at night, she never said a word. She acted as if nothing were wrong. At the same time, she seemed to grow even closer to us children. In the end we had become her refuge.

In moments of solitude—not when the world outside was quiet but when her own heart was still—my mother would take us for a walk. We'd hike one or two kilometers from the house, and she'd tell us stories about the things she saw in the world outside. She'd tell us about the birds, and their habits and food; about the waters of the Lusi as we crossed the bridge above it; about the fields and rice, and the insects that devoured both the farmers' crops and their hopes; about the wind and clouds and the sun and the stars; and almost always about the lives of the poor. The knowledge I found as a child was increased greatly on these walks.

In the evenings my mother would gather us together around the bench in the garden and tell us about plants, the clumps of bamboo swaying in the wind, about fruit trees and ships and trains and automobiles and bicycles. My mother was a good storyteller, and sometimes she'd tell us about cities she had visited and about her own family or her studies and teachers in school. And even though we were just kids, she'd tell us about politics and Indonesia's colonization by the Dutch. I can still remember her stories about people who had been active in the political struggle for independence and had been jailed or exiled as a result. But like all the other things, those times too have been carried away to disappear from the realm of our senses.

My mother's real mother—not her stepmother in Rembang—lived near my hometown of Blora. She had moved there after remarrying, and sometimes she'd come to the house with fruit. She sold vegetables to make a living. Early in the morning she'd stop the farmers who were on the way to the market with vegetables and she'd buy their produce to sell to the city's *priayi,* the "gentry" as it were, or those people who liked to think of themselves as *priayi*.

My grandmother's husband made his living by selling roasted skewers of chicken at the market. About the only time he came to our house was to borrow money. He had once been a farmer, but for some reason his crops always failed. The people of my hometown believed that a man who fathers a child out of wedlock will forever experience misfortune. I didn't hear about this until I was older, but when I did, I began to wonder if that is what had happened to my step-grandfather. Whatever the case, I never had the nerve to ask whether it was true.

Sometimes, when my mother's stepfather came to the house, she'd get a look of intense irritation on her face. Once she spoke to me about him, though somewhat indirectly: "You must never do what is forbidden," she advised. "Just look at your grandfather and you'll see the consequence! Everything he does fails. It's pitiful. His prayers and hopes are wasted."

With my limited mental grasp, I didn't understand what she meant, and I asked her more directly, "What about Grandpa, Mama?"

"When you're older, you'll understand," was all she had to say. I never asked again.

My mother liked to work in the garden and, if I weren't off playing, I would follow her there. As she worked, stories flowed from her mouth—instructive tales mostly, stories with morals to teach us to respect nature, to be proud of what we do, and to work hard. In my young boy's mind I wasn't always able to grasp what she was trying to tell me, and in numerous instances it was not until years later that I came to understand what she had been saying.

"People live from their own sweat, and when you're an adult, that's how it will be for you too. And anything you obtain, if it doesn't come from your own hard work, will not be right. Even the things that people give to you."

But like everything else, that is gone now, never to return, forever to reside in memory and the mind.

The waters of the Lusi flood and ebb; they rise and fall, become shallow and deep. So too with everything that took place in my childhood days.

"You can do whatever you want with the things you justly earn, even your own life and your own body. Everything," my father once told me, "everything you justly earn."

How long does it take to speak a sentence? The sound of his voice was but for a few moments. A momentary tremble of sound waves, and then it was gone, not to be repeated. Yet, like the Lusi that constantly skirts the city of Blora, like the waters of that river, the remembered sound of that voice, coursing through memory, will continue to flow—forever, toward its estuary and the boundless sea. And not one person knows when the sea will be dry and lose its tide.

But all that is gone, gone from the grasp of the senses.

# INEM

AMONG THE GIRLS I knew, Inem was my best friend. She was eight, just two years older than me, and much like the other girls I knew. If there was anything that distinguished her, it was that she was much prettier than the other girls in my neighborhood. She lived at my parents' home, where her family had placed her. In return for her room and board, she helped in the kitchen and looked after me and my younger siblings.

In addition to being pretty, Inem was also polite, clever, and hardworking—not pampered at all—traits that helped to spread her good name to adjoining neighborhoods as well. She would make a good daughter-in-law some day, it was said. And sure enough, one day, when Inem was boiling drinking water in the kitchen, she announced to me: "I'm going to be married!"

"No, you're not!" I told her.

"I am, I really am. The proposal came a week ago. My folks and all my other relatives think it's a good idea."

"Wow! That'll be fun!" I shouted ecstatically.

"It sure will," she agreed. "They'll buy me all these beautiful new clothes. And I'll get to wear a bride's dress and have flowers in my hair and powder, mascara, and eye shadow. I'm going to like that!"

Inem was telling the truth, as we were soon to learn when, one evening, not long afterward, Inem's mother came to call on mine.

Inem's mother earned what money she could from making batik. That's what the women in the area did when they weren't working in the rice fields. Some made *kain,* batik wraparounds, while others made headcloths. The poorer women, like Inem's mother, worked on headcloths; not only did it take less time to make a headcloth, they received payment for their work much sooner. On the average, a woman could make somewhere between eight and eleven headcloths a day. Toko Ijo, the store that bought the headcloths that Inem's mother made, supplied her with the cotton fabric and wax. For every two headcloths that she produced, she was paid one and a half Dutch cents.

Inem's father, on the other hand, liked to gamble—with gamecocks, especially. All day, every day, he spent cockfighting. When his rooster lost, he had to turn it over to the victor's owner, plus pay the owner two and a half rupiah, or at the very least 75 Dutch cents. And when he wasn't doing this, he was playing cards with his neighbors for ante of one cent a hand.

Sometimes Inem's father would go off on foot and not come back for a month or more. Generally, his return home meant that he had somehow managed to make some money.

My mother once told me that Inem's father's real source of income came from robbing travelers on the road that ran through the huge teakwood plantation that lay between Blora, our hometown, and the coastal town of Rembang. I was in first grade at the time and heard lots of stories about robbery, banditry, killers, and thieves. Because of them and because of what my mother told me, I came to be terrified of Inem's father.

Everyone knew Inem's father was a thief, but no one dared to report him to the police. And anyway, because no one could prove that he was a thief, he was never arrested. Besides that, it seemed like almost all of Inem's mother's male relatives were policemen. One was even an investigator. Even Inem's father had once been a policeman, but had lost his job from taking bribes.

Mother also told me that Inem's father had been a thief before becoming a policeman, and that the government, as a means of containing crime in the area, had made him a policeman in order to sic him on his former associates. After that, he'd quit robbing people, she said—but that didn't stop her or others from viewing him with suspicion.

The day that Inem's mother came to call, Inem was in the kitchen, heating water. When Mother went to greet her visitor, I tagged along as they convened to the sitting room, where they arranged themselves on a low wooden daybed.

It was Inem's mother who opened the conversation: "Ma'am, I've come to ask to take Inem home."

"But why? Isn't it better for her here?" my mother inquired. "You don't have to pay anything for her to stay here, and she's learning how to cook."

"I know that, ma'am, but I plan for her to get married after the harvest is in."

"Married?!" My mother was shocked.

"Yes, ma'am. She's old enough—all of eight now," Inem's mother said in affirmation.

At this my mother laughed, a reaction that excited in our visitor a look of surprise.

"Eight years old? Isn't that a bit too young?" my mother asked.

"We're not rich people, ma'am, and the way I see it, she's already a year too old. Asih, you know, she had her daughter married off when she was two years younger."

Mother tried to dissuade her, but Inem's mother wouldn't hear of it: "I just feel lucky someone's proposed," she argued, "and if we let this proposal go by, there might not be another one. Imagine the shame of having a daughter become an old maid! Besides, once she's married she might even be able to help lighten the load around the house."

Mother let this pass but gave me a nudge. "Go get the betel set and spittoon."

I did as ordered, fetching for Mother the brass spittoon and the decorative box that contained all the ingredients for chewing betel.

"And your man, what does he have to say about this?"

"Oh, Inem's dad agrees," Inem's mother affirmed, "especially as Markaban—that's the name of the boy who's proposing—is the son of a rich man, and an only child too. He's already begun to help his father, trading cattle in Rembang, Cepu, Medang, Pati, Ngawen, and here in Blora too."

This information seemed to cheer Mother, though I could not understand why. She then called for Inem, who was still at work in the kitchen.

When Inem came into the room, Mother asked her, "Inem, do you want to get married?"

Inem bowed her head; she held my mother in great respect and always deferred to her. I noticed that Inem was smiling radiantly. But she often looked like that: if you gave Inem something that made her happy she would always respond with a huge smile. "Thank you" was not something she was used to saying. Among the people in our area—simple folk by and large—the expression "thank you" was an unfamiliar phrase. A beaming smile, the happy look on one's face, was the way gratitude was expressed.

"Yes, ma'am," Inem finally whispered, almost inaudibly.

My mother and Inem's mother each prepared a cud of betel. Mother rarely chewed betel, doing so only when she had a female guest. Every few moments the silence in the room was broken by the twang of their spitting into the brass spittoon.

After Inem returned to the kitchen, Mother stated flatly, "It's not right for children to marry."

Inem's mother raised her eyebrows but she didn't respond. I saw no curiosity in her eyes, merely a hint of surprise.

"I was eighteen when I got married," Mother said.

The look on Inem's mother's face vanished. Her unspoken question had been answered. But still she didn't say anything.

"It's not right for children to marry," Mother repeated.

Once again, Inem's mother stared, as if not knowing what to say.

"Their children will be stunted."

Again the look of puzzlement on Inem's mother's face faded.

"I'm sure you're right, ma'am . . ." Then she said evenly, "My mother was eight when she got married."

As if not hearing what her guest had said, Mother continued: "Not only will they be stunted, their health will be poorly affected too."

"I'm sure you're right, ma'am, but my own family is long-lived. My mother is still alive and she's at least fifty-nine. My grandmother is living, too. She must be about seventy-four. And she's still strong, strong enough to pound corn, anyway."

Still ignoring her, Mother added, "Especially if the husband is young, too."

"Of course, ma'am, but Markaban is seventeen."

"Seventeen! My husband was thirty when he married me."

Inem's mother said nothing. She kept moving the betel cud around and between her upper and lower lips and teeth. One moment the wad would be on the right side of her mouth, the next moment on the left. Occasionally she would pluck the cud from her mouth, roll it tightly between her fingers, and then use it to scrub her blackened teeth.

Mother had no more arguments with which to dissuade her guest's intention.

"Well, if you've made up your mind to marry Inem off, I can only hope that she'll get a husband who takes good care of her. I just hope that he's the right man for her, the one destined to be her mate."

Inem's mother then left the house, still churning the cud of tobacco around inside her mouth.

After she had gone Mother said softly to me, "I hope nothing bad comes to that child."

"Why would anything bad happen?" I asked her.

"Never mind, don't pay attention to me," she told me, before changing the subject of conversation. "At least, if her family's situation improves, we might stop losing our chickens."

"Is that who's stealing our chickens?"

"Never mind," she repeated, then spoke slowly, as if to herself: "And just a child! Eight years old. Such a shame. But they need money, I suppose, and the only way to get it is by marrying off their daughter."

Having said this, Mother left the house and went to the garden out back where she gathered some string beans for our dinner.

Fifteen days after her visit, Inem's mother came to the house again, this time to take away Inem for good. She seemed extremely relieved when Inem made no objection to being taken away. When Inem was ready to go and leave me and her foster family forever, she came to look for me at the kitchen door.

"Goodbye," she told me, "I'm going home now."

She said this very softly, but she always spoke softly. In my small town this was one way of showing respect. And then she left, as cheerful as any young girl expecting to receive a new dress.

After Inem stopped living at our house, I felt the loss of my close friend very deeply. And from then on, it wasn't Inem who took me to the bathroom at night to wash my feet before going to bed, but an older foster sister.

At times I could hardly contain my longing to see Inem. Often, when lying in bed, I would recall the image of Inem's mother taking her daughter by the hand, leading her out of the house, and then escorting her to their own house, which was located behind our own, separated from our property only by a wooden fence.

In the first month after Inem's departure, I often went to her house to play, but whenever Mother found out where I had been, she'd get angry with me. "What's the use of going there?" she'd ask. "You're not going to learn anything in that house."

What could I say? I had no answer. Whenever Mother scolded me, she had her reasons, and her words of reprimand were a wall that none of my excuses could ever scale. My best course was to say nothing at all.

But then, when I said nothing, she was sure to continue: "What's the point in playing with Inem? Aren't there lots of other children you can play with? Inem is a woman now and is going to be married soon."

Despite my mother's objections, I continued to sneak over to Inem's house. I found some of my mother's prohibitions surprising; it was as if their only reason for existence was to be violated. And in violating them, I have to admit, I derived a certain pleasure. For children such as myself, at that time and in that place, there were a startling number of rules and taboos. It seemed as if the whole world was watching us children, conspiring to keep us from doing anything we wanted to do. There was almost no getting around the perception that this world was meant only for adults.

For five days before Inem's wedding, her family prepared food and special cakes. As a result, I spent more time than ever at her house.

The day before the wedding, Inem's bridal preparations began. Mother sent me to her house with five kilograms of rice and 25 cents as a contribution to the event. And then, that evening, after Inem was prepared, all the children in the neighborhood gathered at her place to stare at her in admiration.

Inem's eyebrows and the fine hairs on her forehead and temples had been trimmed and shaped with a razor and their lines accentuated by liner and mascara. Her hair had been thickened and made longer with a switch, then ratted and shaped into a high chignon. Sprouting from this was a spray of tiny paper flowers the stems of which were made of fine, tightly wound springs that swayed with the movement of the bride's head. Inem's *kebaya,* the hip-length buttoned blouse, was satin and her *kain* was an expensive length of batik from Solo. Inem's family had obtained these things from a rental store in the Chinese district near the town square. Her gold rings and bracelets were rented too.

The house was festooned with banyan cuttings and coconut fronds. Tricolored bunting of red, white, and blue—cinched at regular intervals to create a series of upside-down fans—ran around the edge of the ceiling. The house pillars, too, had been wrapped with tricolored ribbon.

Mother herself went over to help with the preparations, though not for very long; in less than an hour she was back home. She rarely did this sort of thing, except for our closest neighbors.

At that same time a cartload of gifts from Inem's husband-to-be arrived at Inem's home: a big basket of cakes, a billy goat, a large sack of rice, a bag of salt, a gunny sack of husked coconut, and a half sack of sugar.

As the wedding feast was being held just after harvest, the rice was cheap. And when rice is cheap, all other foodstuffs are cheap too—which is why the post-harvest period is the most favored time for weddings and also why Inem's family was unable to hold a *wayang kulit* performance; all the puppeteers in the area had already been contracted by other families or communities.

Because no puppeteers were available, Inem's family decided to hire a female dance troupe. At first this had caused some contention: Inem's mother's side of the family was well known to be devout, but on this point Inem's father would not back down and, in the end, a dance troupe arrived, complete with its *gamelan* orchestra and female *tayuban* dancers.

In my area a *tayuban* performance was generally reserved for adult males, who participated in the dance, along with young children whose knowledge of sexual matters did not extend much beyond kissing and who were there only to watch. Pubescent boys generally shunned *tayuban* performances because they usually ended up being embarrassed by the female dancers. As for the women, no woman of respect would ever attend. In order to arouse excitement among the largely male audience, a *tayuban* performance was always accompanied by the consumption of alcoholic beverages—palm wine, beer, whiskey, or gin.

The *tayuban* for Inem's wedding went on intermittently for two days and nights. We children had a great time of it, watching the men and women dancing and kissing, clinking their glasses together, and gulping down shot after shot of liquor as they danced and sang.

Although Mother forbade me to watch, I went on the sly.

"Why do you insist on going over there? Sinners is what they are. Just look at your religious teacher. Is he there? No, he's not. You must have noticed that. And he is Inem's uncle!"

Inem's uncle, my religious teacher, also lived behind our house, just to the right of Inem's, and his absence at the *tayuban* performance was widely noted. The comment on everyone's tongue was that Inem's uncle was a pious man and her father an incorrigible reprobate.

My mother justified her anger with an argument I did not at that time comprehend: "Those people have no respect for women. Are you aware of that?" she asked incisively.

When the bridegroom came to the house to be formally introduced to his bride, Inem, who had been seated on the wedding dais, was led forth from her home. At the door to the verandah, where the bridegroom now waited, she knelt before her husband-to-be and demonstrated her obeisance to him by washing his feet with flower water from a brass vase. The couple were then bound and together conducted to the dais.

Guests said, mantra-like, "One child becomes two. One child becomes two. One child becomes two . . ." The women's faces glowed as if they themselves were the recipients of happiness to come.

It was then I noticed that Inem was crying. Her tears had smudged her makeup and left watermarks in the powder as they trickled down her face.

Later, at home, when I asked my mother why Inem had

been crying, she told me: "When a bride cries, it's because she is thinking of her departed ancestors. Their spirits are at the ceremony, and they are happy because their descendant has been safely married."

I didn't give much thought to my mother's reply, but later I found out that Inem had been crying because she had to urinate but was afraid to tell anyone.

The wedding celebration ended uneventfully and Inem's home returned to its usual state. No more guests appeared with contributions. Now, instead, it was the money collectors who began to call. By this time, however, Inem's father had left town on one of his travels.

After the wedding, Inem and her mother spent their days and nights making batik headcloths. If one were to pass by their home at three o'clock in the morning, there would be a good chance of finding them still working, with smoke rising from the pot of heated wax between them.

Often, the sound of raised voices could also be heard emanating from the house. Once, when I was sleeping with Mother in her bed, a loud scream awakened me: "No! I don't want to!"

Later that same night I heard the same scream, repeated again and again, in time with a thudlike sound and then pounding on a door. I knew it was Inem screaming; I recognized her voice.

"Why is Inem screaming?" I asked my mother.

"They're fighting. I just hope nothing bad happens to that little girl," she added without further explanation.

I persisted with my questions: "Why should anything bad happen to her?"

Mother wouldn't answer me. Finally, after the screaming and shouting had subsided, we fell asleep again. But the next night and almost every other night that followed, we heard those screams again. Screaming, screaming, incessant screaming. And every time I heard them I asked my mother what they meant, but she would never give me a satisfactory answer. At best she might sigh. "Such a pity, such a poor little thing . . ."

Then one day Inem appeared at the door to our house. She went to find my mother straightaway. Her face was pale and ashen and even before she tried to speak, she began to cry, but in a soft and respectful way.

"Why are you crying, Inem?" Mother asked her. "Have you been fighting again?"

Inem stuttered between her sobs, "Please take me back, ma'am. I hope you'll take me back."

"But you have a husband now, don't you, Inem?"

Inem began to cry again. "I can't take it, ma'am," she said through her tears.

"But why, Inem? Don't you like your husband?"

"Please, ma'am. Take pity on me. Every night all he does is wrestle with me and try to get on top of me."

"But can't you say to him, 'Please don't do that, dear?'"

"I'm afraid, ma'am. I'm afraid of him. He's so big and when he starts to squeeze me he hugs me so tight I can't even breathe. Won't you please take me back, ma'am?" she pleaded.

"If you didn't have a husband, Inem, of course I'd take you back. But you're married now . . ."

Hearing my mother's answer, Inem began to cry all the harder. "But I don't want a husband, ma'am!"

"You might not want to, but you do, Inem. Maybe in time your husband will change for the better, and the two of you will be happy. You wanted to get married, didn't you?"

"Yes, ma'am, but, but . . ."

"There's no buts about it, Inem. No matter what, a woman must serve her husband faithfully," Mother advised. "If you can't do that, Inem, your ancestors will look down and curse you."

Inem was now crying so hard that she could no longer speak.

My mother continued: "I want you to promise me, Inem, that you will always prepare your husband's meals and that when your work is finished you will pray that God watches over him and keeps him safe. You must promise to wash his clothes, and you must massage him when he comes home tired from work. You must take care of him if ever he falls ill."

Inem said nothing as tears streamed down her face.

"Go home, Inem, and from now on serve your husband faithfully. No matter if he's good or bad, you must serve him faithfully. He is your husband, after all."

Inem, who was sitting weakly on the floor, did not stir.

"Now stand up, Inem, and go home to your husband. If you . . . If you were to leave your husband, the consequences would not be good for you, either now or in the future."

Head bowed, Inem answered submissively, "Yes, ma'am," then slowly picked herself up and made her way home.

"How sad, she's so young," Mother said after she had gone.

"Mother . . . Does Daddy ever wrestle with you?" I asked.

Mother carefully searched my eyes. Her scrutiny then vanished and she smiled.

"No," she said. "Your father is the best person in the whole world."

She then went to the kitchen and returned with a hoe to work with me in the garden.

A year passed by, unnoticed. And then one day Inem came to the house again. She had grown in that time and now looked almost like an adult, though she was barely nine. As in the past, she went directly to Mother. When she found her, she sat, head bowed, on the floor before her.

"Ma'am, I don't have a husband anymore," she announced.

"What's that you said, Inem?"

"I don't have a husband now."

"You're divorced?" my mother asked.

"Yes, ma'am."

"But why?"

Inem said nothing.

"Didn't you serve him faithfully?"

"I think I was a good wife to him, ma'am."

"But did you massage him when he came home tired from work?" Mother probed.

"Yes, ma'am, I did everything you told me to."

"Then why did he divorce you?"

"He beat me," she stated, "all the time."

"He beat you? A young girl like you?"

"I think I did everything to be a good wife, ma'am. But letting him beat me, ma'am, and putting up with the pain, is that part of being a good wife, ma'am?" she asked in true consternation.

Mother said nothing as she studied Inem's eyes. "He beat you . . ." she whispered as if to herself.

"Yes, ma'am, he beat me—just like my parents do."

"Maybe you didn't serve him faithfully enough. A husband would never beat his wife if she's been truly good to him."

Inem said nothing to this. Instead she asked, "Will you take me back, ma'am?"

My mother answered without hesitation, "Inem, you're a divorced woman and there are grown boys here in this house. That wouldn't look right to people, would it now?"

"But they wouldn't beat me," she answered simply.

"That's not what I meant, Inem. For a divorced woman as young as you to be in a place where there are lots of men around just wouldn't look right."

"Is there something wrong with me, ma'am?"

"No, Inem, it's a question of propriety."

"I don't know what that means, ma'am. Are you saying that's why I can't stay here?"

"Yes, Inem, that is what I'm saying."

Inem was left without another word to say. She remained seated on the floor, as if she had no intention of leaving.

Mother bowed and patted Inem's shoulder consolingly. "I think the best thing for you to do would be to help your parents earn a living. I'm truly sorry that I can't take you back."

Teardrops appeared in the corner of the child-woman's eyes. Finally, Inem stood. Listlessly picking up her feet, she left our house to return to her parents' home. From that time on she was seldom seen.

And thereafter, this nine-year-old divorcée—for being nothing but a burden on her family's household—could be beaten by anyone at will, by her mother, her brothers, her uncles, her neighbors, her aunts. But she never again came to our house.

I'd often hear her cries of pain and when she screamed, I'd cover my ears with my hands. Meanwhile, Mother continued to uphold propriety and the family's good name.

## IN TWILIGHT BORN

WHEN I WAS growing up, my family home was filled with young men—some of them my older foster brothers, the rest of them student boarders. One of my foster brothers was Hurip, who had recently graduated from the state junior high school in the provincial capital of Semarang. As is common with young men, one of the group's favorite pastimes was gathering to shoot the breeze. Though I couldn't understand much of what they talked about, I can recall some of what they said. Hurip, who was especially vocal, made the following comment one day: "What this country needs is dynamism. Our people are frozen in time. For once and for all, we need the courage to reject the idea that working for the government as a civil servant should be our ideal!"

Because I was an exceedingly curious boy, I harbored no aversion to rifling through my parents' books or my father's desk whenever I wanted to find answers to my questions. When I thought I had grasped the meaning of something I had heard, I would seek confirmation for my opinion from my mother. Thus it was, I came to ask her the meaning of what Hurip had said.

"You'll understand when you're older," she said with a smile, which was no answer for me at all. I then asked my playmates what they thought, but they could supply no answer either. Even the family's manservant, who was ancient in my estimation, could not give a satisfactory explanation.

Being a graduate of the Dutch-language junior high school, Hurip enjoyed a special position in the family home. Even my mother showed him deference. Not surprising, therefore, when Hurip raised his voice to speak, everyone listened. He was the unrivaled authority in every discussion.

One day Mother told me that Hurip was a politician, which shocked and surprised me. I didn't know what "politics" meant and had understood her to say that Hurip was a "policeman." As young as I was, I was well aware of the family's aversion toward anything having to do with the police.

"But aren't you mad at him for being a policeman?" I asked my mother.

Mother smiled and proceeded to explain the meaning of "politics," adding afterward that any Indonesian who was a member of a political party was an enemy of the police.

Pleased and relieved to hear this news, I ran off to tell my friends the meaning of "politics" but they just laughed when they heard my explanation. Even the manservant was skeptical.

I remember another time—one evening after we had taken our baths but before the older boys had begun to play chess or work on their school assignments—we were all seated in a circle around the low table where they did their homework.

I was seated behind Hurip when he suddenly started to talk about working for the government. "A civil servant's life is boring," he announced. "A civil servant leaves for work at a certain time every morning, he sits behind his desk for a certain number of hours every day, and he goes home at a certain time every evening. There, he has a little fun with his wife, gets her pregnant and, lo and behold, brings yet another child into the world. Day in, day out, from year to year, this goes on—in short, a completely boring existence, no better than that of a draft horse who expects nothing more from life than a bit of hay, a bucket of water, and a place to rest.

"A civil servant spends his days dreaming about better wages. When his boss tosses a compliment his way, like a bone to a dog, he jumps for joy, thinking a raise in position is nigh. But when the boss snarls at him, he runs off like a stray, tail between his legs, fearful of losing the position he has."

I watched as the other boys focused their attention on Hurip. I listened too, even though I didn't understand all of what he said. One thing that did stick out clearly in my mind, however, was my foster-brother's comment that when a man has fun with his wife, she always ends up having a baby.

After we had eaten that night, I asked my mother if what Hurip said was true, that whenever a man had fun with his wife, she ended up having a baby. Mother didn't respond immediately; the expression on her face didn't even change when she asked me to call Hurip and then told me to do my homework. When I didn't immediately oblige, when I remained standing there, expecting an answer, she told me again to do my homework.

Stubborn child that I was, I repeated my question again, and this time Mother became very angry. And so, in the face of her unwavering stance, I finally left to tackle my books.

After I had left the room, I heard Mother herself call Hurip's name. From that point on, I noticed that Hurip was much more reserved in conversation, at least when I was around. If he was in the middle of a serious discussion with the other boys and I made known my presence in the room, he'd suddenly switch to another subject or start telling jokes.

Life was simple in my small hometown, but even in Blora there came a time of change. Not that I actually understood what was happening then. I picked up some information from the bits of conversation that reached my ears about the activities of civil servants, businessmen, farmers, laborers, and so on. And I heard from Hurip, primarily, a number of strange new terms and concepts: *swadesi,* for example, the self-subsistence movement that had begun in India, and about how Japan and Asia were on the rise.

When Hurip talked of such things, he always used the same fiery tone of voice that my father used when speaking in public. "Ever since the rise of feudalism in this country, the ruling class has enjoyed undue and undeserved authority," Hurip declared. "They defend this as their right, even though, mind you, no one from outside their class has ever recognized or ratified this so-called right. They accept it as natural that people from outside their class must defer to them. They spend their time untroubled and at ease because anything that happens outside their class is not their concern. Their attention is focused solely on their own rise in position, power, and wealth. At times, they might worry that their own superiors will turn on them and cut their salaries and benefits, but in the past, this worry was usually baseless. But now, because the country is on the rise, if they don't join the movement, they are going to see their class dissolved."

I also noticed at that time that a kind of frenetic energy had begun to influence the daily life of my small hometown: people began to establish soccer teams, for instance, and in no time at all there were no less than three soccer teams in each part of the city, even some especially for children. Among the upper class, arts-related clubs began to thrive—from traditional theater to puppet theater, from Javanese dance to Javanese vocals and orchestra. Among young people, Western drama and orchestra suddenly found a large following. My father gave his support to a number of such organizations. Mother, too, was active in many women's groups.

Quite a number of the young men from my part of town were recruited to join the police force. From them we learned that the government was actively trying to increase the size of the force. Even so, that didn't prevent masses of people from turning out to see Sukarno, the rising young nationalist, when he came to Blora to speak.

In the early mornings, one could see on the town roads virtual troops of people running in file. Children's choirs sang, in regimental fashion, *"In the East the sun now shines. Awaken and we shall all rise together . . . "*

My father ordered all of the children in the house to join the scouts, and one night, at a bonfire, I watched as many of the parents of scouts, my father included, were sworn in as honorary scouts. A fourfold growth in the Indonesian Scouts provided impetus for the establishment of two more scouting organizations, one with a religious affiliation and another in which Dutch was the official language of communication.

During this time, contempt toward the Dutch also grew. Slowly but surely, this feeling took root until the entire population, it seemed, shared a dislike of the Dutch. I was just seven at the time, but I remember my father saying to my mother one day, "Don't bet on the Westerners here keeping their superior positions forever."

I looked at my mother, who was sitting reading a book and, from the glow in her eyes, I could see that she derived a certain amount of satisfaction from my father's words. Looking more closely, I then noticed that her stomach was distended. She was going to have a baby!

After glancing toward my father, my mother then said to me, "You know that working in an office isn't the only way to make a living. What do you think you'd like to be when you grow up?"

"A farmer!" I said immediately.

"A farmer?" my father asked.

When I reaffirmed my answer, Mother told me, "If you

really want to be a farmer, you can't loaf around like you do now." Her response bolstered my spirit and gave me the will to try my hand at cultivating a small plot of land that my parents had set aside for me out in front of the house.

Sometimes Mother would come out to the plot to help me, and once, when we were planting sweet potatoes, she remarked, with hope in her voice: "The fruits of one's own labor are extra sweet. Just look at you; you're sweating! That's good for your blood and for your health." She also told me that some day our country would be ruled by native Indonesians, and not by the Dutch anymore. "You're just a boy," she said, "but after you have finished school and are able to read the books your father now reads, you will know a great deal more, and the sweet potatoes that you plant will grow and reproduce . . . I know, you're still too young to understand such things, but you will in time. Your father is a teacher," she said, "but do you know what he's really doing?"

I shook my head. "All I know is he's almost never at home."

"That's because he's out there planting sweet potatoes for you so that someday, in the years to come, you'll have a never-ending supply of potatoes for your own."

I had no idea what she was saying.

"Not the kind of sweet potatoes you eat," she said in explanation. "I'm talking about the kind of potatoes that you'll be able to eat when you're older—a situation that is better for you and your friends than it is today."

I stopped working and looked at her, not quite knowing what to say.

The frenzied atmosphere of my hometown affected a change in the life of Hurip, especially after Father put him to work at the school where he was principal. He had very little free time anymore. His days were spent at school; in the evenings he corrected students' homework and at night he studied. What conversations he had now were always serious in tone. One in particular I remember was in regard to the subject of taxes. "Government taxes are killing us," he announced to the other boys one night. "There are taxes on everything these days, and we have to bear their burden. We pay taxes on every meter of cloth we buy and on every step we take on the asphalt road."

Though I didn't understand what he was saying, I could certainly imagine how much happier people would be if they didn't have to pay taxes.

"The Dutch didn't come here to make us all high-government officials," he continued. "They came here for our money, which they get in the form of taxes. If we object to paying, they try to get them from us by force; and if we resist, they send us to a forced-labor camp. Have you ever heard of the Samin people? They are a tribe in far western Java that refuses to have anything to do with the outside world, including payment of taxes. I say cheers to them!"

Because Hurip always spoke in such a serious tone, it wasn't surprising all the other boys believed everything he said.

Another change I noticed was that more people, even people of the upper class, were wearing clothes made out of *lurik,* the coarse, homespun cloth that was so common among villagers but rarely used by those who could afford better material. I might not have been heir to a fortune, but I had no interest in wearing *lurik*. It was scratchy and the colors faded quickly, after only one or two washings. Even so, my father purchased himself a pair of *lurik* pajamas to wear around the house and a set of *lurik* daily wear as well, including a sarong and vest. And then, one day, much to my surprise, he gave everyone else in the household a set as well.

It was Hurip who tried to explain the phenomenon: "It's like in India," he said. "There the people are wearing homespun cloth and burning imported cloth."

Spontaneously, I quipped, "Gosh, I wish I could get some of that foreign cloth!" To my astonishment, my comment caused everyone to laugh, which in turn made me uncomfortably aware that my role in discussions was to listen, not to express an opinion.

Hurip lifted me onto his knee and continued his instruction: "It's things like wearing locally made cloth that give meaning to *swadesi,* the whole point of which is self-subsistence and to provide jobs for our people. Our people need work to live, which means that if you're wearing imported clothing you're depriving them of both jobs and income. In the end it's foreigners who are making all the profits."

It was around that same time I recall a village woman, a weaver, calling on my mother, who immediately ordered twelve sets of *lurik* outfits, one for each child in the household. I noted, however, that she didn't order a set for herself. Apparently she shared my opinion of the cloth.

Naturally, the weaver was delighted to receive the order: "There are so many people ordering *lurik* these days," she informed us.

"Well, it's the age of *swadesi*!" my mother remarked.

The woman nodded. "Yes, *swadesi*—that's what everyone in my village is saying too. My neighbors are working day and night just to keep up with the orders. It's just like when I was a girl," she said with a laugh. "People are planting their own cotton. Even the local sandal maker, who makes sandals from used car tires, has more orders than he can fill. He has fifteen people working for him now."

Mother beamed at this news, and after the old weaver had gone launched into a monologue, though her eyes were fixed on me: "*Swadesi* is giving new life to handicraft production, making it possible for the villagers to live." She pointed toward the home of a neighbor, Pak Kromo, who made bamboo craft ware for a living. "If we can keep the movement going for a couple decades or so, maybe Pak Kromo will have a life that's better than the miserable one he has today. Eight children, and what does he get for a basket? Two and a half cents, even though it takes a day and a half to produce just one!"

Meanwhile, as the weeks went by, my mother's pregnancy advanced and prevented her from strenuous labor. Three months earlier she had purchased a loom and hired a weaver to teach her how to use it. But now, because of the size of her stomach, she couldn't work for more than three hours at a time. It made her whole body shake, she said. And so the loom was placed in the godown and she spent most of her time seated in a chair on the terrace of the *pendopo,* reading and looking at the garden beyond.

My father was rarely at home. He was off planting sweet potatoes for the future, Mother always said if I asked about him. When he did come home, it was usually with three or four people in tow, most of them dressed in *lurik* and either barefoot or wearing sandals made from used car tires. Their conversations—which covered a wide range of subjects and were interspersed with raucous laughter and hushed whispers—were largely unintelligible to me, but it was from them I learned such terms as "cooperatives," "people's banks," "teachers' colleges," "mass reading materials," and "grassroots movement."

Over time, we had more and more people coming to the house. Neighbors whom I knew to be unable to read or write came to talk to my father about signing up for literacy courses. Other people came to enroll in courses on politics, economics, and other subjects—all these, on top of the students from both private and public schools in the area who came to the house professing to want to be teachers or to learn a trade. My older foster brothers were assigned to run the courses that my father established even as he oversaw their growing rolls with a gleam of victory in his eyes. He had three hundred people enrolled in literacy classes, forty prospective teachers, thirty vocational students, fifty people taking general studies courses, fifteen kindergarteners, and twenty English-language students. For the Dutch language course that he established, only eleven people signed up.

Soon after, two duplicating machines, five typewriters, and a large crate of paper appeared at the doorway. Our home suddenly resembled an office. Throughout the day, all you could hear was the tapping of typewriters and the whirling of duplicators shooting out lesson plans.

My father and his work became the focus of attention in our small town. He seemed to be always busy, but his absences from home were frequent too. As the piles of homework for him to correct mounted, the various foster children were delegated to assist. Mother seemed to be heartened by the increasing number of women coming to the house to ask her for advice. She could never say no to their requests. Even though her pregnancy was a difficult one, she always managed to attend their meetings.

Often, when Father was at home, policemen would ride by the house on their bicycles, casting suspicious looks in our direction. When I asked my mother the reason for their surveillance, all she would say is, "They'd like it a whole lot if your father did nothing at all."

"But he's a teacher," I protested, not comprehending the situation.

"That may be," Mother answered, "but the government would prefer to keep our people ignorant and illiterate."

Several years were to pass before I came to understood what was happening at that time in my hometown, but I was frequently made aware of my father's increased stature. Often, passersby would point me out to their companions. "That's his son," I'd hear them say. Virtual strangers would stop me and ask me about my father. Some even gave me spending money, which made me very happy indeed. From all this attention, I knew that my father was an important man in our town and that made me very proud.

But one day, when Father came home from school, he wasn't his ebullient self. When he sat down at the table for his afternoon meal, I noticed a cold and angry look on his face. I lingered in the room to see what was the matter.

"You're working too hard," Mother told him when she came out to serve his meal. "Are you feeling all right?"

"It's not because of work I'm feeling this way," he replied. "The thing is, and this is what I didn't see before, a person has to be the master of his own house before he can do what he wants in it."

My mother looked perplexed. "What are you talking about?"

"I got a letter," my father quipped.

"What are you telling me?" she asked, with growing alarm.

"It was from the government," my father answered with greater force.

"What kind of letter?"

"A threat, or call it a 'reminder,' if you will." He paused. "I've been ordered to close down the school."

My mother stared at my father in disbelief.

Not waiting to hear more, I ran to Hurip's room to tell him what my father had said. To my astonishment, he didn't seem at all surprised; he too looked tired and troubled.

I then went to the kitchen to tell the cook what Father had said.

"What do you mean?" she asked with indignation. "Who could stop your father from teaching? Who would even dare? Even the district officer doesn't mess with your father."

I tried to memorize what the cook had said so that I could repeat her words to others, but the cold look I had seen on my father's face overshadowed my thoughts. I scurried off to find another of my foster brothers to tell him what I had heard.

"I already know," he informed me. "They came when your father was teaching in my civics class. Five police and an inspector! They packed up all the reading books for the first and second levels and took them away. There were at least seven thousand copies of them. Your father put a lot of time and money into preparing them! After that," my foster brother continued, "all the teachers were called together and classes were called off. Before they left, the police also cut the electricity to the school, so there won't be any more evening classes either."

I was stunned by this news. By the time I returned to the dining room, my parents had finished their meal but were now talking about a lending bank my father had also established.

"And what about the five thousand rupiah you put into the bank?" my mother was asking.

My father just shook his head. "It's gone . . ." He then spoke slowly, enunciating his words carefully: "The only thing we can do now is work harder. If the situation isn't always what one hopes for, we should not be surprised."

My mother stifled a sigh. "I always pray for your safety and the success of your work. But, I suppose, if misfortune comes, there is nothing we can do about it." Her voice trembled with a tone of uncertainty I had never heard before.

From that day on we had few visitors at the house; even my playmates began to stay away. Our home, formerly an oasis, was now a small and faraway island. Mother spoke rarely. Hurip sat around the house lost in thought, always with a book in his hand but never reading it.

The number of students at my father's school dropped from four hundred to just twenty-eight in a matter of days. His school, once alive with activity, now looked empty and cold. A classmate whose father was a civil servant informed me that government employees who enrolled their children at my father's school would have their allowances cut off.

One night I was roused from my sleep by the sound of raised voices in the next room. It was Hurip speaking, and I could tell from the sound of his voice that he was angry. The next morning I watched him as he packed his bag and then went to ask my father's permission to leave. "They've got us in a stranglehold," he said. "I can't live in this town anymore."

After he took his leave, our family never heard from him again.

I didn't quite know what was happening, but I guessed that it was for that same reason Father spent more and more time away from home. Sometimes he'd disappear for three or four days on end, not even bothering to check in at his school. And when he was at home, he wasn't reading or looking over students' homework; he never went out to my garden anymore to look at the plants; he stopped asking me to go for walks with him in the morning. He rarely smiled; he hardly even talked unless it was absolutely necessary.

Meanwhile, Mother was more often to be found lying in bed

than cooking in the kitchen or tending to the garden. With my parents' sudden reversal of fortune, I could not help but sense, even in my naive and unformed mind, that something was happening completely outside my parents' control.

One day Mother took me aside to give me some words of advice: "You must learn your lessons well. Hurip was a clever lad but was unable to cope with the current situation. That's why he went away. Your father is also smart, but even he doesn't have the power to change the way things are. That's why you must study. You must become smarter than both of them. And you will! I know you will. You will be far more clever and will not fail in what you do."

I truly did not understand what Mother was saying, but the softness of her voice helped to calm my fears. When she hugged me and kissed my neck, I felt the warmth of her tears on my skin—yet another phenomenon I could not understand.

"Maybe Father can't work, but why is he always gone?" I managed to ask.

Mother held my face in her hands and looked into my eyes. "Your father is very disappointed right now. I'm sure you don't understand what I mean; you're just a boy and haven't ever felt the disappointment that an adult can feel. But your father goes out because he needs to take his mind off things."

As a boy, I'd often disappear from the house to explore the neighborhood. One of my favorite haunts was the local market, and sometimes, during my trips there and back, I'd catch sight of my father and his friends playing cards or engaging in some other form of gambling on the verandah of one of the men's homes. I now guessed that this is what Mother meant by my father's need to "take his mind off things."

After the near failure of my father's school, I would sometimes overhear people talking about him and about how he had forsaken the nationalist movement in order to spend his time gambling. I might have been young, but I was able to sense the negative connotation of that word. I suppose that's why I didn't ask my mother if my assumption about Father's whereabouts was correct. I also suppose that's why when she then asked me if I knew where my father might be, I could not pretend otherwise.

"Then I want you to find him," she told me, "and I want you to tell him to come home."

Leaving the house, I set out to find my father, and indeed I did find him at one of his regular haunts. When he saw me, he gave me an angry look, but that didn't prevent me from conveying Mother's message.

"Tell your mother I'll be home in a minute," was all he had to say.

Not long after my return home, Father appeared at the door. Mother said very little to him. He, too, was taciturn, but that night, after I had gone into my room, I heard Mother say to him, "I think you've had enough time to cure your disappointment."

For the next two days and nights the situation at home appeared to have reverted to normal, with Father coming straight home from his work at school and not going out in the evening. By the third day, however, he had become fidgety and nervous, and that night he suddenly left the house without saying where he was going. Mother made no move to stop him from going, and in the days that followed, whenever he left the house, she never said anything either. But then one day, after he had not come home for four straight days, she called me into her bedroom and asked me to fetch her a pencil and paper. After I had brought them to her, she proceeded to write a letter.

As she wrote I noticed how difficult it seemed for her to put her words on paper. After folding the note, she handed it to me and, without comment, returned to her bed.

"Do you want me to give this to Father?" I stuttered.

Instead of answering, she stared into my eyes and silently nodded.

Unlike the previous time when I was sent to find Father, this time, no matter where I looked, I could not find him. He was at none of the houses he normally frequented. Four or five hours passed as I traversed the town without success, but remembering the look in my mother's eye, I couldn't make myself go home, not without first finding Father. Finally, tired and completely discouraged, I sat beneath a tamarind tree at the side of the road to rest.

Sad thoughts rose and fell in my mind: the confiscation of my father's books by the police, the failed bank in which my father had invested, the bankrupt cooperatives, the falling number of students at Father's school, the silent duplicator machine, the mute typewriters . . . The litany of images went on and on. Suddenly an overpowering feeling of misfortune overtook me and I pushed my body back against the trunk of the tree as if hoping to absorb some of its solidity.

Groping inside my trouser pocket, I took out the note my mother had written. I was almost too afraid to read it, but I couldn't make myself stop:

> *Have you no concern at all for the child I am carrying? Please come home!*
>
> *Honor your unborn child by bowing to the Most High and praying that he becomes a person of honor and intelligence.*
>
> *If, after receiving this letter you are still not willing to come home, then pray for me to die and take this unborn child with me to the grave.*

I began to cry, but then, suddenly, I quickly refolded the note and put it back in my pocket, determined once more to find my father. In the end, I did find him, in the back of the house of a Chinese man where he was gambling.

As before, Father looked displeased to see me, but he accepted the letter that I held out to him.

When Father returned home that night, he didn't go directly to my mother's room. Instead, he stayed in the front room to speak to the children. To my ears, his voice sounded forced and unnaturally loud, as if he were speaking not for us but for Mother to hear.

A week then passed without Father venturing out at night. During that week he was home every night, helping the children do their homework. But then, the following week, three men who were friends of my father showed up at the house. I remember the time well: it was two o'clock in the afternoon and Father asked me to serve his guests refreshments. Naturally, I lingered in the room after bringing them something to drink.

After talking to the men for about a quarter of an hour, Father excused himself and went to find my mother. I didn't hear what he said to her, but from where I loitered in the hallway, I was able to hear her say in an angry tone, "This home is where my children were born and I will not allow you to turn it into a gambling den!"

After returning to the front room, where his guests were seated, Father invited them to follow him to another dwelling, an empty house our family owned about four hundred meters from our home.

To my recollection, that was the only time in her life that my mother refused to receive guests of my father. But what I found even more surprising that day was that after Father and his guests had removed themselves to the other house, Mother quickly rose from her bed and whisked herself off to the kitchen to make bread pudding, my father's favorite dessert. She mixed lots of cheese into the batter to make it taste extra rich. Toward evening, when the pudding came out of the oven, she then ordered me and four of my foster brothers to take the pudding to the house where Father and his guests were gambling.

Father seemed especially surprised to see us appear with the pudding and other treats that Mother had added to the tray. Immediately after serving Father's guests, we returned home, but for some reason not a single word passed between us as we made our way back to the house.

One day, out of the blue, the old *lurik* weaver from the village came to our house to see my mother. I tagged along behind Mother when she went to greet her guest at the door.

"*Lurik* isn't selling well now," the old woman immediately told her. "We're not getting any orders. Even the stock we have on hand isn't selling. The only people buying are people from the village, the same ones without any money to spend. Wouldn't you like to order some more?" she asked in a pleading voice.

My mother said no to the woman, as gently as she could, explaining that she had a pile of unused *lurik* in the armoire.

"I guess the days of *swadesi* are over," my mother said hollowly, tears brimming in her eyes. My mother, who usually had no shortage of time for conversation with the villagers who came to see her, now appeared to have nothing to say at all.

The weaver nodded. With bowed head and stooped shoulders, she turned and left the house.

And Mother was right—or so it seemed, the days of *swadesi* and of helping one another were over. A sense of malaise now pervaded our small town. People no longer delved into fantasies about the greatness of our yet unborn nation. Word had it that the government was recruiting fifty more police officers. Gambling, theft, and murder were on the rise.

At home, the duplicating machine and typewriters were put back inside their shipping crates. A few days later some people came to take away some of our household effects as well. When I asked Mother what was happening to our things, she could only shake her head. Only at a later date did I learn our belongings had been confiscated to pay off my father's debts. Meanwhile, he had disappeared once again.

That very same night, Mother's water broke. When that happened, she gathered the children together and told one of my foster brothers to find my father. She told another to call the midwife. She asked me to help the servant boil water.

Two hours later, only two of us had succeeded in carrying out Mother's orders. The foster brother who had been told to find my father had come back home alone. But the baby was ready to be born, and so, without my father present, my new brother was born. When he screamed, we all breathed a sigh of relief. His was a healthy cry.

The next morning, when I tiptoed into Mother's room to see my baby brother, she welcomed me with a smile. My brother was sleeping peacefully beside her. All suffering and pain seemed to have disappeared from Mother's face.

Just as I leaned down to give my brother a kiss, my father suddenly burst into the room.

"A boy!" he cried, with obvious pleasure. "A boy, who's going to grow up to be bigger and better than both his parents."

My mother stared at him coldly. She then spoke in a voice that at once seemed to be lacking in strength but strangely full of pride: "Yes, you have a boy, a son who will get nothing from you and nothing from either this time or place, a boy who will grow up by himself . . ."

I didn't hear what else she said. I silently snuck out of the room.

And so it was that at the same time my parents' fourth child was born, the country's dream of self-sufficiency was dying. In the end, everything returned to the way it had been before, and it was calm and peaceful in my small hometown of Blora once more. A time of twilight had come, and we knew that before the sun would rise darkness would first descend.

# CIRCUMCISION

LIKE OTHER VILLAGE children, I spent my evenings at the local prayer house learning to recite the Quran. Nothing could have pleased us more than to be there. For recitation lessons we paid two and a half cents per week, which was used to buy oil for the lamps. Lessons began at five thirty in the evening and continued until nine; they were the one and only excuse we had for getting out of doing our homework.

What I'm calling recitation lessons was actually nothing more than telling jokes, talking in fevered whispers about sex, and annoying other devotees who came to say their sunset or evening prayers while we waited for our own turn to be called. This was my world at the age of nine.

Like my friends, I wanted to be a good Muslim, though few of us, at our age, had been circumcised. But then, one day, one of my friends did get circumcised and a large celebration was held for him. This is when I began to think, if I hadn't been circumcised was I really a Muslim? I mulled over this question but didn't let anyone know what I was thinking.

In my small hometown of Blora, boys were usually circumcised somewhere between the ages of eight and thirteen, generally in as grand a style as family circumstances permitted. Girls underwent symbolic circumcision at the age of fifteen days, without any kind of celebration.

One night, my father came home and talked to me about circumcision. I had no idea where he had been, but he was in a very buoyant mood. The house was dark; all the lamps had been extinguished except for one in the central hall, where I was sitting with my mother, listening to her tell me a story about an old man—a pious one, presumably, since he had been to Mecca and was called *haji* to indicate that he had made the pilgrimage to Islam's most holy seat—who kept on getting married. The story was a good one, but because of my father's sudden return it died then and there.

"Do you think you're brave enough to be circumcised?" he asked me, a hopeful smile on his lips.

I didn't know what to say. I wanted to be a good Muslim, but my father's surprise offer terrified me. Then again, my father always terrified me. But, for some reason, his smile that night made all my fears disappear.

"Yes, I am!" I told him.

His smile broadened and he laughed congenially. "What would you like to wear for your circumcision, a wraparound *kain,* or a sarong?"

"A *kain,*" I answered.

He then turned to my seven-year-old brother, who was also in the room. "And what about you, Tato? Are you brave enough, too?"

Tato laughed happily: "Sure I am!"

Father, too, laughed contentedly and the light from the lamp illuminated his even white teeth and pink gums.

Mother rose from the mat she had rolled out on the floor earlier, before starting her bedtime story.

"When do you want to have them circumcised?" she asked.

"As soon as possible," my father replied.

He then rose from his chair and walked away, into the darkness of the house and his bedroom.

Mother stretched out on the mat again but did not continue her story about the marriage-happy *haji*. Instead, she looked at us: "You boys must give thanks to God that your father is going to have you both circumcised."

"We will, Mother," we answered in unison.

"Your dear departed grandmother and all your other ancestors in heaven will be very pleased to know that you have been circumcised."

"Yes, Mother," we said again.

That night I could scarcely sleep as I thought of how much the circumcision would hurt. But then I also began to think of the new *kain* and new pair of sandals I would likely receive—along with all the other new clothes, and a headcloth and prayer mat as well. On top of that, I wouldn't have to go to school and there would be numerous guests. I was almost sure to receive lots of gifts.

I imagined the happiness I would feel from owning my own *kain* and headcloth, for these items were not only a sign of being a good Muslim; they were a sign of being a good Javanese as well, something I also wanted to be.

I was sure to be given at least one sarong, maybe two or even three. My uncircumcised friends would be jealous; that thought, too, gave me a thrill.

The next morning I rose from my bed full of excitement. Tato and I set off for school with plenty of time to spare. Usually, our legs balked at walking to school, but that day they flew. All of our classmates soon heard the news, and the boys who weren't circumcised, especially the older ones, looked on us with newfound respect. Even the teachers cast a kindly gaze on us, for soon we were going to be true Muslims, bona fide circumcised Muslims. And when that happened—and this was the most important thing of all—we would have the right to a place in heaven. We'd no longer have to wish for the many beautiful things that we'd always hoped for but had never been able to obtain, for they would be ours.

At the prayer house, the news also created a sensation among my friends, and our religious teacher gave me the same kindly look that my teachers at school had displayed. I suddenly felt taller, more important than my friends. I could see it very clearly: heaven's gates standing wide open for me. And sure enough, just as our religious teacher had also promised, there they were—the beautiful *houri,* young maidens waiting to tend to my needs. Each one was as beautiful as a certain girl at my school that all the boys talked about.

"After I'm circumcised, I'll be a true Muslim," I told the *kiai*. "I'll have the right to go to heaven!"

The man laughed cheerfully. "And you'll have forty-four *houri* to wait on you!"

"But I don't want any who has six or eight breasts, like a dog," I told him. "I want them to look like Sriati, my classmate at school. She's beautiful."

The *kiai* laughed again.

"And I'll go fishing in rivers of milk every day," Tato chimed in.

Our teacher's mouth opened wider with laughter, baring a disgusting set of teeth that looked like they'd never been brushed.

Our older and uncircumcised friends listened to this conversation silently. I could see fear in their eyes: the fear of missing out on their share of *houri* and the fear of going not to heaven but to hell.

Starting that evening, we followed our recitation lessons diligently and we made sure to finish our homework in short order too. We also fasted, every week, from Monday to Thursday, until the end of the school year. As a result of this extra labor, I easily passed to the next grade.

Two weeks before the end of the school year, my father, the principal of our school, decided to stage a play with the children as actors. Our circumcision ceremony would be held the following day. Father had decided, then and there, to make this an annual event. That way, the poorer boys in school whose parents could not afford to hold a separate celebration would have the chance to get circumcised as well.

For this, my father's first attempt at starting a new tradition, the response of the townspeople was not what Father had expected it to be. Many parents with sons of circumcision age were apparently embarrassed to have someone else pay for their sons' circumcision ceremony. In the end, there were only six boys to be circumcised: my brother Tato and I, a ten-year-old cousin of ours, a sixteen-year-old foster brother, and two boys from poor families who lived outside of town. Another foster brother, who was eighteen and had already had a child with our servant, refused to participate. He insisted that his own father would arrange a ceremony for him.

Five days before the celebration, the boys who were to be circumcised were made to memorize a *panembrama,* a Javanese welcome song. On the night of the play, we were to appear onstage and announce to the audience in song that we were to be circumcised the next day; we were also to request that they offer their prayers for a successful event.

One of our teachers wrote a play about a lost goat in which all the roles were played by the male students.

Finally, the day that we had long awaited approached. The evening before, our grandmother gave Tato and me green silk sarongs. Our mother gave us lacquered wooden sandals and blue shirts. The girls in school gave us switches for keeping flies away during the ceremony, and our father gave us eight Dutch-language children's books. All these gifts made us forget about the pain we were to feel the following day.

On the night of the play, the school was jam-packed with spectators. Food was served: sweet potatoes and boiled peanuts, fermented cassava, *gemblong* made of sweetened sticky rice, and other snacks. Before the performance was to begin, the six of us who were to be circumcised were made to line up on stage. I was outfitted in a *kain* and headcloth, as was my brother, Tato. The other boys were bareheaded. When the curtain opened, the *gamelan* orchestra began to play, and we bowed in respect to the audience. I felt so incredibly proud of myself at that moment. All eyes were focused on us as we sang out that tomorrow we were to be circumcised. The girls looked on us with awe; there would soon be six more eligible men in town.

After our song the audience clapped loudly and we took another bow. The curtain was then closed and we were relieved from further responsibility.

In my hometown, there was very little public entertainment, which is why, I suppose, people came from all parts of the city to watch our performance of *The Lost Goat*. The school's large central classroom, which was usually subdivided into four sections during the regular school day, had been transformed into one large hall that was now filled with people.

The musical entertainment that night varied greatly; besides *gamelan* orchestral works, there were new popular songs such as "Peanut Flower" and "Rose Mary," cowboy songs, theatrical tunes, and older popular songs with a Western influence.

After the performance, many people from the audience patted our shoulders or pounded our backs, giving all six of us greater encouragement and making us feel very special. Later that night, after we had returned home, Tato continued to sing in his bed until he could stay awake no longer; his voice grew softer and softer until it finally died and he drifted to sleep.

In my hometown, the day of a boy's circumcision was a day of great significance, as important as one's birthday or wedding day, the anniversary of a person's death, or even a public holiday.

Although my mother had sent out no formal invitations, news of the ceremony had spread far and wide, and she received contributions for the event from all parts of town.

As was usually the case with major life rituals, even though we had stayed up late the night before, on the day of our circumcision we woke up extra early; by four thirty in the morning the house was already very busy. The candidates for circumcision bathed and were then each dressed in his new *kain* and a prayer cap or headcloth. My sisters wore new clothes and my mother dressed in a new *kain* with a *parang rusak* motif. For a top, she wore a long blouse with embroidered lapels and edging, a gift from an aunt who taught at the girls' school in Rembang. A green rainbow-motif shoulder sash completed her outfit.

My father had on his school uniform: a wraparound *kain* with a broken dagger motif that matched my mother's and a long-sleeved button-up jacket. As usual he was barefooted. (My father never wore shoes; only at home might he sometimes wear wooden cloppers or sandals.)

As if infected by my family's state of readiness, our neighbors rose early too. All dressed in new clothing as well, they then gathered at our house to escort us to the school, where the ceremony was to be held, about a half kilometer away.

Inside the school a small tentlike shelter with sides made of mosquito netting had been erected for the circumcision ceremony. The six of us who were to be circumcised occupied a row of chairs nearby. As the time for the ceremony approached, the number of visitors around the shelter grew larger, both adults and children too. The girls remained at a slight distance.

Finally, a circumcision specialist, the *calak,* arrived, and proceeded to unwrap three straight-edge blades from their handkerchief covers. As he was doing this, an older man offered us words of advice: "Don't be afraid. It won't hurt. It's a bit like being bitten by a red ant. I laughed when I was circumcised."

His was only one of many comforting voices, but no matter how reassuring the tone, we couldn't completely expunge our anxiety and fear.

Then came the time for the ceremony to begin. My father and mother, who were seated in a pair of large chairs among the crowd of visitors, rose and approached the netted shelter. Pride and elation showed on their faces.

The first boy to enter the hut was my parents' foster son, the sixteen-year-old, because he was the oldest one among us. The other foster son, the one who had refused to be circumcised, was nowhere to be seen in the crowd. The children who had come to witness the ceremony crowded so close to the shelter that the adults were forced to shoo them away.

I was incredibly scared. I wanted to be a good Muslim, but that wasn't enough to still my terror. And when the *calak* suddenly began to bawl out an incomprehensible prayer, the pounding of my heart in my chest grew all the more strong. When my foster brother was led out of the hut, he could scarcely walk. His face was drained of blood and his lips looked almost white. He had no strength. The ushers seated him in his chair and placed a large earthenware saucer that was filled with fine ash from the kitchen hearth between his legs to catch and sop up the blood that was dripping from his penis.

One by one, the older boys entered the shelter. As with my foster brother, when they reemerged they looked pale-faced and walked with an unsteady gait. As I stood up to enter the tent, I felt several people take hold of my shoulders, as if they were afraid I would try to run away. I was then ushered inside the hut, where the *calak* was waiting impatiently, with a ferocious gleam in his eye—at least that's how he looked to me.

I was placed in a chair and my head pulled backward so that I was now facing up, toward the roof of the tent. While one of the ushers, an older man, held my shoulders tightly to steady me, another pair of old hands attached themselves to my temples so that I could not look down. Below me, on the floor, was an earthenware bowl filled with ash. I felt a hand grope my penis, and then my foreskin being twisted tightly until it began to sting and feel very hot. Just at that moment, a razor severed that knot of my skin. It was over; I was circumcised. The old man who had been holding my temples back released his hands. I looked down to see blood dripping from the end of my penis.

"Don't move," one of the men said.

"You have to wait until the first flow of blood has stopped," another added.

I stared at the stream of blood—a blackened cord as it began to coagulate—and watched it as it slowly fell and disappeared into the fine ash in the saucer directly below.

Because Tato was the youngest, he was the last to be circumcised; and when his operation was over, he too was led out from the shelter and put back on the seat beside me. Blood continued to drip into the earthenware dishes below our legs. All eyes were upon us. Mother came to me and kissed my cheeks; her display of affection caused tears to well in my eyes. She kissed Tato on the cheek too. Then Father came over to congratulate us: "Well done, well done."

The visitors began to leave, first the children and then the adults, who took their leave one by one. After that, the six of us who had just been circumcised made our way home on foot as well.

We were treated like kings that day. Our wishes were commands. The families of the two poor boys who had also been circumcised came to our home bearing gifts of chicken and rice.

"Now that you've been circumcised, do you feel that something's changed?" my mother asked me.

"I feel really happy," I told her.

"And do you feel like a true Muslim?" she then inquired.

Her question gave me pause; the fact was, I didn't feel any different.

"I feel like I did yesterday," I tried to explain, ". . . and the day before. I still don't feel like a true Muslim."

"Could it be because you don't perform the daily prayers?" Mother then asked.

"No, I always do all five," I told her.

"Your grandfather's been to Mecca. Maybe if you made the pilgrimage, you'd feel the change, and know that you were a true Muslim."

"Would we go by ship?" Tato chirped.

"Yes, you'd sail to Arabia," Mother answered.

"Wouldn't we have to be really rich to do that?" I then posed.

"Yes, you would," Mother said.

And with that all my hopes of becoming a true Muslim vanished. I knew that my parents weren't well off and that we could never afford to make the pilgrimage.

"Why hasn't Father ever been to Mecca?" I asked.

"Because your father doesn't have the money."

Although I suddenly wanted to be rich, I also knew that this would never be the case. And after I had healed, the thought of becoming a true Muslim never again entered my mind.

# REVENGE

THE FOLLOWING SERIES of incidents took place in the space of a week. This is a true story, a story about the faint-heartedness of an individual, that individual being myself. It is a simple tale—yes, with as much simplicity as a tattered cloth or a dead cat in the middle of the road—and, very likely, one that should not be told. But it is a series of incidents that together form the first milestone of my life.

*November 1945. Day One.*

As with other young nationalists at the time, I caught bullet fever. Thus, it's not surprising that when the call went out for soldiers, I enlisted straightaway. I was accepted, but as with other recent inductees had yet to receive my ration of rank. "Ration of rank," you say? Well, let me tell you, in the military, rank has its own value, just like bullets and just like guns. This meant that the soldier with no rank had no determinant role whatsoever to play on the battlefield, in the security affairs of a town, or in the field of love.

Four hours after being stationed at what I shall call Base X, the first thing that stirred my heart was the sight of a company of foot soldiers standing in formation outside unit headquarters. They stood in a line parallel to the main road, their faces hidden beneath metal helmets. It was twilight and it was drizzling, but they seemed to take no notice of the rain, nor did the people who were watching them. No one was talking. Each person's attention was on his own preoccupation: for every soldier, the position of weapon; for the onlookers, the spectacle taking place before them. From the soldiers' waistbands hung various issues of grenades. Each squad had, on average, two carbines and each section one machine gun. Otherwise, all were armed with sharpened bamboo spears. Only one cannon was evident.

The roadside audience that evening consisted mostly of poor people—either with or without rank—but included off-duty soldiers as well. As a new recruit, I was there too, and the sight of those soldiers filled my chest, close to bursting, with a kind of pride in my country that bordered on intoxication. And, to be honest, the sight did make me feel drunk, even though the fighting men were few in number and not fully armed. Every so often a shiver ran down my spine, causing my hair to stand on end. I knew my fellow onlookers were feeling the same thing.

It was no secret that T-Company was to take position on the defense perimeter, which had been pushed forward by seven kilometers. Where the defense posts on the line were supposed to be, however, only a few people knew for sure. All that anyone knew was that the front was to be located seven kilometers from Base X.

At the train station, a formation of train cars sat facing westward in preparation for the move. Four trucks, two cars, and one jeep had already been loaded onto open wagons.

The faces of the soldiers, all of them very young, were gloomy with the prospect of what awaited them: their departure to the front and the field of death. This was normal, to be sure, for they were negotiating with their imagination, attempting to mentally anticipate the battle against their enemy. But it would be different later, after they had left the base and were on the battlefield and bullets were whizzing by overhead with the crackling sound of fat in the fire. Then, their gloom would vanish, as quickly as the promise on the lips of a black marketer. At that time, all minor cares would dissolve, and some major things too—even thoughts about sex and self-preservation. Once the battle had begun and their hearts were beating fast, the only thing these young soldiers would think about was "Ready, aim, fire!" or "Forward, move out, attack!" And later, if fortune was in their favor, they would return home to base singing victory songs.

The drizzle continued, twilight darkened to night. Families in the villages where the soldiers were from were praying that bullets not find their soldier-sons. Meanwhile, far beyond the ocean, in the home of the enemy, other families were praying to God for the safety of their boys who had been sent abroad to free native peoples from terror. Such a perfect illustration of human folly! God, who is purported to be One and Indivisible, was being asked by both sides in the killing to award victory to them, when in fact the reality of the situation was this: that in victory or defeat, as in life or death, it is human flesh that reveals the outcome. Prayers, no matter how long they might go on, offer no certainty of life. And all those lips, moving as one, cannot save the heart from even the pain of a few words that suddenly arise in the penitents' minds, especially the minds of young women whose sweethearts were among those ranks.

Once the commander of T-Company had received his orders from the unit commander, and after he had conveyed his hopes to the soldiers under his command, the company marched off to the train station to the beat of drums and a trumpet's song.

Despite the anxiety apparent on the faces of both soldiers and spectators, pride was also visible. The confidence they exuded caused my own feelings to meld with theirs, making me itchy to follow along. What was wrong with a bamboo spear as a weapon? In skirmishes it was second to none.

Civilians accompanied the troops from behind and at the side, and children hoorayed in admiration. Young women stared fondly, watching sweethearts, prospective sweethearts, and imaginary sweethearts, as they passed.

The troops turned onto the narrow side street that ran behind the station, their shoulders stooped beneath the weight of the load they bore: knapsacks; metal, wood, and leather objects; and their inner thoughts. Most of the men were barefoot. Of the men with footwear, most wore rubber boots. They continued their march toward the station at an easy pace, eventually making their way over the muddy road beneath their feet.

At the station platform, the spectators broke off from the troops to form a chaotic rank of their own. As the drums and trumpets fell silent, the troops quietly boarded the train. In an instant, though, the atmosphere changed when the young women in the crowd began to wave their handkerchiefs at their sweethearts and any other willing soldier. At that moment, the soldiers' gloom vanished and they waved back to the women through the train windows, with bayonets, spears, their heads, their shirts and hats, and noses.

Something alive began to stir, something between the soldiers who were leaving for the battlefront, that field of death, and the young women on the platform. It was something that moved the two genders toward synthesis, a feeling of unity that would not be cleaved by the heaviest of field guns.

The soldiers' songs grew stronger, inviting the crowd of escorts to sing along. Station officials bustled about in an energetic yet friendly manner. A moment later the station reverberated with the thunder of resounding cheers.

Why was everyone screaming? I didn't know the reason, but I felt a deep sense of intoxication pulling and pushing me along. Apparently, for everyone there, the feeling was the same. Everyone was shouting. Everyone felt intoxicated. They cheered for the sake of cheering. They cheered for the intoxication that it produced.

All eyes sparkled, every limb trembled. Then the station bell sounded, followed by the engineer's whistle, as the train began to move slowly out of the station to the west. An even merrier round of song and cheers erupted, and waving handkerchiefs filled the air as the caboose left the station. Gradually the singing faded and died, vanishing into the deep blue gloaming. The people on the platform fell silent and mutely began to make their way home. In the dissipating crowd, young women walked with their heads bowed, saying not a single word.

I remained on the platform, staring toward the west, the direction of the train that was carrying cars of men to the field of death. Because of politics, these men had been yanked from the comfort of their families. On their journey, they would pass through a broad swath of land whose inhabitants were sleeping peacefully, like babies in the cradle of their mother's arms. These same men had been cruelly torn from their own mother's arms, yanked away from the refreshment of deep slumber. Yet they were ready to shed their blood, even as other people found amusement at the cinema, the theater, restaurants, brothels, and gambling halls, even as newlywed couples safely indulged in intimacies. Yes, they were willing, even when knowing that to return to their base in defeat would mean that those very same people for whom they had risked their lives to protect would call them cowardly. And that if they returned on a stretcher, their limbs festering with gangrene, these people might deign to smile slightly as they called them national heroes . . .

I slowly returned to the new-recruits' barracks, my mind awhirl. The time would come, the time I was waiting for, when I would depart for the field of death.

That night I slept a sleep of no dreams.

*Day Three. Twilight.*

I left for the station in my soldier's uniform, an oversized green shirt, trousers of similar disproportion, and tightly fitting shoes that pinched my heels and whose laces were long enough to trip over. But I was proud of my new green made-in-Cipinang-prison uniform. And I was proud of my rank—a no-rank private without a single stripe. I was even proud of my hair, which for two months I had left unshorn. Indeed, I was very proud and because of that I went to the station.

The station was the center of Base X. Because of the station, the base had become a town of its own. It was where the young freedom fighters gathered to preen, to show off their green uniforms, to display their weapons (assuming they had any), and most of all, to publicly present their fetching looks. At least that's why I went to the station. Forever and always, humans are prone to advertising their better features, especially when naked reality can be dressed up in a garb of fantasy such as that of a young revolutionary. But none of that pride means anything, of course, without the admiration of a pair of lovely eyes.

This was especially so when the night train from Jakarta pulled in. If the hearts of the men at the station had lips, there is no doubt that you could have heard them express their fantasy: "Look at me. I am a patriot!" But after the train had gone, the pride would disappear. One's heart would feel empty, one's head completely vacant—or at least this was my experience during my first three days at the base.

After all the tumult had died down, I was forced to ask myself what I had given to the struggle. It was a question I couldn't answer, and I suspect the others couldn't either. Even the devil probably didn't know.

The day before, I had witnessed four of my co-recruits take part in front-line weapons practice using real bullets. Because bullets were so expensive, training usually consisted of aiming the gun, lifting its safety catch, and pulling the trigger—in addition to running and crawling, that is. But on the front, the games were real, with the men shooting other men in green uniforms from behind the trunks of rubber trees, and sneaking through the undergrowth to toss hand grenades at green-painted trucks.

That night, I thought that going to the train station would ease the frustration I felt for not yet being entrusted to engage in combat.

As I was pacing the platform like a person with too much on his mind, a troop of fully armed soldiers came in from the direction of the road behind the station. Following them were civil guards and local notables. The long file stretched itself out along the platform. I couldn't guess what they were there for, but I knew they were not being sent to the front.

Shortly after the station bell rang, a special train came in from the direction of Jakarta. When it came to a halt, I noticed that in addition to passenger cars, there was a Red Cross car as well. The armed troops moved alongside the car. When the order was called out, the men immediately stood at attention. The squad then raised their guns at an eighty-degree angle and fired over their heads three rounds.

I too stood at attention. The civilians in attendance took off their hats and bowed their heads. Thereafter, eleven corpses, each of them wrapped in the Red and White, began to be lowered from the Red Cross car to the station platform. Then the soldiers from T-Company disembarked from the other train cars, not speaking a word, not making a sound. After the corpses had been laid out on the platform, the squad fired another round. Then, all the living soldiers at the station filed off toward the army base.

I followed behind. There were no drum rolls, no trumpets blaring that night, not like when the men had left for the front.

Defeated troops are always silent, but that night I thought I could hear the men's hearts screaming out to be remembered.

At the now forlorn station, the tin roof was dotted with bullet holes.

People believed that soldiers who are killed in battle are martyrs who may be buried in their uniforms with no prior purification. Such is the word that spread that night, along with many other stories about death. Sergeant Major D, a medical student, had died that night, and people talked about his death as easily as they talked about an increase in the price of rice. The fine scent of this young soldier's name, already known beyond the regency's borders, was like the pleasure one finds in restaurant food. Once it has passed the throat, the original taste is forgotten. As another comparison, his life was like a film that had just ended. And now that the show was over, his flesh would dissolve into earth.

The only subject of conversation that night, one that even edged out talk of medicines that would ward off venereal disease, was the defeat of T-Company. The past contributions of the company's commander to the cause—all the blood, sweat, and tears he had given—now had no meaning at all. He was a lily-livered commander, people now said, but of course that was because he didn't return as a corpse. Had he died in battle, they would have been saying, "A true hero!"

Meanwhile, far beyond the demarcation line that separated the areas under Republican and Dutch control, the victorious troops were now celebrating their success in killing 11 terrorists with the same flushed enthusiasm a housewife might employ when recounting to her neighbor that she had just managed to kill 11 mice!

And later that night, when I tossed and turned on my mat, trying to get some sleep, there came to me my life's first revelation: that life is actually very simple, but that man, like a wind in the dry season filling the air with debris, turns simplicity into chaos. It is this self-induced state of chaos that causes men to kill one another. And then, very clearly, came the next revelation for me: that military life was not for me.

Maybe it was fear of an unpleasant death that was speaking to me, but I suddenly wanted to leave the military. But then I thought of the document that had been thrust before my eyes—"All those accepted as soldiers, including volunteers, are bound by the unwritten and unspoken oath that they will entrust their lives to their country . . ."—and I knew that I could not leave. I would have to stay here and wait, possibly until death came to greet me.

That night none of the patrols sang as they made their rounds. I heard no sound of gunfire from night training. The town was silent as its residents chewed on the matter of their own deaths.

*Day Seven. Twilight.*

After drills in crawling and crouching and aiming and firing a machine gun, I washed away my fatigue with bathwater and then went to the station. It was seven o'clock and the station was as busy as a carnival on a night with no rain and a full moon. The number of soldiers there, both with and without rank and with and without weapons, grew larger by the minute. The night train bound for Mojokerto was due to arrive in two hours. Here and there, guards paced, patrolling the station area.

At the entranceway stood the inspectors, a mixture of male and female soldiers, looking more attentive than usual. Maybe they were hoping for another big catch, like the one the day before when they had caught a woman from Jakarta trying to bring in three and a half million in Japanese currency. The troops of Base X were responsible not only for warding off military attacks, but for stemming the flood of unwanted currency as well, especially Japanese currency, the value of which had plummeted to almost nothing since the Japanese surrender. The inspectors from Base X weren't about to see the region's rice reserves turn into a stack of worthless notes. A bitter lesson of the times was that money could not be eaten and was not always all powerful. These days, in 1945, it was rice that occupied the preeminent position. People might have wanted to deny it, but the facts stood for themselves. In the cruel days after the arrival of the Japanese, even a spoonful of rice could determine a person's survival.

Because of the role of our small town as a military headquarters, its popularity in the public imagination was firmly established; but now, situated as it was in the center of the rice belt, it became even more famous. With Jakarta being under Dutch control, the nationalists had established a blockade to cut off the shipment of rice to the city. As a result, our town was deluged with outsiders, and because the arrivals, Jakarta residents for the most part, were also Indonesian who could pass the border freely, the blockade really worked on paper only. For this reason, Jakarta people could breathe a sigh of relief—but this was also the reason behind the beefed-up patrol at the train station. The strictest inspection point for contraband material in the region was there.

The station bell sounded. The train from Jakarta was about to arrive. It was this train that was always filled with thousands of rice dealers. I jumped up from my seat on the platform, as did the other soldiers present. Time to be on the lookout! Time for a change of view—even though my self-pride was not what it had been earlier. I wasn't so proud of my uniform or my hair anymore. Even so, or especially because of this fact, I knew a change was needed—and Indonesian women, even small-time rice traders, are not half bad to look at.

The station was in commotion and the people were acting rowdier than ever. No military police were evident, but at that point, the force was just being established.

I heard the huffing of the train growing louder as it grew closer, like the heavy breathing of a young man in the middle of making his moves on a young woman. Slowly and surely it made its way toward the terminal.

Finally, the train arrived. Everyone seemed excited, and even more uncontrollable. The train stopped and the hiss of steam from the locomotive drowned out all other sounds. A moment later, people from inside the train cars were jumping onto the platform. Passengers clinging to the roofs of the cars made their way down much more carefully.

The soldiers on duty were suddenly busy. The inspectors took care of the female passengers, lining them up before they could make their way out of the station and then giving them a thorough search, from the tops of their heads to other, less exposed, parts of the body. I too was busy, looking around for something I did not seek.

For no reason, I started to watch the male passengers, who had lined up and were waiting to be searched. A man in a thick yellow turban caught my eye. A *haji,* no doubt, who had made the pilgrimage to Mecca and continued to display the trappings. In addition to the turban he was wearing a white shirt and a purple-, red-, and yellow-checked sarong. But it was not his clothing that caught my attention; it was the desperate look in his eyes. He seemed to be constantly searching for shadows in which to hide his face.

Up and down the queue, the inspectors were taking their day's cut—of cigarettes, bread, and cheese, or a pinch of a pretty girl's cheek and, sometimes, a softly whispered promise. All of this was proof of the power of rice. Rice was now king, and as these passengers were rice dealers it was imperative that they knew their place when facing the station guards.

When one of the inspectors approached the man in the yellow turban, he suddenly called out, "Here he is!"

The pilgrim began to panic. His face turned ashen, but he readily collected himself and managed to smile.

Attracted by the confrontation, other soldiers gathered around, myself included. The man was dragged out of the line. With his bag still clutched in his left hand, he was whisked off to the station guardhouse, next to the stationmaster's office. A hundred-watt bulb illuminated his furrowed features.

Being a soldier without rank and having no official role to play in any activity, I stood off to the side but close enough to the guardhouse window so that I could see what was going to happen to the turbaned man.

I watched as the commander rose quickly from his chair and, with a flushed face, strode over to a wooden bench where the soldiers had placed their detainee. He shouted angrily at the man. "You British dog! So, you finally got caught, you son of a bitch. Your face is one I'll never forget. You know me, don't you?"

The captive man panicked again. His ashen face took on a green hue from the lamplight. He bowed his head nervously, almost like a girl being wooed. "Hmm, no, sir," he mumbled.

The other soldiers outside called eerily, "That's him! That's the guy, sir."

The pilgrim momentarily scanned the window and doorway filled with soldiers, then bowed his head again.

The commander yelled at the man again, attracting even more soldiers to the guardhouse, all of them trying to peer inside. A couple of railway officers looked in but just as quickly left.

Hands on hips, the commander screamed at the man, "You're a spy!"

The man looked up for an instant to stare at his accuser and quickly lowered his head again. "No, sir," he said again, in a low and quivering voice.

"You British pig! Admit it!" He nodded his head rapidly up and down, then spoke in a slightly softer voice. "Come on, tell the truth."

When the captive did not answer, the commander's face flushed with anger again. "Confess!" he roared.

"No, sir," the man said yet again with his head still bowed.

"Confess, or I'm going to . . ." The commander's fist flew toward the man and landed in his face, causing the man's turban to fly from his head into the corner of the room.

The man's head was bald and it glistened under the lamplight. Suddenly a visible change came over him: his body stopped trembling and he raised his head erect. His eyes blinked sharply.

And then the beating started. I turned my head to the side, unable to watch, I didn't know why. Maybe it was because I was a new soldier or, possibly, much more cowardly than I had thought myself to be. Whatever the reason, it was clear to me that I didn't have nerves of steel, which is supposed to be a soldier's first requirement. I wanted to leave, I couldn't take it, but something swayed my intent: curiosity, I suppose, the urge to know what would happen. And so I remained there, fixed in place, beside the window.

Next to me was another soldier who couldn't stop grinding his teeth.

"What did he do?" I asked him.

He hissed through his teeth as if chasing a dog away. "What did he do? That pig of a man!" He spat at the ground derisively, but made sure not to hit his shoes. "He's a British spy, is what he is, and there's going to be no forgiving him." His explanation spilled from his mouth: "Here are our guys, out there at the front, and then all of a sudden the Brits attack, smack-dab between our defenses. They routed our troops completely." He pointed his finger at the man. "And did you see that turban of his? Like some holy man, when he's a frigging spy."

"But how do you know?" I myself was curious.

He gave me a teacherly look. "I know everything around here! What happened is one day he comes here and asks to be a cook, and so we take him on, but then what happens? The son of a bitch runs off. When he does come back, he's screaming, 'The enemy's coming! The enemy is coming!' And when we go to check it out, what happens? We find ourselves surrounded, is what! The son of a bitch. Wait till I get a chance to lay into him. He'll see what my fists feel like then.

"Anyway, we put up the best we could but still got throttled. We were going crazy . . ." After throwing a mean look at the pil-gim, he let his story continue to flow. “By that time, they’d taken the best positions and we were being pushed back. It’s just lucky we were able to escape. In the end, they got for themselves a machine gun, two trucks, and the front commander’s car. All we got was eleven dead men and fifty burned uniforms.” He ground his teeth together. “No way we’re going to show him mercy,” he snarled.

Meanwhile, as my companion was having his say, the guard commander was using the captive as a punching bag: left, right, left, right, with a sound like the wheels of a train as they begin to turn. The pilgrim’s head was swinging back and forth with the punches. But then the commander suddenly stopped and ran drunkenly toward the door. His face was lined with pain.

Once he was outside, on the platform, he swore, “Son of a bitch! My hand is killing me!” And then he disappeared.

After that it was his assistant’s turn, and the soldier beside me hissed, “That pig doesn’t deserve any mercy.” And then he yelled into the guardhouse, “You take care of him, sir!”

The assistant to the commander, a corporal, ignored the shouts and eased himself onto the wooden bench beside the pilgrim. His voice was soothing: “Don’t be angry with the commander. He’s upset because of the losses we suffered four days ago. Please forgive him.”

Our pilgrim smiled and his bald head rose and fell like a pigeon wooing its mate. He then looked around with a certain kind of pride in his eyes. I breathed a sigh of relief.

“I know you too,” the corporal said. “You were our cook for a while, weren’t you?”

The man nodded readily.

The corporal continued to speak. His voice was polite, almost seductive to the ear. "We're short of soldiers here, you know. Do you think you might want to join up?"

"Of course I would," the man said happily.

"But we can't have any spies!" the corporal warned.

"If you let me join, you won't have anything to worry about," the man said arrogantly. "I could be *your* spy!"

The corporal raised his eyebrows. "So then you've had some experience?"

"Sure I have . . ." the man started to say, but then stopped, suddenly aware of the verbal trap that had been sprung on him.

"And what kind of experience was that?" the corporal asked, as he calmly removed a hammer from his pack. "You wouldn't be talking about the company at the front about a half week ago, would you?"

The pilgrim cleared his throat but didn't answer. His head was bowed as if in guilt.

The corporal shifted his hammer from one hand to the other. "Can you guess where this hammer was made?" he asked the pilgrim calmly.

Soothed by the corporal's voice, the man raised his eyes to look at the corporal and then at the hammer. "I'd say it's German . . ."

Immediately after, a crack was heard as the hammer smashed into the man's right eye. As the hammer was whipped back to strike again, my vision suddenly darkened, though I could still see clearly in my mind the shudder of the man's bald head as the hammer smashed into the left side of his forehead.

All I could hear was the soldier beside me, screaming, "Let me finish him off!"

When I next opened my eyes, what I saw astounded me: the pilgrim was still sitting on the bench, upright, with a smile on his lips. There was no blood. He wasn't even groaning. I thought I might have imagined what had happened. At that point, I didn't know. Maybe the man was invulnerable. I had heard of such a thing.

Then the soldier beside me began to scream about how the pilgrim had killed his brother. He jumped through the window and began to pummel the man with his fists. Thereafter the other soldiers joined in, rushing into the room for their own share of the action.

I was left alone, along with a few other stay-behinds, trying to avoid the sight of what was going on inside the room. It was then that the revelation came to me again: the military was no place for me. But as before, there followed the recognition that I had pledged my life to the country. If love exists, then I did love my country. But if love exists, there would definitely be something that I would love more than my country . . . Whatever the case, I knew I was in the wrong field. I had to leave the military and get away from weapons.

Just as the pilgrim was being knocked about by fists and feet, I was engaged in a tug-of-war with my revelations. I couldn't bear to watch what was happening, yet couldn't turn my eyes away; there was something I wanted to know. Maybe my heart was screaming inside, maybe my mouth was moving too, but I couldn't hear a thing. War is war; it's the same everywhere, with people torturing and killing one another, generally behind the shield of lofty motives.

No, this is not my place, I said again. But what about that pledge of mine?

What was happening before me was in fact a moral test. Was there even the least bit of humanity still in me? Maybe this was just the feeling of a new recruit. I didn't know.

Between the bodies of his assailants, the pilgrim vanished and reappeared before my eyes. Somehow, he was still smiling; no pain showed on his face. Why was he smiling? Was he smiling disdainfully at his captors' uncontrolled anger? Was his smile one of pleasure from the memory of his wedding night when his new bride suddenly became nervous and hesitated to approach? Or did he smile from the recollection of his pilgrimage to his religion's most-holy site? All these were possible. Isn't it so that when a person is on the verge of death he sometimes recalls his very first love?

Maybe the pilgrim was innocent. Maybe he'd blurted out an unintended confession because he wanted to become a soldier and have the chance to defend his country. It was possible but I didn't know.

War is war, no doubt about it—a constant cycle of man's evil toward man. A tree's branches don't move of their own accord; something has to move them. Likewise, men don't simply turn into savages; there has to be something that makes them that way.

And men then go on to make weapons to kill their enemies because there are enemies everywhere. So very few ever stop to realize that their most important foe is themselves, that therein the seeds of savagery lie.

Outside, the station was dark. Suddenly, an officer made his way into the guardhouse, causing all the soldiers to fall back. With hardly a glance at the pilgrim, he screamed, "That's the spy!" and then whipped out his gun and struck the man on his temple with the pistol barrel.

The pilgrim didn't react, but from his mouth came a weird, chortling sound.

"Are you laughing at me?" the officer screamed. And then, with a nod of his head toward the soldiers, he gave them permission to act.

Again I was forced to hide my face in the shadow of the window frame as the mass of soldiers mobbed their prey. By the time I could make myself look again, the pilgrim had been bound tightly. His hands were in cuffs behind his back. There was a noose around his neck. The men screamed riotously as he was led outside, with their rifle muzzles, bared bayonets and bamboo spears all pointed at the man's back. The pilgrim showed no resistance. He had given up.

I didn't want to watch, but my urge to know how this incident would end made me join this revolutionary procession. The faces of the men looked inflamed, their skin dark red in color, as if they were intoxicated. Among the women soldiers were some screaming shrilly, their breasts swollen with excitement.

At that moment I thought of my family. What would I say, what would I do, if this were happening to my older brother? Right then I also felt rich for still having in me some sense of humanity, but then the refutation immediately followed: that isn't humanity, it's a sign of weakness in a new recruit. It's a sign that I had never tasted betrayal. With that, my arrogance disappeared. If in fact I had any sense of humanity left in me, I would have leaped into the crowd to protect the pilgrim, even if he were a spy. Yet I did nothing. I said nothing. I watched. That is not the way humanity works. I was a coward, which is just a synonym for traitor—and I had in fact betrayed the pilgrim. Humanity has no use or value if it doesn't go hand in hand with courage.

A sergeant appeared at my side, breathing hard. "Aren't you coming?" he asked. I shook my head and continued to walk but his cynicism followed me: "What, you afraid you'll get your makeup ruined?"

I stopped to give the man more distance, to wait for him to go ahead, but he turned to hiss a warning at me: "Watch out, if I find out you're a spy!" He then bounded away to rejoin the procession.

The farther I walked from the guardhouse, the weaker the light became. Finally, the procession passed through the station gateway. I hung back, following from a distance.

Out in the night air, the men became more intoxicated and kept slugging the pilgrim and kicking him in his behind, causing him to wobble unsteadily forward. The men cheered, and in no time at all the quiet little town of X had been awakened by this spectacle of the revolution.

More and more people now joined the crowd, and the pilgrim vanished within the swarm of frenzied bodies. All I could see beneath the flickering light of street lanterns were rustling trouser legs, stamping army boots, and the tips of bamboo spears, rising and falling in the air.

Somewhere beyond the station, the crowd parted as the pilgrim's feet were trussed together. Unable to walk, he was propped up against a lamppost while the end of the rope that bound him was tied to the fender of a small truck. For everyone present, the decision of this ad-hoc court of drunken men was immediately evident, but before the ruling could be carried out, before they would let him slicken one of the country's main roads, they first tested the sharpness of their spears in his flesh.

I was able to get a clear look at the man. He was upright and leaning against the lamppost. His bald head, without the light shining directly on him, had lost its sheen. But what made me stare so long was the smile on his face, which was like that of an innocent maiden in sleep. That, and the fact that his body appeared completely unmarked.

Did my eyes deceive me? I'm not completely sure because vision is not always the most trustworthy sense, but I could swear the man wasn't even wounded. He stood unharmed in the circle of his judges and executioners.

A soldier then leaped into the middle of the arena, a bamboo spear fixed in his two hands, ready to rip open the pilgrim's belly. Like the roar of a Japanese soldier thrusting his bayonet into a sandbag, the soldier thrust the spear into the man's abdomen. Not even conscious of what I was doing, I found myself clinging to the railway crossing bar. My vision blurred completely as my brain refused to see, but I heard a terrible sound—I didn't even want to think of what it was—and after that, nothing. The cheering had died. But then I heard the sound of a man panting, breathing hard, and then another crazy and clamorous cheer. My vision returned and I saw a spear protruding from a billowing white shirt that was now torn. And then I saw a smile. And then a bald head. And then the bamboo spear as it was pulled out. But the cheering died again: the end of the bamboo spear was dry. There was no blood made dark by the night, no guts spilling from the man's abdomen. Just a patient smile. The pilgrim remained unharmed, still the man that he was before.

The crowd cheered again, this time even more boisterously than before. The tips of bamboo spears again danced in the air. With the soldiers flailing their bayonets and the rice traders swinging their carrying pole, I knew, at that moment, there was no one-and-only God with the power to stop this display of independence. The pilgrim was tossed by the blows, to and fro, even as he tried to remain upright. I'm sure I saw a bamboo spear plunge into one of his eye sockets and then retreat without leaving a trace.

The man's clothes were in tatters. Finally, he fell backward, down and alongside the lamppost, but no sooner had he reached the ground when a long sword descended toward his bowed head. After that, what I could see was the backs of men, darkened by shadows and wet with sweat, and the blunted tips of bamboo spears as they rose and fell. What I could hear were drunken cries that suddenly, unexpectedly, faded.

Willing myself to see, I watched the crowd circle around their victim, all their eyes sparkling and focused in the direction of the lamppost's base. Four or five of the men pulled the man up and leaned him against the lamppost. He was half naked, his clothes were in rags. Only the leather belt that he wore still looked solid, but I would swear there was no wound on his body.

For an instant there was a thunder of cheers, but just as quickly the sound vanished, as did the smile on the pilgrim's face when his arms began to move and the knot of rope that was keeping his hands tied behind his back suddenly broke free.

The drunken men suddenly looked afraid as they thought of their own safety. They moved back, away from the victim, as he raised his now freed hands. Frightened whispers quickly spread until someone screamed the order, "Start the truck!"

Then there was silence, at least for a moment, until the pilgrim's hands began to seek the rope that still bound his feet. When he found the cord, the crowd edged farther away from him in fearful anticipation. I watched him. I stared as he collected his inner strength. All the while, his eyes were trained fiercely on the earth beneath his feet.

At that moment, the shrill whistle of the night train from Jakarta to Mojokerto pierced the air as it left the station. And then I heard the roar of a truck's engine as it was put in gear. . . .

The body of the pilgrim flew into the air and then fell back to earth to flop about on the ground. The driver of the truck stepped on the gas and, with the knotted rope on the man's legs attached to the fender, his body leaped forward, feet first. He tumbled over and over as he was dragged down the asphalt road. The people cheered. They clapped and shouted in the lamplight's peaceful glow. As the truck and its baggage made their way into darkness, people ran after it, pell-mell, trying to catch up. I slowly followed in their wake, wandering among the hundreds, or possibly thousands, of people now on hand. Now as before, the atmosphere was one of intoxication.

When the truck reached the second lamppost, near a bend in the road ahead, it slowed down, proceeding no faster than a walking pace. Even so, the pilgrim was unable to make use of his free hands. By this time, I had almost caught up with the tumbling load.

It dawned on me that torture was the only thing these people were capable of doing. It was their second nature, no different from the pickpocket with his innate skill of lifting wallets, the lawyer with his gift of gab, the accountant with his ledger, and the doctor with his cures. And this was the verdict handed down by a court whose members were intoxicated by their own sense of intoxication. It was a court whose members despised the police for never having protected them and who hated informers for revealing to the Japanese their hidden supplies of food. Experience had taught them nothing about the proper role of judges. And now we had the outcome: a trial by drunks who lacked even the knowledge of their own country's long history.

When the soldiers began to tire, civilians took their place, screaming just as drunkenly as the former, "Kill the scum!"

I made myself look more closely at the pilgrim, who was still being tossed about. To my eyes, he appeared completely calm. His body had suffered no great injury from being dragged over the asphalt-and-gravel road.

The soldiers advanced again, their weapons bared, and the procession moved on slowly. No one was thinking about the night train that brought to the area foreign journalists and beautiful city girls.

At the railway crossing the truck slowed to a halt, and a soldier who had just arrived pushed his way through the crowd toward the pilgrim. Beneath the crossing light, he looked at the man and shouted, "That's him!" He then drew from his waistband a short sword, the kind the Japanese used to commit hara-kiri, and shoved it toward the man's face. "Do you know what this is?" he screamed.

The crowd's awful roar suddenly died as all eyes looked at the pilgrim, who never ceased to smile. The truck purred in the background.

The soldier fell to his knees, angrily screaming an exorcist's cry as he repeatedly plunged his sword into the ground, "Back to earth! Back to earth!" He then stopped and raised the sword above his head in both his hands. And then, the sword came down. . . .

For the first time that evening, a great fear appeared in the pilgrim's eyes. The man's features hardened. His eyeballs almost popped out of their sockets. He opened his mouth as if to groan, but the sheer tautness of his muscles prevented him from making a sound. Before he could even blink, the sword's blade slashed open his stomach and in less than a moment his features had finally, and forever, relaxed.

First I saw the man's intestines as they spilled from the gaping hole in his belly and then his blood as it gushed forth from that same cavity. A smell of death rose in the air. I caught the sound of a few brief sighs before every other noise and sound was drowned by the cheers and wild applause of the crowd.

As the truck began to move again, driving unevenly across the railroad tracks and onto the road beyond, the crowd jumped up and down in a wild and insane dance. Even amid the revelry, I thought I could hear, somehow, a man breathing in deep and rapid gasps, and the sound of his trembling voice, calling out for water in utter despair. And even though I hid my face in night's shadow, I could see the man's intestines, the contents of his stomach, his flesh and blood. I continued to follow in the procession's wake but was careful to walk on the side of the road for fear of getting spattered by the blood and flesh with which the asphalt was now painted.

Overhead, the stars twinkled peacefully. Each and every weapon that had ever existed played a role in destroying that man, not only his body but the very memory of him from the history of the revolution, this country and this earth. I no longer knew what I was feeling. I did not understand. Only one thing was certain: the pilgrim was dead and would now be united in the bowels of the earth with the soldiers he was purported to have betrayed.

The man was now dead and his body, which had once

roamed half the world, continued to be dragged on and on while far away somewhere a woman was waiting for her husband to come home with the rice and salted fish that he'd promised to buy. Behind her, their children slept soundly, despite the bedbugs in their bamboo cot.

The voice of a soldier brought me back to where I was. "What are you so quiet for? Does the sight of blood make you sick?"

I nodded weakly.

"It's me who finished him off," the soldier announced proudly. He then gave me an appraising look and shook his head. "It's like that when you first join up. You always feel sick at first. It was the same with me. But after you've been around a while, you'll get used to it."

I watched as he wiped the blade of his sword with a discarded leaf food wrapper that he had picked up beside the road.

"If you'd seen how our men were slaughtered . . . Well, I tell you, it feels good getting revenge." He stopped speaking, then raced ahead to vanish within the procession.

The pilgrim's body kept being dragged on and on. But by now he was no longer human, much less a citizen of a free and democratic nation. Absolutely not! For the crowd that night, he was a wonderful plaything, no different from a rubber ball for a cat or promises for this country's former colonial masters.

In large office buildings far beyond the demarcation line, this act would be called fascist behavior, a Nazi terror technique, or the legacy of the Japanese. In fact, it was pure stupidity, for which everyone present was to blame: the pilgrim, his judges, his executioners, and I myself. But maybe the worst thing about what happened is the pleasure that people took in playing judge. There is nothing more disastrous in life than a stupid judge. The same kind of stupidity that was evident here had also killed Socrates, Giordano, Bruno, Galileo, and Jesus.

This is because judges are very partial to what they themselves love. The judges here very much loved their country. Revenge in a time of revolution feeds a deep hunger. I am quite sure that they, in carrying out their act, were convinced of their service to the country.

By the time the revolutionary parade reached the main Jakarta-Cirebon highway, the number of spectators had swollen. People emerged from side streets to join the massive crowd. When they saw what the truck was pulling, women screamed and fled. At the back of the procession, children cheered and beat on empty cans. The parade went on and on but, finally, by the time the truck neared the recruits' barracks, the crowd had dissipated, the cheers had died.

The rope that had bound the pilgrim's carcass was untied. The truck revved its engine then sped away, leaving the shredded remains of a man in the middle of the highway.

Ten minutes must have passed as I sat on the crossbeam of the barracks fence staring at the naked and abandoned carcass.

As the night progressed the moon rose higher. People coming into town from the west would stop when seeing the mound of flesh on the road and then, when realizing what it was, would jump back and flee in the direction they had come. Such a sight was a sure sign that any business deal they made that day would fail.

Curfew sounded. The base was silent. Slowly I went back to my assigned barracks. There my mates were sleeping soundly from exhaustion. From far in the distance came the smothered hiss of a locomotive as it entered its stable, immediately bringing back to my mind images of what had happened that evening. And after that, the revelation that the military was not the place for me.

But what about my pledge, the promise I had made? A lesson I had learned is that a promise is forever binding. But what if I were ordered to kill someone and that someone was a person I loved? The thought scared me. I knew I had to leave. This was not my calling and these were not a soldier's thoughts; they were the thoughts of a human being. Every person wants freedom, especially in his mind.

And then, for the first time in three years, I prayed. I prayed that such a thing would never happen again. After that, I slept. What I dreamt about in the bit of night that still remained, I do not remember. My next memory is waking to the barking of dogs. It was only three thirty in the morning. I picked up a cane and snuck out of the barracks, intending to drive the dogs away. I grumbled about the fact that guard posts had yet to be installed on the perimeter of the base. There wouldn't be dogs if there were any guards out there.

Moonlight illuminated the roof tiles of the Chinese shophouses that bordered the highway. There was no wind. Nature was still.

When I reached the barracks fence, I caught sight of the dogs, dozens of them, barking frenziedly. Most had their noses to the ground; others sat howling at the moon. And in the middle of the pack of animals was the pilgrim's carcass.

I turned and fled from this gruesome sight. Once inside the barracks, I buried my head beneath my pillow.

Not much later the barracks bell began to ring, waking the soldiers and urging them to hasten into uniform and run to the roll call outside. There we heard the announcement: we would be leaving for the front immediately. I shivered. Now I, too, was going off, either to kill or to be killed. Fifteen minutes later, the unit departed, and the killing machine moved on. It just kept on moving on.

# INDEPENDENCE DAY

EVERYWHERE AROUND THE world, in the United States and Russia, all the more so in the newly founded nations—former Western colonies that were now in a state of turbulence—and even in countries that had been the aggressors during the world war, the call for democracy had sounded. And like an echo repeating the sound of the voice in Kirno's own heart, there came to his ear the spirited cry of a political commentator on the radio, also shouting, "Democracy!"

Hearing the word, Kirno sighed, but because the human sigh so rarely achieves its purpose, he fell silent. But soon he sighed again. Carefully turning his neck, he looked around the room but could see nothing, only darkness, for he had surrendered his sight—not of his own volition, to be sure—to a Dutch bullet. The light in his eyes had faded and now it was only his sense of hearing that sometimes convinced him he was still alive. But what of the bitterness he felt?

"Democracy," he whispered. Democracy is a beautiful thing and national independence a noble goal. About that he agreed, but what rights did he now have in this free and democratic country? He didn't have the right to see. The suffering this caused him was real and because it had so intimately entwined itself with his life, whenever he now thought of his own existence and interests, he derived a strange comfort from its presence. Because he could suffer, he knew he was alive.

Kirno smiled bitterly. When he tried to change his sitting position, the rubber tires of his wheelchair rubbed against their axles. He sighed yet again. When not lying prone in his bed, he was forced to sit in a wheelchair. He couldn't walk, not for a long time now. After the Dutch bullet had blinded him and he had fallen to the ground, a saber had severed both of his legs from the trunk of his body.

"And I don't have the right to walk," he muttered, "not even a single meter."

Despite his infirmity, Kirno felt himself more fortunate than other invalids. At least his parents were wealthy. They even owned a twelve-tube radio. After he had been brought down from the mountains to his hometown of Blora, he had discovered, even in the darkness that surrounded him, that the interests of his fellow townsmen had evolved from what they once had been. Now, with independence being a fact of life, all people talked about were radios, cameras, and bicycles. It appeared to him that he alone continued to focus his attention on democracy, the state of the nation, and, naturally, his own miserable condition.

Like other suffering individuals, Kirno was unwilling to renounce what fond memories he still maintained, which is why he insisted on commemorating Independence Day. In the past,

Independence Day had involved a rowdy and carefree communal celebration. And for independence he had given his eyes and legs.

In years past, even pickpockets forgot to pick pockets on Independence Day, but now, with the newly established government having proved to be ineffectual in serving a starving country's needs, people had to think of their own needs; today the city's pickpockets would be out in force, lifting the wallets and purses of both friend and stranger. But what could he do to fulfill his own needs? Kirno wondered. He couldn't see, he couldn't walk. All he could do now was sigh and listen to the radio's crackle and buzz.

Kirno took a deep breath, filling his lungs with the cool morning air. The house was exceptionally still. He guessed most of the household had gone to the city square to participate in the Independence Day celebrations that were being held there.

He beat his hands on the tray of his wheelchair and called for the manservant. Almost immediately, he heard the sound of footsteps he assumed to be those of Mangun, the servant who had joined his parents' household after he had gone off to the mountains to fight.

"Yes, sir?" The voice was that of Mangun.

"Tune the radio to Jakarta."

As the servant turned the knob to locate the right signal, Kirno listened to the radio's drone.

"Did my mother go to the celebrations?" Kirno asked.

"Yes, sir. She was asked to help welcome guests at the Regency."

"And my father?"

"He's there too."

"And Tini?"

"She left for school early. Said she was going to the parade."

Radio Jakarta began to broadcast light Western music.

"Is that really the Jakarta wavelength?"

The servant grunted in affirmation, then left.

Kirno listened to the music with a rising feel of discontent. He turned his head slowly around, looking in every direction as if expecting to see again, but everything was dark, completely black, without a sliver of light. One year. For a year now he had been like this.

Suddenly, the music playing on the radio died and was replaced by the booming sound of a mass rally, something that Kirno suddenly realized he would never have the chance to see. Cries of "Freedom!" erupted from the throats of thousands of people.

Kirno lowered his head slowly until his forehead touched the tray of his wheelchair. He left it, resting there, as he listened to the distinctive voice of President Sukarno. But then, when hearing a thunderous litany of slogans—"For the people! For the nation! Liberty! Prosperity! Freedom! Democracy!"—he suddenly lifted his head and drew a deep breath.

"The same thing! The same damn thing!" he cried out. "When is it going to change?"

An instant later, his servant was at Kirno's side, asking him, in an apologetic tone, "What is it, sir? Did you call for something?"

Kirno mumbled in a trembling voice, "The government has its income; the people have their own means. Everyone has his income and expenditures . . ."

"I can't hear what you're saying," the servant said. "Is something wrong, sir?"

"No, nothing is wrong!" he barked. "Now go away."

The servant turned away.

"And turn off that radio before you go!"

At once, the sound of the radio died. Kirno again lowered his head to the tray of his wheelchair and rested it there. In his imagination images from the celebrations at Blora's central square appeared. The square was filled with students in uniforms and other spectators as well—farmers, civil servants on holiday, and regular townspeople as well—along with the claque that always came to cheer on the day's orators who screamed out their nationalist sentiments atop the raised podium. Flags were flying. People's clothes were dotted with perspiration from the midday heat. Ice-cream sellers were making a windfall, probably more than on any other day during the year.

In Jakarta, Kirno imagined, the same scene was being played out in the city's Freedom Square, the only difference between Jakarta and Blora being that the former had a much larger pool of prey for pickpockets and young men had much more freedom in finding partners.

Kirno moved his head from the tray of the wheelchair to the chair's armrest and then shouted an order to Mangun: "Find some *gamelan* music."

The radio began to crackle again. Kirno caught snippets of Western songs but no *gamelan* music.

"I can't find any, sir," the servant said in a tone of irritation, even as he continued to turn the radio's knob.

Western music, *gamelan* music, or was it something else that he wanted, Kirno asked himself. "Oh, what is it I want?" he moaned.

To his question, he heard the manservant reply, "I'm an old

man, sir, and from what I've seen in this world, nobody ever knows exactly what he wants."

The kindness of the servant's voice drew from Kirno another question: "Why is it that I think everyone is mad?"

"You're living by yourself, is why," Mangun quipped. "You're keeping a distance from the world."

"Do you think that's what it is?"

"That's what my heart tells me," his servant answered. "And my brain, too. When a man lives alone, he has only himself to listen to," the servant explained, "and sometimes he ends up becoming his own teacher." As if having overstepped an invisible boundary between them, he added quickly, "I think I should go, sir. I've got work to do in the garden."

"Don't go," Kirno suddenly told him. "I don't have anyone here to talk to." His tone of voice changed: "Tell me, Mangun, do you want to work as a servant forever?"

"I didn't choose my life, sir," the servant said reflectively. "I've always had to accept what's come my way, even buffalo dung, if you'll forgive me for saying."

Kirno gurgled to clear his throat. "It sounds like you've had some bitter experiences," he said with understanding. The tone of his voice indicated that he did not expect a reply. "I guess lots of people have to put up with bitter things in life. You can go . . ." he finally added for his servant's benefit.

When hearing Mangun's receding footsteps, Kirno's mind turned to the men he knew who had been crippled before he himself became an invalid. He knew men who had been blinded. He knew amputees. He also knew men who had lost their minds and wandered the streets, screaming about battles.

What happens to people such as those, who lacked the financial resources his own family had? What about them? Kirno asked himself. What happens to them in this free and independent country of ours?

Kirno provided his own answer: they would resign themselves to their fate. Resignation to one's fate, acceptance of one's destiny—these traits had once been seen as virtues in the days prior to independence. But what was their value now, in this modern-day world? Was it a virtue for a person to be resigned to eternal darkness? To reside in a palace that cost a fortune to maintain?

Kirno banged his hand on the wheelchair tray. Every muscle in his body tensed as he strove to control his mounting anger. Somewhere in the back of his mind he heard a song coming off the radio. It was a new one, "Lili Marlene," which he recalled having heard sung by a troop of Dutch soldiers as they rested after jungle patrol. He listened to the song until it ended, until the last syllable had faded. Then he heard his own cry. Bowing his head, he heard the blast of the grenade he had thrown and the rattle of his Tommy gun as he fired on the soldiers. Momentarily, he felt the same swell of victory in his chest that he had carried back to guerrilla headquarters.

These memories suddenly evaporated when he heard someone calling his name from the doorway: "Kirno, *Mas* Kirno!" Kirno turned his head toward the sound and forced himself to smile. "Is that you, Tini?"

Kirno righted his position as his young sister walked into the room. He heard her light footsteps and then the cheerful sound of her voice: "I just came from the parade. It was great! We had a picnic at the school and we sang the national anthem and other songs too."

He reached out for his sister. Finding her shoulder, he drew her closer to him and caressed her cheek with his hand. "Such a child you are!" he cooed. One who knows nothing at all about the world, he wanted to say, but said instead, "But there are lots of adults who are just as childish as you!"

He listened to his sister's giggles but then felt her turn and run away. A moment later she was calling back to him: "It's Ati, Kirno! Ati is here!"

He tensed as he waited for the sound of a voice that once had aroused in him a gamut of emotions, ranging from love to passion.

He listened to the woman he wanted to marry speak to his sister: "Tini, you're such a big girl now!"

He turned toward the voice but could see nothing. Though Kirno had come to accept this fact, his was a forced resignation. He couldn't imagine anyone willing to accept life as an invalid. He bowed his head again until it came to rest on the wheelchair tray and turned his ear to pick up the voices in the hallway.

"Did you go to the parade, Tini?"

Why did her voice sound different? Kirno asked himself. A voice that once excited his passions had somehow lost its special sound.

"I did!" Tini exclaimed. "I sang the national anthem and the proclamation song. And all of us kids got drinks and cakes."

"That must have been great fun!" She paused momentarily. "Where is your mother?" Ati then asked.

"At the Regency. She's welcoming guests or something."

"And your father?"

"He's there too."

"And Kirno? Where is he?"

"He's inside, but . . ."

Tini's voice fell to a near whisper, making it more difficult for him to hear what she said.

". . . but he can't walk. They cut off his legs."

"You mean, his legs were amputated?" Shock was evident in the woman's voice.

"So now he has to use a wheelchair. When he wants to go somewhere, I always push him."

"I see . . ."

There was deep disappointment in that sound.

"And he's blind . . ."

"Blind?"

To Kirno's ears, the question resembled a whimper. He lifted his head and slowly pulled himself erect. He leaned against the back of his wheelchair, waiting, with a furrowed brow.

"It's sad, isn't it?" That was Tini speaking again.

He waited but did not hear an answer. He thought of the freedom and the mobility he once had, even in the days of colonialism, at a time when no one was shouting about democracy or freedom.

He then heard the voice he used to adore: "Take me to him."

Kirno heard the light flip-flop of backless sandals and the patter of a young girl's feet. He bowed his head hurriedly, lowering himself until his head rested listlessly on the wheelchair tray.

He heard his sister call his name and then felt a woman's arms around him. He heard the sobbing of the young woman he used to love—before the Dutch had occupied Blora and he had fled to the jungle. He listened to her labored breathing, then lifted his head and whispered, "Ati, you've come at last."

"What happened, Kirno? Tell me what happened."

Suddenly gasping for breath, Kirno could not answer until he had first calmed himself. Finally, he spoke in a slow, almost sonorous, voice: "My friends are dead, Ati. They died and are now forgotten. And I might just as well be dead for I too have been forgotten. Now that the war is over, there's no time for people like me. Everyone is jockeying for power and position within the country's new social structure."

Not hearing her argue with him, Kirno continued: "You're free to go anywhere now, Ati. You still possess that right. But me? I've lost all ordinary rights. Can you appreciate my situation, Ati? Can you understand how I feel that I no longer have a place in the country I fought for?" He paused. "I'm not complaining, mind you. It's just that sometimes I get lonely, living like this, and sometimes, without meaning to, I have to let out the feelings inside my heart and mind."

He paused again before asking, "Tell me, Ati, are you still as beautiful as you used to be?"

Now it was Ati who sighed.

"If you don't want to answer, I can understand why. I can't hope for you to marry me. I wouldn't expect you to even consider it."

He heard an even deeper sigh before she finally began to speak: "Seeing you like this, Kirno, I don't know what to think. I don't know what to feel."

Kirno smiled. "Sometimes, Ati, a person can only begin to see things clearly after forgetting what he had once considered to be his future possibilities and beginning to think about realities. That is what all of us, too often, forget."

Neither said anything for a moment.

"Will you turn up the radio, please?" he asked Ati.

The sound of the radio filled the room—another Western song.

Kirno shook his head. "God, it's always the same thing. Don't they ever play anything else?"

Ati immediately attempted to find another station. Now, from the radio came a fiery political speech.

"That's just as bad," Kirno complained. "Don't people ever get tired of speeches?"

Ati seemed confused. "What are you asking?"

"That speech! It makes me feel like smashing the radio. It's nothing but nonsense."

Ati turned the knob again until she found a station playing *gamelan* music.

"That's it," Kirno remarked. "I like to hear something soft and unhurried. I much prefer that to Western music."

"You've changed," Ati said.

"It's not that I wanted to change, but what can I do now? Is there anything for me to hope for, anything for me to search for?"

"You never used to talk like that."

Kirno laughed. "Yes, but that was before, when I could hold you in my arms and kiss you when I wanted to. I thought I was strong; I thought a man was the master of his future."

Kirno turned his head at the sound of his sister singing, growing louder as she came closer to him. "Tini," he said, "why don't you sing 'The Butterfly Song' for me? But switch off the radio first," he added.

After Tini had turned off the radio, she sang the song her brother had requested. Kirno and Ati listened intently until the song was finished.

"I used to be like you, Tini," Kirno said to her.

At that remark, Tini suddenly began to cry loudly.

"Why are you crying?" her brother asked.

"Because I'm not like you," she whined. "I don't want to be crippled or blind."

Kirno tried to cheer her: "Of course you don't, and you're not going to be! No one wants to be crippled or blind. I am, but I'm not you. Please don't cry, Tini. I promise you, you're going to grow up to be a healthy and beautiful woman."

Tini stopped crying; now her muffled sobs filled the room's silence.

"Do you still want to sing?" Ati suddenly asked.

Tini shook her head. "I don't want to anymore." Her voice was brokenhearted.

"Please . . ." Ati begged. "Sing 'The Elephant Song'! You must have learned that one at school."

Tini nodded and began to sing, though her sobbing was not fully under control. Her voice bridged the silence that lay between her brother and Ati. When the song was over, Ati gave Tini a kiss on the cheek.

"That was beautiful," Kirno remarked.

"It truly was," Ati added.

"I sang it in the singing competition," Tini explained.

"And did you get a prize?" Ati asked.

"Yes, I did—a slate board and chalk and a kiss on my cheek from the teacher."

"Your teacher must be very kind," Kirno commented.

"She really is," Tini exclaimed happily. Her tears had disappeared.

In the lull, they heard a noise outside—the voices of Kirno's parents—followed by the sound of footsteps coming into the house and then a woman's voice: "Ati! Have you been here long?"

Ati moved away from Kirno to greet his parents. Kirno could make out only part of the ensuing conversation.

"No, fate is not ours to choose," his mother was saying. "Just look what happened to Kirno . . . You've not been around in such a long time," she then added. "Where have you been?"

"I was in the occupied territory most of the time."

"But you never sent word."

"How could I?" Ati asked.

"And now with Kirno like this . . ."

Ati sighed. "The war claimed so many young men."

"He didn't lose only his sight and his mobility," Kirno's mother said.

"What do you mean?" Ati asked.

"You can't tell me that you're willing to marry a cripple, Ati—even if he was crippled because of the war."

In the silence that followed Kirno's mother's comment, Kirno felt Tini tugging on his shirt. He turned and put his arms around her, trying to fill the frightful emptiness he felt in both his and his sister's hearts. When their father began to speak, Tini put her hands on her brother's ears but that did not prevent him from hearing.

"I prayed constantly, Ati. I prayed for God to watch over you and Kirno and for you to come safely through the war. Every night we prayed. I know that in a battle, under a barrage of gunfire, no one can ever be truly safe, but that didn't stop us both from staying up many a night, praying for Kirno's safety and that he might someday find his wishes in life fulfilled."

"It's true," Kirno's mother added. "We prayed as much as was possible for us to do."

Ati's voice sounded suddenly bitter. "What man proposes, God disposes . . ."

After a moment's silence, Kirno finally spoke up, unable to restrain his anger: "What are you talking about? I'm blind and crippled and no amount of talk is going to change that!"

Kirno could imagine his mother shaking her head sadly as she spoke: "I hope you can understand Kirno's attitude. He's angry and often loses his temper. It's only when Tini is around that he smiles and laughs."

"I do understand," Ati whispered.

"Tell me then, what do you think of Kirno now?"

Kirno spoke angrily: "What am I, Mother, a commodity to be weighed and judged in front of the others?"

Silence suddenly filled the room; no one dared to speak except Tini, who, without prompting, suddenly began to sing. The adults in the room listened to her clear and innocent voice.

When the song was over, Kirno called for Ati to come closer. "There's no point for you to discuss my life," he told her. "You know my situation now, you know my position in life. It's useless for you to talk about me." In a lighter tone, he then asked, "Where do you live now?"

"I live in Semarang," Ati replied.

"When did you arrive?"

"Just today, around noon." She paused, before continuing: "You know my family, Kirno. You know I didn't have a choice but to go with them to the occupied territory. After that, I couldn't contact you because you were in the area under guerrilla control."

"By that time," Kirno interjected, "I was at the home of the guerrilla chief. By the time you left, I had lost my eyes and legs." He swallowed before continuing: "You know, Ati, there's nothing more that I would like than to be able to sit beside you forever and to hear your voice. But now, it seems the only thing I can expect to have from you *is* your voice. Only the sound of your voice tells me that you still exist." He took a deep breath. "That's it . . . Your voice and a few memories. You must leave me, Ati," he told her. "Go home. That would be better for me."

Kirno listened as Ati turned and walked away, the sound of her footsteps growing fainter as she made her way to the door. His sister pattered behind. He heard indiscernible bits of conversation between the two of them and then the sound of his parents' voices and then nothing at all. He lowered his head to the wheelchair tray and sat motionless. Around him was a darkness no light could illuminate.

Suddenly he heard the sound of several pairs of feet coming toward him and then his mother's voice as she chastised him: "I say, Kirno, sometimes you can be so rude!" He didn't even attempt to move. "You drove Ati away the same way you'd chase away a stray cat."

Kirno felt Tini's arms encircle his neck. She then hugged him and whispered into his ear: "Ati was crying when she left."

"Don't you have any finer feelings, Kirno?" his mother asked.

Kirno immediately pulled himself erect. "And what good would they do me?" he asked hoarsely.

"Dear God," his mother moaned. "Ati comes to see you and you chase her away like there's nothing you need, like you're the only person in the world! Don't you think she has feelings for you?"

"Shut up!" Kirno snarled. "What's the use of her feelings when all I can do is sit here in this wheelchair? Don't you get it, Mother? I'm going to be here for the rest of my life, until rheumatism, hemorrhoids, and finally death comes to call."

"You're so cold." His mother sighed.

Kirno snorted in reply.

Once again, Tini whispered in his ear: "Ati asked me if I could read, and when I told her I could a little, she said I should read for you. I promised I would, but she wouldn't stop crying. Then she told me to always stay close to you, so that I could help you if you need anything."

Kirno blew through his lips.

"Is there anything you need now?" Tini asked.

Kirno smiled. "Maybe just another song."

Now Kirno's mother spoke up with a trembling voice: "That's all you ever want. Don't you have any feelings left? You punish your sister by ordering her to sing all the time and chase away anyone who comes near you, only because they feel sorry for you. And then you snap at me and your father . . ."

"Shut up and get out of here!" Kirno's voice was unforgiving.

His mother immediately fled the room. After she had gone, Tini began to sing: *"On the seventeenth of August, of nineteen forty-five, independence was declared . . ."*

Kirno's body grew more hunched until, at length, his head was again resting on the tray of the wheelchair.

When the song was over and Kirno didn't move, Tini asked him, "Why are you being so quiet?"

Upon hearing a stifled, barely audible sob, she embraced her brother again. She then chided him: "You asked me to sing that song but you didn't even listen!" When he didn't respond, she then asked, "Why are you crying, Kirno?"

Kirno continued to sob. He didn't raise his head. His body remained hunched. His eye sockets, completely empty, could not catch even the smallest sliver of light. He could not see anything, except in his memory. He rustled, making the chair move slightly. It seemed to him that he had been sitting in that chair since time immemorial.

He heard Tini ask, "If you're blind, Kirno, what can you see?"

"Darkness," he told her, "nothing but darkness."

"You mean dark, like night?"

"As dark as night," Kirno confirmed. "And black as coal. Nothing but darkness."

"You can't see flowers?"

"No, Tini. All I can see is black, and nothing else."

"You mean everything is dark?"

"Yes, Tini, everything. That's why you're never going to be blind like me. You'll always be able to see Father and Mother and all your friends. And you're not going to be crippled either. You'll always be able to walk and skip and jump."

When Tini didn't say anything, he suggested, "Why don't you tell me a story? Tell me about the singing competition at your school."

Tini immediately cheered. "Well, what happened is this: when the teacher asked if anyone could sing 'On the Seventeenth of August,' I told her I could, but I didn't sing as good as Mini, so I lost. But when I sang 'The Elephant Song' I won, and the teacher gave me chalk and a slate board."

"That's wonderful, Tini! And what did you do after that?" Kirno asked.

Tini spoke with greater enthusiasm: "And then we went to the parade. First we lined up outside of school and then, when we were all ready, we walked to the square. Almost all the students were there. It was real crowded. Everyone was waving flags. The band that was leading the parade never stopped playing. They played all these march songs that were really nice.

"But it was really warm in the square. Everybody was hot. When people started cheering, we cheered too. And then, when people started shouting, we shouted too. That was a lot of fun! Then, when everyone clapped their hands, I started clapping too. They set off firecrackers . . ."

"I know," Kirno told her, "I could hear them from here."

"Yeah, they were so loud I had to cover my ears. There were bits of paper everywhere. They fired the cannon too, and when that exploded I almost screamed because I was so scared. There was a lot of smoke. And after that the band played again and we sang the national anthem. I like that song. I liked the way they played. The way they play it on the radio isn't nearly as good."

Kirno suddenly felt a longing for something he could not define. He coughed and cleared his throat. Was it Ati he longed for? He shook his head weakly. His sight? He shook his head again. His legs? No, he didn't know. All he knew was that he felt incredibly lonely. He suddenly threw out his arms to embrace his sister. He stroked her hair and spoke to her lovingly, "You're such a sweet girl, Tini. Do you think you could sing for me again?"

Tini laughed and wiggled from her brother's embrace. "It's *your* turn to sing for me!" she announced. "Why don't you sing 'On the Seventeenth of August'?"

Kirno took a deep breath and began to sing. He sang slowly and with resonance in his voice. While singing, he saw himself as he once was, marching erect and with pride in the city of Pati on Independence Day. A full battalion of men had participated that day; while haphazardly dressed, they were fully armed. But now that drama was over. He then tried to picture Independence Day at the guerrilla camp, but couldn't retrieve any images from his memory at all. By that time he had lost his sight and had only been able to tell what was happening from the voices around him. Voices, that was all he could remember.

Kirno's singing had become a moan. Finally, with tears trickling down his cheeks, he stopped. He kissed his sister, who responded with a hug.

"Why are you crying, Kirno?"

"I'm crying because I can't celebrate Independence Day the way you do, Tini. I used to love to watch our troops marching in parade, but now I can't." His voice suddenly sounded harsh, even to his own ear: "I can't do anything, I don't want to do anything, I don't need anything anymore—not the Seventeenth of August, not a thousand independence days. All I want is death," he said beneath his breath.

Tini attempted to divert her brother's sadness: "Sing something else, Kirno. Why don't you sing 'The Elephant Song'?"

After swallowing, Kirno rose in song again. The song, a simple traditional tune, reminded him of Ati, the woman he loved, the same woman he had driven away earlier that day. He could hear faintly the voice of the woman he had once adored.

But marriage to her now was impossible. She deserved a man who would not bring shame or disgrace on her or her family.

He paused in his song to catch his breath and found himself crying again. He hastily wiped his tears and then hugged and kissed his sister again.

"I want you to do me a favor," he whispered. "Call Mother in here for me, will you?"

Kirno listened to Tini's footsteps as she left the room. Moments later, he heard a different set of footsteps approach.

"Do you want something, Kirno?" his mother asked.

"I want to go away from here," he told her.

"In the condition you're in? How could you?" Kirno's mother shook her head. "You certainly gave us some trouble today."

"I know, Mother," Kirno confessed, "but I don't do it on purpose. I just don't want to have to be taken care of. That's why it would be best if I left. I don't want to give you any more trouble."

All he heard in reply was a long sigh.

"I should go to a home for invalids. There I'd be with people of my own kind. I might even be happy living there. And you wouldn't have to trouble yourself with me, or put up with my temper. I'm not happy here, you know that, and I'm sorry that I was brought back here in the first place."

Not hearing his mother attempt to stop him from speaking, he continued: "And besides, I don't want to poison Tini with this suffering of mine."

"I know that you're not happy, Kirno," his mother said softly, "but I don't want you to go. I don't want anyone else taking care of you."

"But, can't you see?" he argued. "Part of my unhappiness is

due to all the restrictions you place on me here. I can't do this, I can't do that . . ." He stopped and drew in a deep breath, trying to steady his voice. "I was so happy before this happened. I could go anywhere I wanted, do what I wanted to do. Did you ever forbid me then? No, because you didn't have the right to. I'd be happy if I weren't a cripple. I'd be happy if I hadn't taken up arms. I'd probably be happy if I had followed Father's example: when the nationalists were in power, he stood behind the nationalists; when the Reds got the upper hand, he gave his support to them; when the Dutch came back, he worked with them; and, finally, when the Republic was formed, he became a republican."

"You're talking badly about your father."

Kirno detected a tone of guilt in his mother's voice. "But isn't it true?" he asked.

She did not reply to his question, and in the silence that followed, the indefinable longing that he had felt earlier returned.

"It would be better for me to go away from here," he stated again.

"But where would you go, Kirno?" Now it was Tini speaking in an anxious voice.

"I'd go to a place where there are other people like me."

"But where, Kirno?"

"There are homes for disabled people," he told her.

Tini began to cry. "No, Kirno, you can't. Ati told me that I should take care of you. And she asked me to read to you. I can't do that if you go away."

Not knowing what to say, Kirno remained silent.

"She told me that she's not going to come back here any more because you don't want her here. She said that she was going back to Semarang. But if she changes her mind and comes back and you're not here and asks me if I've been reading to you, what am I going to tell her?"

Kirno put his arms around Tini and kissed her. His voice trembled as he spoke: "You have lots of friends, Tini; you should be playing with them. You don't have to sing for me or read for me. You should be playing with your own friends."

Kirno felt Tini's body began to shake and then he too began to cry.

"You mustn't cry," he whispered. "You should be out playing with your friends. I don't have any friends here."

"But *I'm* here!" Tini wailed.

"But when you go to school or somewhere else I don't have any."

"That's enough, Kirno," his mother interjected. "What will you think of next? This is your home. This is where you live."

"This is not my home," Kirno insisted.

"Where is it, then?"

"In an invalid ward, that's where!" he told her. He spoke more softly to his sister: "In the morning you have to go to school, Tini, and in the afternoon you must play with your friends."

"But you can't go away, Kirno. You can't."

"I'll come back, Tini, and when I come back I won't be blind anymore, and I'll be able to walk. When I come back you'll have a fit and healthy brother. We'll go to the city square together. Won't you like that, Tini? And on Independence Day we'll go to the celebration together. We'll walk among the crowd and watch the horserace . . . You'd like that, wouldn't you?"

"Yes, I would," Tini answered honestly.

"Then I can go, can't I?" Hearing no reply, Kirno raised his voice: "Ask someone to take me to the home for invalids. Right now! This is hell here. I hate this place and I hate living here."

Kirno's voice was never again heard in his family home. Never again did he and his sister sing together. Thereafter, Kirno's parents were able to live in peace, without being obliged to care for their blind and crippled son. At first Tini asked them when Kirno was coming back. Later, she never asked at all.

# ACCEPTANCE

NOTHING ESCAPED THE attention of the Japanese, not even villages found on no maps. And because the small town in which I lived straddled the road that linked Rembang and Lasem on Java's north coast with the island's strategic interior, Japanese troops found their way to my town too—to my once peaceful, almost somnolent, town.

They came in a convoy: two trucks full of armed soldiers followed by four more trucks laden with corpses. Tarpaulins covered the bodies, but they had been pulled so taut that rigidly open jaws, frozen with skyward screams, were clearly outlined beneath them. That particular detail wasn't especially important at the time; much more significant was the fact that the Japanese had arrived. Government officials ran around like chickens with their heads cut off, and my poor, forgotten little town, with its own quota of saints and sinners, became a place in turmoil.

In the week that followed the Japanese arrival, those who had been hobbled for so long by the oppressive laws of the former Dutch regime began to take revenge. There was looting everywhere, even in broad daylight. The town was flooded with people from the surrounding areas who had come to see with their own eyes the death of Dutch rule—as well as to take part in the plundering of stores, office buildings, and even schools. During this brief time, no one seemed to understand the meaning of government or what it stood for anymore. That was when the Japanese military stepped in to fill the vacuum of power.

Posters with large red circles were pasted everywhere. Like a dark veil, the threat of death or imprisonment hung over every moment of the day. The looting died down and there returned the reassuring tranquility of a previous century—before modern commerce had wreaked havoc with the life of the town. The town's stores, which in a free-market economy would function as centers for the distribution of goods, had been cleaned out; trade was dead. For a time, stolen goods flooded the local market, but within a matter of weeks, they too were gone and the town began to flounder like a fish thrown up on land. The end was nigh for all trade activity.

Havoc of both the mental and physical kind came to reign and people began to die from hunger and despair. It was at this time, in May of 1942, that Sri's mother died. Sri was just eleven and she shed sad tears for her mother, but, perhaps because of her youth and her ignorance of the true meaning of her mother's death, she did not cry for long.

Sri had been in the fifth grade of a private school when her mother died. However, because the Japanese were bent on eradicating their newly occupied territory of anything that smelled of the former colonial Dutch government—especially educational institutions with ethnic-based admissions systems—her school was soon forced to close its doors. Sri didn't want to leave. The school was a town landmark and was where all her older siblings had received their education. She cried to see its closure, but a young girl's tears had no influence on the Japanese military.

So it was that Sri then enrolled in a state-run school where daily lessons consisted of cleaning the roadside of weeds and cooking rice for *romusha,* the forced-labor conscripts who were more likely to die within a week or two than to survive.

A month after the death of her mother, Sri's two older brothers, Suradi and Sucipto, left home to seek their fortunes. Now it was her older sister Ies who managed the family home. She was thirteen, two years older than Sri, and a graduate of the school that Sri had attended. Also at home were Sri's father; a younger sister, Diah; and three younger brothers, Husni, Hutomo, and Kariadi. With seven people there, managing the house was no easy task.

The landing of the Japanese military on Indonesian shores aroused a sense of dynamism and determination among the younger people of the land. The Japanese had shattered the myth of white supremacy throughout Asia, and young people admired them for it, especially students and recent graduates. An array of new courses was started—initially, Japanese language classes, and later, vocational classes as well.

It was from one of these courses that Ies acquired her typing skills. A certificate of graduation from primary school and another from a typing course gave her the tools she needed to obtain a position as a typist in a government office. But without Ies around to manage the house, Sri was forced to sacrifice her own educational future in the family's struggle to survive.

At first Sri had protested. Why should she have to leave school, when in just two months she would be able to graduate with a diploma and an impressive set of teachers' reports? But she was now just twelve. How was she to oppose the will of her older sister?

Almost every day, when Ies came home from work, Sri would plead with her to stop working so that she could finish school, but Ies would only shake her head, refusing even to consider the suggestion. Instead, she'd eat her meal and then take a nap, leaving Sri with reddened and tear-filled eyes.

Sri felt that her life was being wasted; she felt ignored and when, in such times, she thought of her mother, her tears would flow even faster. Yet she didn't think of talking to her father. Not only had they never been close, he was forever busy outside the house, working for social improvement even as his own household fell apart around him.

Sometimes Sri would look through her mother's armoire, at the mementoes and other items still in there. One was a small stack of pawn tickets for gold jewelry that had been rendered worthless by the Japanese invasion and the subsequent looting of the town's pawnshops by the Dutch authorities, who had taken all the gold in the shops to Australia. The only items of any value still left in the armoire were a matching brooch and necklace and two pairs of earrings, which her mother had deliberately not pawned so that her daughters would have some gold to their name.

In our small town, a common belief was that gold gave a woman value. Thus, to one degree or another, all the women in town, even the youngest among them, subscribed to this view. The jewelry that her mother left had been divided among the three sisters. Ies got the brooch and necklace set, which she had in fact been wearing since childhood. Sri got one set of earrings and Diah the other, both of which were 22-carat gold and weighed four grams.

Another barometer of feminine value in our small town was the size and worth of a woman's wardrobe. Of the many *kebaya* blouses and lengths of batik that Sri's mother had once owned very few remained; most had somehow disappeared the day of her death, after mourners had come to call. In the end, the three daughters had very few items of clothing to divide among themselves. Even so, they did not complain. In our small town, it was expected that young people pay deference to their elders. If their mother's friends had each taken a batik cloth as a memento, that was their right. It was only fair that one's elders received the best, the biggest, and the most attractive share of everything. A younger person had no right to object; to do so would be most inappropriate.

Sri's constant begging to return to school fell on deaf ears. Ies, who was effectively the household elder, had made her decision and would not hear otherwise. "You're younger than I am," she kept telling Sri, "and must do as I say."

Although Sri was forced to acquiesce, she never wholeheartedly accepted the situation. And so it was that while Ies kept on with her job, earning thirty rupiah a month, Sri watched her hopes of obtaining a grade-school diploma fade.

Sri's acceptance of this situation marked the first time in her life that she sacrificed her own aspirations for the greater good of the family, her father and four younger siblings included. While she wished that her mother had not died and that her life had not changed so much, she also prayed that the other members in her family would achieve their own goals in life.

Sometimes when thinking that she might have had a better life than the one she had now, Sri would find herself suddenly crying. But the tears she shed were not tears of regret. She cried only for the relief it gave her. Nothing more. Her mother was dead. The situation had changed and there was no room for protest. Besides, she worried that if she were too vocal in her complaints, she might cause problems in the family.

Had she had the nerve, Sri would have liked to ask her father why he gave the money for household expenses to Ies and not to her. It was she, after all, who managed the house. But, in the end, she didn't; she simply didn't dare. Supposing she tried to force the issue, she expected that she herself would be faulted for being presumptuous. Ies, after all, was two years older than she. Nonetheless, somewhere in the back of her mind, Sri sensed how important it was for a person who was managing a home to have control of the purse strings.

Sri's father, who was a strong-willed person who hungered for social improvement and despised any form of imperialism, very much sympathized with the Japanese military's purported goal of mutual prosperity for the Asian countries in its sphere. (He had yet to discover how cruel the Japanese could be.) For that reason, he studied Japanese intensively until he became one of the most accomplished Japanese speakers in the regency. So inspired was he by the Japanese model, he even talked about how he wanted to have children as heroic as the sons of Imperial Japan. Toward this goal, perhaps, he forced his children out of bed at four thirty every morning to do *taisho* and meditation.

Because Ies was fourteen, an age when most young women begin to think more of their appearance, and because Sri's father was constantly in need of new Japanese textbooks, the amount of money available for household expenses was severely limited, and Sri was forced to provide meals for the seven people in her household on an ever-diminishing budget. Sri grew thinner and more silent by the week, yet it was Ies who doled out the money for shopping. Sri could not help but notice that Ies was always able to set aside a portion of the allotment for herself.

As time went by, the situation grew worse: food was scarce and the thought of obtaining material for clothing was, for most people, nothing but a dream. For an honest person with no savings, cash was hard to come by. As for food, rice as the staple food came to be replaced by corn; then corn was replaced by cassava; and then cassava was replaced by sweet potatoes, sometimes only the leaves and not the tuber itself. While a person of low morals might have easily thought of other ways of overcoming such hardships, Sri's family had always avoided wrongdoing. It was far better for them to suffer than to compromise. Even so, when all was said and done, Sri's sister Ies and her father did not feel the deprivation that much. Having their own incomes, they could afford to opt for a meal at a food stall if they so wished. Sri and the other children, on the other hand, had no choice but to eat whatever was available. In the end, their bodies were nothing but skin and bones. With their heads appearing to be too large for their skinny little bodies, they resembled dried-up tadpoles.

The hardships that Sri was forced to bear sharpened her mind, giving her much greater mental focus and clarity than was normal for a girl her age. She also showed a heightened degree of sensitivity as well as a measure of acceptance that was uncommon for someone so young. Yet in her will to accept things as they were, there remained a certain degree of inner tension, which sometimes revealed itself in a cynical way. If Ies, for example, complained to Sri that she had run out of money for food, Sri might smile and say to her in a dry tone, "That's all right, just think of it as fasting month!"

Comments such as these always earned Sri an immediate rebuke, but she accepted that. She was the younger sister, after all, so she took the criticism silently and suppressed the spiteful glee she felt inside.

Local and family custom dictated that in conflicts between siblings, it was always the younger person that had to acquiesce. Age was the determining factor in almost all social relations and in the link between the two sisters, Ies forever used this fact to her advantage. It was not surprising, therefore, that in time Sri grew apart from her sister and found much more consolation from her younger siblings. In their room she would sew up the rents in their clothing with pineapple fiber and patch the holes that mice had made in them with bits of cloth snipped from her own clothes. Little sacrifices like these made her happy; she felt like a mother who loved her children. Irrespective of the Japanese and their control of the country, she reasoned (even if she could not phrase her thoughts in so many words) schoolchildren had to dress properly in clean clothes. Having once been a schoolgirl herself, she had known the importance of wearing good clothes to school.

As it is in unhappy times, the days passed slowly. In many homes in our small town there was often no man around. The Japanese war effort required immense manpower, and most any man with strength and determination was harnessed for that purpose, Sri's father included. He was constantly being sent by the Japanese authorities on assignment to other regencies, sometimes not returning for days on end. Although he was the only adult male in Sri's family's household, he often had to leave town to attend conferences in other provinces. In those times, after darkness had fallen and the kerosene oil lamps had been lit, the children would gather in the living room to sleep together, one beside another, on a single, frayed mat. Often, when one began to cry from fear of the night's silence or from longing for their mother, the others would also start to weep. In time, however, they became used to the night, and the silent darkness they once had feared became their trusted companion. Similarly, memories of their mother changed from being a source of sadness and longing to a means of honoring her love for them. It was now only hunger that haunted them, at almost every moment of the day, but they even learned to cope with that. "It's fasting month!" they'd scream when their stomachs started to growl. A peal of laughter would ensue.

In one respect, Sri's family was more fortunate than others: their home sat somewhat apart from the other homes in the neighborhood and they owned a fairly large plot of land. That said, like much of the rest of the land in the area, their plot had but a thin layer of topsoil, making it very difficult to cultivate. Even though the children in Sri's family put great effort into the plot, the vegetable plants and sweet potatoes they planted produced far more disappointment than edible matter, at least initially.

Unwilling to give up so easily, the children removed the night soil from their outdoor latrine and spread it on the garden. This was not something that was done in our area, and the neighbors laughed themselves silly at the thought of using human manure to fertilize plants. Sri's family turned a deaf ear to their remarks and saw their crops grow faster and yield larger and more abundant produce that was a delight both to the eye and the digestive system.

When their neighbors started turning up at the house begging for a little of this or that, Sri and her family did not turn them away. Because of the generosity they had inherited from their parents, they forgot their neighbors' former sneers and parted with what they could. Nevertheless, there was little monetary value in the food they produced, and gradually the family's material possessions—dishware, utensils, and clothing—were sold off to supplement the household budget. The kitchen cupboards, which had been filled with goods when their mother was alive, were now empty and bare. For all the family, but especially for the girls—Sri, Ies, and Diah—the sight of the empty shelves was sometimes too much to bear.

After Suradi and Sucipto, Sri's older brothers, left home, the family received no news of their whereabouts. The younger children often thought of them, of course, but were afraid to ask what had happened to them. Even when a visitor to the house inquired after them, they didn't say anything at all. An old crone in the neighborhood, who pronounced herself thoroughly fed up with the ways of the world, strongly advised the children to speak as little as possible. "In crazy times like this, you gotta keep your mouth shut. Life is cheap and death waits 'round the corner, ready to take you anytime." The children took her advice to heart.

But then one day, the family received a letter from the boys. They were working somewhere in Burma, they reported, as laborers for the Japanese. "Hope you're all doing okay," they wrote at the end of the letter. "We think of you often, even though, sometimes, it might be best not to . . ."

They sensed in the message from their brothers an unarticulated sadness. In turns they read the letter through, again and again, and each time found that same melancholy. The six of them then answered the letter together. On the envelope, they printed their brothers' address in large block letters, so there could be no mistaking it. After dispatching the letter, they began to wait for a reply that was never to come.

After a month, the children had almost forgotten that they were waiting for a letter, but then something odd and unexpected happened: the ward office sent them two gunny sacks of rice, ten meters of rough-spun material, and two hundred rupiah. They had no idea about the motive behind this gesture and were especially puzzled by the large sum of money. Sri, who was alone at the house when the items were brought, asked the delivery man where they had come from, but he professed not to know.

"Maybe you've got the wrong address," Sri politely suggested, but when she read the labels on the sacks of rice and the envelope containing the money, she knew there was no mistake. To THE SUMO FAMILY, they read. "Sumo" was her father's name.

When Ies came home that day, she too thought there might have been a mistake and immediately proceeded to the district administrative office to resolve the matter. But there, in answer to her inquiry, she was told that her two older brothers were dead, that they had "fallen like cherry blossoms on the battlefields of Burma."

Ies returned home sobbing and her audible mourning brought neighbors to the house. Soon, the gunny sacks were opened and rice was cooking on the stove. That day everyone ate as much rice as their stomachs could hold. Privately, the neighbors gave thanks for the death of the two young men. Some even entertained the hope that another one or two local boys might end up as cherry blossoms.

A few days later an obituary for the two boys appeared in the local paper. In it was noted how valiantly the two brothers had fought, fending off attacks from every direction. Undoubtedly, the articles were intended to make the Sumo family feel proud, but after that time, Sri's father seemed to lose his former zest. He became introspective and would often sit alone by himself, lost in thought, as if turning over in his mind something he could not comprehend. Thereafter, he began to reduce the amount of time and assistance he gave to the Japanese military. He stopped buying Japanese textbooks and declined the many invitations to meetings and conferences. No longer was he to be found poring over books and memorizing Japanese characters. He began to take notice of the difficulties in his own home and to help the children tend the garden and gather firewood as he had once done before.

Though the children mourned the loss of their brothers, they were grateful to have their father at home more often. With him there, they felt safer at night. He sang to them to raise their spirits, which were weary from the ongoing military occupation. At the same time, in conversations with his neighbors, he would imply that he was proud of his sons who had died in defense of the creation of a prosperous Greater East Asia. As he himself said of this ideal, "It's a good start on the road to our own development as a free and independent nation." But time and events no longer showed special favor to the Japanese and their military. Like other once victorious nations, Japan too suffered defeat, this time, a terminal, irreversible loss.

The news of independence erupted with a force that echoed in each corner of Blora. Resounding in the hills and the mountains around the town, the news drew flocks of people, hoping, perhaps, for another chance to loot the city's stores, schools, and offices. But this time, the young men of the city had organized themselves into defense units that the opportunistic crowd was unprepared to oppose. Even so, they were able to take back something to the village, namely the news that they were now ruled by a Javanese king, one who wore a *peci* very much like the hats that they themselves wore when going to mosque.

At mosques, prayers were offered for the new nation. In their sermons, religious leaders cited Koranic verses that seemed to apply to the new situation. As was common, these sermons usually ended with flowery words about the miracle that was Indonesia—how Indonesians were surely among the world's most heroic peoples and how Islam was definitely the most perfect religion in the entire universe—to which all the faithful gave a seconding amen.

Like other families in our town, the Sumo family was revitalized by the arrival of independence and the end of military rule. For everyone, a new hope began to flicker—and if there's anything that gives an Indonesian satisfaction, it is hope, no matter how vague or uncertain it might be.

Independence came with all the pomp and glory of a hero in one of the country's many ancient tales, but was soon transformed by the mundane difficulties of everyday life into something completely unrecognizable, so much so that people could not decide which kind of life they preferred: their former life under colonial rule or this new one of independence. The only people who continued to exhibit any confidence were either ideologues or opportunists, who made use of every possible occasion to grandstand their views.

Sri's family, who had been infused with a sense of nationalism both at home and in school, welcomed independence wholeheartedly and accepted as natural the tangle of difficulties that came with it. Her father immediately joined the National Organizing Committee, which had been established to formulate guidelines for the new nation. Despite the hardships the family had suffered during the Japanese occupation, they now felt proud, a trait that helped to light up their home.

The days of freedom rolled on, but as much as the people loved their newfound independence, their fascination with it was waning. Following the defeat of the Japanese, the Dutch military arrived with the goal of reestablishing Dutch hegemony over the former colony. To this end, they established a blockade on trade, which had a stranglehold effect on the native populace, particularly those who were not given to nefarious ways of earning a living.

Meanwhile, at the home of the Sumo family, the cupboard remained bare.

Under circumstances such as these, with hopes of productive employment almost nonexistent, young men rushed to join the military, even though the nation's army was little more than a hastily established militia with almost no weapons to its name. Nonetheless, their experience in fighting for independence had given them hope for a better future, and so they left their meager farms behind to eat at the trough of the nation's wealth, or at least they so imagined. Who could blame them? It is a given that people will generally choose the economically advantageous path.

So it was that the roads in town were filled with soldiers on the move, or at least young men who were playing at being soldiers. Having no firearms of their own—because the Japanese had not established a regular garrison in Blora—they instead slipped into their waistbands knives, machetes, and whips. The need for power and the urge to kill, fanned regularly by speakers at mass gatherings, had an effect as these young men began to use their weapons as a means of gaining leverage in every opportunity that arose.

It was at this time a wave of political madness engulfed the town. Politics became the reason for living; it was as if politics, not rice, could sate one's appetite. Even teachers, who served the role of model citizens and generally tried to remain above the fray, became infected by this madness and used their influence to win over their students to their own political allegiances. Everyone vied to bring in new members to their political party and, in this struggle, the schools were a particularly promising recruiting ground.

In our small town, located as it is on a tract of dry and infertile ground, it was Pesindo, the socialist party, that took root. Sri's sister Ies became acquainted with this party's organizers and found from them a far greater measure of acceptance than she had ever enjoyed before. Further, with them her position within the social structure—as a woman, a government employee, and an individual—was much more clearly defined. When she came home at night, she would share with the other children her hopes for the country's socialist future. She was a new person now, with new knowledge and a new vision for the future.

Because Ies and her father were often gone, it was usually the five youngest children of the Sumo family who were at home at night: Sri, Diah, Husni, Hutomo, and Kriadi. Of the four who were still in school, Diah was the most studious. She for one recognized the importance of studying and planning for the future.

Such was not the case with the boys, who gave little thought to life's realities. They showed scant interest in their lessons, and their almost sole concern was playing soccer. This worried Sri, but whenever she reprimanded them, they'd simply shrug it off with the comment: "What gives you the right to tell us what to do? It's Father who pays our school fees, not you!"

Even if her brothers didn't want to study, Sri herself had a great desire to learn and in the evenings she would borrow Diah's school books and ask her to help her with the lessons. She knew about life and worried about what would become of her brothers if they didn't want to study or go to school. This is what pushed her to constantly remind them of the future.

One time she became so angry that she took a broom and started hitting her brothers. "What's going to become of you if you don't want to study?!" she screamed at them. When the three boys suddenly fought back she had been forced to run off in frustration. The weight of responsibility she had borne for the past several years and the hardships she had suffered in looking after her siblings had taken their toll. For her age, Sri was still quite small and fairly prone to illness. There was no way she could defend herself against the united force of her brothers.

Not knowing how to resolve the situation through reason, Sri would defend her position with tears. To a certain extent this worked, and whether abashed or ashamed by the pain they inflicted on their sister, the boys would open their books to study, if only halfheartedly.

At night, after the boys were asleep and the house was quiet, Sri would sit beside Diah, studying with her and frequently asking her sister for explanations about things she did not understand.

Ies rarely came home anymore, preferring to sleep at the boarding house where her like-minded friends lived. The outside world excited her. She was happy now; she was eating well and had lots of male friends. In her eyes, the future looked brighter than ever before.

With regular meals, Ies regained much of the weight that she had lost during the Japanese occupation and she now looked fit and strong. When singing the *Internationale,* her face radiated good health. She was now, as her friends liked to call themselves, a "socialist revolutionary." And because she was one, she felt she had the right to say who was progressive and who was not; who was an agent for change and who was not; who might be used for her party's purposes, and who would be best done away with.

For Sri's father, the advent of the Republican era had rekindled his dynamism, and he too was rarely at home. It was a time for nation-building, and he was active establishing organizations to promote literacy, to provide assistance to families of soldiers, and to tend to the needs of battlefield victims. After these programs could run by themselves, he turned his attention to other matters—providing material support for soldiers on the front line and entertainment for the troops, as well as setting up courses in politics, English, and Indonesian. Pulsating from the frenzied activity, our little town felt much larger than it really was.

As all this was happening, a different kind of change was in the air. A storm was rising of which no one in our town was aware. Although prior to independence, all pro-independence groups had been united in their stance against the return of the Dutch, this did not mean they shared the same vision for the future of the country. There were the secular nationalists, religious nationalists, socialists, Communists and so on, whose conflicting views could not be easily resolved. Independence, when it came, exacerbated the conflict among these groups. In some parts of the country, of which ours was to be soon included, the result was civil war.

In our town the storm broke one clear morning, several hours past dawn. That day the road, usually filled with passing soldiers, was unusually quiet, a fact none of the townspeople seemed to notice. Indeed, the market was open and trade was proceeding as usual, until, that is, a wild scream brought everything to a halt: "The Reds are coming!"

For a moment the hubbub of the market dimmed. No one knew what was happening and activity soon resumed until the terrible scream was heard once again: "The Reds are coming!" Now, in an instant, all activity died as all shoppers and traders realized what this meant. The Communists, now locked in a running battle with the Republicans for power, were on their way. For a moment time stopped, but then the market erupted in shouts of fear; pandemonium was everywhere.

Outside the market, people looked around warily, in confusion and consternation. No Red troops were evident there, yet inside, the marketplace was in complete disarray as everyone sought a way to safety. People's minds were filled with the horrific descriptions of Red soldiers they had read in the newspapers or had heard from people around town.

They need not have bothered to try to escape; by that time the town had been surrounded, and within a matter of hours, Red troops were in control.

After the Reds took over, Sri's father rarely went anywhere

but home after work. In the past, he used to take a nap after coming home, but now he couldn't even rest. He was constantly on his feet, pacing the front verandah with his brow furrowed and his hands linked behind his back.

For the boys in the house, the Red army's arrival in town did not have the same meaning that it did for their father. One day, when they were talking excitedly about the events in town, Hutomo suddenly shouted out the suggestion, "Let's raise the Red flag tomorrow." When their father heard this, he immediately stopped his pacing, turned on his heels, and went to find his sons.

The boys were shocked to see how pale their father looked, but were even more surprised when he shouted at them, "No child of mine will fly the Red flag at this house, and not one of you will wear a red bandana! If you wave a red flag in front of a bull you're just asking to be gored."

The boys had no idea what their father meant, but with him staring at them so intently, they bowed their heads and stared at the floor.

"We have a legitimate government, a nationalist Republican government," he then told them, "and anyone who wants to take down the Red and White to fly the Red flag is a traitor and a renegade. Where have you been getting these ideas?" he asked.

Hutomo avoided his father's eyes when speaking: "At the town square . . ."

"From the Red soldiers on parade, I suppose, the ones with their farmer's hats and red arm bands?"

"Yes, Father," Hutomo mumbled.

As if about to faint, Mr. Sumo stumbled toward the corner of the room. Sri and Diah rushed to his side to prevent him from falling and led him to a chair.

Though he was breathing heavily and fast, he tried to be calm as he explained his position: "Do you know the meaning of the pledge of allegiance? When you say that pledge, you are promising to be loyal to the government. Maybe it's not a written promise but that doesn't make it any less real.

"That's why I don't want you cheering for the Reds, much less ever joining them. We have to be true to the Red and White." Tears were welling in his eyes. "You understand what I'm telling you, don't you?"

The children stood silently, staring, until Diah finally answered, "Yes, Father."

He looked at his children and then, as if seeing them for the first time, he suddenly grew suspicious. His eyes darted among them. "Where's Ies?" he asked.

When no one answered he looked at them again, his eyes growing wide with anger. "Tell me where she is," he demanded.

He fixed his eyes on Hutomo until his son slowly raised his head. His voice trembled as he spoke: "Pesindo headquarters."

"My God!" he screamed. "She's probably become a Red too!" Then, as if losing his strength completely, he slumped in his chair. The children rushed to make him more comfortable. As this was happening, Sri quietly ordered Hutomo to locate their sister and bring her home.

In a flash, Hutomo had left the house, for once doing what he was told.

Diah put her hand on her father's forehead and found it hot to the touch. Immediately, she ran to the bathroom to fetch a towel and cold water. When she returned, she wiped her father's forehead, face, and neck, but he had slipped into unconsciousness.

For a quarter of an hour or more the room was filled with panicky silence as the children wondered what to do. Then, when their father did begin to revive, he spoke as if he were in a stupor, first muttering about the Japanese, then going on to speak about the Republic and, finally, about the Reds and how he had lost his daughter to them. At one point he looked around wildly and drew Sri to him. "Are the Red police here?" he asked her.

Sri could do nothing but try to calm his nerves. "There are no police here," she said to him. She then turned to Kariadi and ordered him to fetch a blanket. When he returned, she covered her father, then she and Diah and Husni knelt around him. Kariadi, not understanding what was happening, stood somewhat apart, watching the scene with widened eyes.

When their father began to rave again, this time about politics, the military, terrorism, and numerous other concerns that occupied both the conscious and unconscious minds of people living in the Republic-held areas at the time, Sri ordered her brother to go to the hospital to find a doctor for their father. As she and Diah took turns placing a cool compress on their father's forehead, he finally drifted to sleep.

Hutomo appeared shortly thereafter.

"Where's Ies?" Sri asked him immediately.

"She's gone and Pesindo headquarters has a Red flag flying over it," he said in a rush.

"I didn't ask about the flag. I asked about Ies," Sri said sternly.

"She's not there," Hutomo repeated.

"Well, where is she then?" Sri screamed, betraying her anxiety. Then, remembering her father, she lowered her voice, "Did you ask anyone where she went?"

"Somebody said she was sent out of town to learn to ride a horse."

"What? Who sent her?"

"The Reds, they said."

The room suddenly fell silent. Sri's eyes widened with anger and confusion. Beads of perspiration dotted her forehead. "Poor Father," she moaned and then looked at Diah, who was changing the cold compresses.

"He's asleep," Diah said, as if to answer the question in Sri's eyes.

"Thank heavens for that," she replied.

Though neither Sri nor Diah spoke, both wondered why the news that their sister had been at Pesindo had been such a blow for their father. Then, as if speaking for them, Kariadi put their question in words: "What's wrong with Father? Why did he get so upset?"

"Be quiet! Stop asking questions," Sri responded automatically, causing Kariadi to seek refuge outside with his friends.

Sri and Diah sat on the floor with their eyes on their father as he slept on the hard, uncovered surface of the teak daybed. Outside, the sun had begun to fall and dusk was descending, cloaking the earth with its haze. The hot clear day had suddenly transformed to gloomy twilight.

Sri turned her head momentarily toward the door. "Husni's not back yet," she said.

Neither Diah nor Hutomo answered.

"I guess we should light the lamp," Sri said.

When Diah went to carry out her sister's suggestion, Sri stood and placed her hands on her father's legs. His temperature was now close to normal.

She sat back down on the floor again. Night had come silently; outside it was still. Her father remained asleep, and though fear, regret, and anxiety were evident in his features, Sri was too young to understand their import; the only thing she knew was that her father had suddenly fallen ill.

With the lamp now burning, its dim and flickering flame cast an uncertain light, leaving the corners of the room in darkness. The chirping of insects in the field outside made its way into the house. Husni then burst into the room, completely out of breath. "The Reds took the doctor," he gasped. "I saw it happen. They had his house surrounded and pulled him out by his shirt. There was no one else around and I wasn't brave enough to go any closer."

Unable to speak, Sri released a heavy sigh. Husni continued in feverish whispers: "One of the Reds caught me. 'Whatcha want?' he said. I told him that my father was ill, that I'd come for the doctor. He asked me if my father was a nationalist and I told him I didn't know. 'Don't try to pretend you don't know,' he screamed at me, and I got so scared I didn't know what to do. They had guns and everything!"

"What else did he say?" Diah asked.

"He said if my dad was a nationalist, like the doctor they'd just caught, he wouldn't be needing no medicine, because tomorrow or the next day after they would be coming around to fix him up for good! And then he shook his gun in my face, which scared me half to death."

"God help us," Sri murmured. "You mustn't say anything to anyone about Father, whether he is a nationalist or not," she said to Husni. Then, as if suddenly surprised by something, she asked him, "Did the man really say that?"

Husni nodded and all the children looked at one another. Their pale faces looked almost blue in the dim light. Sri and Diah began to shake. Sri then turned toward her father and slowly brushed her lips across his feet.

Husni sat beside Diah, not knowing what to say or do; and Diah, upon seeing her father laid out on the daybed like a corpse and Sri kissing his feet, began to weep. Through her tears, she whispered to her brother, "Father's worked hard for all you boys and you've done nothing for it; you won't even study . . ."

"I'm wrong, I know I'm wrong," Husni answered in a hoarse low voice. Then he too began to cry. At that moment Kariadi entered, mouth agape, as if to speak. But when he saw his father spread out stiffly on the daybed and his three siblings crying, he slowly closed his mouth and walked toward them nervously. He sat on the floor beside them, his eyes darting here and there.

The night deepened, bringing its own special gloom. Their father's breathing was more regular now and the two girls had overcome most of their initial fear about his well-being; in the back of their minds, however, was the unsettling question of what would happen if he were to die.

They heard a knocking, light at first and then gradually more insistent; someone was at the front door. Diah got up to see who it was. Standing in front of the locked and bolted door, she could hear men talking. Even the children in the back room were able to hear the sound of their boots on the verandah floor.

"Hello!" a man called out. "Is Sumo home?"

"He's sick," Diah answered.

In the back room the three boys strained to hear what was being said. Sri, on the other hand, tried to block out the sound of the footsteps on the porch by busying herself and rearranging her father's blanket. But she could block the sound no longer when a large number of boots—at least ten pairs or more—suddenly entered the room. In her mind she knew it was the Red police and she became even more unsettled and nervous when one of the group of men said offhand to her, "Don't worry. We won't be bothering you."

"Why are you here?" she asked, but her voice was so quiet no one heard the question.

One of the men from the group stepped toward the daybed to rouse Sri's father.

"He's sick," Sri told the man. Looking at him more closely, she suddenly realized that he was a neighbor.

"Tukijan? Is that you?" was all she could say.

"Yes," the man answered. "So none of you have to worry."

"Why are you trying to wake him?" Diah interjected. "Can't you leave him alone?"

"Government orders," he replied succinctly as he proceeded to carry out his task.

Slowly, the children's father awakened. He pulled himself up to a sitting position, then rubbed his dark and bloodshot eyes. When he saw the group of men around him, he blurted out, "Red police?" but none of the men responded.

Finally, the neighbor spoke up: "The regent wants to see you."

Mr. Sumo suddenly came alive; in an instant, all signs of illness had vanished. He got out of bed, then stared for a long time at his neighbor Tukijan. "Where is the regent?" he finally asked. "Has he left town?"

Tukijan nodded.

Without even looking at his children, Mr. Sumo began to follow the group of men outside.

Tukijan turned back toward Sri for a moment, giving her a sympathetic look. "I don't know what they want."

Sri looked at him quizzically. "But you're a Republican police commander, aren't you?"

The group of men was walking toward the front door.

"I was, until yesterday, that is," he answered.

Sri was becoming distraught. "You mean you're here to turn in my father, your neighbor, who's never done anything wrong toward you?"

Having heard what her sister just said, Husni screamed out, "Don't go, Father! Don't go! They're not real police!"

Whether he heard his son or not, Mr. Sumo paid no attention and disappeared out the door. One of the group of men then returned to the back room and pulled Tukijan's arm, signaling for him to leave. The two of them vanished with the rest.

As the night grew on, the only thing that Sri could do was pray.

A great many changes took place in our small town in the week that followed Mr. Sumo's arrest. Much of the news of what was happening came from Sadikin, a man who owned a cart and oxen and made his living by charging fifteen rupiah a load for hauling things. He had become the town crier, beating on his gong wherever he went and shouting out orders for the inhabitants that had been handed down by the Red troops that occupied the town.

One day, Sadikin announced that all members of all political parties in the area, along with all members of government representational agencies, were immediately required to register at Red Army headquarters. He also called out the warning, "Anyone found ignoring this command will be severely punished!"

Sadikin laughed crazily when saying this. His face was flushed—probably from the thrill he derived from carrying out the order of the victors in this civil war, possibly from the pleasure he found from being able to incite terror in his neighbors.

Sri ran after him to ask what he had meant by "severely punished."

"Well, what do you think I mean, sweetie?" he asked cynically. "Before you eat a chicken, you need to 'punish' it first!"

Sri lowered her head to hide the tears that had suddenly welled in her eyes.

"You understand what I'm saying, don't you?"

Many of Sri's neighbors had joined the Reds and now she knew why. Nonetheless, she persisted in asking, "They took my father. What's going to happen to him?"

"I'll tell you one thing," Sadikin confided, "the Reds aren't wishy-washy, not like the Republicans or the Dutch. You're either Red or you're not, there's no in between, and if you're not Red you aren't worth being called human; you're no better than a chicken that's only good for fattening before it's slaughtered."

Picking up his gong, Sadikin made ready to continue his rounds, but before setting off, he whispered something to Sri.

As the man departed, Sri staggered back to the house in tears.

At home Diah rushed to comfort her sister: "Why are you crying, Sri? Didn't you say that Father had gone to see the regent?"

"That's what I said," Sri reaffirmed, "but Sadikin just told me that Father and the regent went to Pati in a jeep last night."

"So then, why are you crying?" Diah asked again.

Sri tried to explain herself: "Can't you see, Diah? There's going to be war! There will be fighting here in a day or two and Ies isn't home because she's probably gone off to join the Red cavalry. What's going to happen to her?"

The irony—and desperation—of the situation began to dawn on Diah. "Father won't ever switch sides will he? He'll stick with the Republic, won't he?"

Sri could not answer for her tears.

"If there's a war, it's going to mean more destruction," Diah groaned. She paused in thought, then looked at Sri: "And if Ies does come back, should we tell her about Father?"

"I don't know, don't say anything," Sri said through her tears. "If she does come back, let me talk to her."

Just at that moment, Sarmini, a sister of their neighbor Tukijan, appeared at the door. She paused when she saw that Sri was crying, but then went to her and put her arm around her. "Don't cry," she told her, "I've come to help you for as long as your father is gone."

With scarcely a nod from Sri, the matter was settled and Sarmini immediately moved into the Sumo family house. She spent her days scouring the town, pilfering what goods she could find for later resale. The children were aware of how Sarmini made a living, but pretended not to notice.

"Don't ever talk about Father when Sarmini is around," Sri advised her siblings. "She could make things even more difficult for us."

Because of the confusion and uncertainty of the situation, the schools were closed and Sri's siblings were forced to spend their days at home. Even so, the three boys devoted most of their time to lessons; this had been the case ever since their father had been taken away.

One day, Sarmini said to Sri and Diah in passing, "You know, don't you, that Tukijan is only working for the Reds because he's been forced to. If he didn't, they'd kill him too."

"The coward!" Diah screamed. Sri refrained from saying anything at all.

A week after the Red Army came to occupy the town, Ies returned to the house on the back of a Sumba stallion. Dressed in brown jodhpurs, black knee-highs, a white linen shirt, and a red bandana to cover her head, she presented a remarkable sight, especially for her younger brothers. Hutomo and Kariadi could not keep their mouths closed when they saw her gallop up to the house.

When Ies reined in her horse beside the house, Husni jumped off the porch to help her tether the animal to the trunk of a banana plant. Leaving the animal to chew on the tree's soft trunk, Ies made her way up the stairs to the porch, where Diah and Sri were standing. From the smiles on her sisters' faces, Ies could not guess the bitterness they concealed.

"Are you okay?" her sisters asked stiffly, in unison.

"I'm fine, just fine, thank you." Her voice was strong and assertive, even masculine, but when she began to laugh, the discomfort that Sri and Diah had felt when they first saw her began to melt. They hugged her and led her inside the house to the teak daybed in the back room.

After she had caught her breath and rested momentarily, and after all the other children had gathered around, Ies spoke to them about the mission on which she had embarked. As they listened, both in awe and incomprehension, she told them of the "struggle of the masses," how communism will one day rule the world, and how capitalism and all its slaves must be destroyed. She urged them to follow her lead and to help eradicate the running dogs of "American capitalist imperialism." The bourgeoisie was dead, she told them, and now was the time to expunge narrow-minded nationalism as well.

At the end of her monologue, Ies caught her breath, jumped to her feet, and began to sing the *Internationale*.

"Join in!" she told Sri, who was staring vacantly at her.

"I can't," Sri told her.

"Come on. Sing along with me so that later you'll be able to sing it alone." She began the song once more, but her siblings still didn't join in.

"Why won't anyone sing along?" she asked.

With continued silence as her reply, she sat back down on the daybed, disappointed. As if suddenly noticing her father's absence, she asked, "Where's Father?"

Sri's eyes stung with tears as she answered evenly, "He went along with the Red troops to attack Pati."

Ies laughed happily. "The days of nationalism are over. I'm glad Father realizes that. Did you know, the Red Army is setting up a slaughterhouse right here in Blora?"

"A slaughterhouse? Whatever for?" Diah asked.

"For people!" Ies announced. "It's the first and most important step in the plan. You've heard the story about chickens, haven't you?"

"I have," Sri answered honestly.

"Well chickens, as you know, are selfish birds that think only about their own stomachs. That's why they must be done away with. The kind of people who are needed now are those who can work for the common good."

Diah moved to change the subject. "And what are you doing now?" she asked.

"I'm a courier," Ies told her.

"Wow! That's great!" Husni screamed in delight.

"It is great," she told him. "There's no reason that women can't do what men do. Under communism, men and women have equal rights. You boys must remember that. And if you don't join the struggle, you'll be of less value to the cause than the most worthless woman, no better than a Republican."

The boys looked at one another in confusion.

Not noticing their response, Ies added emphatically, "And if Republican troops were to come here, it would be my duty to shoot them."

"Why?" Kariadi asked in surprise.

"Why?" Ies hissed. "Because the only thing Republicans are good for is kissing America's feet, just like women used to do for their husbands in the old days, or like children do for their parents and grandparents."

Sri had started to cry. "But shouldn't we show respect for our elders?" she sobbed.

"Bullshit!" she screamed in answer. "That's feudalism talking. And what are you crying for? Maybe you should go back to the old days when a girl your age would be put in seclusion until she was given away in marriage. Maybe you'd like that—doing nothing but waiting as your life passed.

"That's feudalism," Ies repeated. "It's feudalistic to differentiate between young and old and between men and women. The only thing that our feudal lords were good for was gambling, stealing, and taking advantage of village girls, even while they spouted empty phrases about high moral principles and the like. Well, the days of the nobility are over. Now the workers, farmers, and soldiers are on the rise, with the Red Army at their side."

Excited by his sister's sermon, Kariadi loudly announced, "I want to join the Red Army!"

"You're too young," Ies told him, "but Husni here"—she gave her brother a look—"he's fourteen and old enough to join."

Husni slowly shook his head. "I don't know," he said doubtfully. "What with all that I've seen around here, I think I'd rather stay at home."

"What are you, a coward?" Ies asked. "A good Communist is never afraid."

When Husni didn't respond, Ies asked him, "And what have you seen that's made you so afraid?"

Before he could answer, Diah jumped in: "What are you talking about, Ies? And what's all this about setting up a slaughterhouse?"

"That's for the chickens of this world," Ies huffed.

Diah was growing despondent. "But those chickens you're talking about, they're people!"

"No, they're not," Ies stated flatly. "They're not even human, and as far as the common good is concerned would be better off dead."

"So is that why they shot Dimin?" Husni asked. "He was a puppeteer."

Ies fell silent for a moment, digesting this information before she continued. "What can I say?" she asked flippantly. "Puppet shows have no place in a communist state. The only thing puppeteers do is deprive people of productive working time by making them listen to their nonsensical tales."

"And what about Nursewan, the religious teacher?" Sri then asked. "Why did they shoot him? He was a good man too."

"He was an opium dealer," Ies immediately answered. "He used religion to sap people of their strength, thereby making it all the easier for the nationalists to feed them to the monster of American imperialism."

"Those people have feelings too!" Diah countered loudly. "Don't you think they cry out when they are beaten?"

"That doesn't mean they have feelings," Ies argued. "A tin can makes a noise when you kick it, but that doesn't mean it has feelings."

Diah could say no more as she fought with the anger she was feeling inside. Sri was speechless too, not knowing what to say or how to respond.

Ies examinded the faces of her siblings, then returned to the subject of their father: "You told me that Father had gone with the Red troops to Pati." She looked to Sri for confirmation.

Sri glanced at Diah, who in turn looked at Ies momentarily before bowing her head and staring at her bare feet. She tapped her big toe nervously.

Sri coughed lightly. "That's right," she confirmed. "Right after the Red troops came to Blora."

"Well, if Father himself has gone off to Red headquarters, I shouldn't have to try to convince you of anything."

"He didn't go off," Hutomo corrected. "The Reds took him away when he was sick."

Now Kariadi jumped in, giving his note of support to his brother's declaration: "Yeah, and when Father asked about you and Hutomo said you were at Pesindo headquarters, he screamed, 'Oh my God!' and almost fell down. That's when he got sick!"

Ies turned her head away from her siblings to stare out the open window. She then shook her head, loosening her red bandana and causing her hair to fall free. Raising her hand, she slowly removed the bandana from her head.

"What's the headband for?" Kariadi asked.

"It's a sign the person wearing it is Communist," Ies replied.

"But why is it Red?"

"Red is a symbol of strength, and of blood," she explained.

"Dimin's blood was red, and Nursewan's too," Sri said softly. "All of our blood is red—yours and mine and everyone's," she added sharply.

Ies felt the sting of Sri's comment but didn't respond in kind. "Did they really take Father away?" she asked.

"Yes, they did," Sri answered.

A heavy silence smothered them.

"What else did Father say?" Ies asked after a time.

"That we have a legitimate government and that no child of his would ever fly the Red flag . . ."

Ies turned toward the window once more. Beads of sweat, glistening on her brow, fell to the floor.

". . . that anyone who flew the Red flag instead of the Red and White is a traitor and renegade."

Ies stood and walked to the window. Placing her hands on the windowsill, she breathed in, then let out a long sigh.

Behind her, Diah pleaded, "You have to help him. You must help to set him free."

Ies turned around and walked toward them. She clicked her heels uncertainly, then turned and dashed out of the house. The other children immediately followed but could only watch as she freed the tether of her horse, jumped on its back, and raced off into the distance.

The horse's hooves raised clouds of dust that concealed her disappearance from sight.

"Do you think she'll help?" Diah whispered to Sri.

"What can she do?" Sri asked sadly. "She's as helpless as we are."

With tears running down her cheek, Sri fled back into the house. As she cried, she kept telling herself, "Give in, accept the facts," until she had finally regained her composure. After wiping her tears she left the house and went down to the river to fetch a pail of water. On the way, she heard in the distance the sound of a gong as the town crier made his rounds.

It was common knowledge in town that power had transformed the once meek Sadikin from a lamb into a hungry lion. Wherever he went, he carried a blackjack and whenever he came across someone he took to be a nationalist, he would drag him into the street and beat him until the accused admitted his crime and begged for mercy. After that, he'd turn the person over to the Red police for execution in the town square. This was no rumor, not anymore; people could see what was happening with their own eyes. What they said now, what they whispered about, was that the killings had only begun. The question was, How long would it last?

Other news making the rounds was that owners of the town's larger and better houses were being kicked out from their homes and into the streets. Government employees who were thought to be anti-Communist were taken to the city square to be made examples of. Such tales kept most of the politically ignorant people in town hiding behind their doors. Townspeople who were more politically astute opted either to join the Communists or flee to parts unknown.

Those who had been swept up in this Red wave turned into a pack of wolves hunting for prey. News spread of a local parliamentarian, a man by the name of Kasibun, who had been ordered to choose between life imprisonment or death. When he chose the latter, he was summarily executed in the town square. Life had no meaning, or so it seemed, when such a man, who had been a force behind the town's development, could be put to death for no discernible reason.

Meanwhile, all the yea-sayers in town kept on the lookout for further victims as a means of raising their own public status. It wasn't ideology they cared about—that didn't matter at all; every age provides chances for advancement, and one would be a fool to not take advantage of the opportunities that were presented to them at that time.

It was around that time, in the midst of life's leaps and twists, that Ies returned home again. This time, only Sri and Diah were at the house when she arrived and, before either of them could say a word, Ies held out to Sri a pair of gold bracelets, gold earrings, and a gold necklace.

Sri accepted the jewelry but asked, "What are these for?"

Ies paused before answering. "To cover your household expenses. I have no use for jewelry."

"Are they yours?"

"You don't need to know. Just use them."

"But what about you?" Sri then asked. "How are you?"

Ies spoke in a weary voice: "Government troops are closing in. I have no idea what's going to happen. All I know is that I will continue to struggle for the people." Having said that, she quickly walked outside, mounted her horse, and galloped away. Sri and Diah looked at each other, wondering if the incident had been real, but then they saw the jewelry in Sri's hand.

"We should bury them," Diah suggested. And so, while being careful that no one was watching them or seeing what they were doing, they buried the jewelry beside the house.

No sooner had they finished this task when Ies again appeared at the door to the house, this time with the commander of the courier unit beside her. The commander, a pretty woman with dark skin and short, wind-tousled hair, pointed to Sri and said, "Your name?"

"Sri," she answered politely, though she didn't know why she was showing such honor to the woman.

"Age?"

"Eighteen."

The commander looked at Ies. "Is that true? She's awfully small."

Ies nodded.

"She has to join the troop," the commander said, looking at Ies again. Then she turned to Diah. "And you?"

When Diah didn't respond she asked more sternly, "How old are you?"

"Sixteen," she said.

"You will join us too. And next time when I ask you a question, you will answer right away."

Again the commander looked at Ies, until Sri called out for her attention: "You don't tell me what to do. It's up to me whether I join up or not, and not because you told me to."

The commander, who looked to be in her early twenties, stared at Sri angrily. "That's not a Communist answer. That's the talk of a bourgeoisie. In a Communist state, the life and death of the people is in the hands of the government. I need more people in my troop, and so that means that you, and you"—she pointed at Sri and Diah—"are going to join up."

Sri and Diah stared at each other but avoided looking at Ies, not expecting to receive any assistance from her. But then it was Ies who said, "My sisters are managing the house. They're taking care of three boys on their own."

"Okay," the commander said easily, "then only one of them has to come with us." Without waiting for an answer, she turned around and marched out of the house, leaving Ies to follow.

"I'm a nationalist, not a Communist!" Sri screamed at Ies. "And it's not because Father is a nationalist. I just am one, I don't know why. That's something you have to know."

"And I am too!" Diah seconded. "I love our father and I'll never fly the Red flag."

Ies turned away from her sisters, grumbling, "I had hoped that at the very least you would think of the family's safety. If you want to sacrifice that, there's not much I can do. But if there's one thing I do know, it's that very same kind of blind loyalty that can lead to disaster."

Diah whispered hastily to Sri, "If it means the rest of you will be safe, I'll go with them."

"No," Sri moaned. "You're smarter than I am. The boys will be better off with you here taking care of them." Accepting that once again she must give in to circumstances for the good of her family, she said, "I'm the one who should go."

Ies turned and looked at her sisters. "Well, have you made up your minds?"

Diah could not contain her anger and she jabbed her finger at Ies. "First the Reds take Father away and now you sell your own sisters to them!"

Flushed with rage, Ies clenched her fist. "You have to be able to sacrifice your own interests for those of the common good. One person means nothing when compared to millions, and anyone who can't understand that is nothing but a . . ."

Diah knew what her sister had intended to say. She also knew the meaning of the word "chicken" in the mouth of a Communist.

The tone of Ies's voice was bitter: "Can't you see that the times have changed? Sukarno is a has-been; we're in a brand-new era. We're sisters, Diah, I know that, but we have to consider what is best for the common good."

"Stop it!" Sri shouted at Ies. "You've taken all sorts of political classes and know a lot, but Diah's still in grade school. What she knows, she picked up from books. And I, I didn't even finish sixth grade . . ." She sighed before continuing. "So I will join your unit. Diah will stay here to look after the boys."

Sri's words had put an end to the quarrel and the sisters looked at one another, as if not knowing what to do. Just then, the courier commander came back in the house and barked, "Time to move out." She then looked at Sri. "Get a move on. You're the one who's coming, aren't you?"

"Just a minute," Sri pleaded, "I have to pack my clothes."

"Communist soldiers don't worry about clothes," the commander yelled. "We're leaving now!"

Tears came automatically to Sri's eyes as she threw her arms around Diah.

The commander laughed at the sight of the weeping girls and hooted contemptuously, "Petit bourgeois! Well, we'll make a good Communist out of you soon enough."

Ies took hold of Sri and led her out of the house to where the rest of the unit was waiting. Diah followed her sisters as far as the gate. She watched the troop as they galloped away, tracing their path and the sight of Sri, holding onto Ies on the back of her horse and looking back at her until they disappeared in a cloud of dust. She then ran back into the house, where she cried until she could cry no more. What was she to do now? How was she to feed her brothers? What would become of her family? How were they to survive from one day to the next? Every time she asked herself another question, tears sprang to her eyes.

In our town it was no longer a secret that people were being kidnapped and killed every day. The spread of these stories could not but help to have a disastrous effect. Farmers were afraid to come to the market for fear of being killed, and with the market now empty, economic conditions were worse than ever before. The local doctor, a Republican, had been replaced by a Communist and was never heard of again. But for most people, these things were unimportant; first and foremost in everyone's mind was his own safety. People would have sold all their possessions and perhaps their souls for some kind of guarantee of safety.

Young people who had formerly been associated with the socialist party suddenly joined the Reds. Some of the Republican troops who were fed up with their condition switched sides too. Those who did not join the Communists found their lives to be a living hell. Every day, members of the Red troops roamed the town, forcing people to "contribute to the cause"—an heirloom cloth from one person, a gold necklace from another. The same disease that had spread during the Japanese occupation was back again. Anyone with anything of value had to prepare himself for its eventual loss.

In the midst of this confusion, Diah struggled in the interest of her brothers. Like Sri before her, she too had learned to accept things for what they were. She accepted that she had to struggle, even if it didn't provide assurance of their safe passage from the situation they were in. There was simply nothing else she could do.

To earn a living, she picked banana leaves and sold them to tempe makers for them to wrap their soybean cakes in. What would happen if one day there were no more leaves to pick, if all the trees were bare, was something she didn't want to think about. She silently feared for the life of the plants, but she had no choice but to go on picking the leaves, which meant that the plants would not be able to bear fruit. What a crime, she thought, but she had no other option. As it was, the family had no rice and had been reduced to eating cassava root—not the tuber, which didn't have a chance to develop, but the reddish-colored root instead.

"It's time for fasting!" the boys would sometimes say,

remembering Sri's little joke, causing all of them to break into laughter. Their laughter brought some respite from hunger but also the knowledge that they had learned to resign themselves to the situation, that they had come to accept things as they were. This was no crime, they had decided. Acceptance was a tool for survival, a means to get by.

Time doesn't stop; the world does not cease to turn; days follow each other without end. Time and place are but empty spaces waiting to be filled by a million incidents and events. Changes come, one after another, with the new replacing the old. And just as the people of Blora never thought the Communists would come to occupy their town and change their lives, they had ceased to imagine that the situation could change yet again. But change it did, and very quickly . . .

The day was still new and there was no traffic. Instead, the roads of Blora were filled with thousands of Red troops who had suddenly—almost miraculously, it seemed—converged from the east and the south. They all wore red headbands and thin bracelets and necklaces made of woven palm fronds, Communist symbols for their attack force. They marched into town with an air of confidence, as if victory was theirs. The Red troops who were stationed in Blora and the town's Communist supporters cheered wildly as they welcomed the Reds' main fighting force. Many of the children also screamed delightedly, so enchanted were they by the throngs of people and the sight of so many different colors.

There were other children, however, who ran from the sight and hid under beds or behind doors. They were the children whose fathers or brothers had been picked up and taken away by the Communists. Even at their age, they knew that when that happened, one could not hope for the person to return, not until there was peace, at least. In times of such confusion, certainty was as precious as gold.

The cheering crowd excited no reaction in the troops marching into town. Their facial expressions were frozen, as if their minds were elsewhere. They marched twelve abreast with their ranks occasionally broken by a stretcher team hoisting a wounded soldier crying in pain, or a lifeless corpse.

Almost all their weapons were new and completely unfamiliar to those with any knowledge of weapons that the government issued to its own soldiers. Where all these shiny new arms had come from was a thought that one did not dare to speak aloud.

The troops marched straight to the best buildings in town, removed their contents—living and otherwise—and immediately collapsed on the cool stone floors. People who had come to watch or cheer quickly dispersed and headed home to spread the word of the troops' arrival. In no time at all, the atmosphere in town was tense, especially after word got around that the troops had come to Blora from the front line, having been defeated in a battle at Cepu, a little over thirty kilometers away. They had been routed, it was said, and other Red troops in the area had been crushed by the Republican army's Siliwangi division. "Siliwangi!"—many of the townspeople cheered silently, for the fame of that division as a fighting force was second to none.

Diah and her brothers viewed this change in news cautiously. Diah even forbade her brothers to repeat outside their home any rumors they heard. Rumors can be fatal, she told them. The boys, remembering what had happened to their father, their sister, to the religious teacher, and all the government civil servants, tended to agree. The situation forced these young creatures to compare carefully the worth of the news they heard and the value of their own safety; for that, at least, Diah was very grateful.

Having been forced into retreat by the Siliwangi division, the Red troops left their makeshift barracks that evening to look for weaker prey. As had happened so many times in these years of unending warfare, they searched every house and raided every building, taking for themselves anything of value: items made of gold or silver, goats, cows, and chickens, even fruit still ripening on the trees. Everything was carted to the Communist headquarters to fill the many hungry stomachs there. Other soldiers spent the evening burying those comrades whose lives had been cut short by Siliwangi bullets. Many of the town's inhabitants, allergic as they were to anything having to do with guns and ammunition, fled their homes to hide within the stands of bamboo that lined the riverbanks.

Diah and her brothers also took flight. Rolled-up sleeping mats in hand, they concealed themselves inside a clump of thorny bamboo. And there, like everyone else in town that night, they prayed. While listening with goose-pimpled flesh to the distant sound of breaking doors and windows, they also thought of death and illness. They thought of the meager possessions they owned and, finally, they thought of God.

Many of the self-ascribed religious people in town sought refuge in the rice paddies. Because it was impossible to hide items like gold or silver jewelry in a wet-rice field, they assumed the

Reds would not look there. As for those Republican officials who had thus far concealed themselves from unwanted attention inside their own homes, this time they too were forced to flee, either to the riverbanks through their back doors or, if there was no time for escape, to the crawlspace between the roof and ceiling of their homes.

In every hiding place, parents clamped their hands over the mouths of their young children. No one could make a sound. Noise was a signpost for the menacing troops, a threat to the safety of all. But children are children, creatures who are all too often unaware of the meaning of life but totally cognizant of irrepressible fear, and they used every opportunity given them to bawl as loudly as they could—only to have the hands of their purported loved ones clamp their mouths shut.

Older children, who had some inkling of what the commotion was all about, clung to the earth like house lizards to the wall, too frightened to even twitch. And in between all the shouts and the many bouts of gunfire, the only other sound was that of chattering teeth.

However great their fear, none among those in hiding that night had the audacity to curse the Communists out loud nor to hope for the expedient arrival of the Republican troops. The truth that nothing stands between God and the grave was evident for everyone that night and no name they uttered was going to change their fate. They were afraid and their fear obliterated every other sensation in their hearts and minds.

Diah and her brothers, when sometimes hearing the galloping horses from their hiding place, were reminded of their sisters and their father who had gone off with—or had been taken away by—the Communists. They also thought of Kasibun, the man who had been given the choice of life in prison or death and who was now lying lifeless beneath the banyan tree in the town square. "Why didn't the Communists try to overthrow the Dutch, or the Japanese, for that matter? Why did they wait until we had an independent country to launch their quest?" These were the questions he had asked before he died, and what had it gotten him? A bullet in the head. Diah and her brothers remembered this very well.

In the end, the Red troops did not find it necessary to search for valuables along the river or in the fields. They found enough to tide them over in people's homes, so that by the time the sun next set the owners had returned to their houses. The story they told was the same everywhere: total loss! Having once been robbed clean by the Japanese and then again by the Republicans, they knew enough to keep their despair close to their chests. While they might have longed for justice for both past and present wrongs, no one dared to speak. There were too many Communist spies about—even among those whose belongings had been confiscated. For their part, for some of these people who had snitched and betrayed neighbors and friends in the past, they saw this occurrence as a way to redeem themselves and to improve their hopes for the future.

Night fell, and in the darkness the odd soldier continued to stalk the town, pounding on doors of this or that house and demanding, in a heartless growl, to be let inside. Those who lived near the targeted houses dared not come to their neighbors' aid; all they could do was pray for their own safety. In the still of that night, even the mosque's drums did not sound their soothing call. Ever since the Reds had come to town, the drums had been silent, hidden by their owners under beds. Even on Fridays the mosques were empty; none of the faithful would show their faces, not anymore. Holy books were hidden out of sight; prayer hats and sarongs stayed in the armoire—no one dressed for worship anymore.

Not too much time passed before another event took place. Once again, it started in the morning. Across the Lusi, near the bridge spanning the river's course, a barrage of gunfire suddenly erupted, causing everyone in earshot to wonder what was happening. From the Sumo family house, which stood near the river, the terrifying sounds were clearly audible. Shortly thereafter, soldiers began to wade across the river from the opposite side—the source of the earlier gunfire. As they approached, they called out, "We are the Siliwangi!"

The Siliwangi! A cry of relief from among the townspeople who were witnessing the sight reverberated in the air: "Thank God, the Siliwangi is here!" Townsmen who felt themselves innocent of any crime against the Republic rushed from their houses to welcome the arrival of the government soldiers. In answer, the troops began to shoot into the air. From the direction of the bridge the sound of gunfire grew louder with retorts of rifle shots and machine-gun fire. The world was alive once more.

Suddenly, someone called out, "The Reds aren't fighting back!"

Soon after, the whole crowd was screaming, "The Reds are on the run! The Reds are on the run!"

Troops of the Siliwangi division began to make their way into town, their faces beaming. Soon, they were crawling into the very center of Blora.

As this was happening, Diah and her brothers sheltered inside the family home until the scream of a neighbor drew them to the porch. "You can't hide here!" the neighbor woman was screaming. "They'll think we're Communists!"

They watched as Sadikin, the Reds' official crier, ran from the house and disappeared into the Sumo family field. The neighbor continued to scream, calling the attention of a squad of Siliwangi soldiers: "He's hiding there in that field!"

"What's going on?" one of the soldiers asked.

"There's a Communist hiding in that field!"

Immediately, the soldiers fanned out and, along with hundreds of onlookers, crashed into the Sumo family's field. Even with Diah looking on, in plain sight, no one worried about trampling her cassava plants; all they cared about was finding their prey.

Sadikin, thrashing through the field like a madman, was finally brought to a halt by a thorny hedge. Though he found himself surrounded, he somehow managed, with a burst of supernatural strength, to throw off five of his pursuers, and took off again. He didn't know where was going; he didn't know where to run; all he could do was scream for mercy from his parched throat.

Unfortunately for Sadikin, his pursuers had no mercy left in their hearts and as he bounded crazily through the field, the soldiers raised their guns and fired. He tried to avoid the bullets by dropping to the ground and rolling through the field, but that didn't stop the gunfire, and a bullet caught him in the stomach, stopping him from going anywhere. He gasped for breath. Foamy flecks of spittle dried in the corners of his mouth as he weakly pleaded for mercy.

Once again, his pleas fell on deaf ears. His pain and the hate that was in the eyes of the people now surrounding him kept Sadikin from opening his eyes. His chest rose and fell irregularly.

"Let's drag him out of here!" someone called. A second later strong hands were pulling on his arms and legs, but despite their force, Sadikin was unable to scream; a flower of blood bloomed on his shirt, opening wider until even the man's trousers were red. By the time the crowd had reached the road, his body was motionless.

Diah silently watched the scene from the porch of her house. Though her brothers had run off to join the crowd, she could not make herself move from her statue-like position. She stood, held in place, by the centrifugal force of her own thoughts and memories, her own wishes and desires, and her own hopes for something better in life.

Suddenly, as if released from the force, she broke free and ran to the kitchen with thoughts of her missing family members in pursuit. Dabbing the tears from eyes, she took a crock plate and scooped up some ashes from the kitchen hearth. She then grabbed a hoe and ran out to the spot in the field where Sadikin had been shot. Squatting down, she said a prayer, and sprinkled the ash on the ground, dark from the man's blood. She took the hoe and then, as if deprived of strength, weakly turned the soil. From the expression on her face, she might have been a pilgrim at the grave of a loved one.

After her work was finished, Diah said another prayer and then, balancing the hoe on her shoulder, made her way back to the house. The dead, no matter who they are, she moaned, deserve to be treated as human beings.

Once inside the house, Diah suddenly turned back in the direction of the town, her body drawn by a huge explosion. Through the window, she saw a cloud of black smoke fill the air and flames leaping skyward.

Running out to the road, where her neighbors had already gathered, she heard someone yell in terror: "It's the jail. The Reds set fire to the jail!"

"God no!" another woman screamed. "My husband is in there."

Diah immediately took off, running north in the direction of the jail, pushed forward on her heels by the image of her father. He too might be there, in the jail! The closer she got, the more crowded the road became with relatives of prisoners. Men ran with all their might. Women managed as best they could, trying not to stumble on their sarongs.

At one point, Diah, who was not used to running, was forced to stop to try to catch her breath. As she was standing there, a group of soldiers passed with a scruffy-looking man in tow. He was wearing a red headband. Diah could hear that his interrogation had already begun.

"Admit it, you're a Communist," one of the soldiers was saying.

The sight of the soldiers and the sound of the word "Communist" stopped many people in their tracks, creating an instant crowd around the soldiers and their prisoner.

"You're a Communist, aren't you?" the soldier asked again.

"Yeah, he's a Communist," one of the men in the crowd confirmed.

"He probably set fire to the jail," another surmised.

When asked yet again if he were a Communist, the young man again said nothing. He merely bowed his head.

One of the soldiers then kicked the man's feet from under him, causing him to fall to the ground. The man tried to say something, but no one could hear his words.

"What's that?" a soldier asked. "You're a Red, aren't you?"

The man tried to rise but could not make it to his feet. "Yes . . ." he murmured at last. With his arms on the ground, he tried to lift himself, but before he could stand, a bullet had penetrated his brain. His body fell forward, lifeless, but his limbs began to twitch. With a look of disgust on their faces, the soldiers grabbed the man's arms and legs and tossed his corpse on the back of a truck that was parked on the roadside.

Reminded once more of all the awful things that she had witnessed and experienced, Diah could not help but weep. Sobbing, she used her bare feet to cover the bloodstains on the road with dust. She then set off again, running on and on until she thought her chest would burst. Beside her were old men, women, and children, all hoping to find a loved one safe from the fire at the jail. Many dropped by the roadside, felled by exhaustion, but Diah kept on running.

As she neared the jail, she could see that the rear and central sections of the building were on fire. Hundreds of people, maybe even thousands, had already gathered outside by the time that she arrived. She could hear from the locked cells inside the panicked screams of prisoners, begging for a way out from the inferno. But the front gate to the prison, the only way into the cellblock, was locked.

At each corner of the building, and on top of the towering wall, were soldiers shouting orders; other soldiers were scaling the walls with ladders to help the prisoners inside. From time to time a face and then a body of another prisoner who had somehow made his way to freedom would appear on top of the wall. No sooner would the prisoner have jumped to the safety of the ground below than he would be engulfed by weeping relatives. Each new escapee gave everyone hope and stirred the crowd to a frenzy.

In time, quite a number of the prisoners were saved. Surrounded by their families, they waited for the final outcome at the side of the road or beneath the more distant trees. To the right of the jail, however, the police barracks was now engulfed in flames and beyond saving. No one in there could still be alive.

Diah kept searching the crowd and screaming for her father, but no one paid her attention; they had their own concerns and sorrows to think about. The hundreds of people who were gathered there stared, stone-faced, toward the jail, their eyes fixed on the soldiers as they assisted—or removed—another prisoner. Whenever a victim was lowered from the wall, the crowd rushed forward for a look. If the person wasn't one of their own, they'd fall back to wait until the next victim was brought out. Drenched in perspiration from the heat of the fire and the crush of the crowd, Diah finally collapsed from exhaustion amid the crowd of spectators. Her feeble and pitiful cries for her father were barely audible amid the crackling of the flames, the shrieks of the wounded, and the wailing of people waiting for their loved ones.

After finally regaining some strength, Diah pulled herself to her feet and stumbled to a tree, where she dropped to the ground and propped herself against its trunk. After resting a moment, she stood again to better see the prison. Beside her, an old man paced back and forth, raving about his son who had been a university student. In between his ranting, he would stop and stare at the flames in the sky and then, as if prodded by an electric jolt, begin his pacing again.

Diah summoned her strength and screamed as loud as she could, "Father! It's me, Diah!" Her lips were parched and ashen. She collapsed again but immediately scrambled to her feet and ran to the ladder beside the crumbling portion of the prison wall where a crowd was still waiting for prisoners to emerge. On one side, she could see that the prison gate had finally been breached. On the other side, toward the back of the prison, people were trying to smother the flames with anything they could find—sand, water, even banana-tree trunks. The sand turned into clouds of dust that were carried aloft amid the roaring flames.

One more victim was carried from the prison and lowered to the ground by ladder. Then a second, and a third, whose features were no longer recognizable. "No, it's not him. No, it's not him!" was the common cry that rose and fell as the victims were removed. When yet another victim was brought out, the crowd was told that only one more body remained. But when the rescue workers again emerged, they carried nothing but a human leg, which they placed on the ground.

Though only a leg, Diah knew it had belonged to her father. A distinctive scar told her this was so. She screamed, "Father!" and, without even thinking about what she was doing, she grabbed the leg and cradled it in her arms. She kissed the toes of its foot. Then, holding it tightly, she began to run away but was stopped by a soldier.

"Don't take that leg," he told her. "We'll try to find the rest of the body first."

Diah looked down at the leg in her arms. Slowly, as if holding a feeble child, she kissed the big toe that was matted with blood and dirt and carefully laid the leg on the ground. Righting herself, she then ran crazily toward the prison gate.

Impatient for news of their loved ones and no longer capable of waiting outside, the crowd pushed its way into the building, calling out the names of husbands, fathers, friends, and brothers. Diah followed the crowd, peering inside the cells that had been forced open but finding nothing in them but an occasional pool of dried blood.

The crowd then raced toward a long shed but was slowed from entering by the heat from the flames that continued to burn in the back of the prison. Clouds of acrid smoke strangled the people, making them cough and stumble. Inside the building, they found dozens of prisoners groaning in pain. There were also numerous rotting corpses and parts of bodies.

"There are bodies in the well!" someone shouted, and those people who had yet to locate their loved ones surged toward the well to look inside. At the bottom were bodies of prisoners, floating in a blood-red sauce that sloshed against the well's rounded sides. Some of the prisoners inside were still alive!

The Siliwangi soldiers proceeded methodically from one cell to the next, smashing in their doors with huge sledgehammers.

Inside some of the locked cells, the soldiers discovered men groaning and gasping for words; in others they found silence, for many prisoners had already been shot from outside, through the bars.

Suddenly, a backdraft fire erupted, sending a wave of smoke and ash toward the ground. A soldier grabbed Diah and pushed her forcibly outside. The flames rose higher and more wild. Outside, the onlookers screamed and cried.

As Diah staggered away from the prison entrance, she heard someone scream: "Here's a Red spy!" She saw soldiers run down the man the crowd had pointed out. She watched them tie his hands behind his back, push him to the ground, and shoot him in the head. Brain matter oozed from his skull. She closed her eyes, unable to watch any longer, and when she next opened them, the man's body was gone. Only the sound of a truck driving away told her that a body had been there.

The sudden collapse of the prison's rear wall released a tremendous bellow along with the flames that had been trapped inside. Huge tongues of fire licked the air, and an intense wave of heat rolled over the bystanders, knocking them to the ground. Then, the other walls began to fall. Anyone who had still been in the prison would not be coming out alive.

"Come back tomorrow if you're still looking for someone," a soldier called to the crowd outside.

The bystanders looked nervously at one another, as if not knowing what to do, until a lieutenant told them, "That's right, come back tomorrow!" Only then did the crowd begin to disperse, each person within it taking with him his own tears and news for his family waiting at home.

Diah ran to where the ladder had been leaning against the prison wall, but it was no longer there. Neither was the leg she had been forced to leave on the ground. She bellowed from defeat, but then, like the rest of the onlookers, began to make her way home.

When she arrived at home, she found her brothers waiting outside for her return, but she ignored them and ran to her room to cry. Her eyes were swollen. She ached inside, she wanted to die, but all she could do was cry, to let her tears flow until the well from which they sprang was dry.

Her brothers lingered outside, not knowing what to do but afraid to ask their sister what had happened. Diah herself had no desire whatsoever to relate to them what she had seen.

When twilight came, no meal appeared on the dining table, but the boys ignored their hunger pangs, just as they tried to ignore the images of what they had seen that day—the killing, the vengeance, and the many deaths.

So it was that the situation changed again—but only in its external form; life, as it was, remained the same, and it was no less difficult to get by in the present than it had been in the past.

The Red Army was flushed from town by the Siliwangi troops and driven west, along with their local henchmen. Townspeople who had been forced by the Reds to join them remained behind, waiting for death or a continued life to come to them of its own accord.

Gradually, many of the Red Army's followers from town, young men and women for the most part, returned to their homes. And when they found themselves once more sitting in their favorite chair, they could not help but weigh the merits, both the good and the bad, of their participation in the Communists' mass killings and terror. To regain a place in the local social order, they played the role of penitent, going around to their neighbors and telling them, "If I hadn't done what the Reds wanted, they would have killed me. I'm not a Communist. They made me do it."

Their neighbors, who played the role of confessor, would calmly listen and afterward nod their heads. "Of course, we understand," they'd say. "I know that's what happened." And, in such a way, through this mutual charade, the tension between the two parties began to fade away.

Families with loved ones who had in fact been forced by the Communists to join them and who had yet to return waited with a mixture of fear and worry. Among them was the Sumo family. Though Diah and her brothers cared for their sister Ies, it was Sri whom they missed, Sri whom they waited for. In Sri's absence they had come to realize how much they loved their sister and how very much they owed her for the many sacrifices she had made for them. Ies had voluntarily joined the Reds, the very same people who had caused their father's death. And so, while they might have been prepared to accept her loss as some kind of retribution, such was not the case with Sri.

By this time, the public schools had been closed so long that when they finally reopened their doors, students were forced to repeat the lessons they had studied three months before. When Husni, Hutomo, and Kariadi returned to school, they discovered that some of their former classmates were no longer there.

Now that Diah was head of the household, she herself was unable to reenroll in school. Despite the sadness she felt at being unable to continue her education, she was heartened by her brothers' changed attitude; not only did they now take pleasure in learning, they also listened to her advice. It seemed they had come to realize that Diah was the only person now looking out for them.

Diah spent her days going from one street to the next looking for old clothing which she would then resell at a small profit to any buyer she could find. On occasion she was able to obtain a batch of homespun white cotton from whose sale she made a larger margin of profit. She had never imagined that she could possibly earn a living this way, but the fact that she was able to keep food on the table in the Sumo house raised both her and her brothers' spirits.

And so it was that daily life, for both the Sumo family and their neighbors, began to proceed as it once had, without undue disruption. The market reopened. Traders returned to occupy the empty market stalls. Even so, Diah and her brothers avoided discussion of both their father and their sisters, fearful, perhaps, that vocalizing their thoughts might somehow transmogrify their present situation and bring back into their lives the atrocities and the memories of them that they had valiantly tried to suppress.

Then things changed yet again, and as had happened before, the people of Blora were caught off guard, not thinking that change could happen so fast. Now it was not the Japanese, the Communists, or the army of the Republic that occupied their town. Instead it was the Dutch and their allied forces. Yet again, they conquered with little resistance. In fact, it wasn't until the Dutch were within five kilometers of town that the Republican army put up any fight. But the national army's weaponry was of both limited supply and usefulness, completely insufficient for a lengthy defense of the town, and so the Dutch continued their entrance, virtually unimpeded.

If there was a difference between the town's takeover by the Communists and the Dutch, it was that in the first instance the occurrence took place with almost no gunfire at all. Such was not the case with the Dutch, who employed a scorched-earth policy. Just as had happened when the Japanese came to town, once again the Dutch blew up the oil pumping stations in the town's environs.

The town's daily life, including the educational system, was once again disrupted. The market closed. The townspeople didn't know what to do. To make life more difficult for the common man, when the Republican armed forces began their retreat to the south and the west, they blew up the bridge across the Lusi. All that remained of the span was a twisted skeleton of steel in the middle of the river bottom. This action served to halt the Dutch force's march southward, only one kilometer from the Blora town square. They could not ford the river with their heavy equipment.

Even in times of the most intense guerrilla warfare, a person still has to eat. If one does not want to die of hunger, a source of food is essential. And so it was for Diah, who made daily forays to the guerrilla-controlled area. Rising very early in the morning, when there were few Dutch soldiers patrolling the town roads, she'd make her way to the guerrilla area to find clothes for resale. Because the public schools had been closed again, her brothers helped her in this venture.

Each passing day was marked by the explosion of hand grenades. Once the Dutch had entered the area, they found it impossible to leave because the guerrilla forces had hemmed them in by gaining control of the surrounding regions. Each time a Dutch truck tried to slip through the net, a hand grenade blew it up. The Republican forces might not have had a large array of weaponry, but they did have a huge store of hand grenades, which they had concealed in the teak plantation adjacent to the town.

At one point the Dutch attempted to make a sweep of the area. To stop them, the Republicans sent out troops from Kundaran, a town about forty kilometers away that had become the effective seat of the Republican government in the region. No Dutch boots ever left prints in that place. For as many times as the Dutch sent troops to take that town, they were forced to retreat in equal number.

Because of the ongoing military action between the Dutch and Republican forces, the area between Blora and Kundaran became a no-man's-land. The Sumo family house and those of their neighbors were located on the edge of that strip. Thus, raids on their homes were not uncommon. Just as had happened when the Republican forces arrived, each time the Dutch soldiers appeared, local residents were forced to flee their homes and find shelter in the stands of bamboo.

One night, while hiding in the bamboo waiting out the danger posed by the Dutch troops as they passed, Diah caught sight of a human shape making its way toward her. Even in the dark, she could see that the eyes of the person coming toward her had sunk deep into their sockets. The person's trousers and shirt were little better than rags and his boots were coming apart at their seams. She trembled as the conviction grew that the person was a Red soldier. As if to confirm her belief, other people in her shelter began to whisper, "Look, it's a Red."

Straining her neck forward to look more closely, the approaching figure suddenly became familiar—It was Sri!—and, without any regard for her personal safety, Diah bounded from her hiding place and ran to embrace her sister.

When Diah threw her arms around Sri, her sister suddenly shrank back, wincing with pain.

"My arm . . . It's broken," Sri explained, but then broke into a broad but weary smile when she saw her three brothers suddenly at her side.

A sudden burst of gunfire not far from their place of concealment caused all five to drop to the ground, but even with the very real danger around them, even with Death making its round, each of them felt a measure of contentment they had not felt in a very long time.

After the roar of trunks and tanks had subsided and after the battle had died, the five Sumo children returned to their house. When they finally were able to sit down, none of the boys could take their eyes off Sri's swollen arm.

"How did you break it?" asked Diah, who was bandaging Sri's arm.

"I fell off my horse," Sri answered. "The Siliwangi troops were after us and my horse got hit by a bullet. I was thrown into a ravine. I'm just lucky there was some undergrowth, otherwise I might have smashed my head on one of the boulders."

"And what about Ies?" Hutomo then asked.

"She got away, I guess. She's probably tried to hook up with the Reds' main division."

"Where's that?"

"I heard the Reds were going to try to make a last stand near

Semarang, but I don't know for sure." Sri looked around the room. She sighed, then asked the question that she knew her siblings did not want to hear: "Where's Father?"

In a trembling voice, Diah gave the answer she had wanted to avoid: "He's dead."

Hearing her suspicion confirmed, Sri suddenly lost her power to speak. Tears sprung from her eyes and her chest convulsed with pain. When she then began to sob, Diah and her brothers began to cry, too. Soon the room was filled with the sound of their hoarse wails.

As if unable to stop herself from revealing how their father had died, Diah began to speak: "He died in prison. He was inside when the Reds set it on fire. They shot all the prisoners in their cells before they left. I was there. I tried to find Father, but all I found was one of his legs . . ." Suddenly wailing again, Diah could not continue.

Trapped in their shared pain, it was some time before any of the children could speak, but finally, when her tears had begun to dry, Sri began to disclose her own experience: "After joining the Reds, I saw more sights than Mother ever could have included in one of her bedtime tales. Could she ever have imagined how cruel people could be?"

Outside, a gust of wind shook the treetops, causing Sri to stop. For a moment, she looked afraid, as if, perhaps, she had suddenly found herself reliving her recent past. She listened a moment longer before continuing: "No one thought the Siliwangi troops could move so fast. All of a sudden, they were on top of us, catching us completely by surprise. We tried to run. Oh, and did I run, but without knowing where I was going. That's when I learned the meaning of true fear! All I wanted was to escape, and the only thing we had in our favor was that they had no cavalry. Otherwise, the end might have been different. Instead, they chased us with their gun and mortar fire. All we could do was try to keep out of range, but even then, as you can see . . ."—Sri lifted her bandaged arm—". . . they finally caught up with me."

Sri paused to rub her eyes, then looked at her siblings again. "I don't know why our family has had to suffer so much," she mouthed in weary reflection, as if addressing an audience beyond her vision, "but anyway, that night, the night my horse was shot and I was thrown into the ravine, I blacked out. When I finally came to, it was morning, but my problems hadn't ended just yet.

"After finally making my way up and out of the ravine, I discovered I was near Sulang, about thirty kilometers from here.

"Well, right at that time, with the Red troops on the run, the Muslim parties and their followers were doing a cleanup job in the area and arresting any and all Communists they could find. So, just when I thought I had finally escaped death, danger came to greet me.

"I had forgotten that I still had on my red bandana. That and the palm bracelet and necklace I was wearing gave me away . . ."

Sri suddenly gasped and began to cry. Her body swayed back and forth until she finally gained control of herself again.

"Anyway, they caught me and then they tortured me . . ."

Sri's siblings found themselves unable to look into her eyes and stared at the floor instead, their own eyes glazing with tears.

". . . Male, female, it didn't matter. They threw us all together in a school building where hundreds—maybe even thousands—

of local people had gathered outside. Everyone was carrying some kind of weapon—a sword or crowbar, a machete or spear—and they kept jabbing them in the air and calling us names.

"I thought for sure I was going to die there, and I thought of you all and how you'd eventually grow tired of waiting for me to return. But then, I don't know why"—she took a deep breath—"my life was spared. A Red battalion that was being pursued by two Siliwangi units somehow managed to avoid being snared, and attacked Sulang, causing our captors to flee.

"So we were free again, and that's when I took the chance to make my own escape. I fled to the teak plantation, and that's where I remained, lost, without any bearings, for the last several weeks.

"All I had to eat were young leaves, so I kept filling my stomach with water from streams. I kept walking and walking, day after day, not knowing for sure where I was going. Night was the only time I could find the courage to leave the forest to try to find out where I was.

"One day, a deer suddenly jumped out of the brush, right in front of my path. I took it to be a sign, but didn't know if it was good or bad.

"I came down with a fever, because of my broken arm I suppose, and there were times when I could hardly take another step forward—but I knew that I had to see you, at least one more time, before I died. And finally, I made it back here."

Sri sniffled loudly and her siblings cried as she finished her tale.

"You've gone through so much," Diah said.

Sri amended her sister's comment: "Everyone has suffered, not just me. During my wanderings in the teak forest I thought a lot about suffering and came to conclude that most suffering can almost always be linked to evil. It's evil that makes room for suffering.

"Remember in school how we learned that something exists because it takes up space. I'm not so sure that's right anymore . . ."

The night wind had grown cooler and entered the house through the air holes above the windowpanes.

"Maybe you should rest," Diah suggested.

Sri nodded and smiled at her sister. "I suppose I should if I ever hope to mend." She hesitated, as if remembering something. "First it was the Japanese, then the Communists. After that, the Republicans, and now the Dutch are back. When is it going to end?"

"Don't think about that now," Diah told her. "Tonight you must rest and try to keep from moving your arm. Tomorrow, I'll take you to the Dutch hospital. They're not going to know who you are."

Sri then followed her sister's advice. She stretched out in a large chair and was soon asleep. The other children curled up and slept on floor mats not far from her side.

Sarmini, the neighbor woman, did not stay with them that night and the Sumo children could hardly have cared otherwise. For some time, Diah and her three brothers had been aware of the rumor that Sarmini had in fact moved into their house not out of any kind feelings toward them but as a means of finding a way to take over their house and land.

Sarmini's brother, Tukijan, was now a guerrilla commander,

she had once told them. She also revealed that anyone who was caught collaborating with the Dutch would be killed and have his house burned to the ground. Though it should not have been a worry for the Sumo children, the thought of losing their home was never far from their minds. Perhaps that is why they jumped in their seats when suddenly hearing a pounding on the front door the next evening.

Husni tiptoed to the door to open it up and cried out when he saw his brother Sucipto standing before him. Husni knew it was his brother, even though he looked so very different now. When he left home after their mother's death he still had a teenager's body; now he was a tall and muscular man, with a soldier's bearing and dressed in a Royal Netherlands Indies uniform.

Without waiting for Husni to lead him inside, Sucipto immediately marched to the back room, where his other siblings were seated. Before giving them a chance to react to his presence, he announced, "I've been stationed here in Blora. Just arrived this afternoon!"

Whether because of shock at seeing that Sucipto was still alive or because of his uniform or some other reason, none of his sisters or brothers could say a word.

"What, cat got your tongue?" he said to Sri. "Why don't you say something?" he asked in a softer voice. "How are you?"

"Fine . . ." Sri still found it hard to reply.

"What happened to your arm?"

"I fell from a horse."

Sucipto snorted. "So you joined the Commies too," he immediately surmised.

A flash of anger appeared in Sri's eyes. "The Communists killed Father."

For a moment, Sucipto could say nothing. His reddened eyes glistened with emotion. "And what about Ies?" he then asked. "Is she gone too?"

"It was she who joined the Reds," Sri informed him. "Now, I don't know. She might have been captured by the Siliwangi."

Sucipto suddenly looked extremely weary. Shaking his head, he pulled up a chair and sat down. "I don't understand how it turned out this way. Suradi died in Burma. The war there was a lot worse than it was here, but I survived. I was captured by the Allied Forces and then joined the Dutch in order to get home."

"If you're a soldier for the Dutch, you'd better leave," Sri immediately told him.

Now it was Sucipto's turn to be shocked. "What? Why?"

"You don't know how things have changed around here," Diah said slowly.

"I know that things have changed," he said adamantly, "but I can also see the cupboards in this house are bare. I'd think you might want my help."

"It's not that we don't," Sri remarked sadly. "It's just that if anyone finds out we have a connection with the Dutch army, they'll drive us out and burn the house down."

"You live here. This is your house. Who would do that?"

"Who wouldn't?" came the reply.

The consequences of his return home as a Dutch soldier began to dawn on Sucipto. "You're not going to say anything, are you?"

"We don't have to say anything," Diah told him. "Word has a way of getting around and even the night has eyes."

Sri pointed toward the open front door. "And look at your truck, parked right there in front of the house. What do you think people will think of that?" She breathed in deeply. "I hate to say it, but I think you'd better go."

Now Sucipto was angry, and his bloodshot eyes flashed with fury. "So thank you for the welcome! I thought you might be glad to see me, but it looks like you're more frightened of what might happen than you are of the Royal Dutch Army. We have tanks, you know, and other weaponry. There's no need for you to be afraid."

His words were cut short by the sound of an explosion out front. They looked out to see that Sucipto's truck was now in flames.

"You have to get out of here," Sri whispered hurriedly. "It will be the house next."

Sucipto's anger suddenly died and he turned away in confusion. After a pause, he bolted out the door to disappear behind the flames of the burning truck.

Inside the house, his siblings jumped when they heard pistol shots, but they remained fixed to their seats, staring at one another.

Finally, it was Kariadi who said, "I think we should go outside."

"Yes, maybe we'd better," Sri replied.

A moment later all their fears were swept aside by bitter reality. Outside, people were pelting their house with rocks. Windows shattered and broke. The smell of gasoline was in the air.

When running out the front door, the family saw that Sucipto's truck was still burning but could see no evidence of him. They rushed into their field and kept on running until they reached its far corner, where they concealed themselves behind a clump of tall grass. Kariadi hid his face in Diah's breasts; the rest of the family watched as their house was enveloped by flames. The sky turned red with fire.

"I hope they don't find us here," Diah prayed, but in a sense, she need not have worried. None of their neighbors left their houses to offer help, no one tried to put out the fire, everyone cared more about his own safety than anything else.

As the night passed, the flames grew smaller and the crackling of burning wood faded until, at last, a semblance of silence returned.

"I wish Mother and Father were here," Hutomo softly cried.

A loud creaking and then a cracking sound drew their attention back to the house. The timbers that had once supported the house were caving in.

"Who can we turn to?" Diah asked sadly.

"Nobody," Sri told her. "Not the Republicans, not the Dutch, not even our neighbors. We're going to have to accept that," she added. "If I've learned one thing from all that we've gone through, it's that you can overcome anything if you can learn to forget about yourself. Pretend you're not even there, and all the suffering vanishes."

Sri looked again toward the site of their former home. All that remained was a skeleton of what it had been before. And all that Sri could do was sigh.

Blora is located in an isolated region, a physical and cultural backwater, with incredibly poor soil unsuitable for farming. For that reason, the young men and women from the area enjoyed very few choices for advancement, which is why, no doubt, they were all so eager to join one fighting force or another. The political stripe they opted for was less relevant to them than was the chance to escape from their hometown. And so it was, they made their choices: some joined the guerrilla forces, which operated out of the teak forest; others joined the Reds and then killed or were killed because of that choice; still others joined the Republican forces, to kill or be killed by the Reds and the Dutch. And finally, there were those like Sucipto who, by some twist of fate, found himself joining the Dutch.

By the time Indonesia regained its sovereignty and the Dutch had finally packed their bags, the people of Blora were exhausted from the experience of war. Backwater or not, most people in Blora wanted the town to return to the way it had once been, before. And daily life did gradually return to normal, much as it had been at a time in years past when the word "war" was found only in dictionaries and storytelling, when there had been no bloodshed. What did not return were the bodies of those who had died and, just as sadly, a sense of morality, which, during the war years, had been despoiled by something called revenge.

As the government reestablished itself and the town began to develop and rebuild, Sri and Diah and their three brothers continued to live in the shack they had built on their parents' property. They, too, might have tried to rebuild, but they had neither the necessary strength nor the capital. When a government call went out for public assistance in building its gold reserves, Sri dug up the gold jewelry that Ies had given to her and turned the pieces over to a government representative. The official praised her for her nationalism but neglected to give her any cash or even a receipt of any kind. On this occasion, as had happened so many times before, Sri told herself to accept what had happened, that with acceptance everything would again be all right. Let the wicked be wicked and the good be good. Only through acceptance might there come the possibility of change.

# THE REWARDS OF MARRIAGE

EVEN THE THOUGHT of the upcoming holidays made me greatly distressed. Celebration of Lebaran, the Muslim new year, required cash, a great deal of it, and I needed it soon. Traditionally, Lebaran is a time for visitors, lots of them, coming to ask for and to dispense forgiveness for transgressions one might have committed. That part of the holiday was fine, but the connection between forgiving and festivity (with all the pricey cakes and foods that were involved) was something that escaped me.

I suppose it was these thoughts, rumbling through my mind, that were making it hard for me to sleep. I had shut the mosquito curtain four hours ago. Next to me, my wife floated in the sea of dreams. Yet I just lay there, blinking my eyes, unable to sleep.

*Lebaran!* Yes, it was the thought of the upcoming holidays that was disturbing me. Finally, I decided to force myself to sleep and, from past experience, I knew that one of the easiest ways to do that was to tell myself a story. Maybe I wouldn't get paid for the story and maybe it wouldn't help with my holiday bills, but that is what I decided to do, and this is how it went . . .

There once was a man named Soleiman who felt himself to be the butt of every joke in his hometown. Why it was that way, he didn't know, especially with him having a name like Soleiman, which is derived from Solomon, a man who was renowned for his sense of justice. As such, for Soleiman, this situation didn't seem fair at all but if there was one thing he knew about himself it was that he possessed the undeniable weakness of being unable to ignore public opinion. Wherever he went, whatever he did, in all his dealings, he always felt that he was being swindled or taken advantage of. As a small trader with limited finances and no reserve stock, trying to make a go of his business was difficult at best. Worse still, he had no one to feel sorry for him but himself. In the end, because he had no gift for business, he could only dream of being a successful merchant with millions in capital reserves. He didn't like the way he was; he didn't like the way people treated him, but there was nothing he could do about that.

Finally recognizing that he did not have the power to change the situation, Soleiman began to look at the country's system of administration; he also studied the political system, prevailing religious beliefs, and even the existing moral order. What he came to see was that these systems were now fossilized sets of rules, lifeless obligations, completely devoid of the innovative nature that had marked them during their time of development. Yet his life was shaped and controlled by these same rules, their obligatory virtues, and the powers that supported them. As for the latter, he came to conclude, these people were little more than a pack of liars, swindlers, and cheats. That this was true was self-evident and he felt no need to try to prove otherwise. Or perhaps it was that very need that made him decide to become a writer—at least that's how he began to think of himself.

In a free country, who is to say what a person can or can not be? Soleiman reasoned that if he wanted to call himself a writer, no one had the right to object. A person could call himself a king, a doctor, a lawyer, or whatever else he wanted, at least in his own mind, that is, and no one, neither judge nor policeman, could do anything about it. Soleiman himself had come to doubt whether even God's angels could know what really went on in the hearts and minds of human beings.

A person who has had something that he's written published in a journal or magazine may call himself a writer. Soleiman could point out numerous examples of these so-called men of letters who, after the publication of a short story or two, were suddenly proclaiming themselves to be pioneers of a new writing style, vanguards for the values of a new movement, and forerunners of a generation that would speak its own mind. Who was to say that he could not proclaim the same?

And indeed, Soleiman did proceed to write. In fact, he filled notebook after notebook with his writings. Even so, he had yet to see even one of his manuscripts published.

In a small town such as ours, the opportunity for advancement, much less the possibility of developing a unique personality of one's own, is rare. It's not surprising, therefore, that Soleiman had no idea how to go about publishing the growing pile of manuscripts that was gathering dust in his armoire. Even though his former life of uncertainty as a small trader had become even more unstable as a result of his choice to be a writer, Soleiman still found himself compelled to write and could not stop. He did have to eat, however, and put food in his stomach. To do so, he sold junk or, to put it more politely, traded in secondhand goods—but this was only so that he did not die of hunger.

Anyway, the story goes on as follows: because Soleiman could see the shortcomings in society and social intercourse, he thought that he could choose a better way of life for himself, one far better and more useful that what most other people chose. Of that ability he was very proud. In fact, it served to increase his level of esteem—in his own eyes, at least—and there was no one in heaven or on earth who had the right to tell him differently.

Whenever Soleiman met a single woman of marriageable age, especially one he found to be both beautiful and interesting, his heart would cry out to her, "I am the man who should be your husband! I am the man who knows society's faults and what to do about them. All other men are idiots and fools. I am the man that you must choose. So come with me and follow in my footsteps."

Whenever he met a beautiful married woman (and he paid attention only to those who *were* beautiful) his heart would rail at her, "Look at that husband of yours! What is he? A blind man is what, unaware of your beauty! He is a man locked into society's evil ways. Worse still, he doesn't even realize it himself. He is caught in the grip of empty platitudes, religious beliefs, and political mores. Get rid of him and marry me and you'll be happy forever, that I can guarantee."

Because Soleiman thought so much about society and mankind, his old joy—that of a being a man with zest for life—changed into the pleasure of thwarting public opinion. In his interaction with others, he was forever pointing out examples of social stagnation and societal defects.

The young people in our town—who, it must be said, were not a particularly bright group of people, being isolated as they were from national and world literature—held Soleiman in awe. Had these young men and women been members of parliament, you can be certain they would have passed a motion to support Soleiman despite the man's serious lack of strength, which was so readily apparent in his skeletal frame and skinny butt! And regardless of their opinion, Soleiman did indeed possess great creative powers. Not having read many of the great books from either the East or the West but having plumbed the depth of his own heart and mind instead, much of his creative output was indeed very original.

Soleiman's views on society and mankind changed him into a boastful and arrogant individual. He looked down on the rest of humankind. He had no time for fools and simpletons. But because he did not want to die of hunger, he was still forced to interact with them. In doing so, he always presented a kind and genial face—not because he wanted to, to be sure, but out of necessity, for which he suffered inside.

Sometimes, when alone and remembering how much he had to demean himself just to keep food on the table or how much he needed society and humankind, he felt completely degraded—like a worm that would be better off squished by a servant's foot or, even better yet, washed down the drain with the soapy water from the laundry. Better that than to go on living afraid of the sunlight.

So, that's the introduction to this story about Soleiman, and now that you have it, we can tell you the real story. But because a story is often interesting only because of its tangents, this one too shall have its variations. And because the course of human life would be far too dull if not enlivened by a love song—a clear and mellifluous tune—we shall include here a love story, but not one that is overly long, to be sure, because that too can be boring.

This world would be a very cold place if it contained only men or only women, which is why there are both men and women on this earth. And so it was not Soleiman alone who came into this world, born from the desire of his two parents. A female child named Tijah by her parents also appeared in this overpopulated world.

Like Soleiman, who had also been born in Blora, Tijah never chanced to venture outside of town in all her early years. And like Soleiman, she too had been born into the world through no choice of her own. She had come into being. She existed and she was female, a stroke of fate that would later play an important role in her life. She did not know why she had been born into this world or into a society whose roll of members included a person by the name of Soleiman. No, at the time of her birth she knew nothing at all.

Tijah started off in life as a child, of course, but over the years developed into a young woman who was assured of her own beauty. She was a virgin too—of that she was completely certain, though in the hearts of the young men who were drawn to her, there were those who harbored doubts. One suspects this was because of her physical attributes.

Unlike Soleiman, he of the skinny butt, Tijah had a large

behind that was full and broad. Her breasts were equally proportionate, the sign of a worldly woman, people said, though she herself had never heard that said of her. What she knew was that she was a woman, an attractive one in her own estimation, who would at some momentous occasion in time find herself accepting a young man's kisses. Who this young man would be she did not know, but she accepted the situation and was satisfied with it. The only question for her was when.

Like other young women in our town, Tijah patiently waited for that first kiss on her cheek (because what she knew from her parents was that men always kissed women on the cheek). She waited with a great and silent hope. Silent, of course, because even though she knew herself to be the result of her parents' desire, she also knew that if she were to speak of her hope to them they would probably become angry and possibly even beat her or berate her. "You unthankful girl! You shameless hussy!" they'd say. "A girl like you should never have been born!" Such a situation would provide entertainment for her neighbors, no doubt, and news of it would quickly spread to all corners of town. She could indeed imagine what would happen if she said anything to them. So it was better just to keep her mouth shut.

But then the war broke out. War always serves to loosen gender restrictions, whether for a short time or for longer, and during the war Tijah (and other young women, to be sure) found herself able to travel about town freely. Wherever she went, she always carried that big, silent hope in the bottom of her heart—that of finding a kiss on the cheek. She wasn't quite sure where she had concealed that hope, but she knew it was there inside her, sometimes as large as a balloon pressing her rib cage from inside, sometimes as small as a grain of sand, tickling at her heart.

During the war she was not successful in finding what she desired. Not only was she too young to stir most men's desire, she was also timid and afraid.

But then, following the war and the return of the Dutch, the revolution broke out and whatever restrictions on sexual behavior that had once been in place now fell by the wayside.

Tijah's first kiss came from Mahlani, a sergeant in the Indonesian National Army. His kiss was warm and she shivered at his touch, but because she had waited so long for this to happen, she accepted his kiss and his embraces readily.

Except for the two of them, no one witnessed this meeting of flesh. Mahlani often called on Tijah at her home and her parents welcomed him gladly. While they were certain that this young man kissed their daughter when the two of them were alone, they didn't inquire about the matter. They never forbade it, either. To mention it would not have been polite.

Tijah, for her part, never told anyone either. Again, that would not have been polite. No matter how many times she experienced Mahlani's kisses, she kept word of them to herself. But when she was alone, especially at night when sleep wouldn't come, she'd picture Mahlani in her mind—not as an army sergeant with green uniform and stripes; not as a soldier in a beret and steel-toed boots, but as a man in his completely natural state, with nothing but his own fine hair to hide his body. She explored his body in a state of admiration, growing ever more excited by his physical wonders. And that's when she usually fell asleep.

The focus of a person's concentration rarely remains on one subject only, and so it was that Tijah did not always think of

Mahlani. She thought of other young men too—which was also something she never talked about with others, for that would not have been polite, or so people said—but Mahlani was the man she imagined most often.

In the story of a person's life, characters often change, and so it was in this case when, one day, the man whose body Tijah admired and imagined so often did not return from battle. All that she knew, all that anyone else heard was that Mahlani had taken a bullet in his jaw and fallen near the edge of a ravine. When captured by the enemy, his body had been tossed into the gaping abyss, from which he would never return.

Even supposing that Mahlani's body was found and returned to her, Tijah would never again be able to marvel at his musculature. Nonetheless, even without hope of ever receiving his kisses again, Tijah sometimes found herself prolonging that dream.

Because this story is not about Tijah and Mahlani, hereby ends this story's interlude.

In this particular story Tijah must marry Soleiman. The tale demands it! And because it would be completely wrong if their marriage were not first preceded by some kind of chance meeting, or a mystical union, or secret passion, and love—yes, love!—that is where we must begin.

We must start by saying that it's almost a crime to think that a particular role in life or even a story must always be included among the duties of a particular "character" only. Roles are slippery things. Not only can they change from one person to another, but they can also change from group to group, from people to people, from nation to nation, and even from one period to another. In this particular instance, the role we're talking about is the one that the Dutch army played when they chased out the National Armed Forces and came to occupy our small town.

Soleiman considered himself to be a true-blue Republican, which is why, when the Dutch came back, he exiled himself to a more isolated part of town in order to not have to deal with them. One belief to which he ascribed was that there were times in life when friendship can be a crime.

Tijah, who also considered herself to be a true Republican, frequently visited those parts of town where the young Republican civilians had hidden themselves. It was in this way she came to be acquainted with Soleiman, a man whose name she had known for quite some time. He was, after all, the town's famous writer. Tijah was pleased and proud to meet him. In fact, had she not been embarrassed, she would have liked to shout out, "Soleiman is the man for me!"

It is common knowledge that relationships don't just happen but develop over time. And so it was that after Tijah came to know Soleiman's name, she then came to know his person, and only after that his heart.

Tijah's early conversations with Soleiman confirmed her first impression, that he was the man for her. She found him to be clever and scintillating, by far the smartest young man in the world if not the universe. Had she not been embarrassed to do so, she would have liked to sing his praises to her parents so that they would immediately want to adopt him as their son-in-law. But shame, or embarrassment, as she was to discover, is a treacherous emotion, consummately capable of betraying one's desires.

CITY LIGHTS BOOKS

Open Everyday 10AM to Midnight
A Literary Meetingplace since 1953

711936 Reg 1 2:53 pm 01/28/08

| | | | |
|---|---|---|---|
| S ALL THAT IS GONE | 1 @ | 15.00 | 15.00 |
| S SEL SS TAGORE REV | 1 @ | 14.00 | 14.00 |
| S MARKS OF IDENTITY | 1 @ | 13.95 | 13.95 |
| SUBTOTAL | | | 42.95 |
| TAX - 8.5% | | | 3.65 |
| TOTAL | | | 46.60 |
| VISA PAYMENT | | | 46.60 |

Account# XXXXXXXXXXXX6363 Exp Date 0510
Authorization# 041191

I agree to pay the above total amount
according to the card issuer agreement.

exchange only w/receipt w/in 7 days
sign up for the City Lights newsletter
at www.citylights.com

CITY LIGHTS BOOKS

Open Everyday 10AM to Midnight
A Literary Meetingplace since 1953

711936 Reg 1 2:53 pm 01/28/08

S ALL THAT IS GONE 1 @ 15.00 15.00
S SEL SS TAGORE REV 1 @ 14.00 14.00
S MARKS OF IDENTITY 1 @ 13.95 13.95
SUBTOTAL 42.95
TAX 8.5% 3.65
TOTAL 46.60
VISA PAYMENT 46.60
Account# XXXXXXXXXXXX5363 Exp Date 0510
Authorization# 041191

I agree to pay the above total amount
according to the card issuer agreement.

exchange only w/receipt w/in 7 days
sign up for the City Lights newsletter
at www.citylights.com

There were times when Tijah dropped Soleiman's name to her parents in hopes, presumably, of exciting their curiosity in this young man, thereby giving her the opportunity to speak of his formidable attributes. She hoped in this way to stimulate some kind of reaction from them, but her parents were not psychologists, and neither was she. Her parents' attention revolved around the kitchen and how to keep food in the larder.

When Tijah was alone with Soleiman she found herself playing the role of a silent and submissive listener. She hung on his every word and never disagreed. His voice was that of a god, reverberating with her most fervent hope. To argue with him, she thought, would mean to bring down punishment on herself. And though somewhere, deep inside her, she wanted to tell him, "I am the most beautiful woman in this city. Take me and do with me what you will," she could not let this voice out. In his presence she exhibited attention and submission, which she did willingly, with all the pleasure of her heart.

Because in this story Soleiman is such a hardship case, we have to return to the part about this young man's self-imposed exile.

That part of the story goes as follows: like other young civilians who had exiled themselves, Soleiman lived a miserable life, one that was much more chaotic for him than it had been before the Dutch attack. However, it was precisely this suffering that served as his capital for attracting Tijah's attention. And oh, how he made her listen to his long and dazzling speeches that were sometimes interspersed with philosophical observations. But aside from all that, there was, somehow, an understanding between the two of them—even without direct physical contact.

For her part, Tijah drew Soleiman's attention by giving him things she thought might help him forget his suffering or, in fact, what might better be described as his imaginary sufferings. And even though she was a Republican, to be able to do that she was willing to work for the Dutch. She used her wages to buy food, cigarettes, and clothes for the young man with the flat ass. In this way she was able to convince herself that working for the Dutch was merely a ruse; she was, in fact, contributing to the Republican cause.

Though she herself did not recognize them as such, Tijah's gifts for Soleiman were bribes for his love. Had that idea entered her mind, she might very well have expected the young man to curse her for her betrayal to the nationalist cause. But blindness, it seems, sometimes makes people happy.

Tijah had often heard of people using favors and bribes to win themselves love, especially in cases when one person was old and the other was young, but she never thought of her own actions as such. Soleiman, on the other hand, knew that Tijah's gifts were bribes, but in his case, as in others where the course of life is best traveled with one's eyes shut, he chose to overlook that fact.

For quite some time, Soleiman had wanted to get married—for about as long as the first black hairs had appeared in his armpits!—but he had nothing in the way of material possessions to attract the heart of a young woman. All he had was his ability to talk, a gift with words, as it were, which he did, nonetheless, recognize as a valuable and persuasive tool. He was a writer—at least that's what he called himself—and he had no more capital than that. He knew that if he were ever to find a woman willing to be his wife, she would have to be a woman who could be intoxicated by words. He included Tijah in that category. At the same time, he also retained his high opinion of himself and considered that any woman who married him should be happy to be his wife.

During the Dutch occupation, because so many people's lives were in disorder—at least those who felt themselves to be true Republicans—Soleiman viewed the situation somewhat differently from others. He, whose life had always been in disorder, was secretly gleeful, for now, in the marriage game, he had very little competition.

On one occasion when Tijah brought him a gift, he asked her, "Why do you always put yourself out, thinking about me?" And Tijah, who had long suspected that he might sometime ask that question, answered him respectfully, "But isn't that a person's duty?"

Tijah's answer made him think of how happy he would be to marry a woman like Tijah, a person who recognized the meaning of duty. How many young women were there who recognized that?

At that very moment Tijah was thinking that now was the time Soleiman would ask her to be his wife. The very thought made her tremble.

The silence was finally broken by Soleiman, who remarked, "It's difficult for a poor man to repay a person's kindness." He paused, before adding, "What would you say to me, Tijah, if I were to ask you to marry me?"

Just as a hen will keep her distance from a rooster even when she's willing to receive him, she answered coyly, "But what could you ever hope for in me, Soleiman? I have nothing. My parents are poor . . ." Then, to give additional stress to the actual meaning of her words, she added, "I'm not pretty, not like so many other young women, and I'm not very smart, not nearly as smart as you. What could you ever hope for in me?"

Like other young men when coaxing a woman, Soleiman slowly took Tijah's hand and held it in his own. And Tijah, afraid that Soleiman might suddenly choose to retract his words, made no move to stop him. She took a deep breath to try to calm her nervous heart, but emotion follows its own set of laws and her heart continued to beat wildly.

Such is the classic tale of love, with one body moving toward another, one heartbeat following another. No one can change this scenario; it is something that cannot be outlawed. Love has its own season and its own history.

And then, again, like other young men who are ashamed or afraid to speak to a woman about desire, much less to tell her outright he *wants* her, Soleiman wrapped his wishes in more common words: "It's hard for me to tell you, Tijah, how very much I love you." And though he suddenly recognized that if he were not aroused by Tijah's body, he would not be trying to flatter her, he also saw that he needed to say more to complete the conquest of her heart. "From the very first moment I saw you, I fell in love."

Because such flattery is often, if not always, a complete falsehood, just one part of the larger game and quite incapable of keeping a woman from turning her head away shyly, unless the woman is dead, Tijah urged Soleiman to confess to more: "But what is it that makes you love a woman as unattractive as me?" (Though in her heart she remained sure of her beauty.)

And because Soleiman was worried that Tijah might really turn down his marriage offer, he immediately supplied an answer.

"Oh, Tijah, life is so short and it is our duty to make the best possible use of it. You are my heart's choice; I know that now, and I know that you will be a faithful and responsible wife."

At that instant Tijah suddenly realized that that indeed was what she would be and her heart beat all the faster because of it, as if there were a war drum inside her chest. Even so, she begged for more flattery, not yet willing to be swayed by Soleiman's too brief phrases: "But how can you be sure of this?"

"I know from your eyes," is what Soleiman said. "The eyes are a mirror of the soul."

Tijah beamed from the happiness of knowing that in her eyes Soleiman was able to see that she would be a faithful and responsible spouse. (Besides, it was preferable to believe that than something else.) She wanted to embrace this man so tightly that their two bodies became one and inseparable. However, she was a woman and he was a man and between the two of them stood public sensibilities. That said, the love between a man and a woman is not something new to this world and, therefore, because this interlude about the love of Tijah and Soleiman might become boring if it were continued, it is better to end it here and allow the reader to finish it in accord with his own imagination and wishes.

To give our story a more complex aspect and more multifaceted tone, a number of other elements must be added, the first of which is the fact that the Indonesian revolution ended not on the battlefield but at the conference table. In their attempt to regain their former colony the Dutch did prove to be victorious on the battlefield, but because of international pressure, they ended up having to surrender at the negotiating table. And so it was that they gradually, if begrudgingly, began to withdraw their troops, and when that happened, those self-professed Republicans who had fled the cities during battle now came back in force, shouting cheers of victory and broadcasting their devotion to the Republic.

Having devoted their bodies and souls to the struggle for independence, or at least this is what they proclaimed, they came back to the cities with a great hope burning in their breast—an easy position, a soft chair for their butts, and a high salary.

They then demanded respect as well as a life of pleasure for the price of difficulty they had to pay during their period of self-exile. Such was their logic. And a new struggle ensued, one no less fierce than the battles that had been waged between the Dutch and the nationalists, but this campaign was one for chairs. In the end, there were those who got soft ones; there were those who got hard ones; there were those who got what remained when a tug of war ensued in this game of musical chairs; and, finally, there were those who got nothing but a bash on their noggin from the legs of broken chairs.

While this struggle for chairs was being waged, Soleiman quietly dreamt of getting a bed. Thoroughly accustomed as he was to *not* having a position in whatever government was in power, he paid no attention to the ongoing struggle for chairs. No, what he wanted was a bed, only a bed, with all its legs in place.

For Soleiman a bed was the symbol of desire, both the holy and the unholy (because he recognized that, in terms of essentials, they were the same thing). A bed was a symbol of the natural life force present in every creature.

Leaving that aside for the moment, it was at this time that Soleiman's star began to rise.

One day he ran into an old friend who had just returned from the big city, and this friend was able to provide him a good deal of information about books and the publishing business. For Soleiman, this man's appearance was like the sudden turning-on of a 250-watt light in his darkened room. From the conversations that followed, Soleiman learned from his friend where he had to send his manuscripts if he hoped to see them published.

Quietly, Soleiman began to follow his friend's advice and, lo and behold, one day he received a letter from the secretary to the editor of a large publisher telling him that the firm would like to publish one of his manuscripts and that he was entitled to request an advance against future royalties of five thousand rupiah.

Soleiman read the letter with complete confidence in himself. He had poured his labor into that manuscript, after all, and now had the right to enjoy the fruits of his work. Better still, he now had money—or at least the promise of some—and his dream of having a bed could be fulfilled. And then he could officially propose to Tijah, which was an offer he was sure she would not refuse. He was going to get married!

That day, Soleiman picked up his Parker fountain pen and wrote in his diary, in green ink, "Today marks the closure of my life's past history. I am now a new man with new responsibilities. Today, from this moment onward, is the beginning of my life's new history on this earth."

And Soleiman was indeed a new man with a new life that was about to begin, one that he would share with Tijah. He had never imagined that he would be able to see Tijah completely naked. And now he didn't even have to imagine, for she was now his, his very own! No longer would he have to prepare little speeches, his own love bribes, to keep her at his side. This was something he would not miss, for he knew them to be quite meaningless, as empty of content as his words of advice and his talks about domestic politics. He was thankful that they had served to raise his standing in Tijah's eyes, and no one could fault him for engaging in such a ploy, but he had no use for them anymore.

Soleiman might have thought his speeches to be meaningless, but that was not at all true for Tijah. It was precisely because she had difficulty in understanding what he was saying that she found him so attractive. The more pompous-sounding his voice, the greater trust she placed in him and her choice in him as a husband. In her eyes he was, indeed, the smartest young man in the entire world, and she was proud to be able to claim him as her beloved.

Though nothing was ever said, she trusted that Soleiman was a man who was aware of his duties as a man, as a husband, and as a human being who knew the meaning of both obligation and society's evil ways.

Soleiman's speeches to Tijah had, to a certain extent, influenced her own view about life. In that sense, she, too, was a new person. Like the man she was to marry, she had become suspicious of society. Sometimes she was even suspicious of herself, which was something that made her uneasy.

Now the two were married, a union the local cleric had made official, and love bribes occupied no place in their current lives. Tijah now had what she had wished for. Soleiman no longer had to secretly fear that he would never marry. Their union had changed both of them. Tijah, who was used to spending most of her time going around town, now was a true stay-at-home who spent all her time indoors keeping her household in order. Soleiman, meanwhile, became the older man in his relationship with friends, always ready to give sage advice to these bachelors about the secrets of marital life. His younger friends who wanted to marry could not help but look up to him in awe and admiration. For everyone, Soleiman and Tijah included, their marriage seemed ideal, at least for a while . . .

Now that there was no place in their lives for keeping each other content with love bribes, the mundane problems of everyday life began to occupy their thoughts. Now that the honeymoon was over, Soleiman was forced constantly to think about their need for money. Was it possible to continue providing housekeeping money to his wife ceaselessly, he asked himself, or at least until they were old and gray, sixty or seventy years down the road? Was that even conceivable? He, who had so recently regained his enthusiasm for life and for disputing public opinion, now cowered at the depressing thought of having to fork out housekeeping money for as long as the next seventy years to come.

"I guess that's the reward of marriage," he muttered to himself, for the first time in his life. It was not, however, the last time that he spoke the phrase; for almost every day thereafter, especially on days when he didn't even have a half cent in his pocket to buy himself some cigarettes, he found himself repeating it again.

Sometimes he found himself regretting his choice to marry. Marriage, he had so very quickly discovered, was a two-sided coin. Yes, there was the reward that came from having a wife, but having one almost meant losing one's own sense of self. Was that a reward too?

This silent regret made Soleiman more of a dreamer than ever before. While during the war this had been a survival technique to protect himself from life's harsh realities, now he needed other skills to get by, and the practical ones he had picked as a trader seemed to have all but disappeared. Thinking about this further, he finally came to the conclusion that he was in fact no different from anything else in the world, whether living or not living. And for this, he was grateful. He cheered his state of suffering. He praised empty pockets. He gave thanks to himself for obtaining from marriage a reward that he had not at all expected.

Once talkative, Soleiman was now reticent in speech, but even in silence he still could find no way out from life's predicament. To be silent *and* dreaming can become intolerable for a person who has even a twinge of desire to work or even a hint of aspiration for obtaining something better in life. And so it was that Soleiman began to bury himself in his work.

Day and night, Soleiman immersed himself in writing, and because the public highly valued his creative output for its sprinklings of original thought, he found continued success. This might have brought him some relief except for the burden that came with it, that burden being money.

Even with success, even with money, Soleiman viewed himself as an artist with the right to espouse his views on literature. To a friend of his who now aspired to be a writer because of the example he had set, Soleiman said, "Don't believe artists whose slogan is 'art for art's sake.' Come on! At the very least, they hope to obtain money from their art or, if not that, then fame. And do you know the true value of fame? Nothing, a big fat zero! Just like gold and jewels, whose value is perceived, not real. People love them and will fight over them, but you have to ask yourself what they really mean."

Whether realizing it or not, it was precisely because of Soleiman's fame that people were forced to listen to him, and so he went on: "And do you know why those artists keep talking about art for art's sake? Because they're the ones who have not been able to claim a piece of the market!"

Followers of Soleiman, who had seen his name in books and magazines, rallied to support his view.

"But a piece of writing must be a reflection of society," he also said. "It must highlight social aspects. And because man is a creature in constant search of knowledge, it should support that goal through exposition of more noble human ideals."

When Soleiman was talking and no one was interrupting him with questions, he felt as if he were floating, light as a feather, in the sky. But afterward, when his companions had gone and his feet were on the ground, he felt that all his talk, for all its high-mindedness, was sloganistic too. And in the end, he felt as if he had sinned or, as he himself might have phrased it, that what he had done "was closer to a crime than a violation, but more akin to foolishness than wrongdoing." Even so, when comparing his tales with those he heard from others, he considered himself fortunate. Most other people spent their time talking about things that concerned themselves only—their work at the office, business at the garage, how sales were going and so on. Such conversations were boring and stifled creativity. But about this no more need be said, and the account should end here.

What hasn't been revealed in this story thus far is how Soleiman and Tijah lived after their marriage. Oh, there was some mention of their financial problems, but it is time to extrapolate further. As was mentioned before, after Soleiman began to achieve success as a writer, he began to earn more money. What went untold before was the negative impact this had on his body: the more money he earned, the thinner he became. So sunken were his cheeks that his father-in-law, who was proud of him, warned him to desist from pursuing wealth. What is it doing? he asked. "Your cheeks are so hollow, they look like those of a man who has lost his marrow."

Soleiman was the kind of person who liked to give advice, and not one who liked to receive it, either from his father-in-law or anyone else. He smiled politely, as if in agreement.

"And you should take better care of your body. Sports are important for a person's well-being."

He smiled again, but his father-in-law's advice went in one ear and out the other. He remained unchanged. He continued to be the Soleiman who spent his days wrestling with ideas.

Soleiman's fame as a writer grew; he had mounted the pinnacle of success and there remained, as firmly in place as a nail in a plank. People from the big cities wrote to him to introduce themselves. Critics offered words of encouragement, suggesting that he write more—but not so much that the quality of his work suffered, they said. He also received letters from novice writers, asking him for advice on how to write well. Initially, these letters stirred his sense of pride and he answered them all willingly, but in time, his desire to do so disappeared.

But then, a less auspicious day arrived when he received a shocking letter from one of his publishers, who wrote the following: "If you would heed our advice, you would try to limit your output. If you don't, the value of your work is bound to decline. If you would take our suggestion, try to rein in your passion to write. Take time off to read, for it is only through reading that you will be able to revive your exhausted creative powers. We have great hopes for you and patiently await a new manuscript of a far higher order than was submitted in the past . . ."

Soleiman's first reaction was anger. "Who does he think he is?" he cursed. "What does he want, for me and my family to die of hunger? Is he the only person with a mouth to fill? Giving me advice? He doesn't know his place!"

He went to find Tijah and, after locating her in the bedroom, he waved the letter in her face. "The only thing these guys can give me is advice. If I were to ask them for money, do you think they'd give me that? Fat chance!"

Tijah had no idea what her husband was talking about. Sitting down on the edge of the bed, she pulled Soleiman down beside her and asked him soothingly, "What's wrong, tell me what it is."

Soleiman wanted to shout but, living as he did in his in-laws' house—he still couldn't afford a place they could call their own—he kept his voice low: "It's one of my publishers. He's telling me not to write so much, that the value of my work has declined. Fine, that's his opinion, but what I don't understand is what gives him the right to interfere with my trying to make a living."

Suddenly Soleiman fell silent. When Tijah asked him what he was thinking, he didn't respond immediately. A realization had dawned on him—that he gave too much advice to other people. This was the first time he himself had experienced the distaste of unwanted advice. What was the use of giving advice, he asked himself, if he himself couldn't follow it? Suddenly, he knew what he had to do and he smiled as a result.

"Why are you smiling?" Tijah asked.

The muscles of Soleiman's face, which had been taut with anger, now began to relax. "I promise never to give any more advice," he said.

Tijah, who by this time felt that she had a certain proprietary right over her husband, no longer felt that she had to always listen to what he said. "Those people in the big city know a lot more than we do about some things, especially about writing and publishing. Maybe you should follow their advice. Advice doesn't cost anything, after all."

"What did you say?" Soleiman snarled, but because he was trying to keep his voice down, the tone of his voice seemed to be one of timidity and not defiance. He continued in a whisper: "That's it, you see. It's because you don't have to pay for advice that it makes you sick to take it."

"But I'm sure they have the best of intentions," Tijah said sweetly. "I mean, they do bear part of the risk in publishing your books. So maybe it would be better to follow their advice. Think of all the books you could read."

Now Soleiman truly lost control: "And our stomachs?" he asked excitedly. "How are we supposed to eat?"

Tijah wanted to calm her husband but couldn't think of anything to say.

"So now it's you giving me advice?" Soleiman asked her urgently, but then very quickly bowed his head when seeing his father-in-law pass by the bedroom door. He stood up, went over to the door, and pushed it shut. He then went back to where he had been sitting and repeated himself, this time in a slow and careful voice: "Is that it, Tijah? Is that what you're trying to do? To peddle your advice?"

Tijah, who had already calculated in her head that their future could be even brighter if her husband continued to expand his knowledge, said matter-of-factly, "You have to follow their advice."

"I don't *have to* do anything," Soleiman argued.

"You're just being stubborn," Tijah told him.

"Well, you are stubborn too."

But Tijah, who was much quicker in some things than her husband, who had lost a good deal of his practical sense, embraced him and gave him a kiss, whispering as she did, "Listen to their advice. I'm not forcing you to, I'm asking you. It is I, your wife, who is asking you, not them."

And Soleiman, who was like an unbaked cream puff in his wife's arms, could no longer think about anything but her kisses. The beating of his heart put to flight all other concerns; the power of nature, raging inside him, would not be stilled. And so he locked the bedroom door . . .

After that time, Soleiman wrote very little. He spent his daylight hours reading books on literature for the most part, and even at night he often fell asleep with a book in his hand.

One afternoon, when Soleiman was reading a book on the bed, he came to learn about a new trend currently affecting the country's literary world. It was a trend of frankness. At first he deemed this fad praiseworthy, but before he could give the matter much deeper thought, Tijah came in and sat down beside him, after which he was compelled to lock the bedroom door. At that moment he felt grateful he hadn't been permitted to pursue his thoughts. Otherwise, what pleasure might have passed him by.

After their interlude, he commented to Tijah how authors, through their books, were always trying to win over readers to their point of view.

Instead of agreeing, Tijah laughed at him. "But isn't the purpose of reading about something to learn of what is happening outside one's own circle?" she asked. "I mean, just because you read something doesn't mean you have to agree with the author's point of view."

His wife's laugh never failed to kindle his desire and when she laughed again, Soleiman could only think too, "Of course it's like that." Thereafter, he let himself again submit to nature's way.

Because of Soleiman's secret fear of not having a place of refuge when nature's force arose, he found himself more and more frequently submitting to his wife's control. In moments of greater lucidity, he berated himself for this. Why had he married, after all, if it meant having his own personality subsumed by that of another?

At one point he muttered to himself, "That's what I get for wanting to marry!" But then, when thinking of what he had just said, he began to laugh and his gloom suddenly vanished. It had disappeared, he discovered, precisely because he had been able to laugh at it.

"And that is the reward of marriage!" he said out loud.

Shortly thereafter, Tijah appeared in the doorway, asking him, "Did you want something, darling?"

"You're really sweet," he told her with a smile.

When she smiled back he rose from the bed to lock the bedroom door, but Tijah immediately skittered away, causing him to laugh, even as he moaned. "So this is what married life is like," he thought, "and how it will be for decades to come until death do we part."

Soleiman's story does not end here, for there are other incidents to reveal, ones that further demonstrate the misery of this man's life.

About a month and a half after his marriage to Tijah, Soleiman discovered that he had head lice. He was always wanting to scratch his head, and sometimes lice would fall from his head onto his neck or shirt. This happened once when he was with a friend, who picked up the miniature creature between his thumb and forefinger and gave it a look of disgust. Soleiman felt completely embarrassed and was for days thereafter pursued by a sense of shame. He had just begun to gain a name for himself. What would happen if news of this affliction spread around town? His reputation could be destroyed, and all because of lice!

Whether it was true or not, Soleiman blamed Tijah for his lice and one day told her so: "You've given me lice! Your lice have spread to my head."

Tijah merely smiled at him as if to say that he had to be wrong.

Unwilling to give up so easily, he asked her, "Well, what would you think if I shaved off my hair?"

Please recall, this incident took place shortly after they were married. At that time they liked to go for walks together to display themselves to the people in town. Tijah was proud to have

Soleiman and Soleiman was proud to call Tijah his own. If the one partner was attractive, this only served to increase the sense of pride of ownership in the other partner. As a result, Tijah felt herself to have a vested interest in her husband's appearance. In her mind, she pictured Soleiman walking beside her with a completely bald pate. She also pictured passersby staring at him and smiling for not having to buy a ticket for this roadside attraction.

Before Soleiman could say anything else, she told him, "Don't even think about it." But then she smiled broadly, and it was her smile and not her words that convinced Soleiman to back down from his plan.

And so it was all because of his wife's smile that Soleiman gave in. For months thereafter he served as a courier for the nest of lice in his head, taking the unwanted creatures wherever he went. Only he could tell you how much misery he was forced to endure during that time. There were times when the itching was so bad, he thought he was the most unfortunate creature in the world.

And then there was another incident when, one day, Tijah asked Soleiman, "I was just wondering, why is it you never pray?"

The question took Soleiman by surprise and he exclaimed in a low voice, "What, me? Am I supposed to pray?"

Tijah answered him with a smile, of course, but this time Soleiman wasn't going to give in so easily. "What's the use of praying?" he asked her. "If a man is a jerk, praying eighty-one times a day isn't going to change him. If he's a womanizer, he'll be one until the day he dies. Praying is not going to change him. So what's the use? Every man has a soul and if a man's soul is debauched, no angel in heaven is going to fix that."

Soleiman's retort caused Tijah to lose her own wits. She hadn't supposed that Soleiman could be so defensive, and before she could think of a reply, he fired a second round: "I for one am not going to set my hopes on any of those fine things our friendly prayer vendors say that we can get through prayer. No way, no how!" His temper had begun to get away from him. "And if you ever, if you ever try to force me to pray, I promise you . . ."

Soleiman stopped for a moment. Suddenly, the thought of all the beautiful women that were out there in the world popped into his mind. Yes, he was married but that only proved his desirability. In addition, he was famous and sure to have even greater appeal for any one of a number of admiring women.

". . . I promise you that I will leave this house and never come back."

Tijah bowed her head in defeat, frightened by the terrible thought of becoming a divorcée. She also did some quick calculations, remembering that according to the newspapers she had read, following the war, the ratio of available women to men was far higher than it had been before. In this situation, the only thing she could do was to say nothing and hope that everything would clear up.

But Soleiman wasn't ready to rest. "Supposing you want me to, all you have to do is to repeat that phrase one more time . . ."

Tijah did not raise her head to look at him.

"The world is a big place and there are a lot of women out there . . ."

At this point Tijah's mother came into the room and sat down on the chair in front of Soleiman. After engaging her son-in-law in a bit of small talk, she then reminded him, "You know, when you got married, you promised to pay the agreed dowry no later than six months after the wedding date. Now there are three months left . . ."

Without saying anything more, the woman then left, leaving Soleiman to address his bitter remarks to the empty chair where she had been: "Oh, I remember. I remember very well. Don't you worry, I'm still just as much a man as I was yesterday."

The sound of her husband's voice made Tijah even more frightened of losing Soleiman than she had been before. "What is it you remember?" she asked him weakly.

"I remember that because of our marriage I incurred a debt that I have to repay within three months." His voice was cold. "I also remember there are a lot more women out there."

Tijah grabbed Soleiman's arm and held it tightly. "I'm pregnant," she said, her words falling with her tears.

Soleiman stood and pulled Tijah to her feet beside him. He then led her into the bedroom and closed and locked the door behind him. He kissed her and then whispered, "I love you, Tijah. I do!"

Still trembling from the frightful thought of losing him, Tijah held Soleiman tightly. "What do you want? A boy or a girl?" she whispered.

And Soleiman, who had read the same newspaper article as his wife about the high percentage of women, immediately answered, "I hope it's a boy."

"Yes, a boy," Tijah said, "just like his father."

As time passed and Tijah's belly grew larger, her temper grew shorter. First she'd get cravings and then lose her appetite. She vomited frequently and swore there was something wrong with her stomach. Sour-tasting food helped her to feel better for a while, but then she'd be miserable again. She had never imagined that pregnancy could make a woman feel so awful. She never felt comfortable, she was always uneasy—whether sleeping, or walking, or sitting. And she was always getting angry, usually for no reason, and she always took out her displeasure on her husband.

In the world of women's affairs, Soleiman was a blind man. As a result, his frustration with the situation was not completely unreasonable. "I work hard to earn a living but all I get for it is anger," he said. "I guess that's the reward of marriage!"

Tijah's quick temper had a heavy impact on her husband and he was often angry too. He could hardly bear to stay in the house and often left to go to his old haunts in search of old friends and their consolation, but there was always one thing they asked him, which was, "What are you writing now?" To which he usually gave the non-answer: "Aw, something."

If in former times he had encouraged his friends to find themselves a woman like Tijah to marry, now he never touched on the subject of marriage at all, except to say, "A bachelor should remain a bachelor."

Because being a bachelor, or remaining one as it were, was not yet an accepted thing in small towns, for most of the people who heard Soleiman speak, his opinion caused quite a stir. But when they asked him why he should say such a thing, he never gave an answer. Regardless of his feelings, he wasn't about to divulge the secrets of his own marriage.

Perhaps Soleiman wasn't aware of it himself, but his change in temperament, and his confusion, were very apparent to friends and associates. When Soleiman paid a person a visit, he was treated as an exalted guest, and now that he was making lots of visits to friends, word about his lack of well-being quickly spread.

One day, a sympathetic friend told Soleiman that it was clear to everyone that he was on the down-and-out and had lost much of his former energy. "Open your eyes," he told him, "and look at how irritable you've been. You just can't see it because it's hidden by your own bad temper."

His friend, who was also a married man, then surmised, "If I had to guess, I'd say your wife is pregnant."

The comment took Soleiman completely by surprise. "What, is that what happens when your wife is pregnant?"

"It happened to me," the man told him, "at least when my wife was pregnant with our first child. I was just thinking that this might be the problem with you too."

Soleiman mulled this over. "Maybe you're right," he finally admitted.

The friend smiled solicitously. "You wife is bad-tempered because she's pregnant, and because she's pregnant and feeling miserable, she doesn't want to curb her tongue. Which is why, Soleiman, if your wife is indeed pregnant, you yourself must check your temper and forgive her for her vexation."

Recognizing that his friend had much more experience as a married man and father, Soleiman kept nodding his head in time with the man's words.

"And you know what else old folks say? That the more vile the woman's temper, the more likely she's going to have a boy."

Following that conversation, Soleiman immediately jumped on his bicycle and went home. There, he found Tijah sewing baby clothes. Before he could say anything, her face clouded over and, without acknowledging his presence, she stuffed the cloth in her sewing basket, and went into the bedroom to lie down.

Soleiman's happiness immediately evaporated and the new-found knowledge he wanted to share with her remained stuck in his throat.

Later that evening when the two of them were in their bed-room, behind closed and locked doors, they lay in bed together but alone, listening to songs from the neighbor's radio that wafted into the room through the open window. At that moment Soleiman became acutely aware of nature's force rising within him, but when he turned toward her she immediately turned away.

"If that's the way you're going to be," he snorted, "I'll go find someone else."

He wanted to jump up and shout, to vent his spleen, but with his accursed in-laws being there in the same house, beneath the same roof, he was deprived of that freedom.

"Who cares?" Tijah harshly whispered. "Do whatever you want."

Soleiman's anger changed to intense perturbation. He lashed out at her with the authority given to him as both a man and her husband. "There are lots of other women in the world, Tijah."

Tijah shrugged. "Do what you want. I won't stop you. In a little while this child, my child, will be born, and that's enough for me. I don't want anything else from you."

"Are you serious?" Soleiman asked her.

"Go away for all time, as far as I care. I won't feel the loss."

Soleiman said nothing, but in his head a voice was shouting, "That child is my child too! I am its father."

Staring upward, Soleiman studied the webbing of the mosquito curtain overhead. He then turned toward Tijah and whispered, "Your child is my child, Tijah, and my child is yours." He paused to listen to his wife's breathing before adding, "Perhaps you still doubt my love for you."

Tijah heard her husband's whisper but remained obstinately motionless. When he then put his hand on her body, she growled, "Don't come near me!"

Soleiman immediately turned away, putting his back to his wife and facing the wall, all the while feeling the mounting frustration of his own heart. To console himself, he began to whisper to himself: "Let it go, let it be. It's my child she's carrying and I will do the best possible for him. I will make sacrifices because that child is mine."

In the end, Soleiman was lulled to sleep by his own phrases. Thereafter, he became more diligent in his writing habits and whenever he received a payment he immediately bought things for the baby in preparation for its birth. The child that would be born would receive a magnificent welcome. Tijah accepted the things that Soleiman brought home with a secret and silent joy she never expressed.

After the fourth month of Tijah's pregnancy, the couple rarely made public appearances. No more walks around the town for them! Meanwhile, Tijah's foul temper grew exponentially with her stomach's girth and the itchiness of Soleiman's scalp. He had yet to get rid of his lice, and now they had spread to his armpits!

For Soleiman, the fate of his scalp was a constant irritation and bothered him more than almost anything else (except his wife's temper, perhaps). One day, he decided that he would do something about it, once and for all.

Without giving Tijah the opportunity to exercise her proprietary rights over his hair, he went to the barbershop, plopped down in a chair, took off the hat he almost never wore, and told the barber, "Cut it off!"

The barber looked at Soleiman's face in the mirror. "Cut what off, sir?"

"Everything! Shave it smooth."

"Are you sure about that, sir?"

"Very sure!"

Permission given, the barber's scissors made a first swoop and then the general cleanup began. The nests of lice clinging to Soleiman's hair came under full-scale attack, and within ten minutes, Soleiman was able to cry "Victory!" in his heart. He had won, he would not be itchy anymore.

He looked at his head in the mirror. The thick black hair that had covered it was gone and all that was left was a smooth globe, slightly bluish in hue. He laughed nervously. His lion's mane was gone. The peacock had lost its feather. He ran his fingers over his scalp and, as if receiving a jolt of static electricity, he jumped at the touch, but then he began to laugh freely until he had to force himself to stop.

He paid the barber willingly and left the shop.

Perhaps it's a universal aphorism that when one gains something one loses something in return and vice versa. Soleiman knew this and was very much aware that having had his hair cut off he had lost an element of his natural good looks, but he didn't care. In turn he had regained his self-assuredness. So it was that when he next entered the house, he walked with an air of authority.

When Tijah saw her bald husband she didn't get angry. She didn't feel that her rights over his hair had been usurped. She wasn't even disappointed that he was not as attractive as he had been before. Instead, she gave him a little smile. His in-laws giggled too, and thereafter Soleiman was able to carry his bald head high wherever he wanted to go.

The incident concerning Soleiman's head and its nest of lice must finish here because it no longer has a place in the larger tale. There are other incidents to tell that will round off this story.

One day, quite unexpectedly, Soleiman received a letter from one of his publishers inviting him to come to Jakarta. "We will bear the cost of your trip," the publisher assured him. "It has been the long-standing wish of the people in the firm that we meet you." The publisher then went on to say that his presence in Jakarta would give them the opportunity to discuss his most recent submission and for the editorial staff to get to know him. In fact, he hoped that Soleiman would be able to stay a few weeks, and he ended the letter by writing, "It is fair to say that your name is not foreign here, especially after the publication of your last book."

Soleiman showed the letter to Tijah, who smiled proudly when reading it. "You're going, aren't you?" she then asked.

Soleiman looked uncertain.

"You must go," she told him. "You must accept their invitation."

Though he felt no great urge to go, Soleiman did recognize that in the small towns of this new nation of Indonesia, one could not call himself a true citizen of the country until he had visited Jakarta, the nation's capital. With this thought in mind, he finally answered, "Maybe I should go."

And so it was that three days later, the entire household accompanied Soleiman to the train station.

"May your journey be safe and may you achieve all your ambitions," his mother-in-law intoned as he made his way onto the train.

All hands waved as the train finally chugged out of the station.

In the horse cart on the way home, Tijah began to cry.

"My, my, he just left and you're already crying," Tijah's mother said lightly. "It will be good for him to see the big city," she continued maternally. "It will be an opportunity for him to meet important people and that will be good for him. He won't be gone for long," she added. "There's no need for you to weep."

But Tijah was not weeping because Soleiman had gone; she cried from the realization that she loved him, she truly loved him, and felt regret from so often disappointing him. She vowed that she would never again consciously disappoint the man she loved. She would begin to uphold that vow that very day.

Once again, we must cut this story short, for tales of domestic relations are pretty much the same the world over. Now we must catch up with Soleiman to see the outcome of his journey to the capital.

Time had passed before this particular episode took place, and now that Soleiman's baldness was a thing of the past, when he walked into his publisher's building in Jakarta it was with an air of confidence.

Inside, the receptionist asked him in a bored tone of voice, "And who are you here to see?"

"The director," Soleiman replied.

"Your name?" the receptionist inquired as she shoved a visitor card at Soleiman for him to complete.

Instead of speaking, Soleiman printed his name in large capital letters.

"You're *the* Mr. Soleiman, the writer?" the receptionist immediately asked, wide-eyed.

Soleiman nodded proudly. Now he knew that his reputation had indeed preceded him. In the brief chat that followed, the receptionist made known her admiration for Soleiman and Soleiman made known his pleasure in being admired but that need not be repeated here. Much more significant is Soleiman's visit to the director's office, where he was immediately introduced to the company's employees, in particular members of the editorial staff. A lively conversation ensued, filled with remarks about his reputation, about recent writing trends, about his previously published works and about the manuscript that he was to finish before returning to Blora. The visit that day ended with the director handing him a sum of money that far exceeded the amount of royalties he had expected to receive.

Soleiman left the publishing firm that day brimming with faith in himself. The next objective of his trip was the city's largest household store. On the top of the shopping list in his mind had been things for his unborn child and, after that, presents for Tijah and his in-laws. But earlier, at the publishing firm, when he had let it slip that his wife was pregnant with their first child and that she was due in just a month, the director immediately promised to send a complete set of baby items to the hotel. With that need taken care of, Soleiman was able to concentrate on the rest of the list.

In addition to everything else he bought that day, he purchased several lengths of white silk for his mother-in-law and Tijah to make into prayer robes. For his father-in-law, who was a tobacco addict, he picked up a finely tooled imported lighter.

Back at the hotel that evening, Soleiman packed his numerous purchases in a large wooden packing crate, more than a meter square in size. Even that was too small, however, and he was forced to pack some of the baby clothes inside his own suitcase. For some reason, he felt nervous that night and kept returning to his suitcase, opening and closing it again, to make sure all the items he wanted to take home with him were already there. One after another, he would take the baby clothes out, hold them up before him, and marvel at their size and workmanship.

His son—for Soleiman was convinced that his unborn child was male—would look grand in these clothes, he thought. He wished he were back home already, unpacking the clothes with Tijah. And then he thought of the large comforter he had purchased for his wife. He hoped that she would like it. It was light blue, her favorite color, and made of exceptionally soft material. He'd also bought her a very fine sarong and a prayer veil as well. Though he himself had no time for religion, he recognized that Tijah was pious and enjoyed fulfilling her religious duties. And as she was his wife and the mother of his unborn child, it was his duty to see that she was content.

The cost of living in Blora was not very high, which is why Soleiman had not been the least reluctant in purchasing thngs for his family. But Jakarta, as he was to discover in the time that he spent there, was quite another matter.

During the month that he would spend in Jakarta, Soleiman was introduced to a number of famous artists and writers, but unlike in Blora, where everyone knew his name and showered him with adulation, he garnered scarcely a response from these people. The only person who really paid attention to him was the receptionist at the publishing firm, and the two of them began to see each other after office hours. Just as the young woman had been infatuated by Soleiman at their first meeting, in time he became enamored of her as well. There were nights when he was with her that he was tempted never to return to Blora. He would leave his small-town wife and marry a modern Jakarta woman. Together they would make a new history for him in the capital.

In this story, Soleiman and the receptionist do indeed row far into the middle of the sea of passion, but then one evening, when they were in the outdoor restaurant at Soleiman's hotel, with the full moon shining radiantly overhead, she said something that capsized their little boat.

"If we have a child," she told him, "I hope that he will be a writer too."

That was enough for Soleiman to be suddenly heaved by a wave back to the shore. The image of Tijah pregnant with their unborn child sprang to his mind. And then he thought of his son, the one not yet born, whining for his father to take him on a bicycle ride.

"I'm going home tomorrow," he told the girl.

"When will you be back?" she inquired tentatively.

"I won't be coming back," he said with certainty.

And the girl, realizing that she would not be able to marry Soleiman, began to weep. Soleiman felt the teardrops fall from her eyes onto his hand, but he could say nothing more. The picture of Tijah and his child in his mind had overpowered his ability to speak.

And so it was the very next day that Soleiman set out on the first train to Blora. At the station, the receptionist was waiting for him, ready to continue playing a role in their melodrama.

"I know you have a wife and that you will soon have a child," she told him, "but I am ready to join you, whenever you ask, to help you achieve your dreams."

And Soleiman, who felt as if he really were caught up in some kind of tragicomedy, answered in thespian fashion: "Life is like a path running through the jungle, and sometimes, because our vision is encumbered by dense foliage, we sometimes lose our way . . . I already have a wife and if I were willing to leave her, it is almost certain that I would leave you too if you were to later become my wife."

With the call of the whistle, Soleiman stepped on the train just as it was leaving.

This tale of passion was much too short, but one must remember that not all love stories are lengthy ones. There are many short ones as well, each with the right to be told. But here, in this particular instance, our story of love's failure must end. No one else is going to suffer because of it, because this is only a story for myself, the author.

Now it is time for our story about marriage and its rewards to reach its end and this is how it goes: when arriving home that day, Soleiman entered the front room with an authoritative air and, in the same tone of voice, told the coolie who had come with him from the station where to put his bags and boxes. He then went to his bedroom, which was full of people. Craning his head over the crowd he saw Tijah lying on the bed with her head turned the other way, facing the child for whom he had waited so long.

"Tijah! I'm home!" he called to attract her attention.

Everyone in the room suddenly turned their heads to stare at him, except Tijah, who remained motionless.

A murmur went through the crowd.

"Tijah fell when she was cleaning the backyard," someone said, but he didn't hear that news. He rushed to the bed and there he found Tijah in deep repose. Next to her was a boy, still red from birth, also motionless. Both were in eternal repose; their souls had left this world.

All energy drained from him, Soleiman clung to the edge of the bed as his body slowly crumpled and he fell to his knees. He lowered his head to the mattress. No sound could be heard in the room, except for my own sigh and then my piercing cry: "How can I kill these fictional creatures who are supposed to lead a happy life?!"

After my cry had faded, and was absorbed by the night, the thought came to me: "You must be willing to tell stories about the loss of hope. People must be made to feel the suffering of others. As for contentment, contentment is but a sign that death is at the door."

I turned my body to face my wife and woke her with my embrace. "Tijah shouldn't really die and neither should her child," I told her, regretting the story I had spun for myself. "They should live together in happiness. Why do I want to kill them when they're waiting for Soleiman to come home from Jakarta?"

My wife nudged me. "You're talking in your sleep!"

From outside the room came the sound of my mother reciting the prayer of laudation, "God is Great! *Allahu akbar. Allahu akbar. Allahu akbar walillahil hamid.*"

Of course, tomorrow was Lebaran, and I had bills to pay.

I fell asleep again.

# TRANSLATOR'S NOTE

Having worked as a translator of Indonesian for more than two decades, I can easily attest to the fact that it is impossible to survive on income from the translation of Indonesian literature alone. For this reason, I would like to acknowledge here an important new initiative in the field of translation, that being the International Center for Writing and Translation, which was established at the University of California at Irvine. The translation of this book was made possible in part by a generous grant from the Center.

**FOR MORE FROM PRAMOEDYA ANANTA TOER, LOOK FOR THE**

**"Here is an author half a world away from us whose art and humanity are both so great that we instantly feel we've known him—and he us—all our lives."**
***—USA Today***

THE BURU QUARTET

*This Earth of Mankind*
With *This Earth of Mankind* comes the first chapter of Pramoedya Ananta Toer's epic quartet, set in the Dutch East Indies at the turn of the century, immersing the reader in a world that is astonishing in its vividness. Living equally among the colonists and colonized of nineteenth-century Java, Minke is a young Javanese student of great intelligence and ambition. Battling against the confines of colonial strictures, it is his love for Anneliese that enables him to find the strength to embrace his world.
*ISBN 0-14-025635-0*

*Child of All Nations*
In *Child of All Nations*, the reader is immediately swept up by a story that is profoundly feminist, devastatingly anticolonialist, and full of heartbreak, suspense, love, and fury: the cultural whirlpool that was the Dutch East Indies of the 1890s. A story of awakening, it follows Minke, the main character of *This Earth of Mankind*, as he struggles to overcome the injustice all around him. Pramoedya's full literary genius is evident in the brilliant characters that populate this world: Minke's fragile mixed-race wife; a young Chinese revolutionary; an embattled Javanese peasant and his impoverished family; and the French painter Jean Marais, to name just a few.
*ISBN 0-14-025633-4*

*Footsteps*
As the world moves into the twentieth century, Minke, one of the few European-educated Javanese, optimistically starts a new life in a new town. With his enrollment in medical school and the opportunity to meet new people, there is every reason to believe that he can leave behind the tragedies of the past. But as his world begins to fall apart, Minke draws a small but fervent group around him to fight back against colonial exploitation. During the struggle, Minke finds love, friendship, and betrayal—with tragic consequences—as he goes from wanting to understand his world to wanting to change it. Pramoedya's genius is again evident in his depiction of a people's painful emergence from colonial domination and the shackles of tradition.
*ISBN 0-14-025634-2*

*House of Glass*
A novel of heroism, passion, and betrayal, *House of Glass* provides a spectacular conclusion to a series hailed as one of the great works of modern literature. Minke, writer and leader of the dissident movement, is now imprisoned and the narrative has switched to Pangemanann, a former policeman, who has the task of spying and reporting on those who continue the struggle for independence. But Pangemanann is a victim of his own conscience and must decide whether the law is to control or to safeguard the rights of the people. At last Pangemanann sees that his true opponents are not Minke and his followers, but rather the power of a society awakened. *ISBN 0-14-025679-2*

*The Mute's Soliloquy: A Memoir*
In 1965, Pramoedya Ananta Toer was detained by Indonesian authorities and eventually exiled to the penal island of Buru. Without a formal accusation or trial, the onetime national hero was imprisoned for eleven years. He survived under brutal conditions, somehow managing to produce his masterwork, the four novels of the Buru Quartet, as well as the remarkable journal entries, essays, and letters that comprise this moving memoir.

Reminiscent of the work of Solzhenitsyn, *The Mute's Soliloquy* is a harrowing portrait of a penal colony and a heartbreaking remembrance of life before it. With a resonance far beyond its particular time and place, it is a passionate tribute to the freedom of the mind and a celebration of the human spirit. *ISBN 0-14-028904-6*

*The Fugitive*
Written while Pramoedya Ananta Toer was imprisoned by the Dutch for his role in the Indonesian revolution after World War II, *The Fugitive* was his first major novel as well as the first to be published in the United States. Set during the final days of World War II, *The Fugitive* tells the harrowing story of a young platoon leader who has led a failed nationalist revolt against Japanese forces occupying Indonesia. Betrayed by a coconspirator and forced to disguise himself as a beggar, he sets out to find his fiancée while eluding the military forces who will kill him if they capture him. Combining acute political and social criticism with a gripping, deeply moving narrative, this timeless story of a soldier's return home will haunt all who read it. *ISBN 0-14-029652-2*